CHILDS' PROOF

(Victoria Childs Novel, #1)

NEELEY BRATCHER

Acclaim for Neeley Bratcher:

"This book made me laugh, cry and fan myself all in the first few chapters! This is a must read for anybody who wants to have some fun."

--**Alisha Basso,** Author of *This Blood (The Grace Allen Series)*

"I was thoroughly engaged from the first page...Ms. Bratcher nailed it! Victoria Childs is a fantastic character, and through the majority of the book I actually found myself laughing out loud at her antics. She reminded me of Janet Evanovich's Stephanie Plum, only a lot more entertaining! Kudos to Ms. Bratcher- I cannot wait for more!"

--**Kay Glass**, Author of *Love Bite (Just One Bite)*

"I thoroughly enjoyed this book!"

--**Sarah Simpson**, graphic artist, *A Happy Little Design Studio*

"I love Vic and can't wait to find out what her next adventure holds!"

--**Megan Hilton**, editor

CHILDS' PROOF

Published by Neeley Bratcher

Contact Neeley at:
Neeleybratcher40@gmail.com

Cover design by: Sarah at A Happy Little Design Studio,
Sarah@ahappylittledesginstudio.com

Proofread by: Judicious Revisions LLC

ISBN-10: 1477417656
ISBN-13: 978-1477417652

ACKNOWLEDGMENTS:

To Jami and Tara, the world's best friends and editors. Thank you for the encouragement!

To my family, who never told me "you can't do it!" Thank you for the love!

To Sarah, and her Happy Little Design Studio, for the brilliant cover design. Thank you for bringing Vic's face into focus!

Love to you all!

Here goes nothing.

CHAPTER ONE

I sat in my bouncy, maroon office chair twiddling my pen. Then I flipped it up in the air and caught it, twirling it around my fingers as my dad taught me to do when I was little. The thought of my dad made me smile. He had been gone for nearly two decades, but I still missed him from time to time. He had this way of making everyone laugh and people were immediately at ease with him. My mom always told me that I had inherited those qualities from him. "The Childs' Humor" she called it. Some days I didn't see it. Lately I didn't see it at all.

I signed my name to the letter I had been working on for most of the afternoon. I am a genius when it comes to dragging my tasks out and looking busy when I really don't want to do anything. Actually, rather than signing the letter myself, I had to sign my boss's name with my name under it as Deputy Clerk of Brenton County, Illinois. The title sounded more important than it actually was. There were about ten deputy clerks on my floor alone, and ten more on the floor below us. Sometimes I shortened it to "Victoria Childs, Deputy," thinking it made me sound tough. Normally, I was not tough. Mostly, I was a tiny, wimpy girl. And since this letter was to an inmate at a correctional facility, I decided to just put my initials. This inmate was in prison for raping and murdering his brother's wife. He didn't need to know my name. Names lead to addresses, and addresses lead to phone numbers, which can lead to collect calls from horny prisoners desperate to hear a female voice. I found that out the hard way. I was still having flash-backs.

I yawned and rummaged through my purse for some change to buy a Diet Dr. Pepper. I never seemed to have enough change to feed my addiction to the beverage. At first I drank it because it was high in caffeine, which was the last drug I allowed myself aside from the occasional beer. But I grew to enjoy the flavor immensely. It almost became a comfort for me, a reminder that there was a whole world outside my cubicle walls that had nothing to do with my own working prison. If there were other people drinking Diet Dr. Peppers in other buildings all over the country, there was a world out there. Right?

God, I hope so.

I got up from my desk and looked around. No one was looking, and the only sounds were a few phones ringing and some good natured chatter between employees in the accounting department. The accountants always seemed to be babbling about something. Particularly one of them, who had recently become a grandmother, and had to tell everyone when the child ate, slept, pooped, or yanked fur out of the cat. Then there were the pictures of the poor kitty with a bald butt and the baby who had a scratch across his right cheek. They were looking for a new home for the dangerous cat. If it was me, I'd be looking for a new home for the psychotic, kitty-torturing child.

Maybe that's just me.

Anyway, the coast was officially clear at the moment for my thirtieth soda run of the day. I jogged through the office, out the security gate and glass doors, and down the hall to the vending machines. As I inserted my coins, the last quarter fell into nothingness and did not register on the machine's face. I hit the coin return, but nothing happened. I hit the coin return again and I swear I heard the machine chuckle, insult my intelligence, and call me a very obscene name.

Damn it!

That was all the change I had. Now I'd have to go begging for change before someone gets my soda for a quarter. Or maybe a good swift kick would do it. I punched the machine once before and actually got several free sodas out of the deal. Then they just kept on coming, shooting out like bullets from a gun. And it was, of course, in the middle of a very busy day in the courtroom next door. I stood there trying to catch the flying soda cans without being noticed, and then tried to get them back to the office nonchalantly. Kicking the same machine probably wasn't the best idea. It could explode, or worse. How the heck would I explain how a soda can got imbedded in my forehead? I don't think you can get into heaven if you are killed by a carbonated beverage. Iced tea maybe, but definitely not anything with aspartame.

Eh, screw it, I need my soda.

I looked around, saw no one, and kicked.

Down twenty-five cents, limping and soda-less, I decided to have a nice glass of water. Water was better for me anyway, right?

Have you ever had one of those moments when you wondered what it would feel like to actually kill someone?

I gimped my way back into the office and looked around for a body to give me a quarter. Luckily, Berta was standing at the public counter doing some filing.

"Victoria, what is wrong with you?" she grunted, straightening her back as I proceeded with difficulty through the door. "You got jock itch or something?"

Her abrasive personality could be very lovable at times. This was one of those times actually. She had a tendency to say exactly what she was thinking and it was usually what I was thinking. However, I was trying for a John Wayne gait, not a professional athlete stagger. I just wished she would call me "Vicki" or "Vic" like everyone else. Victoria was too formal, and I was anything but formal. I couldn't remember the last time I had even looked at a dress. And heels? I once tripped over a lettuce leaf and hit the floor like a ton of bricks while wearing my favorite pair of sneakers. So, heels were definitely off the menu for me. God knows what I would trip over in a set of stilettos.

"I don't wear a jock. The straps make my butt look big," I told Berta. "Do you have a quarter I could borrow? The machine ate my money again."

"And I'll bet you kicked it," she said with her lilting laugh. Her laugh didn't fit her looks at all. It was like a cheerful piece of music, which was rather surprising since she looked like a sixty-year-old, gray-haired, English Bulldog with an attitude problem. But she and I were alike with our smart-ass attitudes and I thought she was the greatest. I'm pretty sure the feeling was mutual. Either that or she just laughed at me a lot.

She handed me a quarter and I limped back to the machine, only to find a random punk with an excessively gelled faux-hawk walking away from it, soda in hand, on his cell phone.

"Dude. I got a bottle of pop for a quarter."

A sigh mixed with a growl escaped my lips and I rolled my eyes to the heavens. Or at least the part of the heavens I could imagine through the stucco above me.

At times I wished I could get some sort of debilitating, but not at all unpleasant disease. Maybe something that would require lots of Vicodin. I wasn't a drug addict in any sense, but once when I hurt my back tripping over a lettuce leaf, my doctor gave me some Vicodin and I was pleased with the result. Really pleased. Excessively pleased. I could get in trouble with Vicodin. I would, however, settle for a case of temporary Tourette's syndrome. Then I could tell my boss to fuck off and get away with it.

"Oops, sorry. Illness. Can't fire me though. American's With Disabilities act. WWW.ADA.GOV. Look it up, bitch. Oops. Sorry again."

But that probably wouldn't work when all I had was a caffeine jones and a broken toe.

I shook off the toe thing and reentered the office putting on my best "nobody-mess-with-me" face. Berta laughed again as I handed the quarter back to her.

"You trying to look mean?" she prodded. "I saw that guy get your soda. You should have grabbed it and beat him with it."

"While I'm not in the best of moods, I don't really have a death wish today," I told her. "At least not until Carnie goes on another rampage."

Carnie O'Leary was my aforementioned boss, who had become the source of my slight mood and occasional intestinal disorder. Secretly I liked to call her "Carnage O'Murder," because if I hadn't had certain prescribed medication at various points in my life, that's what she would have caused. I was generally a happy person until she arrived in the morning and began barking orders at me in her voice that could pierce the Earth's atmosphere. I seriously thought her voice was one of the causes of global warming. Maybe I should have called Al Gore.

I wasn't sure what I was thinking when I accepted the job as her assistant. I guess I thought I was walking into a cake job with really good pay. That's how her last assistant made it appear. She sat at her desk and read books all day, mostly about horses like "National Velvet" or "Seabiscuit". After I took the job, however, things were rearranged. Carnie was apparently afraid of her last assistant for some reason. Maybe it had something to do with the horse books. I had met my predecessor. Very sturdy woman. I could actually picture her mule-kicking someone's teeth out with her back leg. Suddenly I ended up doing twice the work of "National Velvet" and Carnie did a quarter of the work she did before I took over the position. She apparently decided that one of her jobs as boss over the entire office was to distract and annoy employees and that this particular activity should take up seventy-five percent of her day. I'm not sure what she did with the other twenty-five percent, but I'm sure it was something vexing to someone.

One of her favorite activities involved bounding out of her office when someone she knew was at the front counter. Then she would bellow something that could be construed as mildly amusing in some circles. She then laughed hysterically at her own joke, took a flying lunge, and put her hands all over the nearest employee. It was rather disconcerting. Disconcerting, hell, it was downright disgusting, especially when she would drool while doing it. However, since she was a woman, and there were nothing but women in the office, what could we do? She claimed to be straight, but was never married. I wouldn't call her attractive, but she wasn't unattractive. She had white, china-doll skin and pretty blue eyes. But she kept her thick blonde hair so short it looked like a fuzzy, yellow hedgehog on her head. And while she was only around fifty, she wasn't aging well, she was developing some kind of senior acne, and her behavior was enough to put anyone off. She lived with her sister Debbie in a "quaint" little house in the middle of town. Her using the word "quaint" made me want to puke. Then again, a lot of her words made me want to puke.

Could the unsolicited touching be considered sexual harassment? Would her jokes be comical harassment? Since her jokes sucked but she laughed at them and pawed all over us, could it be attempted comical and sexual harassment? I cringed every time she went off on one of her imagined humorous tirades, mainly because I knew she was going to rub all over me. And I also knew for a fact she didn't wash her hands after using the bathroom. She said the soap in the office made her hands too dry. Then she'd come back from the bathroom and want to use my phone, or touch something on my desk and I could practically see the E. coli squirming all over it when she was done. I kept a bottle of Lysol in my desk drawer next to my hand sanitizer for just such emergencies. I mean, I wasn't a germaphobe at all, but come on. Wash your damn hands and buy some lotion.

And the woman had the hearing of a freaking elephant. She could hear a mouse fart across the room and would immediately issue a memo, for me to type of course, that the entire office should rid our desks of any food not in a thermos or a burped plastic container.

Then at certain unpredictable moments, the slightest giggle or chuckle from an employee of hers sent her into an uproar of epic proportions. "Keep your voices down. I'm not paying you to sit around and laugh all day."

It was getting worse by the week.

Or maybe I was getting worse by the week.

I knew my attitude needed adjusting, but it was difficult to adjust when I had a college degree and the most interesting part of my day involved sorting the incoming mail. A chimp with communication skills could do my job if you put it in a pair of Dockers. Then it wouldn't be any surprise when the chimp suddenly went berserk and ate Carnie's face. While I wasn't into face eating, I could see myself going berserk, especially after a vending machine ate my last quarter.

I stalked back to my desk and was preparing for the next outburst when the phone rang.

"Clerk's office, Vicki speaking, how may I help you?"

"Thank you for calling Hell. I'm Vicki your hostess for the evening. How may I help you serve The Mistress of all that is evil?"

It had the same ring to it.

"I told you to drink more water," the voice on the phone said. I looked across the room at my confidant Toni who was holding her phone and grinning.

Antoinette Markham was one of those women who was excessively beautiful, but she would fight you if you told her so. She towered over me at just over six feet tall and her hair was the color of smooth, dark chocolate like her eyes. When I went out with Toni, my "Plain Jane" looks were overshadowed by her exotic beauty, and I usually became invisible and ended up paying for all of my drinks. Sometimes I got a few compliments on my long, reddish-brown hair. It was very wavy and ran down to the middle of my back. Men seemed to like it. But, then they noticed Toni and I might as well have been bald. She was the closest thing I ever had to a sister though, and I loved her. She knew me better than anyone on the planet. And we had heard each other fart, the mark of true friendship. Plus I beat her by about two cup sizes in the boob department, so we both had something to flaunt. I inherited mine. She was hoping her husband would get her pregnant so she could catch up.

"Water is boring and it has no bubbles," I replied.

"But it's so much better for you. And you can get water with bubbles."

"Have you ever tasted that stuff?"

"Yes. It's not that bad."

"I'd rather drink my own urine."

"Well that's just wrong."

"I agree, so I'll just stick with soda and you can have the urine," I laughed.

"Be careful, she'll hear you," she whispered into the phone.

"Right now, I don't care," I whispered back. "I just want to get the hell out of here."

"Only twenty-five minutes to go. I think you'll make it."

"I don't know, man. The urge to shove a stapler up someone's ass is starting to overpower me. I'm beginning to tremble."

She laughed. "A stapler?"

"Well, it was in my eye line."

"I won't bend over in front of you anymore."

"But I love it when you do, baby."

She laughed again. "You're too much."

"Yeah, I weigh too much."

"Oh please! You do not."

We both laughed and hung up. I tried to use humor periodically to get me out of my "work moods". It usually worked out better for my co-workers than for me. "The Tears of a Clown" you know?

Or in my case, "The Chainsaws of a Clown."

Yeah, I definitely needed an attitude adjustment.

Or a man. Yeah, a man would be nice.

The clock ticked. I played with my pen. The clock ticked some more. I looked at my calendar. Nothing was scheduled. I was never sure what was going to happen in April. Sometimes the Clerk's office was busy at the beginning of spring. A lot of people wanted file for divorce, probate a will, or over-turn the Court's decision to keep them out of the sunshine and in a nasty, old, prison cell throughout the spring. Then again, how much sunshine a body gets in April in Brenton, Illinois depended on how the weather gods felt about dumping rain on the newly planted corn.

"Tick....Tick....Tick...."

Tonight on sixty minutes, a Clerk's secretary goes insane and staples her boss to death. Post-its were found in the throat of the decedent, and written on each one was the message "You should have washed your hands, (expletive)."

I began typing the memo I had been given long before my trip to the vending machine. It was something about asking attorneys for advice and how it was "frowned upon" in this office. Hell, the only attorneys around here who would consider giving advice would be posing like an Egyptian hieroglyph waiting to be paid. But apparently someone got away with getting free counsel and it pissed someone else off, so rather than dealing with that person directly as a good manager should, I was typing this memo in the hopes of offending everyone equally.

"Vicki. Could you come here for a minute?" the global warmer called from behind me.

My spine stiffened.

What the hell did I do now?

Maybe she saw me kick the machine.

I turned around, got up, and shuffled into my boss's office. "Yes?"

"I know you showed me how to do this before, but could you show me again how to make the little smiley face appear on emails?" she asked, using her magnifying glass so she could see the screen. She had eye problems, along with her many other ailments: fibromyalgia, chronic fatigue syndrome, spinal meningitis, COPD, and every now and then various forms of twenty-four hour cancer.

"Colon, right-parenthesis," I answered, turning to leave.

"I tried that, it didn't work," she moaned, holding her forehead. "I think someone has been messing with my settings."

I never knew someone could get so worked up over a smiley.

Thinking how my taxes were paying for this lesson so technically I was working for free, I blew out a sigh, moved around the desk to her keyboard and typed the colon and right-parenthesis smiley she wanted.

"Oh, there, it worked. I don't know why it won't work for me."

I stifled a snort and thought of a few reasons.

No, Vic, just smile and back out of the room quickly before she tries to engage you in conversation, or tell you about her latest illness.

I knew more about this woman's butt pimples and ovaries than I cared to know about anyone's. Didn't ask about them. I was just told in no uncertain terms about the night she sat in the bathtub and removed the bandage from her…

Ugh. I'm gonna cry.

"Um, Carnie, do you care if I take off a little early? I have a chiropractor appointment."

Okay, I lied a little. I'd do anything to get out of there without committing a homicide.

"You've been going to them a lot lately, are you having trouble?" she asked with obvious fake concern. She was a good politician, I'd give her that.

"Oh just some pain in my neck," I replied. "I've had it for years."

Have I ever. Almost nine now.

"Okay, well, remind Toni to lock the evidence vault before you go, would you?"

In the five years she had worked in the office, Toni had forgotten to lock the evidence vault only once. I had to remind her every day since. She loved it. It gave her a reason to come to work. And she hardly ever left bruises when she punched me for reminding her.

I quickly grabbed my jacket and headed toward Toni's desk. "Don't forget to lock the vault slacker."

"Where the hell are you going?" she questioned, shooting a rubber band at me.

"Chiropractor." I grabbed the rubber band out of the air.

Cat-like reflexes have I.

I'd be a ninja, but I don't look good in black.

Victoria Childs, purple ninja. Fighting evil rubber bands everywhere. HIYA.

"God, you're such a liar," Toni griped.

I grinned my most innocent grin and walked past her desk toward the front door of the office. "Later Berta!"

"Huh? Oh, yeah," she grumbled, not moving her eyes from the computer screen.

Must have been a good email. Either that or an interesting mug shot. She knew every criminal that came into the office. She probably knew the guy who took my soda. Come to think of it, she seemed to know a little bit about everything that went on in the office, from who was getting divorced, to whose kid had gotten arrested for underage drinking.

I pushed open the double doors and walked down the hall toward freedom from the confines of the Brenton County Courthouse. I happened to catch the elevator quickly, so maybe my luck had taken a turn for the day. I hit the "L" button and rocked on my heels in an effort to hurry things along. The door opened on the first floor and a guy dressed in a tailored, navy blue suit ran into me.

"Oh, s'cuse me," he said, stepping out of the way.

"No problem."

He wasn't much to look at, almost slimy, but his scent lingered behind him. The cologne he was wearing was a mixture of good pipe tobacco and naughty stuff, and I loitered a moment to get another look at him.

His suit didn't jive with the rest of him and after a second look I noticed it was wrinkled all to hell. He was obviously unkempt with a three day beard, and his teeth were gray as he smiled at me. I smiled back reflexively and walked away toward the secure glass doors leading out of the building.

"Jesus, I need to find a man," I muttered.

The fresh breeze hit me in the face as I made my way to my little Honda Accord, lifting my spirits considerably and helping me get into a weekend frame of mind. I smiled genuinely for the first time that day as I left the parking lot. I had no plans in particular, other than sleeping long and hard into Saturday and enjoying every second of it. I often had no plans, and just let the road carry me where it wanted me to go.

I wasn't planning on having a life-changing experience that evening.

I mean, if I had known about it, I would have chosen a nicer outfit, or at the very least some fancier underwear.

****

CHAPTER TWO

After dropping off my dry cleaning, dinner was my next assignment for the evening. I wasn't a frequent cook. I certainly had the ability to cook, but there was no sense cooking for one. I either ended up with a ton of leftovers that were ultimately thrown away because I was so sick of eating them, or just enough food to feed a gerbil. I was not a gerbil. Part German, but not gerbil. Irish-German to be exact, which is probably why every hair color I ever used ended up being reddish-brown, and no matter how long I sat in the sun, my skin was either lobster-red or slightly freckled at the end of the day.

It was difficult maintaining my figure by eating fast food all the time, but the occasional skipped meal and a few jogs around the block seemed to do the trick. I mean, I wasn't fighting off the men with a bat, but I had seen a few of them take a second look at the headlights and the caboose. I did have a fear of cholesterol tests, however.

I decided KFC would do nicely for the evening, and it was on the way home. It was populated by mostly Latin folk, but they knew me by name there. "Veekee!" they said when I entered. Kind of like Norm on "Cheers". I was too lazy to go in however, so I pulled up to the drive thru and twiddled my thumbs.

The only problem with KFC was that they tended to be slow.

"Can I kelllp you?" burst forth from the speaker next to my ear and I flinched sideways.

"Damn, yell much?" I barked and then regained my composure. "I'm sorry, I'll take a two piece, extra crispy, with double potatoes."

"You don juan de slaw?"

Did I freaking say I juan de slaw?

I took a cleansing breath through my clenched teeth.

"No, just potatoes please."

"Ho kay, pull up."

I looked down at the passenger seat next to me and reached for my bag.

Shit!

Oh come on!

Really?

In my rush to leave, I forgot my purse at the office. I fished around in my jacket pockets where I found some blue lint and a condom that had been there for about four months. It was surprising to me that it hadn't fallen out in front of my mother. I kept forgetting to put it in the drawer with the lonely lingerie. Some may say I was in a rut. I preferred to think that I had sowed my wild oats and was waiting for the right man to come along to tame me.

Okay, I was in a rut.

And, unless it had weed in it, I wasn't going to pay for my dinner with a condom.

"Hey!" I yelled at the speaker.

"Jes?"

"Cancel that order. I'll have to come back."

"Ho kay."

Crap!

I had my heart set on extra-crispy goodness and all I had back at my apartment was peanut butter and some stale potato chips. Couldn't get groceries without money. Couldn't get chicken without money. Couldn't even get the slaw I didn't want without money. Back to the office it was. Everyone would be gone by the time I got back anyway. I would just slip in and slip out unnoticed.

I must have really wanted that chicken. Rush hour traffic in Brenton was a pain to say the least, mostly because every street downtown was one way. I had to go two blocks out of the way to get back where I needed to be to park. And everyone and their brother was trying to get home quickly and get dinner over in a hurry. It was Friday. CSI came on at seven.

Brenton, Illinois was located exactly in the middle of the state, which meant it was just far enough away from everything to be completely uninteresting, yet not quite small enough to be completely unintimidating. We had gang shootings, not very many, but we had them, and everyone knew to stay away from the east side of town after dark. And even though the courthouse was in the middle of town, I was glad it was April and still light out. If it had been December, there was no way I would have risked the walk back to the office without an armed escort or my pepper spray, which was in my purse, which was in the office, which was seven floors up. I was slightly paranoid about darkness anyway and what may be lurking there. I wasn't sure anything would happen right in front of the building, but a girl can never be too careful.

After five p.m. meant I had to enter through the Sheriff's Office at the back of the building. I hoped Paul Harrison was working. He was sort of a buddy of mine. Well, okay, we had a thing. But it was very short lived, and since he decided to stay married, it got a little too complicated, particularly because I was head over heels for the gorgeous bastard. Paul was one of those shallow, yet incredibly beautiful men that women have a tendency to take one look at and throw caution, and their underwear, to the wind. The trouble with Paul was, he knew this. If he hadn't been unbelievable in the sack, I would have only done it once. Okay, maybe twice. Three times topless.

I mean tops. Yeah, tops.

I entered the Sheriff's Office and proceeded to the desk sergeant. No Paul. It was some round guy I didn't know and my employee ID was in my purse which was obviously not in my possession at that particular moment.

"Can I help you, Miss?"

It was time to turn on the charm, and the headlights. Sometimes, boobs are powerful.

"Yes," I said, fluttering my gray eyes and rolling my shoulders back highlighting the bouncy ladies jutting seductively from inside my gray sweater. "I work on the seventh floor, and I left my purse up there by accident. Can you buzz me in please?"

I flipped my hair back and giggled for added effect. I could "work it" if I needed to, but I always felt silly when I did.

"You got an ID?" he asked.

Dumb ass.

Either that or I was losing my touch.

Actually, I'm not sure I ever had my touch.

"No, I'm sorry, it is in my purse which is upstairs," I said, stretching my hands skyward and giving a little shiver like I was cold.

Come on dude. Look at them. They're right here in front of you.

"Can't let you in without an ID," he grunted, going back to his magazine.

Damn it! Must be a leg-man.

I needed my chicken. KFC attacks are hard to resist and this huge chunk of a human being wasn't going to get in my way.

"Hey, listen, is Paul working tonight?" I asked, leaning against the counter again.

"I don't know a Paul. I just started a couple weeks ago," he scratched his chest and it made the scraping sound of a gorilla with a bad case of psoriasis.

"Great," I muttered. "Look, I swear to God, I work here. Isn't there a way you can look me up?" I plopped my thirty-two D's on the counter in front of him. "Victoria Childs, Room 705, assistant to the Clerk. I should be in the system."

Suddenly I felt a not-so-gentle slap on the ass. "Hey, Sexy Girl, you causing trouble again?"

I grinned.

Thank God!

"Aren't I always?" I said, turning around to Paul's sparkling blue eyes. His chest bulged under his brown, sheriff's deputy uniform and I nearly splattered into a puddle. He had recently started spiking his blond hair, probably in an effort to hide that it was thinning rather rapidly.

But God, he was gorgeous. Like other-worldly gorgeous. Why did he have to be so damn gorgeous?

"Hey Rookie, let her in. She works here," Paul said, addressing the itchy gorilla.

"You got an ID?" Lardo asked Paul.

Paul and I both stared at him for a moment, wondering if he had noticed Paul's uniform at all. Something told me this guy wouldn't have noticed what either one of us was wearing unless we were covered with powdered sugar.

"My name is Sergeant Paul Harrison, and I'm here to relieve you from duty," Paul pointed to the badge on his chest. "You can take off now."

"Just doing my job, sir."

"Well your job is done for the night."

Lardo surrendered, and I thanked Paul with a gentle punch in the arm.

"That all I get?" he grinned.

"What do you want?"

He leaned forward and took a long, deliberate sniff of my hair. "You know what I want."

I leaned into him and put my lips close to his ear. "Get divorced, then we'll talk."

I pulled away and headed toward the door with a sly smile.

"You're not a nice girl, you know that don't you?" he said heading into the security post.

"I know, now let me in."

He hit the buzzer. "Later, Shorty."

He always teased me about being short. I had to admit, I was five-four on a good day in my running shoes. Out of them I was lucky to hit five-three. But he was one to talk. He only stood about five-nine. Toni was taller. Then again, Toni was taller than a lot of men, including her husband. I always wished my height would fluctuate like my weight did. I tended to jump between one twenty-five and one forty depending on how much chocolate I could get my hands on. It would have been nice to be able to be five-ten on those one forty days.

"Thanks. I'll be back down in a few minutes," I said, waving at him.

"Then you can come back here, get under this counter, and really thank me," he said, cocking his chin up a notch and raising an eyebrow.

"I'll consider it, if you can remember my favorite Aerosmith song."

He scowled and rubbed his chin for a moment. "Uh, Love in an Elevator?"

I grinned. "Nope. Dream On, Harrison, Dream On."

He rolled his eyes. "Thanks, I will."

But I had to hand it to the man. He knew what he was doing when it came to women. All I could think about when I turned away from him was jumping on his head.

Unfortunately when the building was shut down, so were the elevators. He buzzed me through the glass doors that led out of the Sheriff's Office. Then I had the choice of taking the public stairs to the immediate left, which tended to smell like various bodily fluids, or I could take a hairpin curve to the left and go around the corner to enter the secure judicial area. Those stairs just smelled like our judges, who were normally very clean by nature and tended not to pee in corners.

I decided to skip the stinky stairs, put the code in the lock and took the clean route. Clean or not, by the time I hit floor two and a half I had to take a break.

"Lord, I gotta get in shape," I told myself as I pressed on.

Must have been a one forty day.

I eventually got to the seventh floor without having a heart attack, opened the code lock to the office, and nearly crawled to my desk. There it was, sitting on the floor under my desk as it has been every day for nearly nine years. I grabbed my purse and headed out the office door and back to the stairwell.

As I rounded the curve to head down to the fifth floor, I was stopped by a strange noise.

Voices. Angry voices.

I took a right on six and peeked around the corner to the left, where I quickly noticed that one of the judge's office doors was open.

"Don't walk away from me!" a man's voice shouted. "We ain't done yet!"

I stifled a snicker. Lover's quarrel. The judge who occupied that particular office was Judge Weinhardt, and it was rumored that he preferred men. I didn't tend to believe rumors without proof, but one can never tell. I liked the man though. He didn't seem to have the "robe syndrome" that was common with the other judges. He never talked down to anyone and always had a smile on his face. He was also very soft spoken and polite which made this even stranger.

"Listen, I've told you I've done everything I can," Judge Weinhardt said, sounding rather desperate.

"No you ain't! You ain't done nothing!"

"If he walks, and does it again, it's my ass! Don't you understand that? I have a reputation to think of here!"

"Fuck your reputation!"

Whoa! Hello!

I knew I shouldn't have been listening and something told me to stay out of sight. I backed up a little, but curiosity got the better of me. I could hear a little more. It's not like I was hurting anything, and maybe I could quash the rumors about the judge.

"I told you, I can recuse myself from the case and say I know the man," the judge said. "That's the best I can do."

Papers rustled and someone gagged.

"Recuse this, mother fucker!"

Then I heard the familiar noise. I had seen plenty of action movies and cop shows to know what it was. It was a gun muffled by a silencer. I put my hand to my mouth and heard the gurgling noises of a severely injured man. More papers rustling, things falling, struggling. Then the sound again.

Another.

Another!

My God, how many bullets did it take to kill a man? And who was killing who? Whom? Whatever!

What the hell could I do? This crazy bastard couldn't know I heard him.

Oh my God.

Oh my God!

I just witnessed a frigging murder!

Footsteps from inside the office. I kept my hand over my mouth and skittered back to the stairwell. Up? Down?

Which way should I go?!

Think, think, frigging think! Okay, okay, just breathe. Calm down and breathe. The answer will present itself if you're calm and breathe.

There were two ways he could get out. He could go through the courtroom, out into the public hallway on the sixth floor, and down the stinky public stairs. Of course he wouldn't do that because he would have to go out through the Sheriff's Office and pass Paul on this way out of the building. If he's covered in blood and carrying a gun, chances are Paul would notice this and detain him.

Then again, it was Paul. He usually only noticed people if they were jiggling up top or wearing something low cut.

Then again, I didn't know what this dude was wearing. I mean, if the rumors about Weinhardt were true…

Ugh!

The logical way out would be to take the judicial stairs down to the basement and go out through the old morgue. It would be spooky as hell, but he could get to the street that way. Then he would pass…

Right where I'm standing.

Oh Jesus! OH GOD! Why the hell isn't the answer presenting itself?!

"I…I killed him." The man's voice was almost as frantic as the voice in my head.

And it wasn't Judge Weinhardt's voice I heard.

Is that good or bad?!

I DON'T KNOW!

I decided to head back up to the Clerk's Office on the seventh floor and call down to Paul to tell him what I heard. But as soon as I hit the first step I heard the door to the office close and feet shuffling quickly on carpet.

Oh sweet Jesus! He's coming! He'll see me!

I backed off the stairs as quietly as I could and ducked into the sixth floor.

What now? I didn't know the code for the lock to get into the office on the sixth floor. Was it the same as the seventh? Chances are I'd be fumbling with it and…

"Oh, hi there. Just little ol' me. Didn't hear nothing, honest. Just go on about your happy, little murder…"

Help! Paul! He's Coming!

I focused all my energy on mentally connecting with Paul. As if Paul was going to hear my thoughts. I'm not sure he even knew I had a brain. Too bad my boobs weren't telepathic. He'd definitely get the message then.

Then I noticed the door in front of me. I crept over to it and tried the knob. It clicked open.

A closet. Thank Christ!

I quickly dove into the broom closet and slid the door closed as quietly as I could. Then I ducked as close to the floor as possible and began praying.

"Dear Jesus, please help me. I don't want to be murdered today."

I heard the man on the stairs next to me, heading down and hopefully out of my life forever. Then I bumped something with my butt, and a long, hard object crashed down on me. It felt like a mop or broom handle. It hit something on the wall next to me and, "CLANG…ANG…ANGG!"

I had always had a slight fear of fire extinguishers, but only that they could explode in my presence like one of those compressed air tanks. I never thought in a life or death situation that my position would be given away by a mop handle hitting one.

The footsteps stopped. I stopped. Everything stopped.

"What was that? Who's there?"

The voice was thick and distorted, as if he'd just been to the dentist.

It was at this point that I was glad I hadn't eaten. I would have puked all over myself.

I couldn't breathe. I couldn't even blink. I heard him ascend the stairs slowly, round the corner to his left, and then he was on the carpet next to me. I reached up slowly and felt for a lock on the door knob. I pushed and turned the lock slowly and begged it not to…

"Click."

Shit!

Running on the carpet now and doors rattling. Tears leaked from my eyes. The door knob in front of me rattled and I put my hands over my mouth to keep from screaming and I closed my eyes. Maybe if I kept my eyes closed and my hands over my mouth and he got the door open, he wouldn't be able to see me.

Okay, Vic, that's just stupid!

Everyone knows you need a special cloak to be invisible. Oh, if I only had the power to disapparate. Was there a spell for that? How did it go? Leviosa? No, that was to levitate.

Where the hell was Harry Potter when I needed him?

Focus, Vic! There's a whole bunch of reality going on here!

There was silence. Time passed, but I had no idea how long. It may have been an hour, or a second. Then I heard him continue quickly down the stairs. I was frozen there, like a big Vic-cicle. Finally, when I couldn't hear him anymore, I wiped a tear off my face and took a deep breath.

"Thank you, God. Thank you. I swear I'll go back to church. I swear I'll lay off the one beer I have a month. I'll never sleep with another married man. I'll stop sex all together. I'll go back to the gym, and I'm never going to KFC again." I whispered promises over and over to the man upstairs. Ain't it funny how important God suddenly becomes when we have near-death experiences?

I had to move. I was locking up all over. After all, my knees were thirty-five years old and they had just climbed seven flights of stairs. I'd lock up too if I was them. I stood up slowly with the pole against my back. My knees creaked and groaned at me and my legs were still twitchy from the climb, but I was alive. I could breathe. I could walk, and think, and jump up and down. I stood in the blackness of the closet and tried to plot out my next move while attempting to make sure that the pole didn't fall on me again. My hands were shaking furiously and I took deep breaths, trying to calm down. Had anyone heard anything? Would anyone come? Surely they would. And Paul would be worried about me, or at least worried about my boobs.

Very slowly, I pushed the door open a couple inches and stopped. I saw the blue carpet in the hallway lit by one single safety light at the end of the hall. I listened. More silence.

"It's now or never," I whispered to no one.

I stepped out of the closet and into the hall. Nothing. Silence. I hated silence. I've always hated silence. There could be boogeymen in the silence.

An uncontainable sob escaped my throat and I was running. Around the corner to the right and I was on the stairs running down. Sixth floor, fifth, fourth…I had to stop. I was going to be sick. I stopped and collapsed on the bottom step before the fourth floor where I gagged a few dry heaves and tried to breathe.

What's going on?

What did I hear?

Who was that man?

Why would he kill Judge Weinhardt?

Why the hell didn't I just go home? Peanut butter would have been way more satisfying than hiding in a broom closet waiting to be killed.

Would the Colts win the Super Bowl next year? That would be sweet. I love the Colts.

What? What the hell am I…?

My brain was firing randomly. I needed to calm down.

I smelled something musty and sweet, like old-lady perfume. And for a second I thought I heard something, but…

There was a quick and sharp pain in the back of my head, and suddenly I had four hands.

Wow, shiny shoes. I wonder where those came from. Are those my feet?

Someone threw me into the blackness as my head hit the tile below me.

****

CHAPTER THREE

I heard voices from far away. Too far away to help me.

"Vic? Vicki? Oh my God!"

Vicki's not here at the moment, would you like to leave a message? She'll call you back when the room stops acting crazy.

I laughed internally at my own joke.

Crap! I'm becoming my boss.

Someone was slapping my face and I wished they would stop.

It's not nice to hit people.

Why was it so cloudy? Buildings weren't supposed to be cloudy. Unless there was a fire. Maybe Carnage O'Murder, the blonde dragon, started a fire with her breath while laughing uncontrollably at her latest hundred-year-old joke.

Am I dying? I can't die here. I don't even like it here. Wait, where the hell am I again?

"Vicki? Please, Sweetie, wake up. Get the fucking paramedics up here, she's bleeding! "

Who's bleeding? Why is everyone being so loud?

I clenched my eyes tighter.

"Huh?" The sound of my own voice echoed in my ears.

Ow! No talking. Vic's not talking anymore.

"Oh, thank God. Vicki, open your eyes, honey. It's Paul."

"Paulie, are you orange?" I whispered.

Someone was squeezing my head too tight. I couldn't think.

"What? Vicki, open your eyes."

Don't want to. The orange hurts.

I tried to open my eyes between the clenches. My forehead was cold. My hands were hot. Everything else was missing.

"Don't move her! Vicki, can you move your fingers for me?"

Who are you? Where's Paul?

I tried to clench my fist.

"Paul?"

"I'm here, Sweetie, you're going to be okay." He was holding my hand, or someone was. "Move your fingers."

I wiggled my fingers. Everything seemed to be where it was supposed to be. But why would someone want to scalp me? They'd better bring my hair back. I loved my hair. It was the only part of me that I ever really liked.

Someone wrapped something around my neck.

It's too tight. Way too tight. I'm choking! He's strangling me! Help!

"Paul?" I squeaked. "Too tight."

"Don't try to talk, Vic. They're here to help you."

"Tell them to turn down the orange. It's too bright. Hurts me. Navy blue is better."

What the hell am I talking about?

Maybe Vic knows. I'll ask her when she comes back.

"She's disoriented," someone said.

"Ya think so, Einstein?" Paul snapped.

Darkness wrapped around me again, cold, like a broken electric blanket that had been in the trunk of someone's car for too long…maybe wrapped around the body…

****

I opened my eyes. There were red flashing lights and chaos around me. People were talking, but I couldn't understand them, and faces were fading in and out of focus. They were all calling me "Ma'am".

"Ma'am, are you all right?"

"Ma'am, can you hear me?"

"Ma'am, do you know what day it is?"

I'm not a Ma'am. I'm only thirty-five. Ma'ams are old. And how the hell should I know what day it is? Is it Spring? Are there lilacs yet?

"April," was all I could get out before someone kicked me in the head.

Ow!

Then I looked up and saw him standing over me. He was surrounded by the whitest light and his gentle fingers brushed my cheek as he smiled at me. His skin was gold, almost incandescent, and his kind smile surrounded me with warm safety. His eyes, a deep hazel tinged with green, like the Illinois sky before a big storm.

And he was the most beautiful thing I had ever seen in my weird, little life.

I reached out to touch his face and he shimmered and held my hand in his, and I was warm all over and tingling.

My mom always told me that everyone has an angel who protects them from harm. This was probably mine. I always thought his hair would be longer.

"It's all right," he said, his voice echoing through me. "You're safe now."

"Angel?" I asked. "Am I in heaven?"

He chuckled. "No, you're still in Brenton."

I closed my eyes. "Damn it."

"My sentiments exactly," he said. "Rest gal. You're going to be okay."

My guardian angel was from the south. Tennessee maybe.

Someone lifted me up, my eyes melted, and I think I faded out again. Someone else was talking about pancakes and monkeys.

I smelled tobacco smoke.

Daddy? Is that you? I miss you a lot.

****

A few minutes, hours, or days later I was waking up. I felt nice, like I was floating on a cloud of rabbit fur and kitties were purring next to me. I might have even been smiling. Then the smell of disinfectant and sickness filled my nostrils, and I snorted. The kitties faded away.

"Vicki? Can you open your eyes for me?" a gentle masculine voice said to me.

Yes Lord, I'm here. Sorry about the whole thing with Paul. I knew he was married but, it's your fault he was so good looking.

I opened my eyes slowly and looked around.

Shit!

I was in a hospital. White walls, mauve curtains, and Mom at the end of the bed.

The guy in the white coat shined a light in my eyes. "Good reaction. Vicki, can you tell me what day it is?"

Why the hell do people keep asking me that?

"Um, Friday?"

"No, Hon, it's Monday morning," Mom said.

"Please, Mary, I need to see if she's oriented," the presumed "doctor of all things" said.

"I'm sorry. She's my baby. I want to help her. Do you have children, Doctor Fielding? Are you married?"

"No, I'm not…please Mary, let me examine her."

Mom was always trying to find me a man. And this one was a doctor. Hot damn!

He held up a finger. "Can you touch the tip of my finger?"

"Are your hands clean?" I asked with slight difficulty.

Lord knows what he was lancing or touching before he got here.

My mom laughed. "I think she's fine, Doctor."

"May I have some water?" I croaked.

Mom skittered into the bathroom and brought me a plastic cup.

"What is going on?" I asked, sipping my water and hoping to get some sort of realization about what had happened to me over the past few days.

"Well, you had a pretty bad concussion," Doc said. "You've been in and out for a while and you had us a little worried. But I think things are starting to turn around for you. Your pupils appear normal and I would say you seem to be focusing. Do you remember what happened?"

I thought for a minute. Then two minutes.

Do I remember what happened? The question of the day…whatever day it is because I obviously don't know.

"Well, I forgot my purse at the office and I went back to get it...and then…oh…" An icy gust of panic rushed up my spine but I wasn't sure why. Then the tears were streaming down my face.

What the hell is wrong with me?

"You're going kind of pale, Vicki, are you all right?" the doctor asked, putting a hand on my forehead.

"I don't remember what…" A sob came out sort of sideways and the corners of my mouth twitched.

Mom rushed to my side. "It's all right, Hon. It's all right."

My mom was a comforting soul with a kind heart, and her arms and hands were warm and just squishy enough to make you feel safe. She wasn't exactly thin, and she wasn't exactly fat. And she had recently let her hair go snow white, and it was always short and beautiful. And she had a way of making it okay to cry whenever I felt like it. But at that particular moment, I didn't feel like it. I felt like kicking another vending machine. Apparently my tear ducts had other plans. I didn't usually handle confusion very well.

"Vicki, the police have been here several times. They want to talk with you," Doc said. "Would it be all right if I called them when you feel up to it?"

He looked at me and smiled. He had kind eyes. Almost like my Angel's eyes.

My angel. I remember my angel. Where did he go? I want him back!

"Yeah, I need to tell the police what I know."

What I knew. What I knew was nothing.

"All right. Here's his card. Um, Detective Varner. I'll tell him to stop by this afternoon. Why don't you get some rest until he comes?" He handed me some sort of device with a button on it. "It's a Morphine pump. Press the button if you have pain."

"Halleluiah!" the choir sang.

I immediately pressed the button. I needed all of that shit I could get. I wanted to float away on the furry cloud with the kitties again. I didn't want to remember what happened, not if it was going to make me cry. I didn't want to remember anything. But I had an annoying thought that wouldn't go away, like a popcorn hull stuck between my teeth.

"Um, Doctor," I stammered, "how was I injured?"

"Well, I just assumed you fell down the stairs and hit your head."

"I didn't. I was sitting down," I remembered suddenly. Or did I actually remember it? It just sort of came out of my mouth and I really had no idea if it was true or not.

He looked at me. "You were sitting?"

Okay, go mouth. You're on your own.

"Yeah, I was sitting on the steps."

I thought about the Indianapolis Colts. Why would I think about them? It wasn't even football season. Maybe because the draft picks were coming up, but I wasn't all that excited about that.

He wrote something on my chart. "Let's see. You have a contusion on the back of your head. I thought you hit your head on the railing. Maybe I better take another look."

I hit the button again and leaned forward.

Jeez Louise! Where the hell did the Clydesdales come from and why are they dancing on my brain?

I whimpered and hit the button three more times.

"Hey, take it easy on that stuff. You only get a few doses every four hours and then the machine shuts itself off." He pulled the bandages back and shined his eyeball flash light on my head. "Let's see here. Yes, there is definite bruising. Sort of rectangular shaped with a gash at the bottom that required staples..."

"My head really hurts," I whispered. "Can I lay back now?"

"And you're sure you were sitting on the steps?" he asked.

"Uh, I'm not sure of anything really," I said. "Can I lay back down now?"

"Hm," he said, ignoring me. "I suppose..."

I hate when people start saying something and don't finish. It makes me nuts.

"You thupoth whaaaat?"

Ooh, boy!

It was getting really hard to talk. I glanced at the kitty at the end of the bed. He was the littlest kitty I had ever seen and he was yellow, no, ginger. A ginger, money cat like I had when I was little, and he was cleaning his ears. I heard somewhere that if a ginger, money cat cleans his ears, then it was going to rain within the next three days. Better tell them.

"Hi, kitty," I said. "Pretty kitty."

"Kitty?" Mom said. "Vic, are you all right?"

The kitty chirped a greeting and rubbed his velvety head against my feet as I let myself fall backwards against the mattress.

"Kitty says it's going to rain," I said. Then I giggled and covered my mouth. "He's a weather-predicting pussy."

My mother gasped. "Victoria!"

The white dude was talking, but his face was all fuzzy and all he seemed to be saying is "Nyaahhhh blabber blabber, who who who."

The kitty licked my toes and I giggled and closed my eyes.

"Sorry, Mom."

****

"Hey! Wake up!"

Someone poked me.

"What?" I said, trying to rub my eyes.

"Watch your IV there."

I rolled my head over carefully and saw Toni sitting in the comfy chair beside the bed, her long legs stretched in front of her casually. The chair was high-backed and had lumbar support, obviously for concerned loved ones. Not for mean people who poke you out of your morphine-induced kitty utopia.

"What are you doing here?" I asked her. "Is it still Monday? Shouldn't you be at work?"

"Yes, it's still Monday. Thanks to you, we get some time off while they're investigating," she said. "You going to eat that brownie?"

I looked at the tray in front of me. Hospital food. Terrific! The brownie was the only recognizable thing on the tray. There was some green slop with what looked like a mushroom perched on the top, and a brown thing that might have been beef at one time, but I don't think the cow had that kind of entrée in mind when she sacrificed herself for the greater good. My stomach gave an involuntary lurch and I shook my head.

"Take it."

She reached over and grabbed it. Then she took a huge bite and grimaced. "Never mind." She spit the bite into the trash can next to her. "Ugh, I'll bet they put a laxative in it."

"What are they investigating? And what do you mean by thanks to me?" I asked her.

"Haven't you heard?" she said grabbing the napkin off the tray and wiping off her tongue. "People are talking about the 'unidentified woman' who is suspected in the murder of a circuit judge."

"What?!"

Ooh, shouldn't have done that.

The horses started the "electric slide" on my head.

"They seriously think I killed someone?" I asked, clenching my eyes shut and holding my forehead.

Toni leaned forward and grasped my arm. "You really don't remember what happened?"

I shook my head. "No. Who's dead?"

"Judge Weinhardt. He was shot to death in his office."

I swallowed. "Why do they think I did it?"

"You were there, Sweetie."

I laid my head back and looked at the water damaged tiles on the ceiling. "Why don't I remember? And how could anyone think that I did that?"

"Well, no one really thinks it, but everyone is saying it."

"Fuck!"

Oops! Nice mouth, Vic.

"Is Mom still here?" I asked.

"I sent her home to get some sleep. She looked exhausted. I mean, with her daughter being a murderer and all."

"Stop saying that!" I grimaced at the pain again. Where was my button? I needed more Morphine. Everything was becoming too real. "What time is it anyway?"

"Um, three," she said looking at her watch. "The doctor says the detective will be here at three-thirty."

Detective. I forgot about the detective. I was going to have to lay here in all my injured glory pouring my heart out to some fat detective with a powdered sugar mustache and a jelly stain on his tie.

"Oh, well, this just couldn't get any better. Call and tell him to bring me a doughnut."

Toni snorted and flipped the channels on the tiny TV mounted to the wall.

"Where are my happy drugs?" I asked, feeling around for my button.

"Oh, um, the doctor came in and disconnected it. He says you can't have any more until you eat and, um, pass a stool. He said you'd have to make due with oral medications."

I looked at the tray again and suppressed a gag. I was not eating that shit, and there was no way I was "passing stool" in a bed pan. Oh, the humanity! I couldn't even pee if someone was in the stall next to me in a public restroom. How the hell was I supposed to do that in a bed pan with everyone watching? I should have kissed the kitty goodbye when I had the chance.

"I don't suppose I could get you to go to McDonald's for me," I asked hopefully.

She rolled her eyes at me. "The usual?"

"Yes, please. With extra ketchup."

"Well, I guess we should be glad you're back to normal."

"Me? Normal? I thought I was the one who bumped her head."

Toni snorted again, grabbed her jacket and left.

****

CHAPTER FOUR

As I was dozing, I was having the worst nightmare. But I knew it was a nightmare, so I wasn't all that worried about it. I was running down stairs that went down forever into blackness, and my legs ached and threatened to fall out from under me. And I was tired and sick, but I kept running. Something kept flying at me. Something black and hard, and shiny, and no matter how many times I ducked or covered my head, it would always hit me in the same spot. Right in the back of the head where my staples were, and it hurt so badly, and I tried to scream and tell it to stop, but it kept coming and coming.

And then there were dogs and horses laughing and playing poker. The navy blue horse had a royal flush, but the puppy on his left thought they were playing spades, and he had the queen.

My head hurts.

"Miss Childs?"

The brown horse was talking to me. How did he know my name? He smiled pleasantly, and I noticed he smelled like leather and a very nice cologne. He had a relaxed voice, southern inflections, and it was deep and soothing. The kind of voice you could wrap yourself in and take a long nap.

"Miss Childs?" he said again and I felt the warmth of a hand on my shoulder.

Uh oh, reality. There's a hand on my shoulder.

I opened my eyes slowly and gazed up toward the source of the voice where I saw a familiar and sweet smile, along with a pair of enchanting hazel eyes.

The angel! He came back to me. But this time he was wearing a brown leather jacket, and his skin wasn't gold and shimmery. It was peachy and normal.

"Angel?" I whispered.

The smile widened. "Pardon me?"

I suddenly became aware of my surroundings and the fact that I sounded like a drugged-up idiot. I grunted a sleepy laugh.

"I'm sorry," I said, stretching my shoulders. "I must have dreamed…have we met before?"

He sat down in the chair next to the bed and leaned toward me. "Sort of. You spoke to me just before they put you into the ambulance. I'm Detective Varner."

"Oh," I said, blinking. I blinked again and he came into better focus.

No powdered sugar or jelly stains in sight. He was meticulously groomed and his gray tie looked as if it had been pressed within an inch of its life. His hair was light brown, cropped to about an inch all the way around, and combed forward covering his hairline which may have been receding insignificantly. His jaw line curved gently into his squared chin. Smooth skin covered his face and neck, not a blemish in sight, and his soft and perfectly full lips smiled warmly at me. The only design flaw I noticed was that his nose was a little bent at the bridge with a small scar on the slope. It had obviously been broken at some point and either hadn't healed properly or there was bit of a botched surgery attempt. But it made his profile very noble and the scar wouldn't have been noticeable if I hadn't been staring so intently.

And the gentle bend of his earlobe caused increased saliva production in my mouth.

And his eyes were so dreamy. My God! They were large, but not overwhelmingly so. Perfectly set, with not too much lash, and the color was indescribable. Hazel didn't seem to cut it. In the darkness of the room, they looked brown, but when he cut his eyes to the light there were flashes of green and gold, with tiny flecks of gray and auburn.

But there was something deep inside them that was so sad.

He was wounded. Someone had hurt him badly. I was betting it was a woman. At least I was hoping it was. If it was a man…jeez! I wish I was a kid again so I didn't have to worry about that kind of thing. Little girls get crushes and never have to question if the guy is gay, which explains why certain fancy little boys are so popular these days. But I guess every generation has their own fancy boys.

"Are you all right?" he asked. "You seem kind of dazed."

"Huh?" I grunted, rising from the fog. "Oh, yeah. You're just not what I expected."

"What did you expect?"

I smiled at him. "Someone different. Older probably."

He sat back. "I get that a lot."

"I'm sure you do."

"But I've never been called an angel before," he said, a trickle of pink easing up from his collar.

I snickered. "Sorry about that."

"Ms. Childs, I'd…"

"Please call me Vicki," I said, "or Vic. Most people call me Vic."

"Okay, Vic," he said, flashing his white teeth and unclipping his badge from his belt. He placed it on the nightstand next to him. Within his smile he had a slightly crooked tooth on the left of center that was very charming and made him the typical "boy next door".

What if he lived next door to me, and he was out mowing his lawn in the hot July sun? Ooh, Detective, it's too hot for that shirt, isn't it? Goodness, look at the sweat dripping down your muscular back and rippling chest. And your big, bulging biceps are simply drenched. Would you like some lemonade? Here, let me towel you off and massage your back while you cool down…

Good God! Hormones anyone? Where the hell did those come from?

"I'd like to ask you a few questions if you don't mind," he continued.

"Not at all."

I must have looked a mess. How was I supposed to seduce him if I looked a mess? How was I supposed to seduce him at all? He was way, WAY out of my league. He was the high school quarterback and I was the chubby girl who admired him from afar.

Then again, I hadn't eaten in more than three days.

Then again, I also hadn't showered in more than three days.

"Would you like the head of your bed raised, or are you more comfortable lying down?" he asked, with his soft, southern cadence.

I fancied myself somewhat of an expert on American dialects. I could usually tell what part of the country a person is from after a few words. I placed him in Louisiana, probably lower. There was a Southeastern United States influence there as well, maybe around Kentucky or Tennessee. I had thought for a while in college that I wanted to be a linguist, so I studied that kind of thing for a couple years.

Useful huh?

I was day dreaming.

Answer his question dip shit.

"Oh, um, uh, I could raise up a little bit."

He stood, reached down beside me and hit the button on the bed rail, brushing my hip with is long fingers in the process.

Oh my goodness. I could seriously pass out from this.

"That better?" he asked.

"Yes, that's fine."

He said "betta." Teehee. Adorable.

He straightened up, and the full length of his body suddenly astounded me. The man must have been six-five. He took his brown leather jacket off and laid it at the end of the bed revealing a neatly-pressed, cream-colored, button up shirt. The obvious bulge of his biceps distracted me as a masculine scent filled the area around us. It was wonderful and I breathed him in and held it awhile. I didn't know the cologne or deodorant, nor did I care. It's amazing how the presence of an incredible-looking man can make the rest of the world disappear.

He sat back down in the comfy, lumbar chair and retrieved a legal pad from his briefcase. He unbuttoned the top button of his shirt, loosened his tie and sighed peppermint into the mix of aromas in the room.

"You'll have to pardon me," he said. "It's been a long couple of days and I'm a little wiped out."

"I know the feeling," I said. I put my hand up to my bandaged head and smiled.

"I'm sorry. I know you've had a rough time. I won't be here long."

"Stay as long as you like, it's nice to have company," I said. Then I had to validate my assessment. "Where are you from, Detective?"

"I was born just outside of New Orleans, but I've lived all over," he said, clicking his pen almost nervously. "I was an army brat."

I smiled in private victory and took a mental bow. "I thought I detected Louisiana in your accent. You said N'awlins which is the obvious give away. Do you say ya'll or you all?"

He smiled. "Ya'll."

"And what's that you're holding in your right hand?"

He looked at his pen. "Why, it's a pen."

I nodded. "New Orleans. If you were from any other part of Louisiana, you'd call it a 'pin' instead of a pen. But I'll bet you catch yourself saying 'worsh' instead of 'wash'."

His eyebrows rose slightly. "Sometimes I do, yes."

"You probably went to school in, let's see, Kentucky or Tennessee, or one of your parents is from there."

He nodded. "University of Tennessee. Impressive ear."

I laughed. "Sorry. I'm showing off I guess."

"Not at all. Maybe after a few more months in Illinois, I'll sound like a native."

"Well don't do that," I said. "Southern suits you."

I scoped out the left hand. No ring or visible tan line.

How interesting.

Yeah, right. Like I had a Popsicle's chance in hell.

"Well, thank you, but I'm here to talk about you," he said, clicking his pen again. "Can you tell me what you remember about Friday?"

Nope, all business. No chance for the Popsicle.

I sighed and tried to flex my brain. I couldn't seem to form the words right away as I rubbed my forehead and willed the pain to go away.

"You okay?" he asked gently.

"Yeah," I replied quietly. "My head hurts, and I'm just trying to remember."

"Let's start with something simple. You had left work for the day. Why did you go back into the building?"

"I left my purse in the office. I stopped for dinner at KFC on my way home and realized I didn't have my purse with me, so I drove back to the office to get it."

"The KFC on Grove St.?"

"Yes."

"That's not on your way home."

I blinked. He was right.

Shit! Why the hell was I over on that side of town?

"Oh," I said, as the memory popped in. "I dropped off some dry cleaning first at that place on uh…"

"Market?"

"Yeah, Market. The KFC is on my way home from there."

"They do good work," he said. "They got a grease stain out of my navy blue suit."

"The KFC or the dry cleaners?"

He blinked a few times and his eyebrows lowered.

Wow! Tough crowd.

I smiled. "Kidding?"

He nodded and sort of smiled, but then went back to scribbling on his pad. "So, how did you get back into the building without your ID?"

"Paul, let me in."

He flipped back through his notes. "Paul Harrison?"

"Yes."

"Y'all know each other well?"

"We're friends," I said, attempting to hide the truth about my relationship with Paul. He watched me analytically, his eyes searching my face like a "Where's Waldo" book.

"Um, Deputy Richards was on duty at the time, he said you appeared to be very good friends," Varner said, reading only the name "Richards" from his pad. The rest of the time, his eyes were on me.

I stared at him blankly. Something about the look in his eyes told me he would know if I hid anything else.

"Paul and I had a relationship about eight or nine years ago," I admitted. "It was also over about eight or nine years ago."

"A sexual relationship?" he asked, writing furiously.

He stopped looking at me. Why did he stop looking at me?

"Yes," I answered quietly.

"Why did it end?"

I sighed. "I woke up."

He nodded and his eyes rose to mine again. "He's married."

"Yes."

He shifted in his chair as if he was uncomfortable. "That didn't bother you?"

"Yes, it did, but I was in love with him," I said defensively. "Is this really relevant?"

"Just trying to establish a few things," he said without emotion.

I laid my head back slowly and bit my lip. Why did I feel like crying? I didn't have to explain myself to him. My love-life was nobody's business but my own.

"Anyway," he said, "Harrison let you in and then what?"

"I'm not proud of whatever it was that Paul and I had, Detective," I gushed, somewhat dramatically. "It was a very low point in my life. I haven't been with him or another married man since I ended it with him." I wiped away an embarrassing little tear. "And whether you believe it or not, I did love him."

He leaned forward and put an apologetic hand on my arm. "I'm sorry, Miss Childs...Vic. I didn't mean to upset you. I just want to make sure I have every detail correct. Kind of my job, you know?"

I sniffled and glanced at him. He caught my eye and he looked genuinely sorry. I attempted to smile. It was hard not to when I looked at him.

"I guess I haven't really let myself be emotional about all this yet," I said.

He squeezed my arm and smiled warmly. "It's okay, Cher, I know you've been through a lot."

He called me "Cher," a common term of endearment used in bayou country. If I had been standing, I would have had to hold on to something to support my weak knees. I looked down at his hand on my arm and had to force myself not to bring his hand up to my mouth and start kissing his fingers.

Maybe he was dropping his guard a little. Either that or he was working his way into my head. Instinct told me not to take the "Cher" thing very seriously, and not to let him charm something out of me to twist around to his advantage. He didn't strike me as the type to do that, but I didn't know the man.

I had to remember, Toni said they were investigating me. He probably thought I was a murderer. "Innocent until proven guilty" always sounded good, but it was rarely the case. If a cop had a suspect, he worked to prove him guilty, not innocent. And don't even get me started on judicial prejudices.

But the look on his face was so sweet and friendly.

And then suddenly, as if he read my mind, his demeanor changed back to "no-nonsense cop." It was as if he had quickly remembered that he wasn't supposed to look at me like that, remembered that he wasn't supposed to be enjoying himself.

"So," he said, leaning back in his chair, "Harrison let you in?"

"Yes," I replied seriously, "and I entered the secure area where the judges' chambers are. I had to take the stairs because the elevators were down for the night. I let myself into the Clerk's Office and got my purse."

I had to stop. Everything was kind of fuzzy from there.

"Take your time," he said, taking on a confidential tone. "Don't force it. Just try to relax and let the memory come to you. I'll wait for it."

I closed my eyes and tried to picture what happened, but all I had were momentary flashes, like I was outside it all with a camera.

"I know I went back down the stairs," I said slowly. "Then I heard something that made me stop..."

Blue carpet...security lights...shouting...obscenities.

"I heard an argument," I whispered.

"Who was arguing?"

"Two men. One was Judge Weinhardt."

Why am I whispering?

"Can you remember what they said?"

I inhaled and exhaled with increasing difficulty.

"Um, Judge Weinhardt said something about letting someone walk. He couldn't let him walk because his reputation was at stake and..." I gasped and flinched as the panic came flooding back. "Oh God! He shot him!"

Strangled, I'm being strangled!

His hand was on my arm again and I tried to focus on that, but the memories were taking me back to the stairwell. Back to where I was horrified.

Someone is after me!

"I'm right here with you, Girl. Just breathe and tell me," he said, but he sounded so far away, like we had a bad phone connection.

I gasped again. "I heard three, four shots. They were muffled like he used a silencer."

I was there in the stairwell and someone else was...

I'm shaking! My hands are shaking! Help me!

"He's coming," I whispered. "He's going to kill me."

My arm jerked from his grasp involuntarily and I lunged at nothing, my breath coming in short, jumpy bursts and I couldn't control it, no matter how hard I tried. Hands were on my shoulders and I thrashed about against them. Something in my brain knew that no one was there to hurt me and that these were just memories. I knew nothing I was seeing was real. But I couldn't handle my body's reaction to all of it, like someone else was pushing the buttons on a Vic remote control.

"Vic, stay with me. It's not happening now." His comforting voice echoed in the stairwell, but I tried to scream and run away. My strangled voice came out in a squeak.

"Help me!" I choked. "Please help me!"

"What the hell are you doing?!" Hands were on my face, different hands now. "Who are you? Get your hands off her!"

Toni?

"Vic? Victoria! It's Toni! Look at me, please."

A slap stung my right cheek.

Why do people keep hitting me? I'm not a frigging punching bag people!

I looked into Toni's eyes, gasping for air. "You're here? Is he…is he gone?"

"Ask her how she got away," I heard behind me. "Why didn't he see her?"

"How did you get away from him?" Toni asked me calmly, still holding my face.

I grasped Toni's hands, and there were more hands on my shoulders and my face, but I focused on Toni, my comfort, my friend. "I hid! I found a…I found a closet and I hid! I heard him…I heard on the stairs and then I just ran."

"Did you fall down the stairs?"

I held her arms, my only link to sanity. "Please, Toni, I can't do this. I can't take it."

The room started spinning and I felt my lungs closing in on themselves.

"I can't breathe!" I sobbed. "I'm choking!"

"All right," came another voice. "I'm going to give her something before she rips her IV out."

I touched the hands on my shoulders and gagged. "He's going to kill me!"

"You're safe, Vic, it's okay now."

"I can't br…breathe. Toni, I'm afraid! Help me, please!"

"I know, Honey, I know. Try to calm down now."

My shoulders went limp and my face began to melt. I felt my chest relax and I could breathe again. Then there were three Tonis holding my three faces, and I looked up at them and tried to talk.

"I have to tell him," I sputtered.

That hottie detective. I can't remember his name…

Someone pulled me up on the bed and I was going down into the abyss of unconsciousness slowly.

"Angel?" was all I could get out. I forced my eyes open. "Where's Angel?"

He chuckled and I felt his hand on my arm again. "I'm here."

"I didn't fall," I whispered. "Something hit me. I was bleeding."

Relief washed over me like a warm bath and I closed my eyes, drifting off into oblivion.

Then I heard, "Seriously? Your name is Angel?"

****

CHAPTER FIVE

"Girl, let's get you up and around a little bit," Mike said.

Mike was an attractive, African-American nurse who was very large and muscular. To put it bluntly, he was built like a brick shit-house. Though I'm not quite sure I've ever seen a brick shit-house, but I'm sure they're well built. We used to visit my grandparents in the back woods of Tennessee when I was a kid and they didn't have indoor plumbing. My father was a first-rate hillbilly. Their shit-house was wood, and kind of scary. There were spiders. The only animal I could consciously kill with relish was a spider.

Mike was also as gay as the day is long. But I just adored him and he was a wonderful nurse. And since there weren't many patients on the ward, and it was my second full day awake there, we were getting to know each other pretty well.

"Ugh," I groaned as he helped me out of the bed. "Every time I try this I puke."

"I know," he said gently. "But we got to get you into that shower. You stink to high heaven."

I looked up at him. "Thanks a lot."

"Well, I ain't nothing if I ain't honest."

I laughed weakly for a couple beats until the nausea came. "Oh, God."

"Now come on, girl, take some breaths. Through your nose in, out your mouth. We can do this."

He walked me slowly to the bathroom and helped me out of my gown. "You all right?"

I nodded. "Aside from being naked in front of an attractive black man, sure."

"You ain't got nothing I ain't seen before, honey," he said, smiling and turning on the water in the shower. "You ain't my type anyway. Too small and pale. I like 'em big, dark and brawny."

"Brawny? Like the paper towel guy?"

"Only kind I use."

I staggered out of my underwear and into the shower. It was the kind that just has a little lip on the floor to keep the water from going everywhere. Good thing too, because I'm not sure I could have lifted my leg high enough to step into a tub without falling on my ass.

"If you all right, I'm gonna get that night gown your mama brought you, okay?"

"Can I please wash my hair?" I begged.

"I'll bring shampoo too," he said. "Just try and avoid that big, old bald spot."

Bald spot?

I had a bald spot? Wonderful! They had just removed the bandages from it earlier that morning, but I didn't put two and two together. I had staples, so they had to shave me.

Duh!

I let the warm water run over me and washed with the scratchy hospital wash cloth which felt surprisingly wonderful against my skin. Mike handed me some shampoo and I wet my head. As I washed my hair I felt the three-inch-square bald spot on the back of my head and I flinched. Terrific. It was a glowing testament of my clumsiness there for everyone to see. I rinsed off and turned the water off feeling slightly human again.

"Ooh, Girl, hurry up!" Mike said, handing me a towel and closing the bathroom door. "That fine detective is at the nurses' station asking about you."

"What?" I shrieked, followed quickly by a horse kick in my head. I was lucky though. The herd of galloping stallions in my noggin was down to about eight from the previous twelve.

But the angelic detective was back. He could heal me with his tongue. I mean his lips. I mean his touch!

Sheesh!

"I said move your little ass, woman!" Mike said, snapping me back to reality for the moment.

I toweled off as fast as I could and threw on my night gown and robe. I tried to brush my hair, but was having a hard time getting the brush through the knots until finally Mike took over.

"Damn, I wish I could have gotten you some conditioner," he said. "We're never going to get a brush through this."

When I was judged presentable, Mike helped me back into my clean sheets just as Detective Gorgeous came into the room. He looked startling in his navy blue suit and I suppressed a gasp.

"S'happenin'?" he said smiling. "Well, don't you look better."

"H…Hi," I stuttered out. "Nice to see you again, Detective."

He held out his hand and I took it. He squeezed gently and I nearly swooned.

"Mm hm," Mike said. "You okay now, Sweetie?"

"Yeah, I think so," I told him. "Detective…uh…"

What the hell is his name? I only ever thought of him as Angel.

He smiled. "Varner."

"I'm sorry," I gushed, feeling like a complete fool. "Varner, this is Mike. The best nurse in the world."

Mike rolled his eyes, "You're just trying to get extra cookies with your meal tonight."

"Ex-Lax cookies? No thanks."

The men shook hands and Mike said, "Enchanted, Detective."

"Uh, yeah. Me too," Varner said.

"You buzz me if you need anything, Sugar," Mike said grabbing my old hospital gown. He looked Varner up and down and then at me again. "Mm hm, now that's brawny."

And with a wink, Mike was gone.

Varner looked at me and cleared his throat uncomfortably. "Are they taking good care of you?"

"Oh, yeah. Mike is very entertaining."

"Yeah, I could tell."

We looked at each other again and we both smiled.

"He's a very good nurse," I said.

"I'm not doubting that at all."

He sat down and loosened his tie and I licked my lips wondering how his neck would taste. He was looser than the other day. His brow wasn't as tight and his eyes were softer. Maybe he found something out to exonerate me.

Or maybe he got laid. Shit!

"What brings you here, Detective?" I asked, making sure my stubbly legs were covered.

"Jason," he grinned. "I've seen you in a fugue state. I think that means we're past the formalities don't you?"

"What's a fugue state?"

He chuckled. "I witnessed your little panic attack the other day."

"Oh, that. I'm so embarrassed."

"No reason to be," he said. "It would have panicked anyone. You're damn lucky to be alive."

I sighed and put a hand to my forehead, willing the pain to subside so I could see him more clearly. I didn't want to miss a thing about him.

"So, what brings you here, Jason?" I asked with a smile.

"Boredom mostly. I was in the area and I thought I would stop by and bring you some lunch." He pulled a couple of sub sandwiches out of his briefcase. "Hope you like turkey."

"You're a wonderful person," I said, trying to forget the lunch the hospital had served. It resembled meatloaf, but I secretly thought it was cut from an old tire tread.

He smiled shyly and handed me the sandwich. "Nah. Well, okay, I'll buy that."

I grinned at him and I could feel my ears turning red as I brushed the hair out of my face.

"Oh, that reminds me," he said quickly. "Can I take a look at the wound on the back of your head?"

"Uh, sure?"

He pushed the tray table away and I slipped my legs out from under the covers as I turned my back to him and hung my feet over the side of the bed. He ran his fingers gently through my hair exposing my baldness, but all I knew was that he was touching me and I liked it. I liked it a lot. So much so that I couldn't contain a little shudder as one of his fingers brushed the back of my neck.

"You all right?" he asked, his voice washing over me like a wave of lust.

"Yes," I whispered, closing my eyes and concentrating on his touch, which probably wasn't the best idea. Having an orgasm just because his fingers were in my hair would probably tip him off that I was attracted to him.

You think?

"May I take a picture of this?" he asked, putting a hand on my shoulder.

I swallowed my slobber. "Be my guest, but no posting on the internet."

He chuckled rather politely and I wondered if the man ever genuinely laughed. I heard the tone of a digital camera and saw a couple flashes, then his hands were in my hair again.

"Hm," he sort of grunted. "Does it still hurt?"

"Yeah, but only when I move around too much or get loud," I admitted. "It's the fingers…hands…I mean the nausea that cripples me."

Sometimes I hear myself say things and I think my brain is no longer connected to my mouth.

"Okay, you can slide back now," he said, giving my shoulder a little squeeze. "Thank you."

I righted myself in the bed and he moved the tray table over so we could share it. I unwrapped my sandwich and he watched me take a bite. Then he smiled.

"Hungry?"

"God, I miss real food," I said, savoring the crusty bread and mayonnaise.

He took a bite of his and flipped on the TV. "Mind if I catch the score of the game?"

I grunted my approval as I inhaled another bite. Baseball? A dog dragging his hiney on the grass was more entertaining to me. But he was close to me. Close enough that the clean scent of him covered the sick smell of the hospital. And he made me feel, I don't know, alive.

We ate in silence for a while and watched the game. Well, he watched the game. I watched his mouth and envied the sandwich. He reached down into his brief case and handed me a bottle of Diet Dr. Pepper.

"OH!" I exclaimed. "I could kiss you."

He chuckled. "Maybe later if you're up to it."

Wow!

"Uh, I wasn't talking to you," I said. Then I gave the bottle a passionate kiss.

He put his face in his hand and laughed quietly. "You're something else."

Ah ha! He could laugh.

"How did you know I love Diet Dr. Pepper?" I asked him.

"I have my sources."

I squinted at him, but he just grinned.

"Checking up on me are you?"

"That's my job," he said, picking at his sandwich. "Did you know the judge well?"

I shook my head. "I spoke with him a few times, but never at length."

"You know what kind of cases he heard?"

"I think he was on felonies," I answered.

He nodded. "Yeah, most of the felonies in this town are drug cases, and there are very few of those. He wasn't a busy man."

"Yeah, not much happens around here," I said, wiping my mouth.

"I heard dat."

He heard "dat." Cutest accent ever.

"He did have that big case a few months ago," I said, snapping my fingers as I remembered. "They caught this guy in his meth lab with a bunch of homemade kiddy porn, but I forget the dude's name. A cop got killed on that one, but then I never heard any more about it."

He grabbed his trusty legal pad out of his briefcase and his pen out of the interior pocket of his suit jacket. With a click the pen came to life and began scrawling its notes.

"I'll have to check on that," he said. "Must have been before my time around here. Do you remember when it happened?"

I thought as I chewed. "Must have been around November of last year that he was arrested. Yes, I remember because it was around my birthday. Then he kept writing letters to my boss asking for forms. I think he was trying to be the jail attorney for a while. I wish I could remember his name."

"Should be easy enough to find out," he said, then he looked at me. "Scorpio or Sagittarius?"

I looked back at him, confused for a second. "Oh, me? Scorpio. Why?"

He smiled. "Just curious."

"You don't believe in that stuff, do you?" I asked him.

"Nah, not really, but some people believe in it adamantly and it can be helpful to know."

"Oh, well, all I know about Scorpios is that we're supposed to like sex a lot."

See? Mouth-brain connection momentarily severed.

I snorted at my own stupidity and covered my mouth.

He grinned slowly, nodded and took a drink of his soda.

"What about you?" I squeaked, hoping to change the subject.

He swallowed his soda and grinned again. "Yeah, I like sex a lot."

Holy crap!

I giggled and covered my face.

"Good to know," I said between giggles. "But I meant what's your sign?"

"Aries. Early April."

"Just recently then?"

He nodded. "Thirty-six unfortunately."

"Hm," I said, as I pondered that. "I have no idea what the signs mean though. Are we supposed to get along?"

He cleared his throat. "I'm fire, you're water, and we both want to be in control."

Oh my goodness! I may just hyperventilate.

Good thing my hair was long to hide the redness creeping up my neck, and down my face, and probably down my whole body.

He looked at me and his eyes narrowed. "So, how is it a charmer like you is still single?"

My eyebrows rose up into my hair. "If that's a line, I'm biting."

He exhaled a laugh. "Sorry, I didn't mean it to sound like one."

I took a nervous drink of my soda trying to think of a clever retort.

Eh, what the hell.

"Damn, I thought maybe I was about to get some."

He laughed again, a little more boisterously. "Down, girl."

"Sorry," I said, flipping my hair back and grinning. "I tend to use humor to avoid questions that I can't possibly answer. I mean, I think I'm hot as hell."

"I couldn't argue with that," he said with a grin.

"Wow!" I said. "Very nice."

"Why thank you," he said.

"Thank you," I said back.

Was the flirting real? Did I care if it was real?

Um, let's see…nope.

Flirting is flirting, and even if it wasn't real, I could still look back on it and feel kind of warm and fuzzy about it.

"You still didn't answer my question though," he said. "How come some lucky guy hasn't snatched you up?"

I giggled some more and squirmed a little.

"I don't know why I'm still on the market. It's an enigma."

He looked at me and chewed his lower lip. "Mystery woman, huh?"

I raised my eyebrows up and down. "I have many layers. I'm like a parfait. Or one of those desserts they put in the big bowls. You know with the whipped cream and fruit and custard…"

He chuckled. "A trifle?"

"Yeah. That's me. I'm a trifle."

He shook his head, rubbed his bottom lip and raised an eyebrow as he looked at me. I stared back with what I hoped was a sexy look. Usually when I tried to look sexy though, I ended up looking constipated.

"Hm," he said, narrowing his eyes again and smiling, and probably wondering if I needed a laxative. Then he looked at his watch. "I should get going. I've got to pass by the office and do some more paperwork. They're going to want a list of suspects from me sometime soon."

"Darn," I said, avoiding the obvious question. "I was just starting to have fun making you uncomfortable."

Pink oozed across his face as he grabbed the empty wrappers and napkins off the tray table and threw them away.

He actually blushed. I made him blush!

It's the little victories like this that make my life seem worthwhile.

He picked up his briefcase and held out his hand to me. I slipped my hand into his and relished the fact that our skin was touching again.

"Well, my little trifle, how about I bring you lunch tomorrow and I'll see if I can make you uncomfortable."

I laughed. "It's a date. Bring tacos. But not from Taco Bell. Go to Taco Johns, they're better."

"You got it."

He smiled, waved, and walked out of the room. I laid my head back and closed my eyes.

"I'm in trouble."

"Damn straight you are, Girl," Mike said, poking his head around the door. "I'm bringing you some make-up tomorrow."

****

CHAPTER SIX

"So, let me ask you this," Varner said as we walked slowly down the hall the following day. "Knowing what you know about the court building, how easily could someone get in after hours to get at a judge?"

"Actually, it wouldn't be too difficult. I mean, you know how easily I got in without an employee badge. But he would have to either know someone in the Sheriff's Office, or have a key to the judges' exit," I said, holding on to the hand rail.

"Any idea who has keys to that door?"

I shrugged. "You'd have to ask the building superintendent."

"Do they check the building after hours?" Varner asked. "Could he have come in earlier and hung around until they closed up?"

"I suppose," I said. "There are a lot of places to hide around there. Luckily I found one."

"And it was definitely a man's voice you heard?"

"Yes," I said. "It was sort of gruff and nasally. His tongue sounded thick. And he almost sounded, I don't know..."

"Slow?" Varner asked as he quickly scribbled something on his notepad.

"Well, yeah, or maybe handicapped in some way."

He looked at me. "You think the killer was mentally challenged?"

"Not profoundly, but that's how his voice and speech pattern sounded. I mean, I'm not an expert, but there was an obvious impediment."

He wrote something else down. We had been walking around for about twenty minutes discussing the case. I didn't realize how tired I was until…

"Ohh, Jeez," I said as the hallway started tilting.

"You okay?" he asked, holding out a hand to me. "I'm sorry. I didn't realize how long you had been up."

God his hands are huge! I'll bet if he put both of them out, I could sit down in them. Then he'd be touching my butt.

I closed my eyes and grasped his hand tightly. "I'm just a little dizzy."

"Come on," he said, keeping hold of my hand and putting his other arm around me. "Let's get you back. Think you need a wheelchair?"

"No, no, I'm fine." I opened my eyes and the hallway tilted the other way as the nausea swept over me and I put my hand over my mouth. "Okay, maybe not."

He supported me around the nurses' station and back down the hall to my room. I stopped and hung on to the railing for a minute, thinking I was about to see the tacos he brought one more time, but it passed without incident.

"Here we go," he said, lifting me up in his arms. Suddenly I felt as if I was on the cover of a romance novel, except my breasts were covered and his nipples weren't showing either, damn it. "Let's get you into bed. Don't puke on the tie now. My mama gave it to me."

Aw, he loves his mama. Could this man be any more perfect?

"Ugh," I said, clenching my eyes closed. "If I didn't feel like hell, I'd think you were trying to seduce me with sweet stories of precious gifts from your mother."

He chuckled and laid me gently on my bed. "You get to feeling better and I might consider it."

"Well let me know so I'll be prepared for it," I said, reclining the head of my bed.

He went into the bathroom and got me a cold towel while I took some deep breaths. He put a pillow under my feet and elevated the lower part of the bed a little, presumably to get some more blood into my head.

Okay, so maybe he was an angel after all. He was the angel of pillows and cold towels. He was the angel of turkey subs and tacos. And he was the angel of making me feel things I had forgotten I could feel.

"Better?" he asked, sitting down next to the bed and patting the towel against my forehead.

I opened my eyes. The world had stopped tilting, and the nausea was starting to go away.

"Yes, thank you. I hope this is all over soon."

"Head injuries can really mess you up," he said. "I know, I've had my share."

"Oh, yeah?" I said, clenching my eyes shut again and swallowing.

"Yeah. One guy came after me with a tire iron a couple years ago. Broke my nose and busted my head open. Thought I was never going to be right again."

"I thought maybe you'd been hit in the head a few times," I quipped.

"Hush now."

I exhaled a small laugh and gazed into his eyes. He touched the side of my face lightly and continued to smile down at me. His eyes started drifting lower, below my neck, and then he appeared to become aware of himself and his smile slowly faded into a look that could only be described as apprehensive.

"I don't want to upset you again. I know you've been through a lot," he said as he took my hand gently. "But I need to tell you something, and I need you to be calm."

I looked at his hand holding mine. This had to be bad. I didn't want any more bad.

"Okay," I said. I took a deep breath and prepared to be annihilated.

"I found your purse on the stairs," Varner said. "The murder weapon was in it."

He squeezed my hand gently and gave me what I interpreted as a look of confidence, like he was sure I could handle it. Then again, what the hell did he know?

"A gun in my purse," I said, rubbing my forehead. "Well, shit!"

He spit out a laugh. "An appropriate response."

"Sorry," I said. "I just can't believe all this."

He dipped his head and caught my eye. "I need you to be honest with me."

"I have been."

"You knew nothing about the gun being in your purse?"

"I've never touched a gun in my life."

"Then how did it get there?" he asked, obviously trying to test my memory. Or maybe he was trying to see if I could come up with a good lie about it.

"I have no idea." I pulled my hand away. "Do you think I killed Judge Weinhardt?"

He sat back in the chair and sighed. "Did you?"

I looked him dead in the eye and set my jaw. "Absolutely not."

He stared at me and bit his bottom lip, which I had already noticed was a sign that he was thinking.

"All right," he said softly.

"You believe me, don't you?" I asked him, on the verge of tears once again.

He shrugged. "I could believe the sky is green, that doesn't make it a fact."

"But, you do believe me," I said, almost pleadingly, holding out my hand to him. "I need to know that. I need to know someone is on my side here."

He took my hand in both of his, and suddenly a feeling came back to me that I hadn't felt since childhood. It was almost as if he were cradling me and keeping me from harm.

"Please say you believe me," I said. "Even if it's a lie."

His eyes met mine again and softened into a gentle look of sympathy as I felt a tear rolling down my cheek. He wiped it away almost tenderly with his index finger and he nodded slowly.

"Right now, yes I do," he said. "I believe you."

I knew right now didn't matter. I knew all that mattered was what he could prove. I laid my head down gently and sighed, but I wasn't sure if it was out of relief or fear, or if there was really a difference anymore. It all felt the same when I looked into his eyes.

"You okay?" he asked stroking my hair.

"We'll see," I replied gazing up at him, and most likely looking like a calf being led to the slaughter, or a woman desperately in love. No difference there either.

"I should go and let you rest," he said, looking at his watch.

"Okay," I said, secretly wanting to beg him to stay.

He shrugged into his beige suit coat. "Any idea when they're going to let you out of here?"

"Doc said maybe tomorrow afternoon."

"Okay, well, why don't you give me a call when you're at home and settled," he said, grabbing his briefcase and sliding one of his cards on the nightstand. "I just want to know you're doing all right."

"I'll do that."

Please, don't go.

He turned and smiled at me. "See you soon."

"Bye," I said, almost bursting into tears.

Why did I feel like this was going to be the last time I ever saw him? He wasn't leaving forever, was he?

He started out the door.

"Wait!"

The word popped out of my mouth like toast.

He turned around and looked at me.

"I'm sorry if I've been, I don't know, a little too forward," I stammered. "I'm just finding it very difficult not to flirt with you."

He winked. "Have you heard me complain about that?"

And with a wave he was gone again.

****

CHAPTER SEVEN

The following afternoon, I was sprung from my white room with the mauve curtains. Part of me was happy to be going home. Another part of me was terrified. I wasn't sure how I was going to handle being alone, out of the constant buzz of the hospital and the comforting presence of my giant nurse, but I knew sooner or later I would have to face it.

"You should come stay with me for a few days," my mom said as I began climbing the stairs at my apartment building.

I didn't know how to tell her that the last thing I needed was to stay with her for a few days. I loved her dearly, but she was kind of a Jesus freak. I mean, I still believed in God, or a higher power of some sort, but "Praise and Worship" music playing round the clock could probably drive me legally insane. Plus all her church friends would want to come over and pray on me, and not only did I find that kind of embarrassing, but some of the men liked to "lay hands" on places that didn't need healing.

Uh, dude, it's my head that hurts, not my inner thigh.

"I appreciate the offer," I told her. "But I really just want to sleep in my own bed."

I negotiated the stairs slowly and got the door to my apartment open. The big purple couch in my living room smiled at me. He and I were old friends. We had been through three previous apartments, four boyfriends, and one failed engagement. Luckily, I had been at this place for two years and I finally found my niche. It was a small, one bedroom place in an old remodeled house that was probably built when God was a child. I could have the place dusted, vacuumed, and mopped in about an hour and I had plenty of space for what little I had, though I never seemed to have enough room for my books. It was a nice place though. I had it decorated with a few Party Lite items that I had picked up over the years, and I loved burning candles. Vanilla was my favorite, but in the fall I liked burning Pumpkin Pie or some of the spicier ones. And at Christmas I always got out my big peppermint candle. It was drippy and getting pretty old, but it wasn't Christmas without my big peppermint candle.

Plus my neighbors were great. I had an older lady with a lot of cats next door to me in apartment three, and a couple with three kids below me in apartment one. I was in apartment two, with a view of the street below where my car was typically parked. My bedroom was just big enough for my full-sized bed and a little dresser, and luckily it had a big closet for storage. The kitchen and living room were surprisingly large, but the kitchen was a little cluttered because I didn't have much cabinet space. It was mostly cream-colored linoleum on the floor and up the walls, and would have supported an island nicely, but I wasn't in it enough for that kind of investment. The living room was furnished sparsely, with only my big purple couch, an old glass-top coffee table, a small entertainment center, and a computer desk. The only problem with the place was that the walls were startlingly white, and it had tan carpeting that didn't go with anything and looked as if it had been installed in the early seventies. And the bathroom was like a bowling alley, long and skinny, and if I fell in the tub, I would be on my own getting out because there is no way they could have gotten a gurney in there or an EMT that weighed more than a hundred and ninety. The wall separating the tub from the sink would have prevented that, with only about sixteen inches of clearance.

But, it was my home, and I was happy as hell to be back to it.

As for the failed relationships, it turned out the guy to whom I was engaged had two other fiancées and he used my credit card to buy rings for them. He was still wanted for that offense. And believe me, if I caught a glimpse of him, I'd tackle and arrest him myself with a two by four and some rope I had in the trunk of my car from when I helped Toni move a riding mower into her husband's truck.

Ooh, I should probably take that out. It wouldn't look to good for me right now, would it?

The guy after him cried on the stairs of my apartment building all night after I broke up with him. Married, criminal, or insane, I knew how to pick them right? After the cry baby, I decided to wait awhile before my next endeavor. Four months had passed, and the excessively gorgeous Detective Varner had me thinking I was ready for romance, even though I had already convinced myself that there was no way in hell he could ever find me attractive. Plain Jane never got the good-looking ones. She got the married, criminally-insane ones who stole credit cards.

"I'll get your garbage out," Mom said as I sat down on the couch. "It's starting to stink."

"Thanks," I told her flipping on the TV and falling on to a throw pillow. My head was still tender, but it was nothing like it was before. Plus, the doctor gave me Vicodin for the pain and another medication no one could pronounce for the nausea. Vicodin was my friend, and the other meds gave me a nice buzz too. I planned on sleeping for the next month.

Mom got back with the garbage can and handed me my pills. "Do you need anything? Want me to make you some dinner?"

I looked at my Charlie Chaplin clock hanging on the wall. The Little Tramp's legs were swinging and his arms indicated that it was five PM.

"No thanks. I'm not really all that hungry. I think I'm just going to get in the tub for a while and then go to bed."

"Okay, well, call me if you need anything." She kissed me on the cheek. "I love you, Hon."

"Love you too, Mom, be careful on the stairs."

She was agile enough for sixty-five, but her bifocals gave her trouble on stairs. She just took her time, and if someone was behind her, she stopped to let them pass. I admired my mom for many things, and her cheerful attitude about everything was one of them.

I began dozing during "Mythbusters," which was my all-time favorite show, and jumped awake to the phone ringing. I picked up the cordless next to me on the coffee table and grunted a sleepy, "Hello?"

"Vicki?"

"Yes."

"I'm sorry, it didn't sound like you. This is Carnie. How are you feeling?"

I rolled my eyes in anguish. "Oh, I'm okay. Still pretty sore and a little light headed."

"Did the doctor say when you can come back?"

I realized then and there, I wasn't going back. And as the thought entered my mind, my heart throbbed in my ears and sweat poured from my hairline. Then my hands started shaking and all I wanted to do was curl up in a ball and cry.

What the hell is happening? I was fine a minute ago. Relaxed even.

"Uh...um...no. I'll have to let you know about that," I choked out.

"Are you okay? Did I upset you?"

No, I was not okay. I was so far from okay. I couldn't even see okay anymore. But I had no intention of telling her that. I knew she was just wondering when her office bitch would be back. I was never going to be anyone's bitch. Never again!

"I'm fine," I said, swallowing my emotions momentarily. "I'll call you later on in the week."

Yeah! Right after I walk a tight rope across the New York skyline in a full hand-stand.

"All right, take care."

I got off the couch, dropped the phone on the charger and stared at the floor. I couldn't move. I couldn't think. I couldn't even breathe. Something was happening to me, and I sure as hell didn't like it.

Somehow I made my way to the bathroom and began filling the tub with extra-warm water. Another good thing about my old, remodeled apartment was the enormous, vintage bathtub on legs that was so deep I could fill it up to my neck. I undressed and opened my hamper. Inside I saw a plastic grocery bag. I reached down to grab it and saw that a pair of my khaki, work pants was inside. Mom must have brought them home on one of her trips to bring me fresh clothes. I pulled them out of the bag and inspected them, realizing that they must have had to cut my sweater off me.

And along the waist band, in the back, was a stain. It wasn't very noticeable, very small in fact, which is probably why my mom didn't see it.

I was wearing these pants the day it all happened. And the stain was blood.

My blood.

The blood I was laying in when they found me.

Good God! My sweater must have been saturated.

I dropped everything on the floor, turned around in a stupor and sank into the hot bath water.

Then the tears came. The feelings rippled through my body in waves as I wept. Soon I was holding my knees and sobbing every emotion I had ever had down my legs and into my bathwater as it rose higher and higher. Then I slowly began rocking, perhaps to comfort myself. It was too much for my mind to wrap around everything that had happened to me in the past week, but I couldn't turn it off. Images burst into my mind. The carpet, the stairs, Paul, my purse, my car, gun shots again, and again, and again.

"Please make it stop," I cried out to no one in particular. I held my face and wept until I couldn't anymore. And I was finally numb.

****

After the meltdown in the bath, I felt surprisingly better. Endorphins at work I suppose. Being clean and smelling like something other than hospital soap helped tremendously as well. Plus I was able to use a deep conditioner on my hair so it wouldn't tangle and break. I brushed my hair as gently as I could and threw on a clean t-shirt and sweat pants. I stepped into my kitchen and had just begun to make a peanut butter and strawberry jam sandwich when I heard the knock.

"Mom," I said smiling. She must have taken pity on me and bought some groceries. Moms are the best.

"You didn't have to do this," I said, opening the door without checking the peephole.

There he stood, all six-five of him, in a green polo shirt and jeans, haloed by the overhead light behind him. And everything was suddenly sultry and foggy. Was that music? Did I leave a radio on somewhere? No, not that I remember. Were those harps? Really?

I shook my head and finally noticed he was holding two delightful-smelling plastic bags of what appeared to be Chinese food. I nearly dropped the jam-covered knife I was holding.

He found me!

He's a cop fool. Of course he found you.

"Oh!" I said with a slight start. "Hi."

"What's up?" Varner said, looking at the knife. "You okay?"

I looked at the knife and laughed. "Oh, yeah. It's jam."

"Hope you like Chinese," he grinned, holding one of the bags up, the muscles in his arms flexing under the weight, causing things to happen to my libido.

The shock at seeing him hadn't quite worn off, but I was suddenly incredibly excited. I was also very aware that I had neglected to put on a bra after my bath. I was sure he was aware too. They're kind of hard to miss, especially when things happen to my libido.

Like high beams on the boob highway.

"Uh, yeah," I stammered. "I'm sorry, come on in." I stepped aside as he entered.

"Where should I put this?" he asked.

I stared at him like an idiot. He looked so amazing and he smelled even better. Joop cologne, I believe. Good enough to eat. And he was in my apartment. And we were alone.

"Um, oh, the kitchen is this way."

Come on, Vic, get it together. It's not like he's the first man who's been in your apartment, after months of nothing, who looks fantastic in a pair of jeans, and has the biggest feet I've ever seen, and who you secretly want to mount on the purple couch.

I cleared my throat nervously and led him into the kitchen. He put the bags on my tiny two-seater kitchen table. I dropped the knife in the sink and put my sandwich in a plastic bag for later. I have always felt that peanut butter and strawberry jam sandwiches were very important in maintaining my functionality as a human being on the planet, and should be savored.

"I wasn't sure what you liked, so I got a lot. Besides, I'm starving," he said, turning and looking at me. His smile immediately fell. "What's wrong?"

"Nothing, why?"

"Your eyes are…You've been crying."

"Oh, yeah well, it's the first time I've actually been alone since…" I didn't finish. It almost seemed like I didn't have to finish.

"Do you have anyone you can stay with?" he asked with a sympathetic nod.

"I could stay with my mom, but I have to be alone with it sooner or later. I chose sooner." I crossed my arms over the bouncy ladies and sort of shrugged.

He smiled. "Strong lady you are."

I smiled back. "Um, I'll be right back. The plates are up there," I said pointing.

I jogged to the bathroom and grabbed the first bra I saw. It was, of course, the most unflattering garment I owned, which was why it was hanging on the back of the bathroom door. It made me all pointy. He was going to think I had torpedo tits. Oh well, you gotta work with what's in front of you. And boy, oh boy, were they in front of me.

Cautionary cones! Boob highway under construction!

"What the hell is he doing here?" I asked my reflection.

My reflection shrugged.

I checked myself out, and was pleased enough, though I was a little pale. Oh well, next time I would be prepared with blush and eyeliner, if there was a next time.

I opened the door and headed back to the kitchen to find the extraordinary sight of his rear end sticking out of my refrigerator. I tilted my head involuntarily and enjoyed the view for a moment, until he reemerged holding a beer.

"I hope you don't mind if I help myself," he said, flashing me a grin.

Dimples. How did I not notice he has dimples? Lord help me.

"Uh, no, please. So, what brings you by?" I asked, figuring it was best to get it out of the way quickly.

The grin continued. "I don't know. I guess I missed you."

My eyebrows jumped. "You…missed me?"

As much as I wanted to, I didn't buy it, and I could tell by the look on his face that he knew I didn't buy it. His answer screamed ulterior motive.

"Sure I missed you," he said. "I haven't been in town that long. So hanging around your hospital room was the most fun I've had since moving here."

I nodded slowly. "I see. So, you just figured you would drop by?"

"Yeah."

I crossed my arms. "What if I wasn't home?"

"I would have come back later."

"What if I had had company?"

"I brought plenty of food for company."

We studied each other for a moment. He broke the stare first and grinned at the floor.

"I win!" I said, rather jovially.

He exhaled a laugh. "You're on to me aren't you?"

"I don't know, am I?"

"Too smart."

"Thank you."

He sighed and held up his hands in defeat. "All right. I've been keeping an eye on your apartment. I knew you were home because the kitchen light was on and I saw your shadow. I knew you were alone because I saw a lady, I am assuming she's your mother, bring you home and then leave. No one else came by after that. So, I popped down the street for Chinese and now I'm here to look around."

I smiled at his honestly. "Don't you need a warrant for that?"

"I was hoping it wouldn't come to that, but I can get one if you prefer."

I turned to the silverware drawer and got out some serving spoons and forks. "It smells too good, let's eat first."

****

CHAPTER EIGHT

We sat on the couch and relaxed with our respective dinners. His consisted of Mongolian Beef with a side of sweet and sour something or other, and mine involved some sort of brown, meaty substance with a lot of vegetables and of course the fried rice with another mystery meat. I honestly didn't care if it was kitty cat, it tasted great, and the company was enjoyable. He seemed to be letting his guard down a little more, but it could have been the beer. He did become a great audience for my half-witted humor. I liked his laugh, when he used it. Lots of times he just grinned and his shoulders shook a little if something struck him funny, like the way I bit into a green pepper and spit it across the room. Green peppers are the work of the devil in my opinion.

I took him on a guided tour of my apartment and he constantly chewed his bottom lip, obviously making his mental notes. I secretly hoped he didn't chew it off before I got a taste, then I kicked myself for thinking that. I opened my messy closet and drawers for him, and he smiled when I quickly flashed the bottom drawer, where I kept the naughty clothing. I hoped he hadn't noticed the dust on the lingerie, but something told me he had. He didn't ask to paw through it though, so I was glad of that. He did ask me if he could take the stained khakis I discovered into evidence. I wasn't sorry to see them go to tell the truth.

I'm sure neither one of us wanted to talk about the case, but the subject was bound to come up eventually. So,as we headed back to the couch for more Chinese, I brought it up.

"So, what do you think? Am I a murderer?"

He started on his third beer. "I never thought that about you."

I sipped my soda, having abandoned the beer for fear of a headache. "What do you think then?"

"About you?"

"Sure."

He smiled to himself and seemed to be avoiding the question. After a few more drinks of his beer, he finally said, "Well, between the checking up I did and what I've seen tonight, I could write a book."

"So start from birth and I'll tell you if you're right."

He sighed and put his beer bottle on the coffee table. "Well, you're a townie, born and raised. You went to Brenton High, and you're thirty-six..."

I kicked his shin lightly. "Excuse me! I am thirty-five. I won't be thirty-six until November."

"Hell to get old ain't it?" he said with a casual grin.

I kicked him again with my socked foot and snorted in a very lady-like manner. "I am not old!"

He snickered. "Seasoned then. And no more kicking."

I laughed. "Proceed, Detective Know-It-All."

"Anyway, your father passed fifteen years ago of a heart attack. You got through college in five years with an English Degree, but you started as a music major, I think." He paused for some sort of validation, like a psychic looking for clues to answers that would make himself look better. I didn't respond and dipped my egg roll in the sauce from my kitty cat combo.

"You've worked for a veterinarian, a podiatrist, an insurance company, and you currently work in the Clerk's Office as a secretary. You've been in the office for nine years, but you have only been in this position for three."

All of this I could explain, and so far I wasn't wowed. "Anything else?"

"You've lived four places in the last ten years. You were engaged, but never married, and your former fiancé is currently wanted for stealing two of your credit cards. He used one to buy another girl a ring." He gave me a quick and obviously uncomfortable look. "Ooh, sorry. I hope you knew that already."

"Yes, I knew that already, and I think it was two other girls actually."

He sighed and went on. "You like silent films, your favorite dog is the Boston terrier but you prefer cats, and your favorite color is purple." He looked at me, possibly trying to find validation again and I'm sure the shock on my face was proof enough.

"You hate your job," he said with a smile. "And you're self-conscious about your height and weight. And…let's see, what else?"

I leaned forward slightly, with wide eyes.

He snapped his fingers sort of rhythmically. "You use Garnier shampoo and conditioner, Jergens lotion on your hands and legs, and Clinique perfume, sometimes. Probably not for a couple weeks. Happy, I think it's called."

Holy shit!

He downed the rest of his beer, sat the bottle down and looked at me. I was aghast and speechless. I mean, the statistical stuff I could explain, but…

"How did you…I didn't see you look in my shower, how did you know about the shampoo?"

"You just washed your hair. I can smell it."

He smiled again. He was playing a little game with me and I wasn't sure I liked it.

"What about the conditioner?"

"Your hair looks much smoother than it did in the hospital. And I can smell that too. Like fresh apples."

"And the dog thing?"

"I saw a Boston Terrier mug hanging on the mug tree in your kitchen, but you have cat magnets all over your fridge."

Okay, Sherlock.

"And the lotion and perfume?"

"You have a bottle of perfume on the shelf above your toilet but it has a thin layer of dust on the cap, probably about two weeks' worth, and the bottle is labeled. Jergens is a favorite among women of seasoned age, and your hands are very smooth." He picked up his beer bottle and cleared his throat. "And since you're a woman, and women shave their legs, I assumed you shave your legs and I just guessed that you used the same lotion afterward. Sometimes I get lucky. Do you have any more beer?"

"You tell me," I cracked.

"You have eight left. You want one?"

"Uh, no, thank you."

Man, this guy was good.

"Oh, and I noticed the lifts in your shoes in here, Shorty!" he called from the kitchen. "Your shoes are next to this old, dial scale in here, which I noticed is set two pounds under zero so you always weigh lighter than you really are. This is pretty common among women who think they are overweight. It's usually a five pound loss though, so you're probably pretty confident about some parts of your body."

He came back in the room and handed me another soda. "Charlie Chaplin clock on the wall means you like classic movies, silent films, particularly the comedies, but you love the pathos as well. You're an observer. You like to let your eyes find the story. And I'll bet your favorite Chaplin film is..."

He paused for a moment, pretending he had to study me.

"City Lights," he said pointing a finger. "The blind girl who finally sees in the end. Right?"

Wow!

I think I nodded.

"And it's obvious, well, let's just say I've never seen a purple couch. You have to have a fondness for the color. What did I miss?"

He sat back down and stretched his long legs out in front of him.

"I hate my job?" I asked.

He looked me straight in the eye. "You're an intelligent and beautiful woman. You should be giving orders, not taking them."

I smiled rather bashfully and looked at the soda can in my hand. "Thank you."

He opened his beer. "You're welcome."

"But they're not lifts, they're arch supports. My feet are kind of flat."

"Arch supports then. You shouldn't worry about your weight though. You look fine. And anyone with that many kitties on her fridge couldn't murder anyone."

I exhaled a laugh as he took a long, self-congratulatory drink of his beer and squelched a burp.

"Oh, and could I make a suggestion?" he asked.

"What's that?"

His eyes dropped. "Throw that bra out. It's not very flattering."

I looked down at my chest, suddenly feeling uncomfortable and exposed. It was like he dissected me, put me on display, and I wasn't sure I liked it. He knew all these little details about my life and I hadn't given him liberty to know any of it. I crossed my arms over my torpedo tits and stared at the TV wondering what else he had noticed.

He said I was beautiful. He thought I was beautiful. Maybe I was beautiful, in some weird universe where everything is the opposite of what it is.

"I'm not sure what to say," I said rather sheepishly. "You know a lot."

"Look," he said, setting his beer down on the coffee table and leaning toward me. "I wasn't trying to make you uncomfortable, and I'm sorry about the bra thing. That was inappropriate. I've had a few beers and two is usually my limit. I just wanted you to know I'm good at my job, and I don't want you to worry." He leaned closer and put his hand on my knee. "I will catch this guy, I promise."

I looked down at his hand and developed a warm feeling in the pit of my stomach. I dropped my hand and touched his. It was soft with just a hint of hard work and age.

"Thank you," I said, looking him in the eye. I could feel the tears spilling out of my own. I couldn't cry in front of him. Not again. I'd look like a weak little woman who couldn't control her emotions. I looked down at my lap.

He scooted closer to me on the couch and put his arm around me. "Hey, it's okay. We'll get through this." He rubbed large circles on my back, over my hair, almost as if he was making a point of touching it. I didn't peg him as a hair-toucher, but I didn't mind. I loved it when men touched my hair.

"I don't know when I became such a cry baby," I said, wiping a tear away.

"Probably the day you witnessed a murder," he said, moving his hand up to my neck. "I've witnessed way too many, and you never quite get used to it."

I turned my head to look at him and he was closer to me than I thought. Close enough that his fragrance wrapped around me like an invisible robe and touched places in me that I had forgotten could be touched.

"No, I suppose not," I said quietly.

Our eyes connected and the air between us was suddenly charged. I felt his warm breath as the electricity slowly drew us closer together. Was he leaning in? I couldn't tell. If he wasn't, I was about to make a big fool of myself. I leaned forward slowly and closed my eyes as our lips brushed together softly.

"I can't do this," he whispered. But he didn't move away from me, his hand still on the back of my neck, massaging tiny circles of lust.

"I know," I whispered.

His head tilted slowly and he almost, but not quite, kissed my upper lip. "I have to stop."

"I know."

I ran my hand up his chest, feeling his toned muscles quiver against my fingertips. Then I grabbed a handful of his shirt, rubbing my lips against his face taking in the close scent of his cheek and back to his neck, just below his ear.

Should I risk a little nibble? God, I don't know!

"But I really, really don't want to stop," he whispered, his voice trembling.

I grinned and pulled back, looking deeply into his eyes. "I know."

Then something took over me. Some kind of sexual beast from ages ago when humans didn't know about self-control. I pulled him forward by his shirt, pulling his lips against mine and knowing it was so completely wrong. He kissed me back hungrily, parting his lips just enough as our mouths embraced and our tongues caressed each other.

Then as things intensified, he stroked gentle circles around my tongue with his, making me anticipate what he would do to other parts of my body with his tongue, or fingers, or other things. And even though he tasted a little like beer, it seemed to add something to the naughtiness of the whole thing, which was a huge turn on for some reason. As if the fact that he was kissing me wasn't enough of a turn on. His lips were so full and so soft and all I could think was, *more*!

His strong arms wrapped around me and pulled me close against him, my breasts pressed against his chest, and he moaned his passion into my mouth.

In my mind I knew he might be playing me, thinking I was hiding something from him, but I didn't care anymore. I just savored the feeling of his lips on mine and his warm smooth body against me.

"God," he moaned as I sucked his bottom lip and gave his shirt a yank, hoping to pull it out of his jeans so I could touch his chest, or back, at least something that was covered.

"This is wrong," he said.

"It doesn't feel wrong," I whispered. "Please don't stop."

"Sweet Jesus," he said, burying his tongue in my mouth again and squeezing me almost breathless against him. His fingers ran through my hair and I damn near had an orgasm right then and there. I know my eyes rolled back for a second.

And then he was lifting me off the couch and carrying me into the bedroom as I kissed his long muscular neck, already moist with perspiration, and he let out a groan as I nibbled his ear tenderly. He laid me gently on the bed and crawled in next to me.

"Are you sure you want to do this?" I breathed as his fingers worked their way under my shirt, lightly touching the soft skin of my stomach. I let out a short gasp followed by a sigh, and the craving for more of him became almost painful.

"Yes," he whispered, leaning down to kiss where he had just touched me. His forehead dropped against my belly and he took a long breath. "No."

He looked up at me in the dark.

I brushed my fingers against his face and up into his hair. "It's okay."

"I'm sorry," he said gently. "God, I'm so sorry."

"Sorry for what?"

"You just feel so good."

"So do you," I squeaked. "But it's all right, Jason. I know this is all so confusing."

"I love hearing you say my name like that," he whispered, nuzzling his lips against my palm. "You make me feel so...alive."

And we smiled as he rose up to my face and reluctantly lowered my shirt back over my stomach. He kissed my lips again softly, lingering there tenderly until I almost couldn't stand it anymore and I wanted to cry out that I needed him closer. I needed his lips pressed harder against mine and I wanted to taste every inch of him. I needed him inside me more than I needed air. But he stopped and settled in next to me, wrapping me in his arms and burying his face in my hair. He took a long smell and sighed.

"Fresh apples," he said. "I don't think I should drive."

****

CHAPTER NINE

I awoke suddenly to darkness. It took me a moment to realize where I was, and figure out why I didn't hear the sounds of nurses chatting the hallway or gurneys squeaking. My head was killing me, but the blanket around me was so warm and comforting. And breathing. And had arms. Long, strong arms wrapped around me and a face snuggled into my hair.

He sniffed and chuckled in his sleep and I remembered what had occurred.

He got tipsy and all we did was fall asleep? I thought I did everything right. I didn't pressure him, I didn't force anything. I let him have control of the situation. And he just passed out.

Maybe the bump on my head knocked the little sexiness I had right out of me.

Maybe he was worried he would poke an eye out on one of my boobs.

And just maybe he was being a gentleman. He didn't want to take advantage of a vulnerable woman by swooping her into bed. And he really shouldn't swoop a witness to an ongoing investigation he was working on, right? I'm sure that was a big no no.

The trouble with that was, this woman wanted to be swooped. This woman hadn't been swooped in a long time. This woman was due some serious swooping!

I looked up at his face. He was smiling. He said I was beautiful last night, and he didn't want to stop himself from kissing me. That's what he said, and he meant it, or he lied very well, which is entirely possible. He was, after all, a detective. Aren't they supposed to lie very well?

God! I just don't know.

I gently lifted his arm off me and slid out of the bed on a mission to find my Vicodin. It was on the coffee table along with four beer bottles. I smiled. Cheap drunk he was. I popped a couple pills and washed them down with the flat soda I had left, hoping it would take effect quickly. These headaches were awful. I staggered to the bathroom and did what I needed to do without turning on the light.

When I got back to bed he had rolled over so his back was to me. I shimmied out of my t-shirt, missile bra and sweats and into my nightgown as quietly as I could. I threw the quilt at the end of the bed over him and snuggled under it against his back slowly sliding my arm around his waist. He took my hand and kissed it, and I wondered if he had any idea who he was kissing in his sleep.

"Night, Vic," he said.

I smiled and kissed the back of his neck, just above his shirt collar. "Night."

Guess that answered that question.

****

Soft daylight filtered through the mini blinds in my bedroom as I felt the bed move beneath me, and gentle lips on my forehead.

Mouthwash. He must have helped himself to my Scope.

"Vic?"

"Hm?" I grunted, covering my eyes against the light.

Is light ever going to stop hurting?

"I've got to go," he said quietly. "But I didn't want to leave without telling you."

"Oh," I said. "Okay."

I squinted up at him and he smiled down at me.

"What time is it?" I asked.

"It's early yet. You go on back to sleep and I'll call you later."

I smiled. "Thank you for staying with me."

He touched my cheek gently and I kissed the soft palm of his hand.

"Thank you for letting me," he said. I could hear the smile in his voice, and even though he still looked fuzzy in my sleepy eyes, he was so beautiful.

"Anytime."

He kissed my lips softly. "Bye, Pretty Lady."

I chuckled. "Bye, Angel."

He kissed me again and he was gone.

I dozed off again feeling like I had just won the Illinois Lottery.

****

Strange dreams. I was getting off the elevator at work as Varner was getting on. I didn't realize it was him until the doors were closed. I hit the buttons frantically, hoping he would be on the next one. The doors opened and he wasn't there. I got on anyway and hit the button for the seventh floor, knowing I didn't want to go there, but for some reason feeling I had to. I had forgotten something I needed but I didn't know what. The elevator shot upward quickly and the door opened. There was Judge Weinhardt with blood dripping out of a hole in his head.

"Why didn't you come?" he asked, "Why didn't you help me?"

I couldn't answer him. I was being choked. Strangled. The judge pulled me off the elevator, pushed me down to the floor and began to hit me in the back of the head. All I could see were his shoes. They were black patent leather and very shiny.

"You should have left," he said hitting me again. I managed to look up at him, but it wasn't him. It was a man with slimy hair in a blue suit. He smiled and hit me again.

I heard ringing.

My eyes popped open and I gasped.

My phone was ringing.

I grabbed it and groaned, "Hello?"

"Hey, how are you feeling?" Toni asked.

"Huh? Oh God. Um, fine, I think." I stuttered.

I looked at my alarm clock and red numbers screamed eight thirty at me. My bedroom was still too bright and I closed my eyes again.

"Did I wake you?" she asked.

"Yeah, but that's okay. I was having a really messed up dream."

My head throbbed as the previous night's activities came back to mind.

"What were you dreaming?" she asked.

"I'll tell you later. I've got a better story for you."

I outlined to her what had occurred the night before and there was silence.

"Toni? You there?"

"You are such a lucky bitch."

"Whatever!" I laughed. "He won't want to see me again."

"Oh, bullshit!" she said. "He's probably just embarrassed because he got drunk. Ten bucks says he calls you today."

"Maybe, but only to talk about where and when he's going to arrest me for murder."

"Stop talking like that, you said he believed you didn't do it."

"Yeah, he did seem sincere about that," I said, rubbing my forehead.

"Well, if he doesn't call you, he's an idiot and I'll tell him so if I see him again."

I smiled. "What would I do without you?"

"Hell if I know. Now, you have to tell me, how big do you think the man is? Downstairs I mean."

"Toni!"

"Well, he's a big guy. I'll bet it's massive."

"Lord!" I put my face in my hand. "Honestly, I really couldn't wager a guess and I really didn't get to, you know, feel anything. But I will say he's the best kisser ever."

She laughed. "Wish I could test that theory."

"You better not!"

"You'd get him back unscathed."

"Hands off!"

We laughed for a moment to cover up the tiniest bit of jealousy that was seeping into our conversation.

"I think I'm going to pop a couple pills and get some more sleep," I said. "My head is killing me."

"Sounds like a good idea. Call me with any updates."

"You know it. Later."

I hung up and set the phone down. I laid there for a few minutes contemplating what to do next. I decided to hit the bathroom and have my PB & J sandwich for breakfast. I sat up slowly.

Just then there was a knock at the door. I jumped. Was it him? Please God, let it be him.

Jesus, my brain was starting to think like a Shirley Bassey torch song.

"Let it please be him, oh dear God, it must be him, or I shall die…"

Ugh! I'm such a girl.

I stood up, grabbed my robe and jogged to the door. I checked the peep hole and it was a man I didn't recognize.

So much for Shirley Bassey. It wasn't him and I was still alive as far as I knew.

"Who is it?" I called through the door.

"Miss Childs?"

"Yes," I said.

"My name is Detective Tom Fisher, I'm with the Brenton Police department."

I opened my door and clutched my robe over me. "I'm sorry, did you say you're a detective?"

"Yes, I did."

He looked to be around fifty-five and was a short, dumpy guy, maybe five-seven, bald with dark hair around the edges, and a bushy mustache and eyebrows. His eyes were brown and kind of close set, and his nose was starting to become bulbous at the tip, or maybe it was always that way. He looked like the "time to make the doughnuts" guy. I smiled at that thought.

"I was wondering if you would accompany me to the station and answer a few questions regarding what you witnessed last week," he said, showing me his badge. He had a rather deep and very commanding voice that didn't match his looks. It made me afraid to tell him no. It also made me think he could be scary as hell under the right circumstances, or the wrong circumstances depending on what side of the law you were on.

"Um, I'm sorry, I'm a little confused," I said as politely as I could, checking out the badge and pretending I would know if it was fake. "I thought Detective Varner was on this case."

"He is," Mr. Doughnut said. "I'm just following up. Would you like to come with me or drive your own car?"

"You'll have to take me. I don't have my car here."

Come to think of it, where the hell is my car?

"Can I freshen up a bit? It won't take long. I just woke up."

"Certainly, take your time. I'll be downstairs."

I closed the door as he headed down the stairs. For some reason, I wasn't exactly comfortable with this. I wondered if I should call Detective Varner.

Detective Jason Varner. Mrs. Detective Jason Varner.

I sighed and stared at nothing for a moment. Then I slapped myself in the forehead and immediately regretted it.

Ouch!

I fished his card out of my purse and dialed his cell number.

It chirped a ring. "Varner."

My heart jumped to the back of my tongue.

"Uh, Jason, it's Vic…toria Childs."

"Hey, you," he said with a smile in his voice. I shivered involuntarily at the sound of it and the thought of his hands and lips on me the night before.

"Hey," I said, after a ridiculous little giggle. "Um, there's a Detective Fisher here."

"Mr. Doughnut? What does he want?"

I stifled another nervous laugh. God, I sounded like a giggling simpleton.

"Uh, he wants to take me back to the station and do some kind of follow up with me. Is this cool?"

"Sorry, Darlin'. I'm still kind of a rookie in this town. He's my assigned partner and has been instructed by my superiors to check up on me during my probationary period at the station. Frankly, he doesn't think I know how to do my job."

I blushed at the "Darlin'" thing.

"What should I do?" I asked, looking out the window. It seemed to be a nice enough day and I would have smiled if the sun wasn't stabbing me in the eyeballs.

"Go ahead and go with him," he replied. "I'm on my way to the office now. I'll see you there."

I giggled again, damn it. "Okay, bye."

"Bye." He was still smiling when he said it.

"I don't have anything to wear!" I squealed, running full tilt into the bedroom.

I splattered some make-up on, ran a brush through my hair and made sure I threw on a more flattering bra. Then I picked a black, girly t-shirt, a clean pair of boot-cut blue jeans and stepped into my purple sneakers before tromping down the stairs to my fate. Fisher was standing there smoking a cigarette and waiting near a black Corolla. He flipped the cigarette, hit the button to unlock the car, and I got in without saying a word.

It was a long and silent drive to the station. Mr. Personality, this one. For some reason I kept waiting for him to fart. It must have been the tense look on his face, like he was trying to hold one back and losing the battle. I hit the button and cracked my window, just in case.

When we got there, he silently took my elbow and walked me toward the building.

"Excuse me," I said. "Am I under arrest?"

"No," he said, giving me a not so gentle nudge toward the door.

"Then would you take your hand off me, please?"

I couldn't believe I said it. What's even stranger was he released my elbow and backed off.

Assertive? Me?? Never!

Where the hell did that come from? Usually I was like a turtle, only poking my head out if there was food.

But it felt good, and what the hell did I have to lose anyway? His respect? I probably didn't have that to begin with. He probably thought I was a murderer.

When we got into the building, he nodded at a bench outside of a windowless door and said, "Have a seat. I'll come get you when I'm ready."

I sat down and wiped my hands on my jeans. I wasn't sure why I was nervous, I didn't have anything to hide, except having the hots for a detective. I hope he didn't ask me anything about Varner. I wasn't sure I could hide my enthusiasm about him entirely. I was staring at the floor going over questions I thought he would ask when I saw a large pair of feet coming toward me.

"Hey," Varner said. "I'm sorry about this."

He was wearing a navy blue polo, very long Dockers, a cell phone and gun clipped to his belt, and a big grin. I don't often use the word, it was so outdated, but it seemed appropriate for him. The man was a hunk!

"It's not your fault," I said, smiling up at him. "He just surprised me, and then he man-handled me on the way in."

"What?"

"He put his hands on me and I didn't appreciate it," I told him. "He makes me nervous."

"You were just worried he was going to cut one in the car, weren't you?" he said with a grin.

I covered my mouth and was actually able to suppress the giggle into a small chuckle, but I had to bite my lip.

"He always looks like that when he's driving. He's a little gruff, but he's generally harmless," he said sitting down on my left. "You look nice."

"Thanks. So do you," I squeaked out.

Smooth, Vic.

The urge to lean over and kiss him nearly took over me, but I restrained myself. I didn't want to create the appearance that he wasn't completely objective about everything. And for all I knew, he still considered me a suspect. The thought still crossed my mind that last night was all part of the game he was playing to get me to trust him. And I did trust him, to a point. I was innocent, he said he knew that.

But Fisher? What if he got me to say something that he could twist around and make me look guilty?

What if he didn't believe Varner, that I was innocent of any crime other than being forgetful?

What if he farted repeatedly until I confessed?

Who the hell am I supposed to trust?

"What do you think he's going to ask me?" I asked, trying to hide the terror rising in my throat.

"Probably all the same stuff you already told me. He's a real stickler for detail." He paused for a moment to bend and brush something off of his meticulously polished shoe.

"Well, I hope I repeat everything to his satisfaction," I muttered.

As he sat up, his right index finger brushed against my thigh so gently, I wasn't sure I even felt it.

"Girl, I can't get you out of my head," he said softly.

Okay, so, maybe he wasn't completely objective about me.

Blood rushed to my face, and my nether regions, as my eyes found their way to his. He smiled shyly, and then his eyes darted across the room quickly.

"He's coming over," he said. "Keep your answers simple. Stick to what you know and told me. You'll be fine."

"Varner, you need something?" Mr. Doughnut asked.

"Nope," Varner said. "Just came over to say hi."

"Well, I need to speak with her now," Fisher said, with authority.

Varner stood up, dwarfing Fisher. "I was just headed back to my office anyway. Take care, Miss Childs."

I smiled at him as he walked away.

I love watching him walk away. He has the best butt in the free world.

"Shall we go in?" Fisher asked, opening the door to the tiny room. It was correction-facility gray, and there was a table and four chairs staring back at me. It looked like the typical "Law & Order" interrogation room, but without the one way mirror.

I stepped inside and he closed the door behind us.

"Have a seat, this won't take long."

I sat down and he sat across from me. He opened the folder he was carrying, perused a few documents, and said,

"I just want to go over some of the things Detective Varner put in his report."

"Okay," I said, wiping my hands on my jeans again.

"Nervous?" he asked, looking at my hands.

"A little."

"Why's that?"

I looked him in the eye. "I've never been questioned in a police station before."

He grunted. "First time for everything I suppose."

Yeah, I'm planning on doing this a lot. Asshole.

"You told Varner that you hid in a broom closet on the seventh floor of the courthouse. Is that correct?"

"No."

He flipped through the file frantically. "What do you mean, no?"

"It was on the sixth floor," I corrected.

"Oh," he said. "Right."

I suddenly wondered if he was trying to catch me in a lie.

HA! Take that, Detective Doughnut.

He blew out a long sigh. "Can you tell me what happened next?"

I outlined again, nearly word for word, what I told Varner in the hospital. I hopped into the closet, waited until I thought I was alone, and I ran like hell down the stairs. I stopped between the fourth and fifth floor to compose myself, and the next thing I knew, I was laying on the landing with paramedics around me and Paul telling me to wake up. Then the next thing I remembered was waking up in the hospital.

"And you don't remember seeing anyone else on the stairs?"

"That's correct."

"Miss Childs, do you always carry a gun in your purse?"

I looked at him again, dead in the eye. "Detective Dough…uh…Fisher, I have no idea how the gun got into my purse."

Heh, oops. Insult the dude, Vic, good idea.

He squinted. "Not even the gun that happens to be the weapon that killed Judge Weinhardt?"

"No, sir, I never touched it."

He shuffled through the papers in the folder. "Well, there were no prints on it at all. It appears it had been wiped clean."

I shrugged. "I know nothing about it."

He stared at me. It was similar to a stare Varner had a few times during our conversations in the hospital. The analytical-cop stare, blank and mysterious, though on Fisher it wasn't mysterious. It looked more like his driving face. I stared back at him, determined to convey that I was telling the truth. And that if he passed gas, I was SO out of there.

Just then the door opened and Varner sauntered in quickly. He grabbed a chair across from me, swung it around and straddled the back of it.

"So," he said smiling. "What are we talking about?"

Mr. Doughnut looked like he was getting pissy. "We're discussing your report, Detective Varner."

"Any discrepancies? Varner asked.

Fisher leafed through the file. Varner caught my eye and winked. I licked my lips slowly, lowered my head, and smiled timidly.

God, his smile would make Hilary Clinton blush.

Fisher closed the file and let out a sigh. "None that I've found."

Varner stuck his lower lip out and nodded. "So, what's the problem?"

Fisher looked at him. "Nothing, Varner, I was just…"

"Checking up on me?" Varner finished. "Didn't know I needed it."

Fisher took a deep breath and asked me. "Miss Childs, is there anything else you would like to tell us?"

I shrugged. "I've told you all I know. But I do have a question."

"Shoot," Varner said. Fisher and I both looked at him just as he realized his unintentional faux pas. He cleared this throat and let out a rather nervous laugh. "Sorry."

I snickered. Fisher looked back at me and then at Varner again and his eyes narrowed in what looked like annoyance.

"Am I a suspect in this case?" I blurted out. "I mean, you both seem to think that I'm hiding something."

They both looked at me, fart-faced and gorgeous.

"Well, quite frankly, your story has some holes in it," Fisher said.

"What holes?" I asked.

"Well, for starters, you can't explain the gun in your purse."

I looked at both of them. Cop stares and Varner was biting his bottom lip again.

I need to play poker with him. I would completely kick his ass.

"You're right," I said. "I can't. And you can't explain how I came to be lying in a pool of my own blood at the bottom of a flight of stairs."

"Maybe your accomplice hit you," Fisher said, leaning back and putting his hands on top of his bald head. "Wanted you to take the fall for all of this."

"What accomplice? Who's my accomplice?"

"Why don't you tell us that?" Fisher asked quickly, his authoritative tone raising ever so slightly.

Varner just sat smiling warmly at me, his eyes saying, "Bedroom, kitchen, living room, wherever the hell you want it, baby."

The proverbial lightning bolt hit me in the eyeball and I finally realized what was going on.

Good cop, bad cop.

My shoulders slumped and I couldn't stop myself from spitting out a frustrated laugh. Varner's perfect little smile gave me all I needed for a confirmation. He was playing me. He drank my beer, slept in my bed, and he was playing me.

You bastard!

I rolled my eyes. "You guys can drop the act, okay? I'm not hiding anything."

"What act is that, Miss Childs?" Fisher asked me with narrowed eyes.

"Well, you're here to intimidate me, and Detective Varner is here to make me all mushy and warm right?"

Varner squinted at me and silence filled the room. Some angel he was. I think I heard one of his wings snap off.

"You seem to have it all figured out," Varner said coolly.

"No," I said, glaring at him angrily. "No, I don't. I don't know what the hell is going on. I'm not sure I want to know."

Varner's eyes left mine and landed on the table. I felt like slipping off one of my sneakers and hurling it at him.

"If I killed the judge, where was his blood?" I asked a little louder. "I'm assuming you have the sweater I was wearing that day. Did you find any of his blood on it?"

"You work there, Miss Childs," he said. "You could have kept a change of clothing at the office."

"What did I do with the bloody ones?"

"You had an accomplice who could have taken them."

I nodded. "Oh, that's right. My imaginary accomplice. I suppose I have an imaginary motive too?"

"Well," Fisher began, "you're a very pretty girl, and you have a rather sordid past Miss Childs. Lots of men, some of them married."

"Lots of men? Five men in 10 years? I know women who sleep with more men than that in a weekend!" I said. "And only one was married and that was almost nine years ago!"

"What about your former fiancé?" Fisher asked.

"What about him?" I was practically screaming now, and the horses started galloping in my head again. I suppose that's what I get for letting the assertive turtle out of her shell and she starts mouthing off a little too loudly. But screw them. This was my life they were bouncing around the table here.

"He was married too," Fisher said, pounding his finger on the table. "Are you trying to tell us that you didn't know that?"

I sighed and leaned back in my chair. "I had no idea, but I'm not really all that surprised. He lied about a lot of things."

"Perhaps you were having an affair with the judge," Fisher barked, leaning forward. "You had a lover's quarrel and it got a little heated, and you shot him."

I laughed rather hysterically and threw my hands up in the air. "The man was gay!"

They froze, then looked at each other slowly.

"At least that's what I thought," I said, subduing my voice and realizing I may have just outed someone without full knowledge of his situation. "I mean, there were rumors about it."

Oh God, Vic, just shut up!

Another excruciating silence as they fumbled through the papers in the file. At least I think it was silence. In my head there was a stampede.

"That would explain a few things," Varner said, rubbing his forehead.

I didn't ask what things. I didn't want to know. I just wanted to go home.

Stupid horses! Stupid Mr. Doughnut! Stupid Detective sexy-angel, New-Orleans-accented, "I'm-too-drunk-to-drive-can-I-sleep-in-your-bed?" man!

"I didn't know the man," I said quietly. "I shouldn't have speculated on his sexual preferences."

I leaned forward in my chair and put my head in my hands.

"You all right?" Varner asked, his voice filled with concern. Concern for what, I wasn't sure.

"What the hell do you care?" I snapped back. "My head hurts and I think I'm going to hurl."

"Detective Fisher, would you mind getting Miss Childs some water?" Varner said gently.

Fisher snorted and trudged out of the room.

"Hey," Varner said touching my arm. I yanked away from him.

"You said you believed me," I said through clenched teeth. "I trusted you and you're fucking playing me."

"I do believe you," he said. "I just can't prove anything yet. Give me some time and I'll get it figured out."

"Yeah, and meanwhile Detective Doughnut...Asshole is doing his damnedest to put me away," I said holding my head. "Jesus, how could I be so stupid?"

"Cher, don't get upset..."

"Cher is a singer, and she won an Academy Award for Moonstruck in the late eighties. My name is Victoria. Actually it's Miss Childs to you now." I said, my teeth still clenched with fury. "You want to maintain a certain formality with your suspects, don't you, Detective Varner? Wouldn't want one of them to think you actually gave a damn."

He stared at me, his jaw set. "I do give a damn."

I scoffed. "Yeah right. You owe me fifty bucks for four beers and laundry fees."

He exhaled, obviously angry. "I only drank half of the last one. And I'll leave you alone if that's how you want it."

"It's obviously how you want it. I don't recall your denying that you've been screwing with me this whole time. Buttering up the little black widow so she will confide in you something she was hiding. And what stopped you last night anyway? You could have gotten a good lay while you were at it. An exceptionally good lay. Probably the best lay ever."

"You're way off," he said angrily, pointing his finger at me. "You don't know a damn thing about me, Miss Childs."

He slammed his hands on the table and stood up heatedly.

Fisher came back in holding a bottle of water. "Where are you going?"

Varner stopped and turned to look at me. I was breathing heavily and had never felt so angry at anyone in my life.

How dare he be so sweet to me and make me feel things I thought I never wanted to feel again? How dare he pretend to want me and make me feel beautiful? How dare he make me want to spend the rest of my life trying to deserve what I thought was an angel?

"She's all yours," he said to his partner and walked out of the room.

Fisher came back in and handed me the water. I opened it and took a sip, the water cool on the lump in my throat. Fisher flipped open the file to some photographs stapled to the inside.

"Hm," he said quietly, "how's your head?"

I stared blankly at the table in front of me as the numbness took over. "I'm sorry, what?"

"How is your head feeling?" he asked, looking perplexed about something. "The wound, I mean."

"Oh, it's okay, I guess. Still pretty sore."

He rubbed his mustache and stared at the folder in front of him, obviously deep in thought.

"Miss Childs, will you come with me for a moment?" he asked, standing up and picking up the file.

"Uh, sure," I said hesitantly, "unless you're going to lock me up."

He smiled pleasantly, and I nearly fell over from the shock of it.

"No, I just want to check something."

"Okay..."

I followed him out of the room and down a white and sterile-looking hallway. We passed Varner's office where he was throwing some kind of temper tantrum trying to get a half-open file drawer all the way open or closed. He kicked it repeatedly. "Damn it! Piece of shit!"

Sheesh! Where was he when the soda machine ate my money?

"Varner, when you're finished, will you meet us in the lab?" Fisher said, almost jovially.

I avoided Varner's glare and continued with Fisher down the hall, feeling like a dog being led by a leash. I hoped he didn't have an electric bark collar with him. I didn't need any more shocks. We entered the lab filled with microscopes and big nasty-looking machines.

I knew it. They're going to hook me up to some kind of machine and torture me to get me to talk. They were going to stick me with hot pokers, or deprive me of water, or put my hand in a glass case full of spiders.

Oh, God! Anything but spiders!

"What's this all about?" I asked as Fisher pulled a stool out from under the counter.

"Have a seat," he said. "Julie, this is Victoria Childs. Would you mind getting us a DNA sample from her?"

He was speaking to a round and cheerful-looking woman of around fifty in a lab coat. She had short, spiky, gray hair, her lips were high gloss lavender, she wore heavy eyeliner, and her fingernails were painted black. She looked like the cool grandma who took you to movies that were rated R under the strict guise that you wouldn't tell your parents ever. I'll bet she bowled in a league and was fun as hell after a few beers.

I let out a sigh. DNA. Of course. No spiders were going to attack me. Not yet anyway.

"I'll be back in a moment," he said, jogging toward a secure room marked "Evidence".

"You okay, honey?" Julie asked me. "You look a little green."

I nodded without enthusiasm. "I'm just very tired and I thought there were going to be spiders."

She gave me a strange look. "No, our lab is pretty clean..."

"I meant..." I stopped and let out another sigh, "never mind."

Julie looked at the file on the counter in front of her. "Oh, the Weinhardt case. That was an awful shame. He was such a nice man."

I nodded again. "I didn't know him very well, but he was always nice to me."

She looked from the file and at me. "They're not trying to finger you for this are they?"

"I honestly don't know what they're doing."

She leaned close to me. "Between you and me, honey, they don't know what they're doing half the time either. Sometimes I think if it wasn't for DNA, they couldn't find their asses with both hands in this town."

We smiled at each other, both of us knowing what it was like to work in a world full of over-confident and bull-headed men.

Varner stepped in silently and closed the door behind him as I was pushing up my sleeve for the tourniquet. We looked at each other.

Why did he look like someone had kicked him in the stomach? It was him doing the manipulating, not me. He was just pissed that I figured him out. Pissed that I caught on to his act.

But he didn't look pissed. He looked wounded, like he did the day I met him.

Did I hurt him? Really? Could I have hurt him after we had only known each other for such a short time?

I was immediately sorry for what I had said to him and I tried to convey an apology with my eyes, but he looked away from me. I felt my heart crack, and tried not to think of how warm his arms felt around me and how good his lips tasted the night before.

"Except for that one there, he's smart as they come," Julie said quietly and she gave him a wave. "Hey, Jason."

She pulled her blood-letting materials from the drawer in front of her.

"Hey," he said, leaning back against the far end of the counter. "Have you seen Fisher?"

"He just went into evidence," Julie said, poking around on my arm for a vein. She pulled the needle out of the cap with her teeth and stuck me gently. She hooked up one of the tubes and I watched my blood flow into it, hoping it would exonerate me once and for all. She hooked up the second tube and I tried to look at him again, but he kept his eyes on the floor.

I'm such a bitch!

"Okay, bend your arm up and hold the gauze there for a while," she said, pulling the needle out of my arm. Then her voice lowered again and her chin jerked to Varner. "That man is something, huh?"

"Yeah," I said, looking at him. "He's something."

Fisher burst through the evidence room door holding a plastic bag containing a large black item that I couldn't make out. As he got closer, I realized it was a gun.

"Miss Childs," Fisher said, rather triumphantly, "may I see the wound on your head please?"

He pulled a pair of rubber gloves out of his pocket, slapped them on, and gingerly pulled the gun out of the baggie.

"What's up?" Varner asked, suddenly interested. He stepped closer.

I spun around toward the counter and reached behind my head feeling for the bald spot. I flipped my hair over my face and leaned forward.

Then all was silent.

"Hm," Varner grunted. I felt something cold against the back of my head, and realized after a moment that it was the gun.

"Superficial bruising matches," Fisher said.

"That chip in the butt caused the wound there," Varner said, touching the back of my head softly. "I don't remember seeing any blood on it, but there has to be traces. That jagged edge couldn't be cleaned completely with just a quick wipe."

"Why don't you just shoot me and get it over with," I said sarcastically.

Everyone in the room chuckled except me.

"I'll run her DNA quick," I heard Julie say as she jogged across the room. "Don't put that back into evidence. I'll swab it while it's out."

Someone put a hand on my shoulder.

"My dear," Fisher said. "You were hit on the back of the head with this gun."

I flipped my hair back and turned around to face them. I stared at the gun and shivered.

"That wound was deep. You were hit very hard," Fisher continued. "You're pretty damn lucky you didn't bleed to death or have any permanent damage."

I continued staring at the gun for a moment, noticing the aforementioned chip, and then my eyes moved between the two detectives. They both looked confident about their assessment.

"Still think my accomplice did it?" I asked.

Fisher smiled again.

"Varner, would you take Miss Childs on home? I think she needs a little more rest."

Varner's eyes moved from me to his partner, who gave him a gentle nudge.

"Sure," he said. "Come on."

****

We sat in uncomfortable silence as he drove his burgundy Chevy Tahoe toward my apartment. Neither one of us was sure what to say, at least I know I wasn't. He was a good man, and I verbally bashed him. He pulled up to the curb in front of my place and shifted into park.

"Thank you," I said quietly, without making a move.

"Yep."

I looked at him. He stared out the windshield.

"I'm sorry for what I said," I squeaked, unbuckling my seat belt and putting a hand on the latch for the door. "I know you were just doing your job."

"It's okay," he said, still not meeting my eye. I had insulted his character which I'm sure was not something he could forgive easily.

"Still want the fifty bucks?" he asked.

"No," I said, my voice squeaking again with impending tears. "Bye."

I opened the door and slid out, hoping against everything that he would grab me and pull me back in the car. He didn't. I closed the door behind me and started toward the building mentally kicking myself for letting him slip through my fingers.

I entered the building and climbed the stairs to my apartment. I let myself in and flipped on the TV to have something to listen to as I grabbed a handful of beer bottles off the coffee table. I dropped them in the trash and went to the sink, grabbing a glass from the dish drainer and filling it with water, and then taking a long drink.

Then I went into the living room, picked up the phone and dialed.

"Mom? Can I come stay with you for a few days?"

****

CHAPTER TEN

"Asshole," Toni said throwing her pizza crust on the table.

Nearly a week had passed without a peep from Varner. I was depressed. Depression required pizza. Pizza meant Betino's Pizza Palace where they made the best sauce in Illinois. They put huge chunks of sausage on their pizzas so when you took a bite you either had to take the whole chunk or make a mess. We both had sauce all over our hands, and Toni had some running down her arm, but it didn't matter. Betino's was home.

The booths were the same as they had been for thirty years, red pleather, some with duct tape, and the chairs in the place were of every shape and size. Mr. Betino was a picker of the highest caliber. In fact, a few of the chairs may have been in my Mom's dining room at some point. The walls were decorated with Red Skelton's Clowns, and I remember being scared of them when I was little. Now they made me smile. There were no drippy candles on the tables or snooty music playing. Mostly Mr. Betino left the radio on the oldies station. The only other entertainment in the joint was the ancient, big-screen TV in the corner that was usually on PBS, unless the Bears were playing. But if you were from Brenton, there was nowhere else to be on a Saturday night, especially when the "family fun center" behind the restaurant was open. In the summer, the line for the bumper boats was usually out into the parking lot and the go-cart track was always jumping. Plus there was nowhere else in town that you could get a deep-fried Twinkie if you had that particular craving

"I'm glad you went over to your Mom's," Toni said, picking up another slice.

"Yeah, I should have done that to begin with," I said, picking the green peppers off my piece. "I just don't know how he had me so snowed. I used to be smart."

"He's gorgeous," Toni said with her mouth full. "I'm married and I was ready for him."

"Well, you can have him."

I wiped my mouth and looked out the window. It was warm and humid for April and the sky was overcast. Rain was on the way. Perfect. A nice spring storm was just what I needed to make me feel worse about not having anyone to cuddle with when it thundered. Not that thunder ever bothered me. It actually did strange things to my libido, which was another reason to be depressed.

"I can't believe he almost slept with you to get you to talk," Toni said.

"He did sleep with me," I said.

"You know what I mean."

I nodded. "Can we talk about something else?"

We both tried to think of a new and cheerier topic.

"Carnie's going nuts without you there," Toni said finally.

"Going? She's been nuts for the past three months."

Toni nodded. "But it's worse now. Plus I think she has dropped more weight. She's probably down about thirty pounds. And that funky skin thing she has on her face seems to be spreading to one of her arms. She looks terrible."

"Ugh, I dread the day I have to tell her I'm not coming back," I said, putting my hand to my forehead.

"Wait," Toni said, "you're not coming back?"

I shook my head and took a bite. "I'm sorry. I just can't."

"Crap!" Toni put her head in her hand smearing sauce across her forehead. I grabbed a napkin and handed it to her.

"What am I going to do without you there?" Toni said, wiping her forehead. "I'll lose my freaking mind."

"I'm sorry," I said. "But I'm not going to make myself go back to a job that I hate."

"I know you hate it, but what are you going to do for money?"

"I don't know. I'll figure something out. I'd rather sell cosmetics door to door than go back in that building."

We ate in silence. Toni was obviously upset by my decision, but I knew it was the right thing to do.

"Look," I said, "I could have died only a couple tiny-little weeks ago. I need to start making things count in my life before I run out of time. I mean, I felt myself slipping away sitting at that desk, almost like I was bleeding to death you know?"

Toni nodded. "I know. And I understand you need to do what is best for you. I'll just miss the hell out of you, that's all."

A sudden throb hit me in the back of the head and I'm sure I made a rather unattractive grimace.

"I just wish these headaches would go away." I rubbed the back of my head. It was slowly healing, but I was having headaches every day and they seemed to be getting worse. Vicodin helped, but it was obviously not a long term solution.

"Have you seen a doctor?" Toni asked.

"Yeah, yesterday. All the scans have been fine. He seemed to think it was something to do with stress."

"Jason Varner stress," Toni said. "Asshole."

"I'm not giving him credit for it," I said. "He doesn't deserve it."

The waitress brought the check and a box for the leftovers. We paid up and went out to the parking lot and thunder rumbled in the distance. And little me without an umbrella as usual.

"When are you getting your car back?" Toni asked as we got into her Kia.

"I don't know. I don't even know where my car is," I said. "I guess I better call Detective Fisher and ask him about it. They still have my driver's license and credit cards too."

We both sniffed the air, which had become hot and smoky. It wasn't a typical smell for Brenton in the spring. Usually all we could smell when it was humid was the dog food factory on the west side of town, and the genuinely unpleasant aroma of processed horse meat.

"Whew," Toni said, closing the door. "Something's burning somewhere."

"I noticed it too. Maybe someone's burning brush or something. Hey, would you mind stopping at my place so I can pick up some more clothes?"

"No problem."

Toni drove down the block and cut across Main Street toward my apartment building. As we went down the street, it started spritzing rain, but we noticed people milling around looking down the street. And as we got closer to my building, realization hit us both in the gut like a sledge hammer.

"My God," Toni said. "It's your building!"

Toni parked and we both got out and ran toward the building.

"It's in my apartment!" I yelled, picking up the pace.

We stopped across the street from my building, breathlessly staring in horror as the smoke poured out of the broken windows of my living room and bedroom. Fire trucks and police cars surrounded the building and my neighbors were all standing in the street. Toni took my arm and moved me under a giant oak tree on the lawn behind us.

I went numb, my knees melted out from under me and I sat down in the wet grass under the tree.

"What the hell happened?" Toni asked, wiping her wet hair off her forehead.

I just stared. Judging from the amount of smoke, everything I owned must have burned. Toni knelt next to me and put a hand on my shoulder. Unconsciously I scanned the crowd to make sure everyone I knew was out of the building, particularly the family with three kids that lived in the large apartment below me. They were standing on the corner, huddled under a large umbrella, as was the lady next door who had five cat carriers clustered around her.

"Thank God," I whispered.

The firemen sprayed in and around the windows as my life burned before my eyes. I pictured my Chaplin clock melting, the Little Tramp's legs shriveling into tiny raisins, and the tears began to sting my eyes.

Then my heart leapt in my chest when I saw the burgundy Tahoe pull up on the cross street. Fisher jumped out of the passenger side and Varner's long legs appeared soon afterward. He popped open a golf umbrella big enough for five people.

"Is everyone all right?" Fisher yelled, jogging over to the scene. "Is anyone hurt?"

Varner walked slowly toward the building. He towered above the crowd, wide-eyed and completely thunderstruck. I watched him scanning the crowd just as I had just done and his eyes met mine from across the street. Relief washed over his face as his eyes rolled up toward the heavens.

He was genuinely glad to see me. The thought made my toes tingle.

He gave his umbrella to one of my neighbors and jogged toward me.

Toni squeezed my arm. "Okay, so maybe he's not such an asshole. Go on."

I stood with rubbery legs and took a few steps forward with difficulty.

"Are you all right?" he yelled, pushing his way through the crowd.

I nodded as he grabbed me up in his arms.

"Thank the Lord," he whispered, swinging my feet off the pavement. "I heard the call come in and all I could think was…"

"I'm fine," I said against his shoulder. "I just got here."

He set me down but kept his arms around me as if he was protecting me from the scene. The scent of his chest was almost enough to make my knees buckle, but I could feel his heart racing against my cheek and I couldn't stop myself from smiling.

He held my shoulders and looked me in the eye. "I'm glad you went to your mom's."

"How did you..." I stopped and smiled at him. "Never mind, sneaky."

He enveloped me again and nuzzled his lips against the top of my head. Toni walked up and picked his hand off my back, her face contorted into a look of disgust like she was flicking away a bug.

"Did you apologize to her?" she asked, dropping his hand.

Way to ruin a moment, Toni.

"For what?" he asked.

"You could have called her if you knew where she was."

"I didn't think she wanted to talk to me," he said, looking down at me.

I shrugged as Toni made a very rude noise. Something between a raspberry and a grunt.

"Men! You could have at least called to see if she was all right."

She went to grab his other hand off of my back.

"Okay, Okay," Varner said grinning. "I'm sorry I didn't call you."

"And?" Toni said.

"And, um, I'm sorry it took a fire in your apartment for me to contact you?" Varner said, looking at Toni.

"Apology accepted. Can we move on please?" I said. "Remember? My apartment? Everything I own in flames?"

"I'm going to go see if I can find out what happened," Varner said, putting a hand on my cheek. "You all right?"

I nodded, grateful for his touch and wishing he would touch me even more.

"Stay here," he said and jogged across the street.

Toni's head slanted in admiration of his receding form.

"Very nice," Toni said. "That is one damn, fine-looking man."

"Uh huh."

"He has really broad shoulders."

"Uh huh."

"And his back makes a..." her hands traced an outline of him in the air, like she was molding a large hunk of clay, "It makes a V."

"You should see his arms," I said, rather dreamily.

"Toned?"

"Uh huh. Biceps and triceps. And have you ever seen a better ass?"

"Whew! Fine specimen."

Then I caught sight of a dark figure down the block walking toward the scene. Actually, it was more like he was shuffling toward the scene, favoring his left leg. I lost sight of him behind a fire truck, so I stepped off the curb and moved into the street for a closer look.

"Where are you going?" Toni asked behind me.

I continued walking toward the building with Toni at my heels. The man reappeared on the other side of the truck and I immediately recognized his slimy dark hair. He turned and looked at me.

And then, he smiled.

I froze.

He was there, at the courthouse, the day it happened. I bumped into him getting off the elevator. He smelled nice then. He looked the same now, aside from his clothing. His red t-shirt was torn at the neck and read in white block letters, "Satan is a pussy."

"Jason!" I called, starting toward the man again.

A black sedan pulled up and the man limped toward it.

"Jason!" I yelled louder. He made no indication that he heard me and continued talking with Fisher and the Fire Marshall.

The man jumped into the passenger side of the car and it pulled away from the curb. Without considering any consequences, I bolted down the street after it.

I had to know. If this was the same man, what the hell did it mean?

"Varner!" Toni screamed. "Victoria Childs! What are you doing?!"

I looked back and saw that he had finally snapped to attention.

The car sped up the street with Toni and me running after it in vain. I repeated the plate numbers in my head over and over in an effort to commit them to memory.

"What the hell are you doing?" Varner shouted.

I stopped in the street and the rain poured down on me. I bent at the waist and put my hands on my knees to catch my breath, willing myself not to puke.

"Are you all right?" Toni asked, breathlessly, putting a hand on my back.

Varner caught up with us. "Are y'all crazy, running down the middle of the street like that?"

"It was him," I said, trying to straighten myself. "He was at the courthouse…that day."

I grabbed at the stitch in my side and grimaced.

"What is going on, Vic?" Toni asked.

I looked up at Varner and tried to speak as I gasped for air. "It was him…red t-shirt…Satan is a…"

I staggered into Toni who caught me and held me against her. Varner took my arm gently and helped me up on the curb.

"Satan is a pussy," she finished for me, mopping the wet hair off my face.

"He was limping," I groaned, bending over again to try and get rid of the cramp in my gut. "Like he was…"

"Handicapped," Varner said, looking over to where the car had been. "Did you get a plate number?"

"Illinois plate," I breathed, "BC5419."

He pulled a small note pad out of his pocket and wrote it down on the soggy paper.

"His ride was late," he muttered. "Come on, let's get you two out of the rain."

We jogged over to Varner's Tahoe. Well, they jogged. I was sort of dragged. Toni and I crawled into the back seat and huddled together in fear, and to keep warm.

Varner hooked up with Fisher and they spoke to the Fire Marshall for a few minutes. Then Fisher and Varner had a short conference after retrieving Varner's golf umbrella. The men lumbered back over to the car, Varner threw the umbrella in the back, and the car swayed as they got in.

"Fire Marshall says it looked like the fire originated from an explosive device that was thrown through that window, there," Fisher said, pointing to the suspect window which used to be my living room. "According to the neighbors below, they heard something hit the floor and then a 'whoosh.' Sounds like someone made up a cocktail."

"My God," Toni said, putting a hand to her mouth.

I just stared at the back of Varner's head, uncertain how to feel.

"Darlin'," he said, his hazel eyes shining at me in the rear-view mirror, "I think you've been targeted."

I took a deep breath and tried to react appropriately, but I couldn't. I knew I should be scared, even terrified at the news, but I wasn't. I was pissed. I knew what was going on, that someone wanted me dead and burned like my Chaplin clock, and I was mad as hell. I felt my fists tighten and I clenched my jaw.

"What now?" was all I could say.

"Well, I don't think you should go back to your mom's," Varner said, rubbing the back of his neck. "Actually, I think your mom should take a vacation. Is there anywhere she could go?"

I nodded unconsciously, staring at the ruin of my building. "Where am I going?"

"We've got a place you can stay," Varner said.

I had a feeling I knew where, but I didn't say anything.

"You okay getting home?" he asked Toni. "You want an escort?"

Toni shook her head. "I'm fine. I live outside of town. My husband is there."

"You guys might want to say your goodbyes then," Varner said quietly.

Toni and I looked at each other.

"Sheesh, he acts like…" Toni stopped.

"Like we're never going to see each other again," I said, the words catching in my throat as it tightened.

We both sighed and held on to each other.

****

CHAPTER ELEVEN

I was wrong about where they were going to hide me. I thought for sure I would end up in the only cheap motel in town that rented rooms by the hour. Then I worried that they were going to lock me up in the jail. Then I was even more worried that Detective Fisher would offer me a room. I didn't relish any of those options. But Varner said he wanted me away from town. Away from where someone could drive up, unnoticed, and throw something through a window to blow me up.

Varner decided that I would stay with him that night, at his house off Old Fort Minonk Road, way out in the country. A car could be spotted easily that far away from town, especially in the dark. The roads were so treacherous that there was no way to drive without headlights, and headlights could be seen for miles in that kind of darkness. It was too far to walk to from town, and the house had an alarm that patched directly through to him and the police department at the same time. Plus he apparently had an armory in his basement.

If I hadn't been so stunned, I would have been anxious to see where he lived. He drove several streets out of the way to make sure we weren't being followed. When he was sure, he drove us out a long country road. He pulled into the gravel driveway of an old, two-story farmhouse and parked. It was too dark to tell much about the house other than it was large and lonely, somewhat like its owner.

I slowly got out of the car, the refreshing night breeze scented with rain and wet earth hitting my face, and I began to take stock in my situation. I was here. I was breathing. I was all right. Everything else was secondary.

"This is it," he said, and I followed him to the front door.

"Wow, it's really nice," I said, without much enthusiasm.

"Keeps the rain off me," he said, unlocking the door.

He held the door open for me and I went inside. He flipped on the lights and I almost gasped. It looked like he had just polished all of the original wood work, and the result was beautiful. A warm and inviting smell of vanilla and fabric softener greeted me as I shuffled into the foyer. The hardwood floor gleamed below me and I slipped off my shoes for fear of scuffing the polished surface. The sitting room was dark off to the left, but he flipped on the lights above the stairs on the right revealing a polished banister that must have been a hundred years old.

"Wow," I said. "Did you do all this?"

"Yeah. It kept me busy before I started at the station. Why don't you come upstairs and get a shower and I'll find you something to wear," he said, taking the first few steps. "No sense you sitting around in wet, smoky clothes."

"Can I call my mom? She's probably frantic," I said.

He handed me his cell phone and I dialed. She answered quickly.

"Mom, it's me."

"Oh, thank God! Are you all right? I saw the fire on TV and when I realized it was your place…"

"I'm fine, Mom. But listen, can you go stay with Aunt Martha in Kentucky for a while?"

"I suppose so. What's going on?"

I explained to her that she may be in danger and it would be best for her to get out of town. She cried, but agreed to go to Aunt Martha's for a while.

"Where will you stay?" she asked.

"I'm not sure yet. I'm with Detective Varner now. He's going to put me up for the night until we can decide what to do."

"Oh," she said, her tone suddenly changing. "I've talked to him on the phone but I never met him in person. What's he like?"

I took that to mean, "Is he a nice Christian boy who will give me lots of grandbabies?"

"He's a nice guy, Mom, and he has offered me his guest room for the night, that's all."

"All right, I'll call Martha now and I'll leave in the morning. Are you sure you're all right?"

I bit my lip and sucked in a breath. "Yeah, I'm fine. Just kind of numb."

Varner put his hands on my shoulders and I had to fight the tears back once again.

"All right, Vic. Call me when you know what's going on."

"I'll try, but please stay in Kentucky until you hear differently."

"All right. I love you."

"I love you too, Mom."

I ended the call and looked up at him.

"Come on," he said with a smile.

I followed him up the stairs and he opened the second door on the left. "Here's the guest bedroom, you can rest some in here."

There was a twin bed, dresser, and a small night table. A hand-stitched quilt was on the bed and it looked as if it had been made from baby clothes. I smiled unconsciously. I had a feeling his grandmother made it for him for some reason. The walls were white at one time, but appeared to have tobacco stains running down from the ceiling. It smelled clean though, and looked comfortable enough for at least one night.

"Sorry about the state of it," he said, looking around. "I haven't had much of a chance to work in here yet."

"It's fine," I told him, sitting on the bed and touching the quilt gingerly.

He left the room and brought back a t-shirt and a stretchy pair of workout shorts.

"This should do you until the morning. Come on and get a shower. You'll feel better."

He led me to a white, comfortable bathroom with tiny black and white tiles underfoot. "Bring your clothes down when you're done and I'll throw them in the washer," he said. "Take your time."

"Thanks."

****

I went downstairs after my shower and found him sitting in the living room. He was watching an enormous television and snacking on what smelled like kettle corn. Boxes lined one wall and the back part of the room was a little cluttered. He was obviously meticulous about everything work related, but his house didn't reflect it. It was almost like he didn't want to deal with what was going on at home.

I wondered what his desk looked like at work. Probably immaculate.

Oh well, I could prod him about that later.

"Lord, that's a big damn TV," I said, realizing quickly how childish I sounded.

"Sixty inches," he said when he saw me. "Feel better?"

"Somewhat." I looked down at what I was wearing. The black shorts hit me around mid-calf and the gray t-shirt hung almost to my knees. I looked like a little girl in her daddy's pajamas.

"Thank you for the flattering outfit," I said, trying to smile.

"You're welcome."

I sat down next to him on the brown leather couch. It had deep, long cushions, so when I scooted back on it my feet hung just off the edge. It was quite a contrast to the long legs next to me and I smiled at the comparison and wiggled my toes.

He chuckled. "You're so tiny."

"No, everything you have is big," I said.

Then I needed a moment to compose myself.

He scooted closer and put his arm around me. "You've been pretty quiet. Are you doing okay with this?"

I stared at the TV. "Um, yeah, I guess. Right now I really don't feel anything."

He put his hand on my wet hair and I put my head on his shoulder. We sat like that for a while, watching, but not watching the TV. I felt comforted with his arm around me and the feeling almost scared me, but I wasn't quite sure why.

Probably because I had a feeling it was all temporary.

"I'm going to head up and shower too," he said. "I smell like a smokehouse steak."

He stood up and handed me the remote. "I'll be back in a few minutes."

I flipped channels for about twenty minutes and finally settled on a M*A*S*H rerun. M*A*S*H is one of those shows that I could watch over and over and never get tired of it. And from the time I was little, I always had a little crush on Hawkeye. A man with a sense of humor was always attractive to me and Hawkeye had a tendency to make me giggle.

Varner padded down the stairs in his bare feet in an outfit similar to the one I was wearing. But he obviously filled it out much nicer than I did. He went to the basement and the mechanical "whooshing" of a washing machine began. Then, I heard him coming back up the stairs and, without thinking, I straightened my back and fluffed my hair a bit.

Okay, so maybe I wasn't completely numb. Even the sight of his long calves made my mouth water.

He entered the room and sat down next to me. "Hi."

"Hi," I said, smiling.

He scooted a little closer and kissed me gently on the cheek. "You sure you're okay?"

I nodded and stared at the TV. "Would you mind if I bunked here on the couch tonight? I think I'll feel better with the TV on."

"Wherever you're more comfortable."

He got up and went into the kitchen.

"Here," he said, handing me a glass that was filled halfway with a brown liquid.

"What is it?" I asked.

"Just a little brandy. It will calm your nerves so maybe you'll sleep."

I looked up at him. He smiled and I slammed the drink. My chest was immediately warm and tingly.

His eyes widened. "You're supposed to sip it, fool."

I coughed a little. "Whew. More please."

"Why don't you wait a few minutes?"

"Are you trying to get me drunk so you can take advantage of me?"

He chuckled and sat down next to me. "Would I need to get you drunk for that?"

I gazed at him for a minute, my eyes lowering to his lips, remembering how wonderful they felt against me and how good he tasted.

"Probably not. I've kind of got a crush on you, you know."

What? What the hell did I say?

His eyes sparkled in the light of the television as they moved around my face slowly.

"I thought I was the one with the crush," he said quietly.

Whoa!

I was suddenly very glad I shaved my legs before meeting Toni for dinner.

"Really?" I asked. "You've got a crush on me?"

He sort of smirked but didn't really answer, just shuffled some of the magazines on the coffee table in front of him.

"What are we going to do about that?" I asked, putting the glass on the coffee table. I scooted back into my typical TV watching position, with my knees up in front of me on the couch and my arms around my legs. I was apparently more comfortable than I thought, or the brandy had made me so. It had obviously affected my mouth.

He shifted his chest toward me, put his right elbow on the back of the couch and ran his fingers through a lock of my hair. I was immediately covered with goose bumps which made their way to my chest and my nipples reacted accordingly.

"Until this case is over, it's best if we leave it alone," he said.

"I know," I agreed, turning my head to look at him.

Then the sex monster returned. Apparently the sex monster likes Brandy.

"But, don't you ever just feel like being bad?"

He looked at the TV again and smiled, slowly turning pink. I shifted my knees toward him so they were touching his leg. "I mean, don't you ever bend the rules just a little?"

He looked at my legs and cleared his throat nervously. "Nope, never have felt the need to."

I leaned forward and ran my fingers over his right hand that had somehow found its way to my thigh.

"Hm," he said quietly. "But I haven't thought about anything else since that night in your apartment." He looked deeply into me. "You and your beautiful gray eyes."

My home had just blown up, and I didn't care. Everything I owned was probably gone, and I didn't care. All I wanted in the world at that moment was to be naked in his arms.

"Well, if you have this crush on me, you can hardly remain objective about the case," I said, scooting closer to him.

He shrugged. "I don't know about that."

"Have you ever had a crush on a suspect before?"

He laughed nervously. "No. But then I don't really consider you a suspect."

"Why not?" I purred. "You don't think I'm naughty enough to be a murderer?"

I leaned and kissed his newly shaved cheek near his mouth, the smell of his aftershave turning my insides to jelly. I scooted closer so my unfettered breasts were against his arm as I reached up and moved his chin toward me. We both instinctively tilted as we kissed each other gently and I ran my fingers up his thigh under his shorts. He let out a short exhale and the muscles in his leg quivered.

He smiled and shook his head. "Oh, you…you're, uh, you're naughty enough."

I ran my lips up his long neck to his ear. "It's fun to break the rules sometimes, Detective Varner."

I nibbled his ear lobe and a sigh of pleasure escaped him.

"Please don't do that," he whispered. "I can't."

"No?" I said softly. "You sure?"

I moved my hand higher on his thigh, tracing his muscles softly with my fingernails.

"Uh," he grunted and bit his bottom lip. "I want to, Vic, but…"

He pulled away quickly and got up. I fell face first on to the couch and groaned as he walked to the doorway and pounded his forehead on the frame a couple times.

"I can't do it, Vic. It's my job."

I laid there mentally pounding my head on the door frame along with him.

"Denied," I said quietly, sitting up. "Again."

"I'm sorry," he said turning around. I looked up at him and my eyes traced down his body to his noticeable semi-erection. I felt a quick contraction of muscles and my pelvis sort of thrust itself forward involuntarily.

Jeez, Vic. It's not your first boner you know. Calm down.

"I'm sorry too," I said, sitting back against a throw-pillow. "I just wanted to feel good for a change."

"Please, don't think I don't want you," he said gently. "I want you more than anyone I've wanted in a very long time."

"That's kind of obvious," I said, my eyes lowering again, excessively dirty thoughts playing out in my mind.

"But, I can't get involved with a witness. It could mean my badge. You can understand that, right?"

"I understand," I said, "And thank you for upgrading my status to witness."

He ran his hand through his hair and left the room, immediately returning with a quilt and a pillow and dropping them at the end of the couch. He stepped over to me and kissed me on the cheek. I grabbed the back of his neck and kissed his lips deeply. He groaned again and stood up slowly.

"You are just pure evil," he said, smiling down at me.

I looked up at him and licked my lips, slowly moving my face closer to the front of his shorts. Then I gave his thigh a little nibble.

He jerked back and away from me. "Oh, God. Evil to the core."

He walked to the doorway, pounded his head against the door frame again, a little harder this time, and squeaked, "Good night."

I watched him climb the stairs holding his forehead. Then I whimpered, and fell face first on to the couch again.

"Damn it, damn it, damn it!" I moaned, pounding my fists into the cushion.

****

CHAPTER TWELVE

"What the hell was that?" I said, sitting bolt upright on the couch.

You didn't hear anything. You were dreaming. Go back to sleep.

I rolled my eyes and let out a deep breath as I lay back down. I looked at the clock on the cable box which told me it was two-forty a.m. and I had only slept thirty-five minutes.

A quick thump came from the front porch. I sat up quickly and turned down the TV.

Okay, you weren't sleeping that time.

"Jason?" I whimpered. "Jason, please come downstairs and say you heard that?"

Scratch. Thump. Rattle.

ACK!

I jumped up and ran to make sure the door was locked, and I noticed the key pad for the alarm as I passed it. It wasn't armed.

Shit!

I distracted him and he forgot to set it. Sometimes I do shit like that and then later on I'm completely astounded. And I couldn't exactly run upstairs and wake him. He would just think I'm crazy and a big, old slut who was just trying to go to bed with him.

"Jason?" I whispered, looking up the stairs. "Please?"

I stood at the door and listened, my eyes darting around like in a horror movie. Then my mind drifted and I wondered why the hell people actually do that. It's not like it does one any good to stand there with your eyes looking left, right, up, down.

Jesus, Lord, God, I'm so tired.

I thought about standing there and screaming my head off, and I actually opened my mouth and took a deep breath. Then I heard another sound, a sort of chattering, and I recognized it. It was an animal, most likely a raccoon or an opossum. I blew out my scream breath and opened the door a crack.

There he was, Rocky Raccoon and his little bandit mask, sitting on the rail of the porch. He couldn't have been a year old and he had obviously been trying to get the big, metal garbage can open. Varner had put a large rock on the lid for that very reason. I had a weakness for animals, so my heart immediately melted. Poor little guy, he was just hungry.

I closed the door and went into the kitchen and poked around for something to satisfy a raccoon. Cheerios? Maybe. I opened the pantry door and ran across a jar of dry roasted peanuts.

Perfect.

I went back to the door and opened it slowly, slipping out into the chilly night. He saw me and froze, his eyes shining in the soft moonlight.

"It's okay, little guy," I said quietly.

I poured some peanuts into my hand, put them in a pile on the porch and backed away, sitting down on the top step. I stayed completely still as he sniffed the air. Then very slowly, never taking his eyes off me, he climbed down the rail and headed toward the peanuts. I smiled.

I'm the Raccoon Whisperer. Get me a damn reality show.

"It's okay," I said again. "Come on."

Closer, closer, his eyes shining blue, and he sniffed the nuts.

Suddenly the door burst open and Varner lunged through, his gun drawn, and my new friend snorted and skittered to a tree in the front yard. I nearly jumped out of my shorts.

"Jesus!" I screamed. "Oh, way to go Robocop, you scared him away!"

He dropped his gun arm and stared at me, breathing heavily. It was then I noticed his lack of a shirt and perfection shining in the light behind him. I swallowed audibly. The smooth skin on his chest rippled in what moonlight could get to him on the porch, and my arms were quickly covered in goose bumps as I thought about lying on that chest, sweaty and spent, after he had brought me to ecstasy over and over.

"What in God's name are you doing?" he asked frantically.

I wiped the drool off my mouth.

"I…I think I dreamed...and I woke up and couldn't sleep and I heard him scratching around, so I just…"

We both exhaled and he laughed.

"I thought," he began," I thought you were…raccoons are dangerous you know."

"I wasn't going to try and catch it or anything. He was just a baby."

"Babies have teeth." he said, sitting down next to me on the step. "You could get rabies."

"If it was light out I'd show you the scar I got from one littler than him. I used to work at a vet's office, remember?"

"Start taming wildlife around here and he'll end up in my attic."

I chuckled. "Sorry."

"If I'd have shot him we could have made a nice stew."

I gasped and slapped his bare shoulder. He laughed.

"Sorry I woke you," I said.

"It's okay," he said, stretching his muscular back. "I really don't sleep that much."

"You did at my apartment."

He smiled at me. "Yeah. Must have been the beer."

I fought the urge to bite his shoulder. "Or the company."

"That too," he said, putting a gentle hand on my back. "What did you dream?"

"I keep dreaming about shoes. They're always chasing me."

"Shoes?"

"Black shiny shoes. Sometimes they're attached to legs, sometimes they're not. I never see faces, just shoes."

He bit his lower lip. "Your brain might be trying to tell you something. Shoes can mean you're trying to get away or get to something. How do you feel after you dream about it?"

"I don't know. Anxious I guess. But I'm always anxious lately."

He nodded. "Maybe you should talk to someone about it."

"I am talking to someone about it."

"No, I mean, maybe you should talk to a psychiatrist."

I smiled. "You sound like one."

He smiled back. "I've studied it, but I'm not a professional. Can we go inside now? I'm freezing."

I grabbed the nuts, the ones in the jar unfortunately, and we went back inside. He closed and locked the door and pressed a few buttons on the keypad arming the alarm.

"No more adventures for you tonight, raccoon girl," he said, shivering. "If you start foaming at the mouth, I'm going to have to shoot you."

Great. I'd better not drool in front of him again.

I sat down on the couch with a handful of peanuts and began chewing. He sat next to me and shivered. I grabbed the quilt on my right and threw it over his smooth chest with a sigh of disappointment. Then I couldn't stop myself from blurting out the oldest cliché.

"If I said you had a beautiful body, would you hold it against me?"

He groaned out a laugh and snuggled into the quilt. "Against my better judgment, I probably would. I'm about to freeze to death."

I smiled. "Then give me some of that quilt."

****

I awoke with the sun shining on my exposed toes. I stretched and tried to roll over, but fell to the floor with a "clunk." Then a quilt fell around me and over my head.

"What the hell?" I struggled to get the quilt off of me and heard a low-pitched laugh above me.

"You okay?" Varner laughed, pulling the quilt off my head.

I brushed the hair out of my face and my neck crunched. "Ow! I don't know."

I looked up at him and remembered where I was, and that we had fallen asleep on the couch, him spooning behind me.

"You kind of have a thing for spooning don't you?" I asked, trying to de-mummify myself.

"I guess so," he said, trying to help me. "I didn't use to. Damn, I can't feel my arm."

He yanked part of the quilt out from under me. I fell over again and banged my elbow on the floor.

"Stop helping me," I commanded.

He lay on his back and laughed. "I swear woman, your life needs a soundtrack sometimes."

I struggled free, stood up and pointed at the quilt. "Stay!"

He continued laughing and sat up.

"What time is it?" I asked, trying to untangle my hair.

He looked at his watch. "Eight."

"Aren't you late for work?"

He yawned and rubbed his eyes. "I'm at work."

"Huh?"

"I'm your bodyguard as of last night."

I reached around and gave my neck a crack and he cringed. "Don't you ever do that in my presence again."

"But it feels good. Come here, I'll do yours."

He held up his hand. "No, no. My neck is fine."

For a moment I contemplated tackling him on to the couch and finding his ticklish spots, but decided that I had already pressed my luck a little too much last night.

"So you get to stay home all day and get paid for it?" I asked him. "While not using up any of your vacation or sick time?"

"It's called, 'on assignment'," he said. "I need to take you in to make a statement about your apartment and we need to go get your car, but other than that, yeah. As long as you're with me, I'm on duty."

"So, this is a permanent arrangement until the case is over?"

"Unless you'd rather go to a hotel."

"With room service?"

He yawned again. "You could get that here. Go on up to the guest room and I'll bring you up a Pop Tart and some orange juice."

I rolled my eyes. "Okay, what do you want for breakfast?"

"You're cooking?"

"It's the least I can do. You didn't have to take me in."

He grinned. "I've got bacon and eggs in there."

"Scrambled okay?"

"I prefer over-easy."

"Don't push it, Varner."

****

Later that day we went and got my car out of hock and I drove it to a storage facility at the police station. I hated leaving it, since it seemed to signify the only ounce of freedom I had left, but Varner insisted that it be kept out of sight.

"What if I'm at the house alone and something happens?" I asked him, locking my car and touching the door almost lovingly.

"We'll find you something," he said. "Your license plates are rather conspicuous."

I always thought that my VICS HOT plates were cute, but I had to agree they were a dead giveaway to my identity. I said goodbye to my little, green Accord and left her in the garage.

"Your landlord called the station earlier," he said as we piled into his Tahoe. "Your apartment is a total loss. Did you have renter's insurance?"

"Of course not," I said. "I didn't have anything worth insuring except maybe my Chaplin clock and my…" My voice trembled and the corners of my mouth twitched.

My purple couch was gone. I sighed and looked out the window. He put a hand on my knee.

"I'm sorry, Darlin'. I know this has been tough on you. But you're safe, and your mom is safe, that's what's important right now."

I nodded, but didn't look at him. If I looked at him, I was going to bust out crying again.

We drove over to the lot where they kept the seized vehicles and right away I spotted a shiny, purple mustang with some kick-ass rims.

Hot damn! Maybe this won't be so bad after all.

I got out of the car and headed, rather excitedly, toward the gorgeous automobile of my dreams.

"Nope," Varner called after me. "You'd be less conspicuous in your own car."

"You're no fun at all." I pouted, following him to the office. "You'll probably have me driving a freaking Pinto."

He laughed and held the door open for me. "Not with your luck."

I entered a greasy office and saw a greasy guy behind the greasy desk. Varner followed me.

"Hey, Bill, what have you got for me?"

"Bill" was gigantic, and I don't mean he was tall. He had to be the biggest man I'd ever seen, probably weighing about four bills. He looked me over and grinned with his greasy teeth. "She'd look awesome in that little mustang out there."

I elbowed Varner. "See?"

He looked down at me. "I said no, young lady."

I pouted again. "You big poop."

Bill chuckled and looked at a bulletin board. "Let's see. I've got a Dodge Neon out there that's in pretty good shape except for the bullet hole in the back."

"Let's stay away from bullet holes," Varner said.

"Oh yeah, I just got a little Ford Focus in," he said, reaching for a sheet of paper under the counter. "It's got low miles and has been maintained pretty well."

"Hm," Varner said. "What's the story?"

"Well," Bill scratched his greasy head and looking at me. "They found an old lady who had, um, expired in it. She had her seat belt on and everything. Looked like she was headed for church."

"No!" I said.

"Let's take a look," Varner said to me.

"No!" I said again.

"Come on," Varner said. "You can at least look at it."

Bill grabbed a set of keys and the men headed out the door. I followed reluctantly. We all trudged out to look at the dead old lady car. I had to admit, it was adorable and it totally looked like something I should be driving. It was small and dark blue with a silver tinge through the paint. Bill unlocked it and I opened the driver's side door.

"She mustn't have been in here long," Varner said, sticking his head in. "Doesn't stink."

I dropped my hand from the door and took a step back. "Now why'd you have to go and say that?"

He laughed. "Well, it doesn't."

"They think she was only in there a few hours," Bill said. "Poor lady. Only had one son and he lives in Chicago and didn't want the car."

I swallowed the stuff rising up the back of my throat and Varner smiled down at me. "Hop on in, Vic."

Trying to get the image of the old lady dying and emptying her bowels and bladder simultaneously out of my head, I slid into the seat and put my hands on the steering wheel.

"How does it feel?" Varner asked.

"She didn't have anything contagious did she?" I asked Bill, my hands popping off the wheel.

Bill laughed. "No, she was just old."

I held out my hands for the keys. "All right."

Bill dropped the keys in my hand and Varner closed the door. I watched them walk away. Well, I watched Varner walk away and rubbed my lips together. His retreating form was enough to keep a nun up at night. Bill went back in the office and Varner hopped into his car, and I followed him out of the parking lot.

The Focus did pretty well on the narrow, bumpy roads to his house. I half expected it to fall apart when I hit some of the pot holes, but it held together. I parked next to him in his gravel driveway and got out. I noticed he didn't get out right away, so I sauntered around the front of his car and observed he was on the phone in a heated discussion with someone. Actually, he was yelling and looked like his eyes were about to explode out of his face. I backed away from his car slowly and headed up to the front porch. I took a seat on my favorite step from the night before and noticed the peanuts were gone. My friend must have returned in the night. I scanned the trees around his house. It really was a beautiful area, and the closest neighbor was a couple miles down the road, which is why I needed a vehicle. The air was cool on my face, with just a hint of spring, and I started to feel optimistic about things for the first time in a while.

"Well that's just fucking wonderful!" he snarled into the phone as he got out of his car. "You go ahead and take me back to court! How much do you think I have on your extra marital activities that I kept out of evidence to help you out? You take me back to court and I'll be forced to produce all of it! I'm not an idiot, Claire! You're not getting another fucking dime from me!"

He started up the walk angrily, stomped up the steps next to me, and shoved his key into the lock.

"Yeah, that's what I thought!" he said, ending the call and stepping into the house. I snuck behind him and silently sat down on the living room couch. He just stood there in the entryway staring at the floor and breathing hard. I wasn't sure what to do, so I flipped on the TV which seemed to bring him out of his stupor. He dropped his keys on the table by the door and stalked into the kitchen. I heard the refrigerator door open and the clinking of bottles. He came back with two beers and handed me one.

"Don't make me drink alone," he said.

"Okay," I said, popping the top. "Everything all right?"

He took a long drink and sighed. "My ex is trying to get more money out of me."

He guzzled the rest of his beer and I handed him mine.

"Thanks," he said. "She cheated on me for years. Then she left me to shack up with my best friend, and he gambled away half of her settlement. The other half probably went up his nose. Now she wants more, plus the alimony I'm sending her."

My eyebrows shot up. "You're giving her alimony after she cheated on you?"

"You sound like my dad," he said, waving his hand. "I know I don't have to, but I still feel obligated I guess."

He looked at me. "She was my first love. It was a hard winter without her."

I nodded and tried to look sympathetic. Inside me the nasty, green, jealous monster was starting to growl.

"I guess maybe subconsciously I thought if I paid her enough, she would come back," he said sadly, picking at the label on his beer bottle.

"You really want her back?" I asked.

He took another long drink, looked at me and smiled. "Not at the moment, no."

I smiled. "Good. Because I think you deserve better."

He continued smiling and picked at his bottle some more. "Nice of you to say. I think I'm a pretty good guy. Although she would call me a bastard who's obsessed with his job. She never told me she was unhappy though, so I was pretty damn shocked when I found out what she had been doing."

"I'm sure there was a lot of crime to be obsessed with in New Orleans."

He nodded. "We had a lot of unsolved homicides. People were afraid to cooperate because of what might happen to them. I moved up here to get away from all of that, and everything that reminded me of her."

I started to touch his shoulder and then thought better of it. "I'm sorry you've had such a tough time. But it's not your fault. You're dedicated and she should have seen that. I mean, if I was her I would have…"

He slowly turned his head to me. "You would have what?"

I smiled shyly and exhaled a laugh when he nudged me playfully with his shoulder.

"You want to go shoot something?" I asked him, hoping to lighten the mood.

He thought for a minute. "Hm. Might not be a bad idea."

"What?"

****

"Okay, relax your shoulders, all the tension should be in your arms. Keep your wrists straight. Lock that right thumb down. Finger right there. Try to keep the trigger against the crease of your finger, not the pad, so you'll be able to fire again quickly if you need to. Now bend your knees a little. There, that's it. That's good. Now aim, gently squeeze…"

POP! POP! POP!

I took a step back and pulled the ear protectors off. "Did I hit it?"

"Yeah you did, right in the center again. Are you sure you haven't shot before? You're a dead- eye. We should try you out on a damn rifle."

I rolled my shoulders. I couldn't believe I was holding and shooting a gun. Varner decided it would be a good idea to learn how to use one, just in case. I was practicing with his "Smith and Wesson, double action, semi-automatic, nine millimeter pistol". Honestly, a gun is a gun to me. It felt good though, now that I was actually holding one. He had lectured me on the do's and don'ts before he would even let me touch it, but once I got over the apprehension and actually hefted the weight of it in my hands, I went all bad-ass.

Victoria Childs, the macho chick from Brenton. All I needed was a swat suit and full body armor to complete the look. Or a leather vest, tattoos and a mullet. I already had the enormous boobs, but mine were real.

We had gone outside and he began teaching me some self-defense moves, but we stopped after I stomped on his foot and slammed the heel of my hand into his chin like I saw on Miss Congeniality. I almost knocked him out. He wouldn't admit it, but I knew he was seeing little birdies. We then started shooting at an old archery target he had in his shed.

"But, if someone is coming at you, I don't want you to aim. I just want you to shoot. It doesn't matter where you hit, as long as you hit," he told me. "But try and aim low."

I looked up at him. "I don't think that will be a problem."

I secretly hoped I wouldn't have to use anything he was teaching me, but I felt more confident that I could handle myself if I needed to. Then again, I knew he didn't really want to hurt me. The boogie man did. The boogieman wanted me dead.

"Um, isn't this against the law? I don't have a gun license or anything," I questioned, unloading the gun and handing it and the empty magazine to him.

"You have an honorary one for now," he said with a smile. "We should get you fitted for a vest though, in case you ever need to go out."

"Sweet! I'll be one bad-ass bitch when you get through with me. I'll be a sharp shooter and suited up in body armor. Then I'll piss my pants with fear if that guy ever shows up to kill me," I said. "We should get some of those adult diapers too."

We both laughed at the image, but mainly to cover up the fear that it would actually happen that way.

"What if he shoots me in the head?" I asked, suddenly serious.

He bit his lip and looked at me. "We try not to think about stuff like that."

He handed me another magazine and I slapped it into place. Then I unloaded it and slapped it home again, just for practice and because I liked doing it. The sound of it registered something in me. To me, it felt like power.

His phone rang and he pulled it off his belt.

"Varner," he said, smiling at me.

He was thinking how cute I was. I could tell. At least the smile on his face made me feel cute. I practiced my grip and aimed at the target while he was talking.

"All right, I'll be there as soon as I can."

He flipped his phone shut. "I've got to run to the office. The DNA on the gun is back, but there's a problem."

"Figures," I said, stretching my arms skyward.

POP!

Oops.

I heard a quick "squawk" above me and a bird fell out of the tree next to us.

"Oh, no!" I exclaimed, running over to the bird. "Oh, no! I killed him!"

Varner spit out a laugh. "I told you to keep your finger off the trigger."

"It's not funny." I said strongly, looking down at the bird and dropping the gun next to me on the grass. "I've never killed anything in my life."

He didn't appear to have a wound and I didn't see any blood. The next thing I knew the bird jumped up, shook himself, hopped a couple steps and flew away.

I looked at Varner.

"Hm," I said. "Guess I just scared him."

"Give me the gun," Varner said, when he could compose himself enough to talk.

"It's not funny," I said again, grabbing the gun and handing it to him.

He unloaded it, checked the chamber and put it back in the case.

"You're right. Not funny. Sorry," he squeaked.

He looked like he was going to swallow his own lips. I started to smile, then I snickered. His eyes were watering by that time.

I grabbed the gun case in a false huff, and headed for the sun porch connected to his house. He followed me, trying to compose himself, but he had to stop and hold on to the rail of the stairs. I put the gun in the closet and headed into the kitchen.

He flopped down in one of the kitchen chairs and put his head on the table.

"I'm glad I amuse you," I laughed, grabbing a soda from the fridge.

That started him up again. "I need to start carrying a video camera. I could win some money."

"All right, all right," I said. "You tell anyone one about that and you're next."

"What?" he asked, wiping his eyes. "You going to shoot me out of a tree too? That would probably be a felony."

I threw a dish towel at him and started out of the kitchen. I went into the living room, flipped on the TV and sat on the couch suddenly realizing how tired I was. It had been a long couple days, including a long night thinking about him and sex with him and showering with him and the like, and I was wiped out. I curled up on the couch and flipped channels.

"Hey," he said, as he walked into the room, "I'm going to go make groceries too. You need anything?"

"Clothing?" I said, assuming "make groceries" meant he was going to the store. I loved the way he talked.

He chuckled. "But you look so good in my t-shirts."

"You look better in them," I told him.

"I bet you'd look better out of them."

"Cool it!" I ordered with a laugh. "I'm the one who's supposed to be torturing you."

He laughed. "I'll stop by your mom's house and pick up some clothes for you."

"Okay, my stuff is in the bedroom, second door from the left off the kitchen."

"Got it," he said, grabbing my keys off the table by the door. "And no taming or killing the wildlife around here while I'm gone. You hear me, Girl?"

I hurled a throw pillow from the couch at him as he set the alarm.

"Don't open the doors or windows or it will go off," he said, kicking the pillow back at me. "I'll be back as soon as I can."

I smiled to myself as he left. "All right, you big cutie."

****

CHAPTER THIRTEEN

I was going insane.

I had a cell phone that only dialed him or Fisher and couldn't receive incoming calls. I had a gun to shoot any intruders. I had a car to drive away from danger. I had a house with an alarm that went straight to him. I knew I was safe from harm.

But I was going insane!

I know people say that all the time, and usually it's a figure of speech, but I seriously thought I was going to lose my mind from the boredom. The only contact I had with the outside world was when I had conversations with Hawkeye and Radar on the TV. I was told to stay away from the phone house phone, so I couldn't even call my mom's cell to see if she was all right. I did happen to notice that it rang about the time he was due to come home from work every evening, around the time the telemarketers come out to play. But I loved it when he came home, though I tried not to seem too enthusiastic. I jumped up and down a few times before he actually got in the door, but then I played it calm and cool.

And I cooked. God help me, I cooked! He had one cookbook that looked to be about a hundred years old, and I made just about every recipe in it, except the seafood ones. The only seafood I can cook is fish sticks. Then when I ran out of recipes in there, I used the few I knew by heart. Then I made stuff up. He liked it all, or at least he acted like he did.

I moved into the guest bedroom after a week of my incarceration and was given the green light to fix it up a little. I polished the wood and painted, and by the time I was finished it looked great. He was so impressed, he bought more paint for the hallway. Then I put together two book shelves for the living room and loaded them with his books that were cluttered in boxes in the back of the room. They were mostly about criminal investigation techniques with a few books about sports in the mix. While I wasn't doing manual labor, I read about preferred interrogation, murder scene investigations, and a couple books about how to tell if someone is lying which I found completely fascinating. Some people blink a lot. Some don't at all. Some twitch or pull their ear lobes or play with their hair. I looked at myself in the mirror and told some lies, but I couldn't find my own cues.

Maybe Varner could work with me on that. I could sit across from him and tell him that I was *so* not attracted to him anymore. One hell of a lie.

I was in the middle of putting together an entertainment center I found behind the book boxes when he came home one evening, looking tired and a little forlorn.

"Hey," he said, managing to smile and throw his keys on the table by the door. "I forgot I bought that. You don't have to do all this stuff you know."

"I'm bored," I said, smiling back. "Everything okay?"

He nodded. "I'm just tired. What smells so good? I could smell it from the porch."

"I've got a roast in the oven," I said, getting to my feet and brushing my hands off on my jeans. "Should be about an hour."

"You little homemaker, you," he smirked. "Are there potatoes too?"

"Of course."

"Wow."

"You making fun of me, Varner?"

He chuckled. "No, I'm just kind of glad I got to see this side of you. You're an amazing cook."

I grinned. "Thanks. I'm kind of glad I got to learn that too. I guess I'm a little more complicated that I thought."

"I'm learning that a little more every day."

Uncomfortable silence followed and he shrugged out of his suit jacket.

"I'm going on up to take a shower before dinner," he said, his forehead flushing slightly.

"Okay," I answered, checking my fingernails and avoiding his gaze. His eyes tended to make my stomach flutter and caused moisture in places I had forgotten could get moist. Picturing him in the shower wasn't helping.

The worst part was, I didn't know if he was having the same feelings about me. He did at one point. I mean, I knew he had been attracted to me at one point. His body gave him away on that. But I wasn't so sure anymore. He was hard to read sometimes. Incredible, but hard to read. He knew how to hide things better than I did. Hell, just the sight of his bicep would turn my face the color of a beet.

He headed upstairs and I went into the kitchen to check the roast. I heard him in his bedroom above the kitchen and remembered that I forgot to tell him that I did some of his laundry today. I put his clothes away that were still stored in boxes up in his room..

"Vic?" I heard from the top of the stairs.

"Yeah?"

"You know what happened to all my workout shorts?"

"They're in the dresser, bottom drawer!"

I heard him the bedroom again, and smiled when I thought I heard a stifled, "Wow."

****

"Mm," he said, wiping his mouth. "This is awesome."

"I'm glad you like it, I haven't made it in a while. I was afraid I used a little too much Worcestershire."

He got up for his third helping and sat back down. "If I had known you could cook like this, I would have asked you to move in a long time ago."

"You didn't know me a long time ago," I said, sipping my water.

"Wish I had," he said, shoving a forkful in his mouth. "Are there more green beans?"

I smiled, wondering if he realized the implication of what he had said, and got up to get the pan of beans. I had let them simmer for several hours in some of the beef stock and a little bacon, like how my dad's mom used to make them. She was the best cook in the world. Maybe that's where I got it. I dumped a couple spoonfuls on his plate and cleared my own place.

"How's the case going?" I asked, standing at the sink with my back to him, swallowing the sudden lump in my throat.

"Slowly," he mumbled, his mouth full. "Very slowly."

"What's the hold up?"

I looked out the window at the purplish sky and closed my eyes.

God, no! Please don't do this to me, not now. Why can't I have the crying fits when I'm alone?

He sighed. "I shouldn't really discuss it with you."

I nodded and quickly wiped away the tear that was rolling down my cheek.

"Eh, what the hell? The plate number you gave us was from an impound lot in Elgin," he said, after a few minutes. "They reported it stolen three months ago and we haven't gotten any hits on that. We couldn't get any prints from the judge's office. We got several sets from the handrail in the stairwell, but none of them match any in our system. We're running them through Interpol and I'm hopeful that…"

But for once, I didn't give a shit about the case. I didn't give a shit about dinner or putting furniture together. I didn't even give a shit about the plate I was holding. I couldn't get past the waves of emotion that were crashing through me at that very moment.

This wasn't just crush anymore, at least not like any crush I'd ever had.

I was in love with him. As much as I'd tried to fight it, it was something I couldn't deny any longer. I loved every little stinking thing about him. I loved the way he walked, talked, ate, smiled and fell asleep on the couch watching ESPN. I loved that cute little way he crooked his mouth to the right when he was disgusted with something or making a joke. Jesus, even the way the man breathed sent me into fits. I was honest to God in love with him, and it ached deep inside my chest. It hurt that I couldn't say it to him. Not to mention the fact that it scared the hell out of me. Love tended to kick my ass whenever I happened upon it.

It was usually unrequited or just plain bad timing. Bad timing was an understatement in this case.

And I knew he didn't love me. He couldn't. He was an angel and I was…

Who the hell knows what I am?

I started the water and scrubbed the hell out of the plate I was holding, hoping to get rid of the tears before he noticed anything.

"We're still waiting on DNA from the gun," he continued. "They botched the first sample in the lab because Julie went on vacation."

I nodded again and tried to sniffle and sob without making a sound.

"I mean, I hate to say it, but the resources they have in the department are from the Middle Ages, and when the only staff they have that's worth anything leaves town for a week…"

I gasped out a quiet sob and bit my bottom lip.

"I think the plate is clean," he said, suddenly next to me. His fingers touched my chin and moved my face toward him. I turned away quickly and went back to scrubbing.

"What's wrong, Vic?"

"Want to dry?" I asked, rinsing my plate and putting it in the dish drainer.

"Tell me."

"Nothing," I said, taking his plate. "I'm fine."

"You cry when you're fine?"

"I'm not crying, the steam is making my eyes water."

He opened the drawer next to him and grabbed a dish towel. "Fibber."

"All right then, I probably have PMS."

"I'll hide the firearms."

I washed and rinsed his plate and handed it to him.

"Did I say something to upset you?" he asked as he dried.

"No. You're fine."

Fine, hell, he was perfect. Damn him.

He put the plate in the drainer, took me by the shoulders and turned me toward him. I dropped my head and tried to look away, but he caught my chin.

"Tell me what's wrong, woman."

His eyes. His beautiful hazel eyes. His incredible angel eyes. And once again, everything I had inside me was exposed.

I gasped out another sob and stuttered, "I…I lo…I just…could you just hang on to me for a minute?"

He slid his arms around my shoulders and held me close to his chest and the clean scent of him wrapped around me like a warm, comfortable bath.

"You want your life back don't you?" he said gently, rubbing my back.

Sure, that sounded good, even though it wasn't true at all. I loved my new life with him.

I nodded against him and continued sobbing, hoping he wouldn't mind if I wrapped myself around his waist. He didn't mind. In fact, he squeezed me a little tighter.

"I was wondering when this would all get to you," he said, his cheek against the top of my head. "You've lost everything and you've been so strong."

"I'm not strong," I cried. "I'm a wuss."

"Not even close," he said. "You know, people have gone insane over less than what you've been through in the past few weeks."

"I'm such an idiot," I whispered.

"Why do you say that?"

I looked up at him and something in my brain screamed, "Tell him you love him, fool!"

"If I hadn't gone back to that damn building, if I hadn't forgotten my purse...I'm just an idiot."

He grabbed a Kleenex and wiped the tears from my face gently. "You're a human being. We're not perfect. And if you hadn't gone back in there we wouldn't have a witness."

I sniffled pathetically. Sure, maybe I was human, but he was an angel. I was in love with an angel. Sooner or later he was going to have to go back to heaven and I'd be stuck in my stupid, boring little life again. How could I go back to that? How could I go back to a life without his arms around me? Without his touch, his scent...his damn laundry.

"Girl, if you hadn't gone back in that building, I never would have met you," he said with a gentle smile. "Which in itself would have been a tragedy. Nobody can make me laugh the way you do."

I sniffled again. "I'm such a coward."

"You're one of the bravest people I've ever met."

"I'm a fool."

"You're smart as hell."

"I'm ridiculous."

"You are wonderful," he said, touching my cheek. "And if this is about the roast, I wasn't lying when I said it was good."

I smiled and spit out a laugh. "Okay, I'm a good cook. But that's it."

"That's not it," he said. "You're a dead-eye shot, you painted the whole interior of my house without a single spot on the floor, and you put furniture together for God's sake."

I laughed again as he pulled me closer. "I'm sorry. I guess I'm having one hell of a pity party, huh?"

"Don't be sorry," he said. "Believe it or not, I know how you feel."

I nodded, knowing he was referring to his bad divorce. His life had gone up in flames before his eyes too, and he survived it. He survived it alone. And his love was unrequited too.

He hugged me closer. "It's going to be okay, I promise."

"You really think I'm wonderful?" slipped out of my mouth.

He pulled back and smiled down at me. "A little."

I smiled back. "Just a little?"

"Well, not completely wonderful, I mean you have a few flaws."

"Like what?"

"Dirty dishes make you cry."

I smiled. "I'll try to quit."

He smiled and touched my hair that was still swirled up in a careless rubber band bun. "Your hair's kind of a mess."

I pulled the rubber band out and shook my hair down around my shoulders. "Better?"

His smile turned into a grin. "And you're too damn cute for your own good."

"Thank you," I said, laughing quietly. "You're not so bad yourself."

"I know."

I giggled and grabbed another Kleenex.

He palmed my cheek again and we gazed at each other for what seemed like an eternity.

God he was beautiful. Too beautiful to be anything from this stupid little planet. Maybe he was an alien instead of an angel. Maybe that's why he was so tall, because he was really a little, tiny alien inside a big robotic body like on "Men In Black." Maybe this wasn't his true form and he was actually a wonderful, glowing creature from somewhere else in the universe.

Whatever, Vic. Are you going to kiss him or not?

Then he leaned down and kissed my cheek softly. I was very tempted to turn my lips toward his, but I chickened out and accepted the cheek kiss gratefully.

"Listen, I think you've done enough for today. Why don't you go in the living room and relax," he said. "I'll finish up in here."

"Okay," I agreed. "Thank you for, well, just everything."

"Anytime, Darlin'."

I started out the door, but turned back and my eyes traced the long line of his back, down his legs, and on down to his bare feet. He was the epitome of perfection under the soft, white, kitchen light. Just the sight of him made everything beautiful and calm in my world.

"Yep," I muttered. "Alien."

"What? Did you say something?"

"Huh? Oh, nothing."

****

CHAPTER FOURTEEN

He was late.

He usually got home around six p.m. and it was nearly seven p.m. I always panicked when he was late. I mean if he was dead in a ditch somewhere, no one would think to call his house and tell me. Except maybe Detective Fisher, and I got the distinct feeling he wasn't thoughtful like that.

Maybe he just went to the grocery store. He didn't mention going before he left this morning. We were out of a lot of stuff though.

He's dead in a ditch! I know it!

I lay on the couch watching and not watching an episode of ER, like a puppy waiting for its owner, when the phone rang and I nearly jumped through the ceiling.

Without thinking I grabbed it.

"Hello?"

Silence. Breathing.

Ooh, shit! Shouldn't have answered it.

"Hello?" I said again, pressing the heel of my hand against my forehead, hoping and not hoping that someone would answer.

"Is…Jason Varner there?"

It was a woman. She sounded young. Tentative and young. Too young to be his mother.

"No, he's not right now, can I give him a message?" I asked.

"Who is this?" she asked, the tone changing so that she might have been saying, "All right, bitch, who the hell are you?"

Okay, she was young, pissy, and an Illinois native. It wasn't his ex.

"I'm a friend of his," I answered.

"Oh, okay, friend of his. Will you tell him his girlfriend Deborah called?"

What?

WHAT???

A cool realization swept over my stomach and down my arms followed quickly by the accompanying nausea.

Girlfriend? He has a girlfriend.

Of course he has a girlfriend. Come on, Vic, how naïve could you be? That's why he wouldn't go to bed with you.

But if that's true, why didn't he just tell me? I could understand a girlfriend better than abstaining for a job.

He doesn't want me and he was using his job as an excuse. Oh, God!

Yes, he does. He said he wants me. He doesn't lie.

Does he?

"Uh, his girlfriend?" I asked, after swallowing several times. "I wasn't aware he had one."

"Well, he does. Just tell him I called, okay?"

The line went dead and I dropped the phone from my ear as I sat up slowly.

I should have known he was too good to be true.

I sat back against the couch, stared at the floor and the stewing began.

"Oh, I'll fucking tell him, you bitch," I said to no one. "I'll tell his ass all to hell."

****

Another half hour passed before he pulled into the driveway, just long enough for me to work myself into a wonderful, jealous rage while I paced in front of the bay window like a caged animal. I watched him walk up to the house carrying a few bags of groceries, obviously the reason he was late. But in my mind he was late from all the sex he was having with Deborah, the girlfriend. A low growl emanated from my throat, and I tried to calm the green demon that was tearing out my heart and stomping it into a big glob of nothing on the floor.

Apt description of you, Vic. A big glob of nothing on the floor.

I knew I didn't really have a reason to be mad. He never promised me anything, and God knows we weren't "together" at least not in a romantic way. He never led me on or made me believe we were going to be something amazing, the kind of thing Lionel Ritchie wrote love songs about. That was all me. All my fantasies. And he didn't know that he was my sole reason for getting up and showering in the morning, for brushing my teeth and hair. He was the only reason I had mascara in the house.

I didn't have a right to be angry.

But I was mad as hell, and it felt like I was supposed to be.

"Don't you fucking cry," I told myself as he put his key in the lock and opened the door.

"Hey," he said. "Can you help me carry this stuff in?"

He disarmed the alarm quickly before it went off and almost dropped a bag in the process.

I grabbed a few bags from him and headed into the kitchen where I started unloading and putting things away. And I didn't slam or stomp. I kept my composure and I breathed.

It doesn't matter. It doesn't matter. It doesn't matter that he's a liar and a cheat and a snake!

He came in with another arm full and put them on the table, handing me a carton of milk.

"DNA from the blood on the gun matches yours," he said with a grin. "And they found someone else's DNA all over it, even inside the barrel. Once we have a match on that, you're clear."

"I figured I would be eventually," I said, swallowing my anger and putting the milk away. "Unless Fisher still thinks my accomplice hit me."

He laughed. "He never thought that. He was just trying to get a rise out of you."

"It worked," I said, putting a case of soda in the fridge.

It doesn't matter. He doesn't matter. He's nothing to you. He's nothing but the man of every damn dream you've had since you were five years old. Ever since you gave up on Paul McCartney.

"Something wrong?" he asked, after a few minutes of silence.

"No!" I snapped quickly. "Why?"

"Well, your face is all red and I've never seen that vein in your forehead before."

I swallowed and took a deep breath. "Nothing is wrong."

"You sure?"

"Yes."

"Then why won't you look me in the eye?"

I shrugged and tried to get some canned goods on the second shelf of the overhead cabinet beside the sink. I jumped a couple times but the cans kept falling and I was just damn near fed up with everything at that point.

"Damn it!" I barked, throwing one up and denting it on the shelf.

"Here," he said, grabbing the can I was holding above my head. "I'll put them up. You'll end up conking yourself in the…"

"Your girlfriend called," I blurted out.

Jeez! It was like I vomited. Like I puked a declaration of betrayal all over his striped tie. I couldn't have stopped it if I tried.

I looked up to see his reaction. He was frozen where he stood and his eyes slowly dropped to mine.

"What?" he asked, his face contorting into a sort of nervous grimace. It was cute as hell, but I was so pissed that it didn't matter how cute he was.

"I think you heard me," I said, turning and grabbing a package of cheese off the table. "Deborah called. Girlfriend. Your self-proclaimed girlfriend, Deborah. She called. Maybe you remember now?"

I tossed the cheese in the fridge and slammed the door.

"Oh," he said, turning a very strange shade of crimson. "Why did you answer the phone?"

"You were late," I said, getting madder by the second. "I thought you were dead in a ditch."

I opened the fridge again and put the ice cream on the top shelf.

Shit! Smooth, Vic.

"Uh, that goes..."

"I know," I growled, slamming the fridge door and opening the freezer.

Victoria, don't you cry!

"I guess I wasn't aware of your current situation," I told him slamming the freezer door, opening the fridge, and grabbing a beer. I popped it open, took a long drink and put it on the counter.

"Dead man walking," he muttered.

I wasn't going to argue that point.

He finished putting the canned stuff up in the cabinet and turned around to face me and my wrath. He cleared his throat, shrugged out of his suit jacket, and pulled on his tie like it was a noose.

"Okay," he said, unbuttoning his top button and dropping his jacket on the table. "Truth. She's a woman I was seeing for a while when I first moved here."

"Was?" I questioned, under some sort of shriek-laugh I didn't recognize. "She doesn't seem to think she WAS seeing you. She said she's your girlfriend. As in, the woman you're currently poking!"

He walked around me, opened the fridge and grabbed himself a beer. I fought back the urge to punch him in the gut and kept my fists clenched at my sides. He sat down at the kitchen table and sighed.

"I suppose she thinks she is. I guess I never really made myself clear."

"Oh! Okay! That's just great!" I took another long drink of beer. "I guess you never really made yourself clear to either one of us!"

"I'm sorry. I didn't think this would be a problem. She usually calls my cell phone."

My mouth dropped and I stared at him wide-eyed. "Oh, so she wouldn't be a problem if I didn't know about her? Oh, that's wonderful. Perfect! Fan-fucking-tastic!"

He sat in silence looking at his beer bottle. Just then I had a sort of revelation and I put my fist to my forehead.

"Oh, I see! I get it now! How could I be so blind? My staying here was all part of the game wasn't it? Some sick little fucking game that you and Fisher are still playing to see if I'm hiding anything about the murder!"

"No!" he said strongly. "I mean, it…this whole thing may have started like that, but no, not anymore. And wait a minute, who is playing who here? I'm not the one making all the sexual advances."

"Bullshit!" I yelled. "You strut around here without a shirt all the time! Flexing your biceps and stretching your back! You come up all sweaty from your workout in the basement, smelling all musky and, and, all that shit! Like I haven't noticed you trying to show me what a stud you are!"

"Bullshit yourself!" he shouted back. "You and your short, purple satin nightie thing with the tiny little straps! And why is it that one strap always seems to fall off your shoulder when I'm around? Whoopsies, here's my breast! Try not to look, Varner!"

"It's the only nightgown I have, and I have never once showed you my breast!"

"No, but you might as well have, wearing that skimpy thing around! And your hard, little…upper chest…things sticking out! I mean, well, it's pretty obvious you're cold! Put a robe on for Christ sake! How am I supposed to sleep at night knowing you're over there half naked?!"

"You don't have any trouble sleeping at night!" I yelled. "I can hear you snoring across the hall!"

"I don't snore!"

"You, sir, are a window-rattler! And what about you in those tight jeans you always wear! Trying to flaunt that big old bulge? Like I haven't noticed that! That's probably why you always have one sock missing! You're stuffing your junk!"

"I do not stuff my junk!"

"Right! You don't leave all your freaking beard hair in the bathroom sink either! And how does it get on the mirror, Jason? Can you explain that to me please?!"

"Don't talk to me about hair!" he growled. "How much of your hair have I had to fish out of the shower drain so it doesn't clog? Are you shedding your winter coat or what?!"

"Shedding my what?!" I hollered. "Are you calling me a dog?!"

"Trust me, lady, if I was going to start the name-calling, I'd come up with something better than a dog!"

"Don't you fucking 'lady' me!" I snarled. "If you had any regard for the fact that I'm a woman, you wouldn't leave the seat up all the time! Have you ever doused your ass in the middle of the night in a freezing toilet?! It ain't pleasant!"

"Believe me! I'm perfectly aware you're a woman! Maybe if you'd stop leaving your frilly, lacy, panties drying on the shower curtain rod and you're damn tampon wrappers everywhere, I might have more consideration for your cold, little ass in the middle of the night!"

"I haven't even used tampons since I've been here!"

"Diapers then! Whatever!"

"They are called MAXI PADS, dumb ass, and you're just pissed off because you got caught!"

"Caught doing what?!"

Wow, I didn't know his voice could get that high!

"You wanted your live-in slut and your outside fuck, huh?" I said. "Indoor/outdoor carpeting right?!"

"I'm not fucking anyone, and I have never, EVER referred to you as my live-in slut! Not to anyone! I have nothing but the highest respect and admiration for you!"

"Yeah, well…thank you!"

"You're welcome!"

Some sort of growl left my throat. I grabbed my beer, stomped out of the kitchen, into the living room and slammed myself down on the couch.

"What the hell am I going to do now?" I wondered aloud.

He followed me and flopped down next to me on the couch. We sat in an excruciating silence, nursing our beers and licking our wounds, and for once I didn't want to lick anything else.

"Look, Vic, can I explain?" he asked quietly, after a few minutes.

"Explain what?" I laughed. "Explain how you've been lying to me?" My voice left me and I had to swallow a few times to get it back. "I haven't intentionally sexually advanced as you call it, on you for a long time. But you want it to stop? Fine by me! It's not like I couldn't get some of that whenever the hell I feel like it! I know plenty of guys who would love to go to bed with me!"

"They're probably all married," he grumbled.

"Oh, fuck you!"

"Sorry, cheap shot."

"Yeah, it was, you jerk."

He fell silent, staring at the floor in some sort of trance. Maybe he was processing what I had just said. I was too mad to care. I stood up and paced across the room.

"You still think I had something to do with killing the judge, don't you?"

"No," he said weakly. "Of course I don't."

I scoffed at him with a quick burst of something that sounded like a laugh. In reality I was about to cry, but there was no way I was going to let him know that.

"You're good, Detective, you're really good. You really had me fooled into thinking you gave a shit about me."

"I do give a shit about you!"

"Oh, right! Because I'm the only witness you've got!"

"Please sit down," he said calmly. "Let's talk about this rationally."

"We have nothing else to talk about!"

I started around the coffee table toward the door. He popped off the couch and grabbed me by the shoulders. I struggled, as if it would do any good, but he just held me harder.

"The hell we don't!" he said, his teeth clenched in sudden emotion.

I struggled harder as he pulled me closer to him. I slapped and clawed at him but he grabbed my wrists in his giant hands and there was no way I was getting away.

"She and I are over!" he yelled, shaking me a little. "I'll call her right now if you want me to!"

"Let go of me you big, nasty…MAN!"

"Not until you calm down and listen to me for a minute!"

I wriggled from his grasp and backed away. "Fine! One minute! Start talking!"

He stopped for a moment and took a rather long breath.

"All right," he said calmly. "The only reason I didn't tell you about her is that I didn't think she was worth mentioning. She's nothing to me. Less than nothing. I never even liked her. She's attractive, but she's boring as hell. No sense of humor at all. And I haven't seen her for weeks. But she was there, and for a while it was, I don't know, I was lonely. I hadn't been alone in so long and I hated it. But she's....she's not..."

"Thirty seconds!" I yelled. "She's not what?!"

"She's not anything like you!" he yelled back, immediately followed by a deep breath as if he was trying to calm himself. "She's not...she's not you, okay?"

He sat down on the couch and dropped his face in his hands. I stayed rooted to my spot on the floor, not sure what to do.

"You said you thought I was wonderful."

"I do," he groaned into his palms. "God help me."

"How am I supposed to believe anything you say now?" I asked, fighting back a sob which sort of made my voice sound like a chipmunk.

He looked up at me. "You're just going to have to trust me. I'm not playing any games with you. I have genuine feelings for you."

"Feelings for me?" I hollered. "What feelings? I haven't seen you have an actual feeling about anything! Oh sure, I'm great when you need someone to laugh at or pity, but it would be too much to actually like me!"

"I don't pity you."

"Well, what then? Just what feelings are we talking about here, Jason?!"

"Do I have to spell it out for you?" he shouted, slapping his hands down on the couch. He got up and gave the coffee table a shove, sending it sliding across the hardwood floor. For a minute I was frightened by the quick show of violence against his own furniture, but it was quickly replaced by a small twinge of frustration that he scuffed my newly polished floor! Then again, I guess it wasn't going to matter if he splattered my blood everywhere when he punched me. The floors would have to be done again anyway.

He lunged toward me in one long stride and grabbed me by the shoulders, his eyes fiery with something like anger, but I wasn't quite sure I was reading it right. He looked ready to explode. Then he quickly pulled me against his lips and kissed me.

This wasn't right. Kisses weren't supposed to hurt. I didn't want him like this. I opened my mouth to protest and his tongue plunged in, apparently searching for my tonsils that had been removed when I was twelve.

I shoved him away with all the strength I had and dashed toward the door. He grabbed my hand, fiercely at first, but softening quickly as if he suddenly realized he was losing control.

"You're hurting me," I cried.

"I'm sorry," he said. "Oh, God. Please, Vic, Honey, I'm so sorry."

"Let me go," I said, tears streaming down my face.

"I can't," he said, pulling me gently to him and holding my face in his hands. "Don't you know that?"

"I don't know anything anymore," I squeaked through the tears. "Everything I thought I knew about you was a lie."

"No," he whispered, tracing my tears with his gentle fingers. "Haven't you noticed how I can't take my eyes off of you? How I can't stop myself from touching you?"

I shrugged and looked away.

"You're all I think about," he said softly. "And it's killing me, knowing that you're sleeping just across the hall, and all I want to do is throw open the doors between us and slip into that bed with you." He ran his fingers down my arms and I shivered and pressed my hand against his chest, pretending I wanted to get away and not meaning it in the slightest.

"I stand outside your bedroom door almost every night," he whispered. "I know that may sound kind of creepy, but I feel better there than alone in my room. And I've tried to think of other things to distract myself so I can sleep at night, but my mind keeps drifting back to you. To wanting you. Wanting to kiss you and touch you until we just melt together and make love all night."

Make love? All night?!

"Please, Vic, look at me."

I let my eyes find his and was almost shocked at what I saw. It was as if he had finally opened himself to me, dropped whatever mask he was hiding behind, and I saw such a desperate need that it nearly took my breath away.

His fingers stroked the back of my neck delicately and I gasped quietly as my heart started doing cartwheels. Then he slowly leaned in and kissed me again, softly, tenderly, like he should have before. Tingles bubbled up from my toes and shot up to the top of my head. It felt like my hair was standing on end.

"I can't let you go," he said, wrapping me in his arms, sliding his hands across my back. "If I even think about it I can't breathe."

"Jason," I whispered. "How can you possibly want me when everything around me is such a mess?"

"Vic," he said, with a tenderness in his voice that weakened every part of me. "You have no idea what you do to me, do you?"

He kissed me again, his lips so soft against mine, and he sighed like all the tension was leaving his body. His armor was dropping off, one piece at a time, as if he was beginning to realize what a weight it had been.

"How could I not want you," he said, resting his forehead against mine. "I want you so bad that it almost scares me."

"Why does it scare you?"

"Why do you think?" he whispered. "I don't want it all to happen again. I'm not sure I could survive it."

Love had abandoned him before, and he was afraid it was going to happen again. I ran my hands up his muscular arms and to his face as he kissed me again, gently. His lips trembled softly against mine and I could feel how terrified he really was. My heart immediately melted, and if at all possible, my love for him grew stronger and almost consumed me.

"I'm not going anywhere," I said, smiling and running my fingers through his hair. "It took me too damn long to find you."

"You're so beautiful," he whispered, caressing my face with his supple lips. "I would never hurt you, you know that don't you?"

"I know that, Jason."

I kissed him deeply and we embraced again. He slowly backed up to the couch and sat down, and I crawled onto his lap. We held each other for a while, breathing, and being close, and then I felt the caress of his lips on my neck.

"I haven't felt this way in a long time," he said against my ear. "I'm not sure I ever have."

"What way?"

He ran his hand up my arm and touched my face. "Like I'm on the first drop of a giant roller coaster."

I chuckled and kissed his cheek and nose gently as I stroked his long neck lightly with my fingertips. Then he leaned into my lips and we were kissing each other again as I turned on his lap, putting my leg around his waist so I was straddling him. We kissed again and again, the excitement between us becoming more palpable with each passing second. His hands ran up my thighs under the shorts I was wearing and I slid tighter against him.

"Are you sure you want to do this?" I whispered.

"Yes," he said breathlessly against my ear. "Absolutely positive."

I giggled quietly as he ran his lips down my neck. "You won't talk yourself out of it this time?"

"No. I need you, Vic."

He kissed and nibbled his way across my collar bone and my eyes started rolling back in my head like I was in some kind of sex trance.

"I need to be inside you," he whispered, as if it was a secret just for me. And his voice was husky with want, and I felt a quick contraction just above my thighs, like my body was trying to draw him closer. Our lips found each other again, our embrace tightened passionately, and my clothes were sweltering and too tight. I had to get them off quick or I was going to completely incinerate. He pulsed between my legs and I slid my hand down and gently rubbed his raging erection. He whispered a groan in response and it was the sexiest thing I had ever heard in my life.

"Okay, so you don't stuff your junk," I said, after a giggle escaped me.

He laughed against my neck. "I still can't believe you said that."

"I was caught up in the moment. I'm sorry."

"It's okay."

"And I've never heard you snore. And I really, really like it when you come up from your work out and you're all sweaty and…"

He interrupted me with a kiss and I totally forgot what I was babbling about. I tended to babble when I was nervous, and even though I knew I didn't really have anything to be nervous about, I couldn't help it. What if I didn't measure up to what he was used to? I did a quick mental check list. Showered and shaved just before six p.m., check. Deodorant on, check. Teeth brushed, fingernails filed, clean bra and panties on, though I couldn't remember the color or if they even matched.

Did I do the quick spray of perfume in the panties before I put them on?

Crap! No, I forgot. How could I forget? I always do that.

It's okay. I should be all right. Right?

Oh, God!

I couldn't remember ever wanting a man as much as I wanted him at that moment. Actually, I couldn't remember ever wanting another man. There was no comparing Varner to the men I had known before him. It was like comparing a sleek thoroughbred to a ratty old goat. The goat was cute for a while, but after he ate your drapes, he wasn't so cute anymore. Okay, so, none of them actually ate my drapes. One of them chewed a hole in a pillow one night though. He said he was dreaming. I didn't want to know what he was dreaming.

Varner laid me back on the couch and slid his knee between my legs, straightening up to remove his shirt, button by agonizing button. But he was only half way down before I couldn't stand it anymore. I yanked his shirt out of his waist band and plunged my hands underneath so I could finally touch him. I wanted to feel the play of the muscles in his chest and shoulders against my fingers. Feel the warmth of his naked flesh and run my hands all over his unbelievable body.

And then he was kissing me again, rubbing my stomach gently and slowly up to my breasts.

"Can we take this off?" he whispered, tugging at my shirt.

I sat up a little and lifted my arms as he slid my blue t-shirt over my head.

Oh yeah, the white bra with the lace, one of my nicer ones.

Whew!

"Pretty," he said, running his fingers over the lace.

He kissed down my chest and between my breasts as he slipped the straps over my shoulders.

"Your skin is so smooth," he said, nuzzling my neck and running his lips over my shoulder. He stopped and rose up slowly, running his fingers down my chest as he slid the bra down to my waist.

He looked.

Then he smiled.

"Wow."

"What?" I asked, suddenly feeling self-conscious.

He just stared for a moment, a stupid grin plastered across his face, like a teenager who had seen his first nudie picture.

"Haven't you ever seen a set of boobs before?" I laughed, covering them with my arm.

He laughed and pushed my arm away. "No! Don't cover them. In fact, never cover them again."

I covered my face with my hands and giggled. "Stop it!"

He chuckled, moved my hands away from my face and started kissing me, lips, chin, jaw, and on down my neck. He kissed his way down my breasts, running his soft tongue over and around my left nipple, and after a quick nibble, kissed his way over to the right. Then he straightened up again.

"I'm sorry, but I just gotta have another look at these. Hot damn!"

"You'll have plenty of time to gawk at them later," I giggled. I slid the bra around, unhooked the clasp, and dropped it on the floor. Then I sat up and ran my hands over his smooth chest as he dropped his shirt behind him. "If I had a nickel for every time I fantasized about touching your chest."

"Right back at ya, Babe," he said.

Somehow we ended up on the floor, in a frenzy of tangled limbs and heavy breathing and then my shorts were on the lamp. His pants ended up on the banister. Once again, I'm not quite sure how that happened. I think he kicked them off before we hit the floor.

"We should probably talk about something," he said, running his tongue down my belly and flicking it around my navel.

"I'm on the pill," I said, smiling and sliding both hands into his hair. "You're safe."

"That's not all to consider," he said, running his fingers under the waist of my white "frilly little panty things."

"It's been almost six months for me, and I've, oh God, I've always been really careful. But if you would prefer to use a..."

"Let's go upstairs," he whispered, lifting me up in his arms. "We'll be more comfortable in the bed."

"Am I safe?" I asked quietly, nuzzling my lips against his neck.

He chuckled. "I've been divorced for five months and I haven't had sex since, mm that feels nice. I got tested for everything when I found out she was cheating, but she cut me off way before that."

"I think you're about to be rewarded for your patience."

"So are you."

I kissed and nibbled his neck as he carried me up the stairs in his unbelievably strong arms. We got to his bedroom and he nudged the door open with his foot. He laid me down on the bed and stood up, reaching over and flipping on the lamp next to the bed.

"I need to see you."

I slid my panties down my thighs and threw them toward the end of the bed as I watched him finish undressing in front of me.

Holy cow!

I knew he was a thoroughbred. Part horse, part angel. Maybe Pegasus was real, and I was about to sleep with him. Nah, I was never really that crazy about horses, and this man's body was way more beautiful than any equine I'd ever seen. Toned and defined thigh muscles, smooth speed bump pecs and abs, a butt that would repel any coin you threw at it. But all that was nothing compared to…holy cow! The only thing that could have made it more spectacular was if it vibrated. My mouth watered and I silently thanked God for answering all my prayers from the last twenty years with a drop of one pair of strategically placed boxer briefs.

He lay down beside me and I could feel him, hard and throbbing against my thigh as he kissed and touched my entire body, from ankle to lips, and worked me into a hip-grinding fury. He took his time, teased and tickled around all the most sensitive spots and made me almost insane with desire for him. Finally I'd had almost more than I could take, and I slid my hand between his thighs, wrapping my fingers around him gently. His skin was silky and hot and a quiet gasp left him as I gently rubbed the naked object of my obsession.

"Now," I whimpered. "Please."

"Be patient, girl," he said. "I want to savor this as long as we can."

"I feel like I've been waiting my whole life," I moaned against his moist lips.

"Maybe we both have."

He rolled on top of me slowly and hovered over me supporting himself with his arms.

"Are you real?" I whispered, running my hands up his beautiful muscles and into his hair. "Is this really happening?"

He kissed my lips and slowly pressed his body between my thighs. "If it's not, then this is one hell of a dream I'm having."

"What happens if you wake up?"

He chuckled. "Then I'm getting up, going across the hall and kicking your bedroom door down."

He slid his arms under my back and lifted me to his mouth, our bodies pressed tightly against each other and the heat between us over-powering me into a tiny squeak of pleasure as he slid himself inside me slowly.

"Baby," he sighed, nibbling my chin and running his tongue down my neck. "Is that what you wanted, Baby?"

I managed to moan a soft "yes" before something animal in me took over, and he was suddenly on his back. And after I realized where I was, I started riding him like a crazed Lady Godiva

"Whoa! Slow down, Girl," he laughed. "Keep going like that and I won't make it much longer."

"It will be over in a minute," I said, clinging to his outstretched hands. "Just think about football and hold on."

I was right, but it was less than a minute before I worked myself into a frantic orgasm that rocked through me like long, intensely-satisfying bolts of lightning and almost knocked me off of him in the process. He sat up quickly and grabbed me around the waist to steady me, and I clung to his neck as I shuddered through the aftershocks, each pulse causing me to sigh with pleasure.

"Jason," I moaned. "Don't let go of me."

"Damn," he said, wide-eyed and grinning. "You're a little hellcat!"

I giggled and tried to catch my breath. "You got me all wound up. I should have warned you. I'm sort of a maniac when I'm wound up."

"No warnings necessary," he said, rolling us over. "That was awesome."

I ground my hips against him and shivered with pure delight. "Trust me, there are a lot more where that came from."

"Good God," he laughed. "I've hit the mother lode."

We kissed and touched and tasted each other, and he was continually inside me. He seemed to be trying to keep track of how many bolts of lightning hit me. I should have told him it was impossible, especially when they all merged together and I constantly quivered with pleasure. Every place he touched me, every kiss, and every word he moaned against me sent me over the edge again. Some women told me I was lucky to be blessed with my "multiple" abilities. On that point I had to agree. But it was so easy with him because he was every fantasy I'd ever had.

And after a very thorough investigation, I came to the conclusion, over and over, in fact, that he was neither angel nor alien. He was definitely a man. An extraordinary, powerful, relentless, and somewhat insatiable man.

God should expect about a thousand thank you notes for this one.

****

CHAPTER FIFTEEN

I lay breathless against the tight muscles in his chest as he ran his fingers gently up and down my moist back. For a moment he sounded like he was asleep. I couldn't blame the guy really. He had already, um, fired the cannon twice in the short time we had been in his bed together. According to the alarm clock it had only been an hour, and in my love life, two full-throttle romps in one hour had never been seen before. I lost count of how many orgasms I had. It had to be into double digits. I hoped I hadn't worn him out completely, and for some reason I knew I hadn't. He could do things with his body that I couldn't even explain, especially for a thirty-six year old man. Eighteen maybe, but thirty-six? He was in incredible shape, and I was already craving more. How any woman in her right mind could give him up was beyond my comprehension.

I kissed the smooth skin of his chest, salty with sweat, and lay my head back down with a long and satisfying exhale. I ran my fingers gently over his well-defined pectoral muscles and smiled.

"Mm," he sighed, obviously content to be where he was. "I have never in my life had sex like that. Ever in my whole life…I mean never in my…shit, I can't even talk."

I looked up at his face and grinned. He smiled back at me and traced the side of my face with his finger.

"Where have you been?" he asked quietly.

"Here," I answered. "Wandering around."

He chuckled and ran his fingers through my long hair. He lifted me, sliding me up against his body and kissed my lips gently. I snuggled back down against his chest and felt the sweet thump of his heart against my cheek.

"Girl, you are amazing," he whispered.

I looked up at him again. "You're the amazing one."

He smiled. "You certainly seemed to be having a good time."

"I'm sorry I yanked your hair that hard."

He snickered. "Did you? I don't remember that part."

"I think it was right after you yelled 'touchdown'."

He laughed harder. "Oh yeah. Number six."

"And the extra point."

"More like a two point conversion."

"Well, you're…you're very gifted," I said.

"Gifted huh? What does that mean?"

I ran my fingers across his smooth chest lightly, watching goose bumps rise, and then followed the path of my fingers with my lips. "You know what I mean."

He shook his head and grinned. "Don't have a clue."

I grinned back him. "All right, to put it bluntly, you have an incredible penis."

He laughed. "Well jeez, Vic, say what you mean."

"Hey, any woman who says size doesn't matter is lying. You've got something to be proud of there, buddy." I lifted up the sheet covering him. "I mean, look at it. It's perfect."

He laughed again. "I'm not a braggart."

"You should be."

He lifted me up and kissed me again and I snuggled in against his neck.

"I'm sorry if I hurt you, I mean, I didn't mean to grab you like that," he said quietly.

"You didn't hurt me, Sweetheart. You just scared me a little."

"I don't let myself get angry," he said. "So sometimes I just, kind of…"

"The tea kettle blows?" I asked, kissing up the line of his jaw.

"The tea kettle blows," he repeated.

"I'm sorry I made you so angry."

He ran his fingers lightly down my back. "You didn't."

I chuckled. "Did too."

He laughed. "Okay, maybe a little. But I've been angry for a while now. And when the antidote to the anger started yelling at me, I went a little nuts."

I smiled. "I'm the antidote to the anger?"

He pressed his lips to my forehead. "You are the only thing on this planet that makes me smile anymore."

An uncontrollable "Aw" escaped my mouth and I snuggled closer.

I felt his smile against my forehead. "I know, it sounds all corny and mushy. But it's been a dark year. You've been the only sunny spot."

"And I had to stop myself from actually wagging my tail when you got home from work every day," I giggled.

"Ooh, if you had done that we probably would have been in bed together a lot sooner."

"Well, shit."

We laughed together and it felt almost as good as the sex. Okay, it wasn't even close to the sex, but it did feel good. And the snuggling, kissing and hand-holding were more than I could have hoped for. I had never really experienced that before. In the past, when I went to bed with a guy, usually all I'd get afterwards is a slap on the ass and a "that oughta hold you!"

It was different with him. Satisfying, obviously, but it was more than that.

It was like I was finally home after a long, weird journey.

"What happens now?" I whispered, not intending for him to hear me, but knowing he did.

We looked at each other.

He sighed. "This really sucks."

I moved my head back on to the pillow and my jaw dropped. "What?"

"No, no," he took my hand and held it against his chest. "This part doesn't suck, this part is unbelievable."

He scooted closer to me and kissed my hand.

"What part sucks then?" I asked.

"No one can know about this," he replied quietly. "They'll take me off the case. I could lose my job."

"I know," I said. "Let's not think about that now."

"But if Fisher or anyone at the station finds out..."

I slapped him lightly on the forehead. "I said no more thinking."

"Hey!" he said with a laugh. "No hitting!"

"Sorry," I apologized, cuddling closer to him. I reached up to stroke his face, and slapped him lightly on the cheek. "Oops."

A really girly squeal left me as he rolled over on me, caught both my hands with his left hand, and wrapped his legs around mine in some sort of Judo-cop hold thing.

"Why don't we see if you're ticklish," he chuckled, starting in with his free right hand.

"No, I'm not!" I giggled when he found a spot on my side that always sent me into fits.

"Oh, just right there, huh?"

"OW!" I yelled.

"Oh, sorry, did I hurt you?" he asked, rolling off me.

"No," I said, leaping out of bed, naked as a new born piglet, and running out the door.

"Ooh! Officer in pursuit!" he called, running after me down the hall. "Code six-nine, nekkid woman on the premises!"

I tried to barricade myself in the bathroom, but he was just too damn strong and pushed his way through. Then I slipped on the bathmat and landed on my butt. He let out some sort of battle cry and he was on the floor in front of me, tickling the crap out of me.

"Stop it!" I screamed through the giggles. "Help!"

"Motor boat!" he yelled, burying his face between my boobs and shaking them vigorously.

"Let me up, you big dork!" I giggled when the cartoon noises started. "My butt is sticking to the Linoleum!"

He got to his feet and held down a hand to me.

"Dork, huh?"

With a quick yank, I was practically in the air.

"Police brutality!" I laughed as he hoisted me over his shoulder and carried me back into the bedroom. "Where's a camcorder when I need one?"

"You're into that?"

"With an ass like yours I could be."

I tried to reach down and give his tight backside a slap but his back was too long and I ended up slapping the air.

He threw me down on the bed, crawled over me and grinned. "Perp apprehended. Commencing body cavity search."

"Oh my!"

****

The next morning, I woke up warm, naked and curled up with a naked giant spooning me. He threw his arm across me and continued snoring quietly against my back. I smiled and snuggled back against him. I closed my eyes and enjoyed the feeling I was having, the comfortable feeling of exhausted passion. Then I started analyzing it. Then I started wondering when it was going to go away. Then I realized I needed to stop thinking like that and enjoy him while I had him. If it turned into something permanent, so much the better.

I squeezed out from under his arm and replaced myself with a pillow. It was still very early, and we had had a long night, but I didn't feel like sleeping anymore. I threw on one of his t-shirts, tossed my hair up in a ponytail, and headed downstairs, with some difficulty, to make breakfast. He deserved breakfast after all the energy he used up during the night. And that morning. Damn! No wonder I was having trouble walking. It had been ages since I'd had sex all night and I had forgotten some of my muscles could bend the way they did.

I made my way into the kitchen and put on some coffee. Then I checked the fridge for options. Ah! I decided French toast would do nicely and got out the eggs. I also grabbed the bacon. Normally he tried to stay away from it, but he needed his protein. I smiled as I thought of ways we could work it off.

I was pretty impressed by the way I was handling the culinary activities lately. Even this morning's breakfast was moving along nicely considering my sexually-exhausted condition. I flipped the toast and it was a perfect golden brown. I even caught some tips from the Food Network and put the bacon in the oven on a baking rack rather than fry it in a pan. It turned out crispier that way, and most of the fat drained out the bottom of the rack and onto the cookie sheet under it.

Perhaps there was a little June Cleaver in me after all.

I heard the shuffling of bare feet behind me and then there were lips on my neck and hands around my waist.

"French toast," he said. "I must have been a good boy."

I leaned back against his smooth, bare chest and smiled at his disheveled bed-head. "Phenomenal."

He smiled. "Looks good." Then he leaned down and kissed my cheek. "All of it."

God, what that man did to me! I spun around quickly as he wrapped his long arms around me and lifted me to his lips. A good morning kiss soon turned into a make out session that threatened to set me on fire, literally. My hair was dangerously close to the burner on the stove.

"Mm," I moaned. "We have to eat."

He chuckled. "I know, I'm starving."

"Have a seat. It will be ready in a minute."

He went to get the paper, poured himself some coffee and sat down. I plated up for him and then myself, and got maple syrup and butter. I watched him take his first bite hoping I didn't poison him.

He smiled. "What?"

"I was just hoping it was okay."

"Oh yeah, it's perfect, just like everything else you've cooked."

"Cool," I said grabbing part of the paper. I read the funnies as he read the sports page and we ate in silence for a while. I was just finishing my bacon and Beetle Bailey when I saw fingers coming up over the top of the paper. Then I saw his face.

"Come here," he whispered.

"Why?" I whispered back.

"Because, just come here," he whispered, letting the paper flop back up over his face.

I got up and went around the table to him. He grabbed my hand and pulled me down on his lap and started kissing me and I felt what he wanted against the back of my thigh.

"Again?" I asked incredulously.

"You wanna?" he grinned.

"Hm, let me think," I giggled. "I had no idea your passions were so voracious."

"Neither did I," he said with my earlobe in his mouth. "Let's do it in here."

"In here?" I was all for exotic locations, but the kitchen?

He lifted me up, set my butt on the kitchen counter, slid himself between my legs and leaned me back against the kitchen cabinets. It wasn't a bad position. He was so tall, that it was actually kind of perfect.

I laughed and wrapped my legs around his waist. "I didn't know French toast turned you on."

"You turn me on," he said with his lips against my neck.

"I've created a monster."

"Sorry," he said. "I just can't help myself."

"Sure you can," I smiled and lifted the t-shirt up slightly, revealing my lack of underwear. "Help yourself."

He growled and bit my neck and I let out a squeal.

"You are a very, very naughty girl," he said, kissing my lips gently.

I giggled. "You figured that out a long time ago."

"I know," he said, leaning his forehead against mine. "I'm starting to really, really like it."

We stayed like that for a moment, holding each other, our foreheads together and our eyes closed, contemplating what to say next or even what to do next. It was simple and warm, yet somewhat awkward. It was as if neither one of us wanted to be the first to break the silence.

"This is nice," he said finally. "It almost feels, I don't know..."

"Like you're home?" I practically whispered, almost hoping he didn't hear me.

"Yeah," he said. "I'm home."

"Are you still afraid?"

He kissed my lips gently and then took a huge breath. "I'm terrified, but it's a relief not to be numb anymore."

"I'm scared too. I've never felt this way before."

He smiled. "Neither have I. Not like this."

"I don't want it to go away," I whispered, pulling back and looking into his beautiful eyes. "Please, Jason, say it won't go away."

He tilted his head and our lips clung to each other.

"It won't go away," he whispered. "I promise."

****

CHAPTER SIXTEEN

It was the longest sexual marathon I had ever had, and once again I couldn't fathom how any woman in her right mind could give him up. Living in a constant state of ecstasy must be tiring for some. Nah, his ex was just a complete idiot. Every few hours we were on each other again, touching, kissing and rubbing up against one another. By three that afternoon, we were both completely exhausted and nearly unable to move. I dragged my sorry butt up the stairs and flopped down into the bed after he had fallen asleep on the couch.

I woke up to his soft fingers in my hair. I opened my eyes and looked up at him sitting on the edge of the bed.

"Hi."

"Hey," he said softly.

Uh oh! His eyes were very red and very sad. He looked like a little boy who had lost his puppy, and not at all like a man who had spent the last twenty-four hours playing slap and tickle.

"What's wrong?" I asked, propping myself up on my elbow.

He ran his hands through his hair. "Deborah is dead."

"What?" I yelped, unable to hide my shock.

"Yeah, Fisher just called me. She apparently committed suicide last night. She shot herself up with something and drowned in the bath tub."

I sat up and put my hand on his shoulder.

"God! Are you all right?" I asked, kissing his prickly cheek.

"Yeah, it's just a shock that's all. I mean, I knew she was unstable, but I had no idea she would do something like this. I guess she left a note. Most of it was about me."

I wrapped my arms around him and cuddled him close. "You know it's not your fault, right?"

He nodded. "I know, but I should have seen it."

"Jason, there's no way you could have known."

"I know that," he said quietly. "But she was sick and I was too wrapped up in myself to notice."

"You had a lot going on," I said, pressing my lips against his shoulder. "I'm so sorry."

"She never asked for help. She knew I would have helped her if I had known."

I snuggled my head into the curve of his neck and hung on to him for a while. He didn't cry or even tear up, but I could tell it was really eating at him that he didn't do anything to help her.

"You can only change what is within the reach of your hand," I said quietly. "She was out of your reach and not your burden to carry. We can only hope her soul is at peace now."

I felt him smile against my forehead. "Who said that?"

I lifted my head and looked at him. Then I waved my hand in front of his face and grinned.

"It's me, Jason. It's Vic. Can you hear me?"

"I thought you were quoting someone."

"No."

He chuckled. "You mean you just sat here and made that up? Just off the top of your head?"

I nodded. "Sorry. Did it sound stupid?"

He shook his head and smiled. "No, it just sounded like something the Lord Jesus himself would have said."

I exhaled a laugh. "I'm not that good. Saint Paul maybe, but not Jesus."

He just grinned at me for a moment, and if I didn't know any better I would say he was looking at me in complete adoration.

"You constantly amaze me," he said.

"Too many nineteenth century novels in college," I said with a giggle. "You have the greatest smile in the world."

He leaned in and gave me a gentle kiss just as I froze.

"Wait. I just thought of something. Your phone rang around six o'clock every evening. You know, when most people are sitting down to dinner and the telemarketers like to call. Anyway, I never answered it, until I talked to her yesterday. I wonder if she always called at that time, hoping to catch you when you came home from work."

He grabbed his cordless off of the night stand and checked the numbers on the face.

"It was always from her number," he said. "Yesterday there was a call at six thirty, and then again at six forty-five. The day before there was a call at two, then another at six sixteen. I didn't know she had been calling so much."

"I'm sorry I didn't tell you. I never looked at the number or anything. I figured if it was important they would leave you a message. Like I said, I figured it was a telemarketer."

He continued scrolling. "Strange that she never left a message, and she never called my cell. She knew I always have my cell on me."

"Maybe she wanted privacy so she tried you at home. Cell phones aren't exactly private when you can use them everywhere."

"Could be," he said. "I should have called her back. I should have looked at the damn caller ID on my landline more often and called her back."

"Don't beat yourself up about this," I said. "You couldn't really call her with me here. I didn't exactly act rationally when I found out about her. Imagine how I would have reacted if you called her where I could hear you."

"You'd have tanned my hide," he said with a grin. "Ugh, I can't think about this right now. I'm not ready to go back to reality yet."

He rubbed his face vigorously and then crawled into bed with me.

"Pretty lady," he said, after a long kiss. "I need a snuggle."

"Aw," I cooed, wrapping myself around him. "If I didn't know you better, I'd say you were a big, sweet, teddy bear."

"Don't spread it around," he said, cuddling his head against my breast and sliding his long arms around me. "Might ruin my bad-ass reputation around here."

"My lips are sealed," I said, kissing the top of his head and hugging his warm body against mine. I stroked his hair and whispered that everything would be all right, and he sighed as he relaxed against me. The romantic bliss I was feeling nearly overwhelmed me to tears. I'd never known a man who liked to cuddle so much. He couldn't seem to get close enough to me, it felt so affectionate and true, and completely right. It was also terrifying in ways that I couldn't explain.

We had almost fallen asleep when the phone rang.

"Ignore it," I begged as he began untangling himself from my arms.

"I'm a cop," he said. "It's impossible for a cop to ignore a ringing phone. Better get used to it."

I smiled at the implication. The only reason I would have to get used to it is if he wanted me to hang around awhile. If he wanted me to hang around awhile, that probably meant that he loved me, or at least liked me a whole lot, and he wanted to keep me and make me his girlfriend, or maybe even his…

"Holy shit," he exclaimed, popping up off the bed. He flipped me over as he sprang up and I rolled off the other side of the bed. My head hit the nightstand with a loud "clunk!"

"Ouch! Jerk!"

"Sorry, but it's Deborah's number." He hit the talk button. "Hello?"

I scrambled to my feet and crossed my arms against the chill that suddenly ran up my spine.

"And who are you?" he asked.

He stared at me as he listened.

"Why should I do that?"

"What's going on?" I whispered, rummaging around for a pair of underwear. I found the ones I had on earlier hanging off the head board and slipped them on.

He held up a finger at me and then took the phone away from his ear. "She's gone."

"Who?" I asked rather more excitedly than I meant to.

"The woman on the phone."

He hit a few buttons and placed a call. "Fisher? It's Varner. I just got a call from a woman claiming that the man who killed Weinhardt is at Skinny Moe's on Lapidos Street."

An uncontrollable gasp escaped my lips and I put my hand over my mouth.

"Yeah," he continued. "The call came in on my landline. She said he is wearing a blue t-shirt, black jeans, and black boots. I'll meet you there."

He disconnected and scanned the room, presumably for clothing. "I'm sorry, Darlin', I've got to go."

He threw on a pair of jeans and a t-shirt and ran down stairs. It was kind of amazing to see him get dressed that quickly, but I think he put his jeans on over the shorts he was wearing. I didn't even have time to enjoy the view of his nakedness. I jogged after him as quickly as I could, but he was three long strides ahead of me, and I had to take sixteen steps for every two of his.

"Please be careful," I told him.

He kissed me quickly. "I'm always careful." He grabbed his forty-five, holstered it, put his jacket on and pocketed his badge and phone.

"I'll be back as soon as I can. Keep the phone by you."

"Okay."

"Don't answer unless it's my number."

"Okay."

"And keep the nine millimeter with you just in case."

"I will."

He kissed me again and I was almost overwhelmed with the need to grab him and beg him not to go. I wanted to wrap myself around him and pin him to the floor. But I knew he had to go and it was stupid of me to think he would stay. He would pry himself away from me if he had to, because no matter how much our day together meant, he still had a job to do.

He dashed out the door and sped away, tires kicking up dust behind him.

I immediately ran to the sun porch, found and loaded the gun with shaky hands, and went back into the living room. I carefully sat on the couch and put the phone on the coffee table. I held the gun close to me and closed my eyes.

"God, I know it's kind of stupid of me to ask you for a favor after what I've been doing for the past twenty-four hours," I said to the ceiling. "But please keep him safe."

****

Two excruciating hours ticked by. I hadn't moved from my spot on the couch and there was no word from Varner. I kept switching channels hoping that something would come up on a local news station, but there was nothing. And every time a phone rang on the TV, I jumped out of my skin.

I should have heard something by now! What if he's hurt?

How many ditches are there between Lapidos Street and here?

I leapt off the couch and started up the stairs.

I thought better of it and started back down.

"No!" I said aloud. "I'm going to find him!"

I turned around and headed back up.

"He's fine," I said after a deep breath. "He's fine, he's fine, he's fine."

I descended the stairs slowly, flopped down on the couch and blew out a frustrated breath.

"Please, Jason, please call me."

Another twenty minutes went by on a snail's back, and I spent most of it switching positions on the couch. I sat. I lay down. I knelt. I hung over the back.

"Fuck it!" I barked as I got to my feet and started toward the stairs.

The phone rang. I jumped and lunged, hit my knee on the coffee table, fell on the couch and grabbed it.

"Hello?" I blurted out quickly. "Jason?"

"Hey, Darlin'," he replied. "You all right?"

I sighed and my stomach trembled at the sound of his voice. "There are several schools of thought on that. What happened?"

"Not a damn thing. We sat there for an hour waiting for this guy and not so much as a hair."

I sighed again. "Jesus."

"Yeah. I'm sorry I didn't call sooner, but we've been patrolling the area awhile and this is the first chance I've had to myself. Then I heard your voice, and if they saw this big old grin on my face, everyone would know what we've been doing all day."

I smirked and broke into a grin of my own.

"I miss you, Girl," he said, his voice lowering a little.

"Aw," I said, stroking the back of the phone. "I miss you too. I'm so glad you're all right."

"Something bugs me about this whole thing. I keep getting the feeling I've heard that woman's voice before, but I can't put my finger on it. I'm sure she was trying to disguise it."

"I know the feeling," I said, running my fingers through my hair. "I keep thinking I'm forgetting something really obvious and important."

"Well," he said, after a long sigh. "I've got to go back to the office and fill out a report. I should be home in about an hour okay?"

"Okay, grab a pizza or something, I'm starving."

"You got it. Maybe we can pick up where we left off earlier."

I grinned. "Sex addict."

"I've had sex before. This is different. It's you that I'm addicted to."

"Well, you can snort me anytime you want."

He chuckled. "See you soon."

"Okay, bye."

"Bye."

I disconnected and put the phone on the coffee table. What a freaking joke. I thought it was all going to be over. What the hell did I know? I headed upstairs and decided to take a long, hot shower to hopefully loosen my tired muscles so I could maybe go a few more rounds with the Vic addict.

The Vic addict. Too adorable. The thought made me smile and I stared at nothing for a moment. I couldn't remember the last time I had walked around with that special and stupid grin on my face. You know the grin that tells everyone who sees you that you're completely smitten with someone and that someone thinks you're pretty neat as well. New love is always so warm and happy, and completely disgusting all at the same time.

And it felt so wonderful and terrible, glorious and painful, and just everything.

I let out a long, audible sigh. Then I was appalled with myself. I needed to focus on what I was missing and where this case was going, not stand around sighing like a drunken fool.

I stood in the shower, letting the water run over me and tried to think. There was something I was missing in all of this. I was usually pretty observant, sometimes insanely so. I always figured out the ends of books and movies way before anyone else, especially murder mysteries. It pissed people off too. I'd never forget the time I went to a movie with a high school boyfriend. I pointed out the killer about ten minutes into the thing and he was so mad he broke up with me.

Movies were easy. Real life usually gave me fits. But as hard as I tried to focus, my brain kept drifting back to the tender feeling of being in Varner's arms. His fingers tracing my curves and touching me in sweet places no one else ever seemed to find. His eyes on me, making me feel beautiful and sexy. His lips moving up my neck and against my ear where he could whisper anything in that accent and it sounded erotic as hell.

Heavy sigh!

Okay, Vic. Focus.

"I must be getting old," I said aloud, running the razor over my armpit.

Who the hell was the woman on the phone? And why would she send him on a wild goose chase like that? I hit the other pit and started on my legs. What the hell, I might as well be smooth for his return.

I finished up, washed and conditioned my hair, washed and conditioned my body, and shut the water off. As I was toweling off, I heard someone on the stairs.

"Hey!" I hollered, wrapping the towel around me. "I'm in here. You must have dashed."

The door opened slowly, and he was there, and I gasped.

Slimy hair, slicked back in its own grease. Slimy face, grinning at me, but breaking into a grimace as if he was in pain as he moved forward. He was wearing a blue t-shirt, black jeans, and black boots, and he was standing not six feet in front of me.

"I did," was all he said.

I froze as my eyes took in every inch of his oily little body. "What the hell are you doing here? How did you get in?"

"Your boyfend foegot to lock duh basement windows," his thick tongue slurred as he took a step into the room. "And he foegot to set de alarm. Tsk, tsk, tsk."

He came closer, favoring his left leg, and looking me up and down. His eyes stopped at my breasts under the towel. I backed away until I was against the wall, holding the towel tightly around me, and gulping down oxygen to remain upright.

"You sick bastard! You get the hell out of here!" I yelled in the toughest voice I could muster.

Yeah, Vic, that's going to scare him. Tiny, little you, naked and unarmed. Real intimidating.

"You gonna make me?" he said, his gray teeth glinting in the light.

Yuck. Even his voice was slimy. The kind of voice a slug would have. Where was a salt shaker when I needed one? Then I started singing "Margaritaville" in my head.

"Searchin' for my lost shaker of salt…"

Jeez, one day of awesome sex and you have orgasm-induced Attention Deficit Disorder. Focus! Slimy douche bag at six o'clock, wants to take your life. Remember?

"Look," I said, holding my hand out in a ridiculous effort to keep him away. "I don't remember anything about that night. I swear. I didn't see you. I'm not even sure what happened."

"Hm," he grunted. "Is that what you told your boyfriend?"

Think, Vic! Think! Think! Think!

There weren't any closets to hide in this time. And I left the damn nine millimeter downstairs.

Shit!

Should I play the sympathy card and start crying? No, that wouldn't work with this little bastard.

He stared at my chest and I saw the tip of his tongue flick against his teeth as he sneered at me.

Drop the towel?

No, I couldn't do that! There had to be another way to handle this situation. I could talk to him, reason with him, tell him to leave and never come back and I'd never tell a soul he was there.

But he was staring at my boobs and practically drooling.

Sometimes boobs are powerful.

Oh, God!

I swallowed loudly, attempted a sly seductive smile and licked my lips.

"Maybe we can work something out here," I said when I finally found my voice.

"Huh?" he questioned, his eyes darting up to mine.

I took a step toward him, loosening the towel a little, which is surprisingly difficult to do when your hands are shaking like crazy.

"I mean, you're a man. I'm sure you have…guh…desires…or something," I took another step and let the towel fall a couple inches so he could see the top of my breasts. "I mean, why don't we talk about this?"

"This ain't gonna work," he said thickly, his voice shaking slightly. He reached around to his back and brought out a pistol, pointing it at me.

It was the nine millimeter I left downstairs on the couch. I had a momentary lapse into childhood and considered throwing a "THAT'S MINE" tantrum. But then I noticed a small tremor in his hand, and thigh. Trembling thighs, I had been around enough to know what that meant.

He liked what he saw.

GAG! HACK! PATOOEY!

"You sure?" I asked, moving closer to him until I was almost to the end of the gun. "You don't know what you're missing."

I licked my lips and let the towel down another half inch.

Peek. Was that a nipple? Maybe it was you scum bag.

He stared. "You are so pretty."

"You know," I said, with the giggle that turned Varner on, "I think guys with guns are sexy."

His hand shook again. I let the towel fall below my breasts, which was actually an accident because of the shaky hands, oh well. I'll take embarrassment over death any day.

His jaw dropped. "Damn. I didn't think you was actually going to do it."

I smiled again and stepped past the gun. "You want to touch them, don't you?"

I rubbed the fingers of my free hand over my nipples and he stared, open mouthed, at me, or I guess I should say at them. His arm dropped several inches so the gun was pointed at the toilet.

Great! If he decides to shoot now, there's going to be a hell of a mess.

Then I caught movement in the hallway behind him.

God! Does he have friends with him?

"You want the rest of me too, baby?" I said, trying to sound breathless with horniness.

Mostly I was breathless from trying not to vomit on him.

"Uh…uh huh," he stuttered out. I stepped closer and our lips almost touched.

A long arm attached to a Glock forty-five entered the bathroom. I let out a small squeak and my eyeballs popped out of my head and landed on the floor next to my jaw.

"Good evening," Varner said calmly, pointing his gun at the slimeball's temple. "My name is Detective Jason Varner. I'm with the Brenton Police Department, and you're in my house."

The slime ball gasped. I covered myself quickly, jumped back into the tub and squatted near the floor shivering and trying not to barf.

"Now, you have a couple choices," Varner said. "You can drop the gun and we'll walk quietly out of here or..." he paused as he chambered a round and clicked the safety off, "I can shoot you in the head which I have a legal right to do since you are, as I said, in my house, and threatening my guest with loaded a firearm."

I heard a gun hit the floor. Then, I heard handcuffs being locked into place.

"Good choice," Varner said, and I heard him holster his gun and fish his phone out of his pocket. "You're currently under arrest for breaking and entering. And I'd like to thank you for not shooting out my toilet. That would have made one hell of a mess."

I peeked around the tub and saw Varner hauling the guy out of the bathroom by his shirt. Varner smacked Mr. Slimy's head against the door frame as he dialed his phone.

"Oops, my fault." Varner said. "Still with me there, Sparky?"

I snickered.

"Yes, this is Detective Jason Varner," I heard from the hallway, quickly followed by a loud WHACK! "Ooh, sorry pal, my fault again. I am requesting assistance with an intruder I just apprehended in my home. My address is...yes, that's correct. Will you alert Detective Thomas Fisher as well? He may want to come along for the ride. Thank you very much." I heard a couple of strong pats, like he was rapping the guy on the back.

"Come on, and let's go downstairs and make you more comfortable shall we?" Varner said.

SLAM!

What was that? The banister? Youch!

"Oh, sorry, Captain, I'm all thumbs tonight huh? That one might leave a mark. We'll take care of that, don't worry. Rub some dirt on it, it will be fine."

I covered my mouth and giggled as I heard them tromp down the stairs, Varner chatting away like they were old friends. Something told me he treated all his "perps" that way, with his sweet, Southern charm.

Then I heard something that sounded like a smack and a body hitting a hardwood floor.

"You all right, Vic?" Varner called.

"Uh, yeah, I'm fine," I said, struggling out of the tub. "Are you all right? What just happened?"

"Clumsy bastard ran into my fist and fell asleep!"

"Oh," I replied. "All right then."

Jeez! Why couldn't I have done that?

Probably because I was naked. Yeah, that's it. You can't beat someone up when you're naked. Everyone knows that. Right?

I dashed out of the bathroom and into the guest bedroom. I got dressed quickly, picked up the nine millimeter, laid it gently in a dry towel and took it downstairs trying not to smudge any prints. Varner was in the living room locking the guy's ankles in something that looked like garbage bag zip tie.

He looked at me and smiled. "You okay?"

I nodded, handed him the gun, and crossed my arms over my chest. "I feel like I need another shower."

"Get me a plastic bag would ya?"

I went quickly into the kitchen and heard sirens in the distance. I grabbed a baggie and trotted back into the living room. He put the nine millimeter into the baggie and closed it. He laid the gun on the coffee table and held out his arms to me. I melted into him and began shivering uncontrollably.

"Shh," he said, kissing my forehead. "It's all right."

"Thank you," I whispered. "If you hadn't gotten here when you did…"

"Baby," he soothed, stroking my wet hair. "I've got you. It's okay now."

And it was. Everything was okay.

God help me if I ever lose this man, would everything be okay then?

The sirens pulled up outside and there was a flurry of activity in the driveway. Varner let me go after a reassuring hug and opened the door for them. Two uniformed officers came in followed by Fisher.

"Hey," he said. "Caught the bastard, huh?'

"Yeah," Varner said, stepping close to me again and putting a hand on my shoulder. "He had my nine millimeter on Miss Childs here when I came home." He grabbed the gun off the coffee table and handed it to Fisher.

"Uh, who knocked him out?" Fisher asked him.

"He, uh, resisted," Varner said, looking at me and grinning. "Fell down the stairs after I cuffed him."

Fisher nudged Slimy with his foot. "Looks like a fist print on his jaw there."

Varner snorted and jerked his thumb at me. "She's a maniac."

I poked him in the ribs and he squeaked like a dog toy.

Fisher looked at me. "You all right?"

I nodded and hugged myself. Suddenly the fact that Detective Doughnut acknowledged me made me feel kind of warm and fuzzy. The uniformed officers lifted Mr. Slimy to his feet and he slowly opened his eyes.

"Huh?"

"Think you can walk, sir?" the taller of the two officers asked him.

"Uh, yuh."

"Have you Mirandized him?" Fisher asked.

"We didn't get to that," Varner answered.

They unlocked Slimy's ankles.

"We'll take care of it, Detective Varner," the taller one said, attempting to get the prisoner to move.

He took a couple steps and looked at me. Then he grinned, slowly, deliberately, and the wound on his lip stretched open so it began to bleed.

"Thanks for the show," he said.

I heard a low snarl from somewhere, like a wolverine caught in a trap.

Took me more than a second to realize it was me.

"Fuck you!" I growled as an uncontrollable rage took over me. I lunged at him with claws out and scratching.

Varner caught me by the arm and held me back against his chest. "Whoa, Girl! Calm down!"

Fisher chuckled. "Damn, I wouldn't want to mess with that."

"Get him out on of here," Varner said quietly to the officers. "We'll be down in the morning to make a report. I think she needs some rest."

Fisher nodded. "You take care of that young lady, son."

Varner regarded Fisher with a look of respect. "Thanks, Chief, I will."

Am I breathing? Yes, I can feel it. And my heart is still beating, like a hamster on a treadmill. Too fast…it's all just too…

The room swirled, my vision tunneled, and I heard a painful clunk. Then it was all nice and quiet.

****

I felt a cool towel on my head and cool leather on my legs.

"Vic? You there?" A warm, smooth hand was rubbing my thigh.

My eyes fluttered open and the sickening realization hit me as I met his eyes.

"I fainted, didn't I?"

"Yep," he smiled. "Welcome back."

I rubbed my face with the back of my hand and tried to sit up.

"Wait a second. Maybe you should just lay there awhile." He handed me a cool glass of water. "Here, sip this."

I took a slow drink trying to swallow the nausea.

"I've never fainted before in my life," I admitted, slightly embarrassed.

"You did it very well," he said with a grin. "Like a pro even."

"Shut up."

He chuckled. "You probably just hyperventilated. It happens to the best of us. Take some slow, deep breaths."

My heart was pounding in my ears as it all flooded back to me. The lovely scene in the bathroom, I had flashed my boobs.

Did I really flash my boobs?

"Did I, um," I stammered, "did I just seduce my way out of being killed?"

"Yep," he said. "You ever considered a career in law enforcement?"

I handed him the wet towel. "You're hysterical. Put this on your own head."

"I'm dead serious."

"Because I showed my tits to a guy who was holding a gun on me?" I asked incredulously.

"No. You stayed calm, assessed the situation, and took action. That's what makes a good cop."

"Then I fainted," I added.

"First time I saw a homicide victim, I puked my guts out. It gets better. With the right training, you could do some damage."

I rubbed my eyes. "Well, I'm not going to start today."

He chuckled. "I'm sorry I forgot to set the alarm on my way out. When I finally realized it, I broke every speed record getting here."

I smiled weakly at him. "That's okay. I'm glad you got here before I had to sacrifice my virtue."

His eyebrows shot up. "Your what?"

I laughed. "Well, I try to only be sexual with men who want me to keep breathing."

He laughed, then looked at his watch. "I'm starving. Pizza's in the kitchen. You feel up to eating?"

"I probably should eat something."

"Might make you feel better," he said, rubbing my thigh again. "Ooh, very smooth."

"Yeah, I had to shave before I seduced the slimeball."

He laughed again and headed for the kitchen.

****

CHAPTER SEVENTEEN

I awoke the next morning completely mummified in the sheets. I always wondered what the hell I did in my sleep to get myself in that sort of position. Sometimes I woke up with no pillow under my head, no blankets on me, and my nightgown in a knot at the end of the bed. I needed a sleep study. I needed a lot of studies.

I heard the shower running so I struggled to get out of my cocoon as quickly as I could, hoping to maybe get a morning quickie, or at least a peek at his fantastic body. I jogged down the hall and opened the bathroom door quietly. He was humming to himself, I think it was "Friends in Low Places," and I smiled as I lifted my nightshirt over my head.

I pulled back the curtain a little and took a long look at his yummy backside as he washed his hair. Before I realized what it was doing, my hand was on his left cheek and it was squeezing.

"Whoa!" he yelped, spinning around.

"Sorry," I chuckled, stepping into the shower. "I couldn't help it."

He took a deep breath and laughed. "Well, hello there, young lady."

"Hi," I said as he leaned down to kiss me. He stepped back and rinsed his head and the suds rolled down his chest and I had never seen anything sexier in my life. My hands suddenly had a mind of their own and rubbed the suds around his chest, down his flat stomach, and down to his thighs. He smiled and looked down at me.

"I don't think I've ever been molested in the shower before," he said.

"What a tragedy," I said, running my lips over his wet chest and teasing his left nipple with my tongue.

"Why don't we get you wet too," he said.

I looked up at him and smiled slyly. "Too late."

"Hm."

We switched positions with some difficulty and I leaned back under the spray of the shower. He poured some shampoo into his hand as I turned my back to him. My eyes closed as he began washing my hair. He ran his fingers through my hair down to the middle of my back and I let out a long sigh of complete bliss.

Varner! Take me away!

Then he gave me a tall shampoo horn and started laughing. "You look like a unicorn."

Okay, so, he didn't have much of a talent for erotic talk.

I rinsed my hair and felt a rough sponge against me as he washed my back. He took my shoulders and turned me around to face him. He dropped the sponge and used his hands to soap my arms. He ran his fingers, slippery with soap, gently up my arms and over my breasts. I closed my eyes as the fingers of his right hand slipped down my stomach. His hand went lower and I gasped as his fingers moved between my legs.

He kissed me deeply and continued "washing" me, his tongue teasing little circles around mine. And just as I was about to reach the point of no return, he stopped.

"Don't stop," I begged, grabbing his hand.

He kissed me again and opened the shower curtain. "We should get going if we're going to get to the station by ten."

He closed the shower curtain on me and laughed.

"You tease!" I yelled. "Big meanie!"

A few seconds passed as I sulked, and then I heard the curtain open a little.

"Aw, shucks," I heard him say behind me. "Guess we'll be late."

****

We hit the police station a little after ten thirty to make our reports. Fisher happened to be headed toward the coffee room next to the front desk and greeted us rather warmly.

"Hey, I was just about to call you," he said. "I need to talk to you."

He was looking at me.

"Me?"

"Yeah," he answered. "Come on in to my office."

I followed him down the hall with Varner close on my heels.

"What's up?" Varner asked as we sat down amongst Fisher's clutter. There were boxes of files stacked almost to the ceiling against one wall and they were leaning ominously toward us. His desk was a mountain of papers and he dug through them like a French pig looking for truffles.

Fisher finally found the file he wanted and tossed it across the desk to Varner. "George Ridley's up."

"Hm," Varner said opening the file. I leaned over for a look. Mr. Slimy's mug shot stared back at me, complete with his Varner-induced fat lip. I cringed and sat back.

"High as hell on Methamphetamine," Fisher said, folding his hands on top of his bald head and leaning back in his chair. "He has three out-of-county cases for petty theft and burglary, but no violent priors."

"Hm," Varner said again, and read aloud from the file. "Previously found to be emotionally and mentally disturbed with possible borderline personality disorder and developmental disabilities. Terrific."

Fisher grunted. "Apparently the meth is relatively new to him. He came down pretty quick without much withdrawal. And he's willing to make a full confession." His black eyes shot to me again.

I shifted my eyes from Fisher to Varner and back. "What?"

"He said he will only talk to you."

My jaw dropped. "Me? Why me?"

"Nope, not happening," Varner said.

"A full confession, Varner," Fisher said.

"Mentally disturbed, Tom," Varner retorted strongly. "God knows what kind of sick shit he wants to tell her. You heard him thank her for the show last night. He's a twisted little fuck, and there is no way in hell she is going near him again."

Fisher's eyes narrowed. "Tom? You never call me Tom. And I sure as hell have never heard you drop the F-bomb at work, or ever, for that matter."

Varner's eyes shifted nervously. "Well this is informal right? Off the record?"

Fisher looked at me for a moment and lowered his head as if he was checking my neck. Then his eyes went back to Varner. "Glad to see you're relaxing a bit."

I felt around on my throat for a minute, pretending I had an itch. Did I have a hickey or something? I don't remember him sucking there, except for that bite in the kitchen, but it was just a nibble. Nothing that would leave a mark.

Great!

"Look, I'm just telling you what he wants," Fisher said. "And I really don't think it's your decision, Jason."

They both looked at me. I felt like I was in the middle of an intervention and bit my thumbnail nervously. Something told me it was going to be a long freaking day. Something else told me that I only had one option.

I let out a long sigh. "Okay."

"What? No!" Varner said. "I mean, maybe if I talk to the guy…"

"You beat the shit out of him," I said. "He's not going to talk to you."

"My case, my call."

"Our case," Fisher said, his tone changing to authoritative. "And I do believe I have seniority over you, Detective."

"You're pulling rank on me now?" Varner snarled, leaning forward in his chair.

"If I have to, yes." Fisher replied. "Don't make me have to."

Varner sighed and looked at me. There weren't daggers in the look, but there were certainly a couple of butter knives. "You're not trained on interrogation procedure."

"Why do I need training to talk to someone who wants to make a full confession?" I asked him. "I won't be interrogating him. I'll be chatting with him...in an interrogation room."

Now there's a sentence I never thought I'd utter.

Varner stared at me. I stared back, almost defiantly. I was getting a little tired of him trying to tell me what I could and couldn't do. What was all that talk about "you should be a cop" last night? Was he taking it back now?

Fisher leaned forward in his chair. "He's been pretty cooperative so far. I honestly don't think he's doing this to scare her further."

Varner sighed and pressed his fingers against his eyes. Then he looked at me. "Are you sure?"

"No," I said. "But I'll do whatever it takes to end this."

Fisher smiled at me and looked at Varner.

"All right," Varner conceded. "But I'm going to be in the room with them."

Fisher stood up. "Go on down to interrogation room one and I'll make the arrangements."

Fisher slumped out of the room, barking orders to the nearest uniform.

Varner looked at me for a while. I think he was studying my posture and probably wondering whether or not he could trust me with this new task. I didn't even know if I could trust me with the new task. What if Ridley went nuts? I mean, more nuts than he already was? What if he attacked me and started eating my face?

But I guess, if all else failed, I could flash the boobs again. It would probably distract him long enough for them to tackle or shoot him if he got out of control. Then again, it could distract everyone, and I'd be up the creek without the proverbial paddle.

"You shouldn't be doing this," Varner said quietly. "I should be the one talking to him."

"I know," I said. "But I need practice for my new career in law enforcement."

He grinned. "True. But this makes me very nervous."

"You?"

"Yes, me."

"What have you got to be nervous about? I'm the one questioning the scum bag."

He leaned forward, his nose brushing against my hair. "I have a very strong need to protect what's mine."

His husky voice made me shiver, as did the fact that he called me "mine". I liked it a lot, and at the same time I hated that I liked it a lot. I didn't belong to him. I wasn't his property.

But God, it sounded so good when he said it

"Am I yours, Detective?" I asked, unable to contain my smile.

He ran his long finger down the length of my forearm. "Oh yes. You're mine. Every cute, little inch of you."

Go away goose bumps! You'll give him the wrong idea.

"Listen," I said quickly, hoping to steer the conversation into another direction. "You better cool it with the touchy-feely stuff. I think Fisher suspects something about us."

"What do you mean?"

"Do I have a mark on my neck or anything?"

He scanned me for a minute. "No."

I touched my neck again and sighed. "I guess I'm just paranoid."

He smiled. "Don't worry about it, Darlin'. He can suspect all he wants. Unless it's confirmed, he has nothing to go on."

"I just don't want anything to happen to you or your job because I couldn't control myself," I whispered.

"You weren't the only one in that bed," he said with a grin. "Or the kitchen, or the living room, and the stairs were fun…"

I laughed. "All right. So we're both culpable. I still don't want you to get in trouble."

He sighed. "If I do, it was so worth it." He took my hand and kissed it. "Okay, let's go on down."

I followed him out of the office and down the hall to a set of elevators. We took them down to the lowest level and he led me down a row of gray doors. There was another elevator at the end of the hall that said "Inmate Transport Only" in big, black letters. We stepped into the room closest to that elevator, marked with a giant, red "One," and I took a seat at the table. Varner sat next to me. I turned and looked at the one way mirror and camera above it. I thought about waving, but I didn't.

"Keep eye contact, even if he makes you sick," he said. "Try not to show any emotion, especially fear, they feed on that. Keep a straight and confident posture, like you've done this a million times."

I bit my lip and ran my fingers through my hair.

"Sympathy is a great weapon," he continued. "Use it. Let him think you're sorry he's in here. Be his friend and gain his confidence. And he thinks you're pretty. Use that too. Flirt if you have to." He made a face and swallowed. "Play this right and he'll be eating out of your hand."

Well that was an image I didn't want. Anyone have a brain scrubber?

"You okay?" he asked.

"Yep." I sat up straighter and my feet barely touched the floor. My insides rumbled with terror, but I tried not to let on to him. If I could hide fear from Varner, I could hide it from anyone.

He smiled warmly. "My little hellcat."

"That's me," I said, returning his smile. "Now stop looking at me or I'll get scared and crawl into your lap and cry."

He chuckled and squeezed my arm. "You'll be fine. I'm here the whole time. Say the word and I'll take over."

We sat in silence for a while, waiting. I heard the elevator doors open and chains rattling, and then he was there in the doorway. He was clean, cleaner than when I saw him last, but he looked tired and pale, and the neon orange jump suit made him look almost jaundiced. Two uniformed officers led him in, and seated him in the chair across from me. His head drooped as Fisher walked in.

"All right, Ridley, Miss Childs has agreed to talk to you. Aren't you going to say hello?"

He raised his head slightly and looked at me. "Hello, Miss Childs."

The hairs on the back of my neck stood up at the sound of his voice, but there was something obviously different about it. Varner shifted out of his chair and walked behind me as the uniformed officers left.

"Well," Fisher said. "Start talking."

Ridley looked up at me. He looked exhausted, sad and completely used up. I almost felt pity for him. Terrified pity, but it was still pity. The kind of pity I'd feel for a starving pit bull who was barking his head off at me.

"I want to talk to her by myself," he said quietly.

Fisher pulled a small tape recorder out of his pocket and sat it on the table. He flicked it on and stepped out of the room, closing the door behind him.

Ridley's eyes shot to Varner. I heard Varner's feet shifting behind me as he leaned against the wall.

"George," I said gently. "Why don't you go ahead and get this over with?"

He looked at me and a tear dripped from his eye.

"What about him?" he asked, jerking his chin toward Varner.

"You're out of your damn mind if you think I'm leaving," Varner said.

I held up my hand, telling him to cool it. I wasn't afraid of this man anymore. I knew he wasn't the same man he was the night before.

"Can you forget about him?" I asked George. "You just talk to me, okay?"

He stared at Varner, obviously fearful but I moved my head into his eye line. "I won't let anyone hurt you."

His mouth twitched and he almost smiled at me. "Promise?"

"I promise," I told him, folding my hands on the table. "Can you tell me what happened the night the judge was killed?"

"I shot him," George said. "I hid in his courtroom and when court was over I snuck to his office and shot him."

He mimed a gun with his fingers, like a child playing cops and robbers.

"Why did you do that?" I asked.

"He was a bad man."

"No," I said. "I don't think he was."

George shifted in his chair and relaxed somewhat. "She told me he was a bad man."

I leaned forward a little. "Who told you that?"

He looked at the table. "The lady did."

"What lady?"

He shrugged and another tear rolled down his face. He looked at Varner again and I turned to follow his gaze.

Varner's eyes narrowed and I felt physically ill. Damn! No wonder he was good at his job. He looked like a tiger eyeing his prey. He was intimidating to me at that moment and I had seen him in his birthday suit only a couple hours before. I couldn't imagine what George was feeling about him. I knew George would tell me more if Varner was out of the room, but I was powerless to do anything about it. Resentment started to bubble in my gut, along with a few other sensations.

Varner was sexy as hell when he glared.

"Detective Varner, could you leave us alone for a minute?" I asked.

He shook his head. "Nope."

I sighed my defeat and turned back to the prisoner. "I want to help you, George, I really do. But you have to tell me who the lady is."

He shrugged again and looked at me. "She had black hair and big sunglasses. I never saw her before."

"Did she say why the judge was a bad man?"

"She said he hurt people. A lot of people. Then she gave me a shot and I felt funny."

"Did she tell you what was in the shot?"

He shook his head.

"How many times did you shoot the judge?" I asked him.

"I dunno, til the gun wouldn't shoot no more," he sobbed. "I never shot nobody before. I was scared."

"What happened after that?"

"I ran down the stairs to the secret door to get out. But the lady was slower than me. I don't know where she went when I ran away."

"The lady was with you when you shot the judge?" I asked, trying to hide my complete shock.

Someone else was there that day? Did I hear someone else? No. No, I only heard him.

I only heard him talk. Someone else could have heard me banging around in the closet.

"Yes, she was there," he said. "But I don't know where she was after that. I just ran away."

"And you're sure you hadn't seen this lady before?"

He nodded.

"Okay, George," I said. "What happened last night? Did she give you another shot?"

Big, elephant tears dripped down his face as he wept. "Yes. I didn't want to hurt you, I promise. I saw you the night your house blew up, and you were so pretty. But she made me promise to, to, to hurt you bad. And then he came back." He indicated Varner with his chin.

"Did you…did you blow up my house?" I managed to choke out.

"I'm sorry," he cried. "She gave a bottle to me and she told me to throw it as hard as I could and I just threw it, and it went through the window and…"

"It's okay," I said gently. "You didn't know."

"I'm sorry," he whispered.

"Did the lady…did she give you money?" I asked him.

"Yes, and a motel room."

"Where were you living before that?"

He cried harder. "With my sister. But she's gone now. Everything's gone."

"Okay, George," I said softly. "It's going to be all right now."

He looked at me with his tearful eyes and my heart melted for him. He didn't have a clue what was going on, and some woman was controlling him. Some woman with black hair and big sunglasses was pulling his strings. The woman Varner talked to on the phone last night.

"You're so pretty," he whispered. "You're a nice lady."

"Thank you, George," I said, smiling at him. "Everything is going to be okay."

Fisher opened the door and George jerked violently and fell from his chair. Varner lunged just as George started wailing.

"No!" he screamed, kicking at Varner. "No! She promised no more hurting!"

Varner lifted him up with brute strength. "Come on, take it easy, Sparky."

Fisher caught one of George's shoulders and jerked him toward the door aggressively.

"Don't hurt him!" I yelled as I got up and circled the table toward them. "George, please calm down. They won't hurt you if you calm down."

But he just kept screaming and thrashing and kicking. The two uniformed officers entered the room and helped Fisher get George out of the room. I heard him struggling in the hallway and into the elevator.

I put my hand over my mouth and tears dripped from my eyes. Varner turned to me. He put his arms around me and I shivered against his chest.

"What a heart you have," he said. "You genuinely pity him, don't you?"

I nodded and sobbed against him, once again wanting to crawl into his lap so he could enfold me in his muscles and protect me, and at the same time hating myself for it.

"I need to stop doubting you," he said quietly.

"Yeah, you do," I said, looking up at him.

"You okay?" he asked, holding my face in his hands and wiping my tears away with his thumbs. I nodded and leaned against his chest again. Fisher came in breathless and Varner released me quickly.

"Good job," Fisher said, clicking the recorder off. "I think we got all we're going to get out of him."

"Is he going to be all right?" I asked.

Fisher nodded. "He's been pretty calm until now. Don't get too attached, honey. Remember he's a psycho with a crush."

I shrugged. "He's not a bad guy. He's just easily manipulated, and some bitch is fucking with his life like she's fucking with mine."

The men looked at me with equal looks of astonishment.

"How about we go out for lunch," Fisher said, looking at his watch.

"Sure," Varner said, putting a hand on my shoulder. "Unless you don't feel up to it."

"Food? I'm always up for food."

****

CHAPTER EIGHTEEN

We went to the local Greek eatery, The Bird of Paradise, which was affectionately called the BOP by almost everyone in town. The BOP served a great salad in a bread bowl and breakfast anytime you wanted it. The staff was a family from a tiny town in Greece that I couldn't pronounce, and they always welcomed everyone with subdued relish.

"Sit where you want," was the typical greeting, followed by, "What you want to eat?"

The place was decorated with flags from all over the world, and the aroma was always a mixture of freshly baked pies and flaming feta cheese.

"OPA!"

If I had to guess, I would say that "feta" means "fart" and "OPA" was originally yelled as a warning to prepare for the stinkiness. I loved the place, but as soon as I heard an "OPA" I knew I would be leaving soon afterward.

I decided on the grilled chicken salad for lunch and the men ordered gigantic breakfasts.

I sat across from them and their enormous spread of breakfast food and watched in awe as they packed it all away. Never in my life had I seen two men eat so much. It was like watching a couple lions eating a freshly killed zebra. I picked at my salad, envying their hunger. For some reason I had no appetite. Maybe it was because Fisher poured ketchup all over his over-easy eggs and made it into an orange chunky slop.

Ugh.

"You're not eating," Varner said to me. "You all right?"

I nodded. "I'm not really all that hungry."

"Stress," Fisher grunted, shoving a forkful of swill into his mouth. "I get that way too sometimes."

My eyebrows raised and I looked at Varner. He smiled and looked at Fisher's plate and I knew he understood when he grimaced. I picked up a piece of chicken with my fork and chewed it slowly.

"You did a damn good job with Ridley," Fisher said with his mouth full. "We oughta have you interrogate all the retards we pick up."

I swallowed. "That's a little more than offensive. Can we stay away from that term?"

Fisher looked at me. "What?"

"He's not a 'retard', he's a man like the both of you," I said strongly. "He just happens to be a little slow."

"Sorry," Fisher said, taking another fork full, orange dripping down his chin. "I'm a little old school I guess."

Varner looked up from his plate at me. "Yeah, well, Ridley and I have a little more in common than I'm entirely comfortable with."

I looked at him and smiled, knowing what he meant. They had both seen me in all my nakedness, and they both liked it a lot.

Fisher, however, appeared to be in the dark.

"What are you talking about?"

Varner cleared his throat. "Uh, well…"

"They're both psychos," I said with a grin. "And they both have crushes on me."

Fisher nodded and looked at Varner. "Oh, that. Yeah, I knew that."

Varner's eyebrows shot up and he looked at his partner.

"Well, it's pretty damn obvious you've got the hot pants for this young lady," Fisher laughed, wiping his mouth. "You've been strutting around the station for weeks like a rooster in a hen house. Never heard a man whistle so much. And you're starting to pack on a belly so she must be a good cook."

Varner made an indescribable sound, kind of a grunt mixed with a squeak. "I don't…I just…hey!"

I covered my mouth to try and hide the giggle that was begging to come out of my face.

"Can't really blame you," Fisher continued. "She's quite a looker. Hell, if I was twenty years younger I'd go for her myself."

"All right," I laughed, pushing my plate away. "I'm going to the ladies room."

The thought of Fisher "going for" anything on me made me lose my appetite completely. I left the tension of the table and retired to the solitude of the one-seater in the back of the restaurant. I did my business and washed my hands while catching a look at myself in the mirror? A looker? I cocked my head and flipped my hair over my shoulder. Cute maybe, but a looker?

Eh, I'd do all right in a pinch. Varner obviously liked the package.

I found my way back to the table only to find that it had been cleared and the men were standing in line at the cash register. I walked over and stood next to Varner while he took care of our check.

As we were heading toward the door, I heard hysterical laughter coming from behind us.

I froze. I knew the laugh well.

First there was the laugh, then the lunge, then the pawing.

"You just went really pale," Varner said quietly. "Is something wrong?"

I turned slowly and there she was, coming toward me.

"Vicki!" she hollered, waving furiously.

"Oh Jesus," I cringed quietly. I had forgotten what the voice did to me. I grasped Varner's sleeve for my very sanity.

"Who the hell is that?" Varner whispered.

"It's my boss," I said through clenched teeth. "Get me the hell out of here."

She ran to me, and I stiffened as she caught me in a tremendous hug. "I'm so glad you're okay. I haven't heard from you since I heard your apartment caught fire. I was worried something happened to you."

"A lot has happened to me," I said, looking up at Varner. He smiled and held his hand out to Carnie. I grabbed his sleeve and pulled his hand back knowing that she didn't wash her hands in public restrooms either.

He looked down at me for a moment, a little confused, and then back at her.

"Hello, Miss O'Leary, I'm Detective Varner. I believe we spoke on the phone a while back about the Weinhardt case."

"Oh yes," she said, fluffing her fuzzy blonde hair. "How are you, Detective?"

"Fine, just fine. Well, Miss Childs, we need to get going if we're going to make that appointment." He smiled, put his hand on my back and tried to direct me away from her.

Appointment?

He cleared his throat and gave me a nudge and I finally caught on. Sometimes it takes me a few minutes, especially if I haven't eaten or slept well.

"Just a moment, Detective," she barked, throwing an arm across my shoulders and turning me away from him. "When are you coming back to work, Vicki?"

I looked her dead in the face. "I'm not. I'm sorry."

She stopped in her tracks. "You're not?"

"No," I said as I grabbed Varner's hand. He laced his fingers into mine and pulled me away from her and toward the door of the restaurant. For a moment, I was amazed at how completely safe I felt when his fingers were wrapped around mine like that, and I smiled at the tinglies I felt.

"Why not?" Carnie almost shouted, killing my joy.

I turned and looked at her. "Because I can't do it anymore."

She looked at Varner's hand holding mine.

"Oh, I see," she said. "You're giving up your job for a man."

"No, I..."

Her chin stiffened and she walked past me. "You surprise me, Vicki. You really surprise me."

I watched her walk away and the exhilaration shot through me like Morphine. She went out the glass doors and I flipped the bird to her back.

"That's strange," Varner said, almost to himself.

"What's that?" I asked, trying to contain my excitement and looking up at him. He was looking at the door she had just gone out with a strange and unreadable face.

"Her voice just then," he said in a daze. "It almost sounded like…"

He looked down at me. "She sounded like the woman on the phone yesterday. The one who told me where to look for Ridley."

I squinted at him. Then that familiar feeling of realization came over me. The feeling in the pit of your stomach when your brain finally figures something out and your whole body tells you you're a big dumb ass. I put my palm to my forehead and pushed.

"What was Deborah's last name?" I asked, rolling my eyes to him.

"What does that have to do with anything?"

"What was it?" I pressed.

"Uh, um, her married name was Newton and she kept that after her divorce. I'm not sure what her maiden name was," he answered. "Why?"

"Carnie lives with her sister," I said. "Her sister, Debbie."

He blinked a few times and then it looked like someone let the air out of him. "Jesus, you think she…" His words trailed off and he looked out the door for a few seconds.

"We need to get her maiden name," I said, giving him a poke in the back.

"Let's go back to my office."

We rounded up Fisher and headed back to the station.

****

Fisher went to get the files on the case and the transcript of George's confession as Varner and I went into his office. I stood behind his desk chair so I could peek over his shoulder at any search results. Even though he was sitting down, I had a hard time seeing over his shoulder, so I stood on my toes a lot.

"Where did Deborah live?" I asked as he booted up his computer.

"Somewhere on the south side of town. I forget the street name. We never went to her place. We always met at restaurants or she came to my house."

I had to ask. "You didn't sleep with her did you?"

He looked back at me. "Is that really relevant?"

"No, but I want to know."

He sighed. "Well, we kind of got close once but then she sort of bolted. I'm still not sure what that was about. Actually, that was the last time I saw her."

I smiled. "She was an idiot."

His ears turned red.

"You're amazing, Jason," I told him, bending down to kiss his cheek. "I want some more."

"Just giving back what I'm getting," he replied. "And you'll get some more, believe me, but not on city property."

"I'll bet I could talk you into it," I purred against his ear.

He closed his eyes and whispered, "Football, football, football."

But the damage was done. He was beet red and grinning like Batman's Joker, which drew a quiet giggle out of me.

Fisher came in with the files and I straightened up quickly.

"All right, what's this all about?" he said.

Varner looked at him. "Well, we're thinking Carnie O'Leary may be involved in this somehow."

"Carnie O'Leary. The Clerk at the courthouse?"

"The very same," I answered.

"Let me make sure I understand you," Fisher said, sitting down in a chair across from the desk. "You think the Clerk, an elected official in this county, had something to do with the murder of Judge Weinhardt?"

"She may not have pulled the trigger, but she had something to do with it," Varner said. "I would be willing to swear she was the one who called me last night and told me where to find George Ridley. The phone call that came from Deborah's number."

"Deborah? Your dead girlfriend, Deborah?" Fisher asked, plopping into the office chair behind him.

"She was never my girlfriend," Varner snapped back. "We dated a few times, that's it."

"All right, all right," Fisher held up his hands. "Don't get your thong in a bunch. I can't keep track of all your women."

Even though I knew for a fact that Varner was wearing boxer-briefs, the thought of him in a thong made me laugh and lots of blood rushed to my face.

"All my what?" Varner squeaked. "What women?"

"Well there was your ex-wife who called you constantly for a while. Then there was that cute little desk sergeant who you..."

"We had lunch once," Varner said quickly. "Once!"

"Then there was that hooker you busted who kept stopping by to see you."

"Oh, for the love of God, don't bring her up again. She's a crack addict and has no teeth."

"Uh, guys, as much as I would like to hear Varner's laundry list of females, can we get back to the task at hand?" I asked.

"Ooh, right, sorry," Fisher said. "Now tell me about Miss O'Leary."

I brought Fisher up to speed about Carnie and how I thought she and Deborah were connected.

"Okay, let's see, Deborah Taylor. Check on aliases here. Oh, Christ," Varner said leaning back in his chair.

"What?" Fisher asked. "Deborah Christ? She didn't look Jewish."

I stared at Fisher for a moment, completely astounded at his political incorrectness.

"How does one look Jewish, Detective Fisher?" I asked him.

"Not Deborah Christ," Varner moaned, pointing at his computer screen. "Look under maiden name."

"Ridley," I read aloud.

"What?" Fisher said loudly. "She was related to the scumbag? How?"

Varner clicked around. "It says here next of kin, George Ridley. Brother?"

"George said he lived with his sister and then she was gone," I said quietly. "Does it mention any other sisters?"

"I don't see any. Latest address is Twelve Fourteen Bradford Road, Apartment Eleven. Before that she lived on Lexington," Varner said.

I swallowed audibly. "Carnie lives on Lexington."

He went back a few screens and typed in Carnie O'Leary.

"Same address," Varner and I echoed.

"Man," Fisher said. "This is making me damned uncomfortable."

Varner spun his chair around and looked at me. "We're missing a motive here."

"Did you ever notice any kind of special relationship between Carnie and the judge?" Fisher asked me.

I thought about it for a minute. "No, nothing unusual. I mean, I never saw them together. But she did have a tendency to disappear from the office for an hour on occasion and not tell me where she was going. But I just figured she was wandering around annoying people. She liked to do that."

Fisher chuckled. "Yeah, she has one of those voices that makes you want to punch her in the throat."

I smiled at him. I think he was starting to like me more and more. I knew I liked him a lot better since the "I wouldn't want to mess with that" comment. Plus he had the endearing habit of trying to embarrass Varner which tickled me to pieces for some reason.

"Was she ever married?" Varner asked me.

"Not that I know of."

He rubbed his face. "We can't even prove she and Deborah were related, the names are different. There's no record of Deborah having a sibling other than George."

"They lived together?" Fisher asked.

I nodded. "At least Carnie always talked about living with her sister Debbie."

"Sister," Varner said, scratching his head. "They sure don't look anything alike. Carnie's as blonde as they come and Deborah had dark brown hair and olive skin tone."

"Was she a real brunette?" Fisher asked, a slow smile spreading across his face. "Did the collar match the cuffs?"

"I wouldn't know," Varner said snidely. "And shut up."

I chuckled and thought for a minute. "Maybe Carnie was adopted. Maybe she kept her birth parents' name," I suggested.

The men looked at each other.

"Adoptions are impounded files," Fisher said, looking at me. "We don't have access to those."

"I do," I said. "At least I did a couple hours ago. But Carnie couldn't have gotten the codes for the locks changed yet."

They both looked at me. I felt like a bug in a jar. I hope they poked some holes in the lid because I was suddenly having a hard time breathing.

"Can you get me into the office?" Varner asked.

I smiled and batted my eyes. "You'll have to get my employee ID out of evidence."

****

CHAPTER NINETEEN

We waited until around five-thirty to go to the courthouse so everyone would be gone. I went in the security entrance and flashed my employee badge at Lardo who was back on duty.

"Hello, Miss Childs. Did you forget your purse again?" he asked suspiciously.

"No," I said with a smile. "I just need to get a few personal things from my desk. Could you buzz me in please?"

"Sure thing."

He hit the buzzer and I went into the building. I made sure he was focused on his doughnut. Then I ran down the stairs and through the old morgue, toward the outside door on the side of the building. Varner was waiting for me, nonchalantly pacing around.

"It should be all clear. Lard-ass Richards is working and he only gets up when he's out of doughnuts or he has to pee."

Varner snorted and followed me up the stairs.

The climb was long and strenuous, at least for me. Varner didn't seem to mind it but then he had the shape of a Roman god. I had the shape of a Roman pizzeria owner. We reached the fourth floor landing and I was about to die.

"We need to get you in shape woman," he said, slapping my ass. "Come on."

"Shut up," I said breathlessly. "I bet Ridley and Fisher like me the way I am. And you said no hitting."

He laughed and ran up the stairs ahead of me.

I took a deep breath. "When I catch you I'm gonna kick your ass."

He stuck his head around the corner. "You'd need a ladder. Come on."

We finally made it to the seventh floor. I went on ahead of him and slogged my way toward the office. I looked around. Then I grinned because I could almost hear the theme from "Mission Impossible" in my head. We should have lowered ourselves through a hole in the roof, in SWAT suits. He would look incredible in a SWAT suit.

I would just look like something you should swat.

"Okay, come on," I said. Varner poked his head out of the stairwell and followed me.

I put the code into the lock and it clicked open. We entered the office and Varner wiped the doorknob off with a handkerchief. "No sense leaving any prints."

He pulled out two pairs of rubber gloves and handed me one. We slapped them on, ducked below the security cameras, and headed for the storage room where the old ledger books are kept. I put in another code and opened that door.

"Shit, I can't turn the light on. The cameras will catch it," I said. "And we can't keep the door open. That would show up too."

"Will it lock if you close it?"

"I don't know, and I don't want to chance us getting locked in."

Varner went to the door and shoved the nearest book against the frame and closed the door against it so it appeared to be closed. Then he reached into his pocket and slipped out a flashlight.

"Were you a criminal before you were a cop?" I asked him.

"Nope," he said, his little crooked tooth gleaming at me in the beam of the flashlight. "I was a Boy Scout."

He shined the light around the ceiling and found the security camera in the southwest corner.

"If we sit on the floor behind the shelves here, the camera won't catch us," he said.

I laughed. "You do realize you're breaking the rules again."

He rolled his eyes. "You're a bad influence."

We pawed through the ledger books one by one.

"I think she's around fifty, so we should go back that far," I said.

We flipped through the books as fast as we could. I think I sneezed nineteen times before we found the one we needed. Apparently I'm allergic to history, or criminal trespassing.

"Nothing under Ridley or O'Leary," I said, looking through the impounded file listings. "She wasn't adopted in this county."

"She's from here originally?"

"As far as I know. But she's lied about a lot of things, she could be lying about that too."

"Well, let's get out of here before the desk sergeant gets suspicious," he said. "I'll check on legal name changes tomorrow when the office is open."

I closed the book silently and we headed for the door. We left the storage room taking care not to be seen on the security cameras. I went back to my desk, grabbed a picture of my mom and a few other personal items, and jogged back to the door.

I went back through security, and he went on down to the judges' exit and we met up outside in the parking lot. Fisher was napping in the back of the Tahoe. He woke up as we got in.

"Anything?" he asked.

"Dead end," Varner said, looking slightly unsettled. "Could have been another county. We'll have to call State Vital Records."

"I can make a few phone calls too," I said. "I still have a lot of connections around here."

Varner glanced at Fisher in the rearview mirror, cleared his throat and started the car. We took Fisher back to the station where he left his ride.

"Call me later about that, uh, thing we discussed," Fisher said getting out of the back.

"Right," Varner said.

"Oh yeah," Fisher said opening his car door. "Here ya go."

He threw my purse to me and I smiled at him.

"I don't think we'll be needing this anymore," he said with a wink.

"Thanks, Tom," I said.

He waved, got in his car, and drove off.

"What are you calling him about?" I asked.

Varner shifted into park and turned to look at me.

"I don't want you involved in this investigation anymore," he said.

"What? Why?"

"We're handling it," he said, rubbing his hand on the steering wheel nervously. "And, I think you need to move out of the house for a little while."

I stared at him, my mind suddenly blank and going numb.

"It's too dangerous," he said strongly. "If Carnie's involved in this and she knows where you are, you're not safe anymore. Fisher has a cabin up by Brenton Lake and he said you can stay there until things cool down."

I sat back in the seat and looked out the windshield. I knew he was right, but the thought of leaving him made me sick to my stomach. I had lost everything and he had become my whole world. And the truth was, I was having a good time. I loved helping him investigate. It was exciting and even though we didn't find anything useful, it felt very satisfying to be active. But, while I didn't like it, I knew he was right.

He put his hand on mine. "It's not what I want, Vic. Please believe that."

I turned my head and looked out the side window, but I knew he felt my emotions. He always did, even before our connection to each other grew into passion.

He sighed and shifted the car into reverse.

****

It was a soundless drive back to the house while I tried to think of excuses for me to stay at the house. He needed someone there to watch out for him too. Nah, he'd never buy that. I even thought of faking a pregnancy, but it was too soon and that was just wrong. The fact was plain, he didn't need me. He was a smart and savvy detective and he didn't need my input. Knowing he didn't want my brain around was completely infuriating.

Then I considered doing some investigating of my own. But how was I supposed to do that from a cabin on Lake Brenton, ten miles from town with no access to anything?

We pulled up into the driveway and he blew out a long sigh. I glanced at him, opened the door and got out without a word. I walked up to the house slowly, thinking about what I was going to pack. He opened the door and I followed him in. He threw his keys on the entry way table and turned to look at me.

"Please talk to me," he said.

I sighed. "What's there to say, Jason?"

"You have to know I don't want you to leave," he said tenderly.

I swallowed and nodded. "I'm going on up to pack."

He looked defeated. "Okay."

I headed up the stairs. I found my duffel bag in the hall closet and started throwing clothes into it. And every piece of clothing that hit the bag was one more reminder that I was leaving. I heard him on the phone downstairs. He was probably making arrangements with Fisher about getting me into solitary confinement. I went into the bathroom, and grabbed my necessities, trying not to bawl like a hound dog which was becoming more and more difficult. I threw my toiletries into the duffle and zipped it up.

"Hey," he said from the doorway. I looked up at him and he smiled sadly.

"I'm finished I think," I said quietly.

"Come on downstairs," he said.

I followed him downstairs and dropped the bag at the door.

"It's all set," he said. "Fisher will be here soon to take you to his cabin."

I scanned his face. "You won't go with me, will you?"

He sighed. "If I disappear too, she'll know we're still together. This way is better."

Swallowing was becoming difficult. "So that's it, huh?"

"What's it?"

"I'm back to being just a witness to a homicide."

He nodded. "It has to be that way for now. Just for a little while."

I exhaled heavily. "I've never been thrown over for a job before."

He stepped forward and tried to take my hand, but I pulled away from him.

"I'm not throwing you over for anything," he said, touching my hair. "I love you."

I looked at him, trying to decide if he meant it. Trying to decide if I should say it back. I knew the emotion was real, but it was the first time either one of us had said it and it seemed to be a worthless statement.

"I want to believe that," I said.

"Want me to say it again?" he asked with a grin. "I'll shout it from the roof if you want me to."

"Was it just a ploy to get me to do what you want?"

His grin fell. "God, no. How can you think that now?"

I shrugged. "Maybe I'm jaded."

"Vic," he said, "Darlin', it's not a lie, and it's not any kind of ploy. I love you, and quite frankly, I don't care anymore who knows about it."

I swallowed back a sob. "How can you love someone you don't trust?"

"I do trust you."

"Not enough to let me help you. Your job won't let that happen."

He sighed and we stood there in silence. I ached to touch him, to be in his arms, but that was all fantasy once again.

"It's not just a job to me, Vic," he said. "It's all I know."

I nodded, sucked in a breath, and finally realized what I had to do.

"Call Fisher and tell him I'll make my own arrangements," I said, grabbing the keys to the Focus off of the hook by the door and picking up the duffle bag.

"Wait," he said. "Where are you going?"

I opened the door. "I don't know. I'll let Fisher know when I get there."

"Vic, stop, please," he begged, lunging toward the door and pushing it shut. "You can't just leave. We have to know where you are."

"I said I'll let Fisher know where I am."

We stared at each other. I straightened my shoulders defiantly.

"You going to let me out now?"

He didn't move, just stared at me. "You're not being very reasonable about this."

"So, I'm unreasonable. I lost reason a while ago. Now let me out or arrest me, but unless you can find something to charge me with, I'll be out in forty eight hours and then I'll leave anyway."

He sighed and rubbed his face. "You read every damn book on criminal procedure in this house didn't you?"

"Pretty much," I replied. "It was either that or sports and I'm not much of a jock."

He studied me for a moment, saw that I wasn't budging in my decision and took his hand off the door. He reached around behind his hip and unhooked the holster from his belt.

"Here, you might need this," he said, handing me the gun and holster. "Try not to get caught with it."

I took it from him, dropped it into the duffle bag, and opened the door again.

"Be careful," he said quietly.

I looked up at him, bit my bottom lip and closed my eyes as his fingers ran down my cheek.

"Please, Darlin'," he said gently. "Don't go like this."

He leaned down and I let him kiss me. I clung to his lips and fought the urge to wrap myself around him. Then I turned and headed toward the car. I threw the duffle into the back seat and hopped in to the driver's side. I started the motor and backed out of his driveway and floored it up the road and away from him.

I didn't cry. I didn't rant or rave to myself. I'm not even sure I breathed. I just drove.

I went on to a motel just outside of town and checked in for the night.

I stripped the bed down to the bleached sheets and lay there, numb, until I drifted off.

****

CHAPTER TWENTY

The next morning I went to the Bank of Brenton and withdrew most of my life savings. I took around five grand and left around fifteen hundred to draw interest in case I ever got out of this alive. Then I went and turned in my cell phone for a pre-paid one, complete with a new number, so he couldn't trace me. I bought the plan with a year's worth of minutes hoping I wouldn't need the phone for that long. Then I drove to the airport just outside of town. I parked the Focus, went to the nearest rental car counter and got myself a nifty little Celica. Luckily, I went to high school with the clerk, so she took my cash and I didn't have to give a credit card.

Track me now, Varner. Told you I've got connections in this town.

I decided to go on up north past Chicago for the night so I could figure out my next move. I checked in to a Holiday Inn off the highway, got settled into my room, and decided to call Fisher.

"What the hell are you doing?" he barked after my greeting. "Are you out of your ever-loving mind?"

"Maybe," I said. "I'm not sure anymore."

"Where are you? I'll come get you."

"I'm north of Chicago, but that's all I'm saying."

"Listen," he said. "I talked to Varner. I know what's going on between the two of you, and I'll tell you right now, I don't give a shit. We need you here and we need you safe."

"I am safe, and he doesn't need to know you've talked to me."

"You need protection."

"Yeah," I said. "That protection helped me out a lot when I was naked and Ridley had a gun pointed at my face. I can take care of myself."

"All right, we got sloppy. You've become a major distraction to Varner. But that's no reason to take off."

"I think it's a hell of a reason to take off!" I yelled. "So while you guys are sitting around and scratching your heads or whatever the hell else itches, I'm going to solve this damn case for you and get my life back!"

I hung up the phone. I felt almost vindicated. I had taken control of things for the first time in my life. I felt, incredible, invincible, and really hungry, but invincibly hungry.

I walked out of the hotel and saw the wonderful sight of the golden arches across the street and a drug store right next to it. I bought a pad of paper, some pens, a new can of pepper spray, and a Big Mac value meal and walked back to my room.

****

"Where the hell are you?" Toni said excitedly. "Varner has been calling every hour to see if I've heard from you."

"Don't tell him I called, okay?"

"He's worried, Vic. He came to the house looking for you and he looked like he'd been run over by a truck."

"Good, let him worry his pretty, little head off."

"Where are you?"

"Can't tell you," I said. "But I'm safe."

"I haven't heard from you in forever. I've been worried sick."

"I know, I'm sorry."

"What's going on?"

I sighed. Where the hell did I begin?

"I was staying with Detective Varner, but now I'm elsewhere."

"Why are you elsewhere?"

"Because I'm going to try and figure all this out on my own. I have to. These guys are getting nowhere, and I'm tired of waiting around like a victim."

"God," she groaned. "What are you going to do?"

"I don't know yet, but I'll figure out something. Besides, since I've been with Varner I've almost been killed. Twice."

"Twice? What the hell happened?"

I explained to her how I showed my tits to a drugged up guy to keep from being killed.

"Only you would think of that." she laughed. "I would have peed my pants and hit the floor."

"I wasn't wearing pants," I laughed.

"You know what I mean."

I laughed again. "Oh, it's so good to talk to you. I'm tired of not knowing who I can and can't trust."

"I know, sweetie," she said, her voice shaking slightly. "I've missed you."

I bit my lip and a tear rolled down my cheek. "I miss you too."

"Now, you have to tell me, did you seal the deal with that gorgeous man?"

I bit my lip and sucked in some air.

"Repeatedly."

She gasped. "Good God! How was it? And I need every tiny or giant detail."

"It was…being with him was incredible. And, God, I love him. I mean, I never knew I could love someone so much that being away from him physically hurts me. My stomach hurts constantly and my head and chest are throbbing, and sometimes I can't even breathe. He told me I'm beautiful, Toni. And I didn't realize until that moment that no one has ever said that to me before. And when he said it, I was. I was the most beautiful woman in the world to him, and maybe to myself for a while." My voice squeaked and started shaking. I sniffed and wiped another tear away.

"Aw, Vic," she said sympathetically. "You are beautiful and it's about damn time some stupid man noticed."

She let me cry for a few moments and then I remembered why she was my best friend in the world. Only a best friend can make you feel all right about being nauseatingly pathetic for as long as you need to, and then kick your ass out of it when it's time.

"But if he doesn't want my brain around, then he doesn't want me around," I said after I regained composure. "And who knows what will happen when this is all over, right?"

"That's right. Whatever is supposed to happen will happen."

I smiled. Toni always had a way of putting things into perspective for me.

"Has Varner asked you about anything else? I mean, has he been calling the Clerk's Office lately?" I asked, after blowing my nose two-hundred times.

"Yeah, well, he's been talking to Berta mostly. He's been at the office several times over the past couple weeks looking at the Stephen Fletcher file. You should see the women in the office fighting over who's going to wait on him. But he always asks for Berta."

Smart man!

"Stephen Fletcher?" For a moment I couldn't place the name.

"Yeah, the guy with the meth lab, and they found some kiddy porn at his place. It was one of Judge Weinhardt's cases."

"Hm," I said, writing Fletcher's name down. "He must think Fletcher is connected to all this somehow."

Apparently little Miss Deborah wasn't the only thing the secretive Detective Varner was not telling me.

"Well, remember that cop who was killed during the raid on Fletcher's place?" Toni said. "Raymer, I think his name was."

"Oh yeah," I said. "Varner must have replaced him."

"That's what I figured. But Fletcher didn't kill that cop. They never figured out who did."

I wrote furiously. "He has to have found a connection in all of this. He doesn't strike me as the type to abandon the Weinhardt case to research something else."

"You should call Berta tomorrow and see if she can tell you anything."

"Good idea, I'll call her in the morning."

I yawned, suddenly exhausted again. "I should have called you a long time ago. I feel a hundred percent better just hearing your voice."

"Well, I feel better knowing you're all right," she said. "What should I tell Varner if he calls?"

"I don't care."

"I'm telling you, Vic, the man is a wreck. He loves you and he's going to be frantic until he finds you."

"Yeah, well, I wish I believed that right now. I'm never quite sure where I stand with him."

Toni sighed in exasperation. "I'm going to tell him I've heard from you and you're all right. I can't in good conscience lie to him."

"Whatever," I said in the midst of a yawn. "Well, I'm going to try and get some sleep."

"Okay," she said. "Call me again, soon."

"I will, I promise."

"Love you, Vic."

"Love you too. Night."

I hit the "End" button and lay back on the bed. I wiped a remaining tear away, picked up my pad and pen and continued on my notes.

****

The next morning I woke up sideways on the bed with the TV on and the pad and pencil under my arm. I had only slept around five hours, but I was suddenly wide awake. I went down to get my "complimentary continental breakfast" and informed the desk clerk that I would like to stay another night.

I went back to my room and looked over my notes. I had written what I knew about Carnie. She supposedly lived with her sister Debbie on Lexington Avenue. She was excessively high strung with many imaginary health problems. She had dropped a lot of weight recently but claimed to be on some new crash diet. Then I did the math in my head. Carnie had lost approximately thirty pounds within a few months, and her behavior had become increasingly unbearable. She was jittery and couldn't seem to sit still.

"Drugs," I said aloud. "Hm." I wrote "symptoms of meth and/or crack addiction" on my pad and circled it.

Then I smiled at who I sounded like. Him and his little "hms". I checked the hotel-provided clock radio that read eight-thirty AM.. I picked up my phone, dialed the number of my former employer, and asked to speak to the woman who knew a little bit about everything.

"This is Berta," she grunted. I smiled again and pictured her Bulldog stature.

"Hi Berta, it's Vicki. Victoria Childs."

"Where have you been?" Berta asked quietly.

"Well, I'm sort of in hiding. Don't tell anyone I called, okay?"

"Yeah, yeah, what's up?"

"I hear you've been speaking with Detective Varner."

"Yeah," she said. "He's pretty cute, but he's too tall. Hurts my neck to look at him."

"So, what have you guys been talking about?"

"He's been asking a lot of questions about Stephen Fletcher."

"What do you know about Fletcher?"

"Only what's in the file," she said. "Drugs, child pornography, and a cop got shot but they never found the person who shot him."

I scratched my head. "Has he asked any questions about Carnie?"

"Yeah, he's been asking a lot of questions about her. He wanted to know if she and Fletcher ever contacted each other."

I thought for a minute. "Does the file say anything about correspondences between them?"

I heard her pecking away at her keyboard. "There is a lot of correspondence entered here. It says she sent him a lot of forms."

"Forms," I said, wondering if she ever sent him anything other than forms. "Did Varner give you any indication that he thought she and Fletcher were connected in any other way?"

"Nope." Berta hardly ever said more than was necessary to get her point across.

"So where is Fletcher now?"

I heard her clicking around on her screen. "He's in Chicago at the Metropolitan Correctional Facility."

How convenient.

"Okay, thanks Berta. Please don't tell Carnie or anyone else that I called, okay?"

"You already said that," she said. "Bye."

The phone went dead. I chuckled and started to place another call to Detective Fisher to check in, when something stopped me, and adrenaline rush down my arms. How I came up with it, I'll probably never know, but it hit me like a barrel of bricks.

They never found the weapon that killed Detective Raymer.

He was shot.

Weinhardt was shot.

The gun!

That was the connection. The gun used to kill Detective Raymer was the gun used to kill Judge Weinhardt, which also happened to be the gun that was found in my purse. I would wager it was a stolen gun. Stolen from an evidence locker in the Clerk's Office.

I dropped the phone in my lap and a slow smile crept across my face.

"Who needs training?"

****

CHAPTER TWENTY-ONE

I stayed at the Holiday Inn for the next week, trying against everything to clear my mind. A few days were spent relaxing by the indoor pool and going to museums in the city, but my nervous little brain wouldn't stop churning, even when I slept. Most of my time was spent trying to figure out what I should do next. I contemplated going to stay with Mom in Kentucky, but decided against it. I had to get to the bottom of what was going on, even if it killed me, which I seriously hoped it wouldn't.

I drove into Chicago several times and tried to get myself acclimated to the area. I finally found the Metropolitan Correctional Center after a few days of driving around and doing some investigating at several libraries, and decided what to do.

I found a strip mall just down the street from my hotel and bought a smart-looking business suit that showed just enough leg and cleavage to be somewhat sexy. I figured I may need something like that eventually. Then I went on down to another store and bought a couple new pairs of jeans, shirts, and some underwear and socks. Some of the clothes I had been wearing were getting kind of thread bare, and nothing lifted my spirits more than buying new clothes.

After my shopping trip, I phoned information and asked for the number of the Federal Prison in the Chicago area. There were two facilities, but one was for "rehabilitation services". I called the other one.

"Metropolitan Correctional Center, Arthur speaking."

A guy. Cool! I could work a guy into telling me something. Well, at least I'd have a better shot anyway.

"Good mornin' Arthur," I said, putting on my best Southern accent and sexiest phone voice. "My name is Victoria Childs and I'm with the Brenton Star. I'm working on a story about Federal Prisoners convicted in Illinois, and I understand ya'll have an inmate there by the name of Stephen Antoine Fletcher, is that correct?"

"Yes ma'am," he said, after a few clicks.

"I'm wondering if it would be possible to schedule a short interview with him."

"I'll connect you with the Warden's Office. He has to schedule all special visitors."

Uh oh. The warden? I may have been digging deeper than I meant to. My story might have to be modified. Maybe I should just hang up.

No! See it through, Vic. See it through.

"Warden Lowe's office," a very baritone and very velvety voice crooned on the phone. This man should have had his own radio show. A radio show for women. For lonely, horny women!

"May I speak with the Warden please?"

"Speaking."

"Well, I like a man who answers his own phone," I said sweetly, pressing my fist against my forehead in the process.

Varner's words rang in my head. "Flirt if you have to…"

Okay, you asked for it.

"Well, thank you, what can I do for you Miss…"

"Childs, Victoria Childs, I'm with a small newspaper in the Brenton area, and I was hoping to schedule an interview with one of your inmates there for a story I'm working on."

"How charming. It is Miss Childs, isn't it?" Warden Lowe asked.

Oh, jeez.

"Why, yes it is, sir."

This man's voice was like smooth, milk chocolate and I wanted to pour it all over some ice cream and start slurping. But my own fake accent was starting to annoy me. I sounded like Scarlet O'Hara on an aphrodisiac.

"And which paper are you with?" he asked.

Shit! Which paper am I with?

"I'm with the, uh, the Brenton Gazette," I said. "And may I say, Warden Lowe, your voice could charm the dew from the honeysuckle."

Gag!

He'd never buy it.

"Well, thank you, Miss Childs," the voice replied. "Why don't you come on up we'll make the appropriate arrangements for you."

"Sounds good, Warden," I said. "Would tomorrow be too soon?"

"No, not at all. I look forward to meeting you."

I cleared my throat. "Great, I'll be there around one."

If that man looked anything like he sounded, I was going to be in serious trouble.

I called and booked a reservation at the downtown Chicago Hyatt. I figured I might as well hide out in style.

****

I was less than an hour from Chicago, but I gave myself extra time to get around. I checked out of my hotel at eleven a.m., stopped at the drug store for provisions, and hit the road. Right away I started talking myself out of going.

"What the hell are you going to ask him? What if the Warden won't let you in? What if they figure you out? Why the hell did you tell the Warden your real name?"

I could tell I was getting close to the city. The traffic started picking up in speed, and everything became very gray. Chicago always seems to be gray for some reason. Probably the fog off of the lake. Or it could be the fact that all the buildings, sidewalks, streets and even the people were gray. And no one ever smiled. I could never figure out why. I always found Chicago to be very exciting, but I guess if you had to live there, it would get old eventually. I found the Hyatt with little difficulty, thanking God for GPS systems, and got myself checked in. I got settled in my room, went back down and caught a cab to the prison which was only about five minutes away. In the meantime, the wind whipped me and my hair into a frenzy. I also contemplated throwing my high heels out the window of the cab. But excitement lapped at my belly. I was in Chicago. By myself. Investigating a murder! By myself!

Good God, if my father could see me now.

I blew in to the Federal Correctional Facility around twelve forty-five p.m. and found the closest public restroom. My hair was a disaster, but I had luckily found enough common sense to bring a brush with me. I fixed myself up the best I could, rubbed the forming blister on my heel, pulled the skirt down a little, hoisted up the bouncy ladies, and made my way to the sergeant at the front desk. He was red-headed and pale and didn't look to be in the best of moods.

"Excuse me," I said, putting the accent back on. "I'm looking for Warden Lowe's office."

"Name," he grunted.

"Victoria Childs."

"Mm," he rumbled, flipping through a list.

The man obviously loved his job.

"Take the elevator to the seventh floor and take a right, then down the hall. His office is the first on your left."

I did as instructed and entered Warden Lowe's office five minutes later.

"Good afternoon, may I help you?" the cute young thing at the desk asked me. She looked to be about twenty-five, was blonde, tiny, and a suspicious wife's worst nightmare.

"I have an appointment with Warden Lowe. My name is Victoria Childs."

Why the hell did I put on that accent? Idiot.

"Okay, Miss Childs, have a seat, he'll be with you in a minute."

I yanked the skirt down a couple inches and sat down. I felt like I was on display. I should have shaved higher on my thighs. And what if I forgot myself and flashed the cha cha region?

I looked up at the door that said "Taylor Lowe, Warden" on it just as it opened.

Holy crap! I'm in trouble.

Big trouble!

Big trouble with hair on it!

He stood maybe six-two and looked to be about forty years old, or an excessively maintained forty-five. He had very short brown hair, brushed forward and gelled "roman style" and he was tanned and toned with an almost insignificant pouch around his stomach area. It was just enough imperfection to make his look approachable and charming. And if he had a whip, a leather jacket, and a brown fedora, I would have asked him to help me find the lost ark. This was definitely the type of man you would want in your bed if you heard a noise downstairs in the dark, so you could climb him and tear his clothes off and ravage him.

Okay, forget the noise downstairs.

His deep blue eyes twinkled and his warm smile greeted me as I turned thirteen shades of crimson.

"Miss Childs? Taylor Lowe," he offered his hand to me and I took it and let his voice trickle down my spine. He liked working with his hands, I noticed. They were soft, but with calluses in a few areas, like he had been using a rake or some kind of gardening tool. Gardening would account for the tan. No wedding ring, but his uniform shirt was neatly pressed so he obviously took pride in the way he looked.

Good grief. Why God? Why do you do this shit to me?

"Nice to meet you, Warden," the horny Scarlet O'Hara said.

"Please, come on in." He stepped aside and I walked into his office. I was surrounded by dark wood and maroon. There was just a hint of a pleasant cologne in the air, Givenchy I believe, and it mixed well with the leather from the high-backed maroon chairs. The only word to describe his office would be manly. There wasn't a throw pillow or anything pink in sight.

He motioned to a chair and I sat down. He sat behind the desk and leaned back in his brown, tufted leather chair. I half expected him to prop his feet up on the desk in front of me. This man was way too relaxed, and it was unnerving to say the least. And his smile was captivating and completely terrifying at the same time. Like a cat with a secret.

"So, you want to talk to Fletcher?" he asked.

"If it's convenient."

"Why would you want to talk to a scum bag like him?"

I was slightly taken aback by the question. "Well, I'm working on a story…"

"No you're not," he interrupted, his smile never fading.

"Excuse me?"

"You don't honestly think we would let anyone in here without doing a background check first, do you?"

I gulped loudly and looked at my fingernails.

For lack of better phrasing, I was fucked.

"You don't work for any newspaper in the Brenton area, do you, Miss Childs?"

Okay, time to level with him, and maybe turn on the charm. Both of them. But how was I going to undo a button on my blouse without his noticing?

"No," I said, lowering my voice to what I hoped was a seductive tone. "I'm not a reporter."

He leaned forward in his chair, the confident smile still plastered across his face.

"Why don't you tell me what you're really doing here?"

I smiled at him, rolled my shoulders back and crossed my legs "Basic Instinct" style, except I was wearing panties. "I'm investigating a murder case in Brenton, Illinois."

"You're not a detective."

"No."

"P.I.?"

"Not officially."

He looked at my legs and slowly moved his eyes up to my face. "So what's your interest in the case?"

I glanced at my chest to make sure my blouse was showing sufficient cleavage, and leaned closer to his desk. "I witnessed it. I was a suspect. Then I was a target. Now I'm sort of on the run."

I was actually kind of amazed that it could all be summed up that easily.

His smile dropped somewhat.

"Why didn't you go to the police?" he asked, glancing where I wanted him to glance.

"I did, and I was almost killed twice," I said, flipping my hair back. "I figured I would do better on my own."

"So what does this have to do with Fletcher?"

"I think he knows someone who may have been involved. I want to ask him a few questions."

He put his hands behind his head and leaned back in his chair again. "That accent didn't suit you."

I smiled. "I'm kind of new to all this."

He nodded. "Why didn't you just tell me the truth?"

"I'm finding it all hard to believe myself, and I'm part of it. How could I expect you to believe me?"

"I suppose that's a good point."

He propped his elbows on the arms of the chair, pressed the tips of his fingers together and looked at me for a moment. Then the moment became two and I became uncomfortable.

"So," I said hesitantly. "Should I leave, or are you going to have me arrested?"

"I'm not going to arrest you," he laughed. "And I'll let you see Fletcher on one condition."

"What's that?"

He folded his hands on the desk. "Have dinner with me tonight."

Crap! I was afraid of that.

Oh well, could one dinner really hurt?

I smiled at him. "Sounds like a fair trade to me."

He picked up his phone.

****

CHAPTER TWENTY-TWO

"Sorry, but I can't let you take that pad and pen in," Lowe said. "You never know what these guys are going to do."

"That's okay," I said, dropping them in the bucket outside the visiting room. "I'm pretty sure I'll remember what he says."

"I'll be right behind you the whole time," he said, leading me in between the security doors.

The door behind us slammed shut ominously and when the lock clicked my hand jumped to my chest.

"I thought you weren't arresting me," I squeaked.

Lowe chuckled as the door in front of us slid open to the visiting room. It had several long, gray tables, but only one was occupied. Sitting there was a short, stocky man of around forty-five. He was African-American, but his lips were bleached almost white, I assumed from prolonged drug use. He looked shriveled and tired, but he smiled when he saw me.

"Good afternoon, Miss Childs," he said. "Warden Lowe, how are you?"

"I'm doing fine, Stephen."

"May I sit down and speak with you a minute?" I asked him, remembering that Hannibal Lecter only ate rude people.

"Certainly," he said.

I sat on the bench across from him as Warden Lowe took his place behind me, and two guards were posted on either side of Fletcher.

"Now," Fletcher said, "you have got to be the prettiest thing I've seen in months. What is a fine, young lady like you doing here?"

"I came to ask you some questions about your case. Specifically about the detective who was killed the night you were arrested."

"You're not a cop," Fletcher said, looking me over. "Why do you want to know about that?"

"Just call me a concerned citizen," I answered.

"Okay," he said, looking up at Lowe. "Well, I didn't know anything about a detective getting shot that night until after I had been arrested. I had nothing to do with that."

"Was someone else with you when the police arrived?"

His dark eyes narrowed as he looked up at Lowe again. "What do I get if I spill my guts about this?"

"Not a damn thing," Lowe said.

Fletcher snorted and looked at me.

"Okay, let me ask you this," I said. "Do you know Carnie O'Leary?"

Fletcher smiled, his teeth exceptionally white in contrast to his dark skin.

"Yeah, I know Carnie."

"Was she with you that night?"

He laughed and nodded. "Man, you're good. You sure you ain't a cop?"

I noticed how his mannerisms had changed since he knew he wasn't getting anything out of this deal. He was starting to act like the usual "gangsta" rather than the polite man he had been a minute before. Nothing could have made me angrier. If he was trying to intimidate me, I was way beyond that. Besides, there was a whole armory standing beside him on either side, how gangsta could he get?

It was then I realized that a couple months ago, he would have intimidated me. A couple months ago, there was no way in hell I would be sitting where I was sitting.

Necessity, the mother of invention, or courage, or complete insanity depending on how you looked at it.

"So, do you think Carnie killed the detective?" I asked.

"She was high as hell, for all I know she could have. But I don't know. I was too busy getting arrested. They tried to pin that murder on me, but I ain't never fired a gun in my life and there were too many witnesses to say different."

"If she did it, how do you think she got away?"

"The detective was the only one in the house at the time, other than Carnie, and that retard she always hung around with. The back door opens up to an alley, that's where she usually parked. She probably went out that way."

"Was the retard George Ridley?" I cringed at the term.

"Damn! You're right. You're too smart to be a cop anyways."

I smiled and blew out a long sigh. "Maybe, or I've just been hanging around this damn case for too long."

"She kept trying to get him to shoot up with meth, but he never did want to. Finally one night I saw her do it for him and he went all crazy, talking about how he was gonna kill this person and that person, trying to get Carnie to fuck him. But George wasn't high the night that cop was killed. When George wasn't high, he was gentle as a puppy dog."

"So, Carnie bought a lot of drugs from you?"

"She was at the house all the time talking about how meth was the Holy Grail or some shit like that. She said the only time she didn't feel pain was when she was high."

I rolled my eyes. "I think most of that pain was in her head."

"You got that right. She's one crazy-ass bitch, but hell, I figured as long as she was paying me, I'd help her out."

"I was her secretary. I figured the same thing."

He laughed. "Who would think to look at the two of us that we got the same problem?"

"Did she buy anything else from you? Guns or any other drugs?"

"She bought some K one time. But I never sold no guns. That wasn't my thing."

I knew what his thing was. Getting little girls stoned and videotaping them while they took off their clothes. Pervert.

"Did Carnie ever mention someone named Debbie or Deborah to you?"

Fletcher shook his head. "Nah. She only ever talked about herself."

"So she never mentioned Judge Weinhardt either?"

"Nope."

I looked up at Lowe who was looking at his watch.

"Why haven't you told anyone this before?" I asked him.

He shrugged. "Carnie wrote and said she would help me out, get me a good lawyer on the drug rap if I kept her name out of everything. She got me a lawyer all right." He rolled his eyes. "Bastard wants me to cut a deal, but they ain't got nothing on me in Brenton."

Lowe cleared his throat and I heard him shifting his weight behind me.

"I think they're about to kick me out of here, but I appreciate this, Stephen, I really do."

"You come back and see me anytime, girl. In fact, if you need to make some extra money, I'm in the film business and I could hook you up."

"Well, thanks for the offer, I'll keep that in mind."

"I'm serious, you think about it. You got the right look. You know what I'm sayin'?"

Lowe put his hand on my shoulder and I almost jumped out of my skin. Fletcher stood up and shuffled out of the room with a guard at each shoulder and shackles on his hands and feet. Lowe sat on the bench next to me and I shivered involuntarily. He laughed.

"Stephen's something isn't he?"

"Yeah, a sick bastard."

"Was he any help to you?"

"He confirmed a lot of the information I needed."

"Good, I'm glad your trip wasn't in vain then."

I smiled at him. "I've made some interesting contacts."

He smiled back, but there was no blushing involved, which was kind of refreshing.

****

We sat in a dimly lit Italian restaurant right on the lake. My mind was still racing after the conversation with

Fletcher, but I tried to focus on the handsome man across the table from me, but not too much.

"So," he said, looking at his glass of red wine in the light of the candle, "what made you decide to take all this on yourself?"

I sipped my wine. "I told you. I didn't think the detectives on the case were going anywhere. They were dragging their feet about everything."

"You mean they wouldn't tell you everything."

I shrugged. "Maybe. I was never quite sure what I wanted to know."

"But that's not all, is it?" he asked, with his all-knowing smile.

This man could see right through me. I wondered if he knew I was wearing my black, lacy panties.

"No, that's not all," I replied quietly.

"You tried to get too involved in the investigation," he said. "And you pissed off people you shouldn't have."

"I don't know that I pissed them off per se, but I definitely made them uncomfortable."

He studied his wine again, and then studied me again. "And, I think maybe you got a little too involved in other things."

I narrowed my eyes. "I really don't feel that's any of your business."

He smiled again, his blue eyes working over my face like a search light.

"Fair enough," he said after a sip. "But you do realize you answered my question with that response."

I rubbed the back of my neck. "Let's just say things got complicated."

"I got ya."

Thankfully the food arrived at that moment and we began eating. I had ordered what turned out to be a giant plate of spaghetti and meatballs and everything was cooked perfectly.

"So Fletcher supplied drugs to this woman you're investigating?" he asked me.

"That's right. Carnie O'Leary, my former boss."

"And she was involved with the murder of whom?"

"Judge Weinhardt, a circuit court judge back in Brenton," I said after I swallowed. "But I don't really know why."

"Sex, drugs, or money," he said. "Those are the most common motives."

"I'm working on a theory," I said. "But God only knows if I'm even close."

"Enlighten me."

I cut my meatball in half with the edge of my fork and savored it for a moment. "Well, the judge was on Fletcher's case in Brenton so I figured she was trying to stonewall things. But I don't understand what could be gained by killing the judge. Fletcher was already convicted."

"He was convicted in federal court for possession and distribution of child pornography, not for housing a meth lab in Brenton."

"I thought they would all be heard together."

"No. The FBI tracked down his website. Because he was selling kiddy porn over the internet and shipping it over state lines, it's a Federal case. But since they can only prove that he had illegal drugs within the state of Illinois, the drug case would be handled on the state or county level. From what I understand, they didn't find enough meth to build a case for possession with intent, so he's only been charged with possession and manufacture of meth. Still a felony, but not as bad as it could have been. He's a smart little bastard though. My guess is he stashed his drugs somewhere else."

I swallowed. "So killing Judge Weinhardt would delay his prosecution in Brenton. And if Carnie could get George Ridley to confess to killing the judge, he would be essentially confessing to two murders."

"Two murders?"

I nodded. "Again, just a theory, but I think the gun used to kill the judge was the same gun used to kill the detective on Fletcher's case. The M.O. is the only thing connecting the two cases. So, if George had the gun and he killed Weinhardt, it would be safe to assume he killed Detective Raymer too. I mean, if the same gun killed both men, but I don't have any evidence to that effect."

He grinned, "The M.O.?"

"Modus Operandi. The way the killer worked."

He laughed. "I know what it means. I'm just surprised you used the term. It's not typically used in casual conversation."

"I've been studying criminal procedure for a while now," I said. "Guess I'm trying to show off a little."

He chuckled. "Well I'm impressed. And your assumption about the two killings sounds logical to me. He confesses to one, he confesses to two if the bullets match. But you think Carnie killed Detective Raymer?"

"She must have."

"Why?"

"She's nuts and she's using meth," I said. "Can't drug-induced insanity be a motive?"

"Sure it can, but it's a shaky one. It's really difficult to prove that someone committed a crime because they are or were insane. The only way to prove insanity is to prove that the suspect didn't know what she was doing was wrong. If she's trying to hide her involvement in the murders, it's obvious she knows she did something wrong and illegal. So in the eyes of the law, she is not insane."

I shrugged and played with my napkin, praying to God I didn't sound like an idiot to him.

"Maybe Raymer had something on her," I suggested. "Maybe he threatened to expose her drug use."

"That's a lot of maybes, Vic."

I sat back in my chair and sighed. "All I have is maybes. I don't even know what I'm doing. I'm just floundering around."

"Well, you're floundering in all the right directions," he said. "At least that's what I think. Keep digging."

Suddenly it was getting hard for me to swallow and tears formed at the corners of my eyes.

"The night before I left town, she shot Ridley up with meth and sent him after me," I said, staring at nothing. "She knew the drug made him violent. She knew he would either rape and kill me, or he would screw things up and get caught."

He stared at me, his jaw lax in surprise. "She did that?"

I nodded but kept my eyes on the table.

"God, what happened to you?" he asked with genuine concern in his voice.

I felt a sob coming on, but I swallowed it back. "Let's just say I'm still here and Ridley is in jail."

He reached across the table and touched my hand but I pulled it away. If he touched me, or looked at me wrong, or breathed wrong, or made any eye contact at all, I was going to lose it, right there, all over my spaghetti.

"I'm sorry," I said quietly.

"Jesus, you've been through the ringer haven't you?"

I nodded, bit my lip, and looked at my lap. "I've lost everything."

For the first time, he obviously didn't know what to do or say. And I had completely lost my appetite, which sucked because the spaghetti was phenomenal. I looked up at him and he exhaled and held my gaze for a moment, his face saying everything he couldn't. He was sorry, and he would help me anyway he could.

"This spaghetti is fantastic," I said, hoping that actually talking about it would make me want to eat it.

"Yeah, this is my favorite place to eat," he said. "Well, not my favorite place really."

"Where's your favorite place?" I asked, finishing my meatball.

He raised an eyebrow and looked at me rather seductively. "The Y."

"Where's that?"

He chuckled and glanced under the table.

I gasped and my eyes bugged. "Warden Lowe!"

He chuckled quietly. "I was hoping to see that beautiful smile again."

I discovered a couple things right about that time. One, it's impossible not to blush when Indiana Jones is coming on to you. And two, if he had his whip with him, things were going to get very interesting.

****

After dinner, he drove me back to the Hyatt. Luckily he had Federal government plates so he could pretty much park anywhere he wanted. We lingered in the car for a while after he found a spot on the street, talking about this and that and nothing in particular, but enjoying each other's company all the same. And then there was the awkward silence that comes when two people are attracted to each other but can't do anything about it.

"How long are you in town?" he asked.

"I'm not sure yet. I think I should get back and share a few things with the appropriate parties."

He nodded and stretched his neck to see the hotel entrance. "Crowded. I should walk you in, it's pretty late."

"Sure, that would be nice."

Oops! Shit! Victoria, you dumb ass.

We got out and he walked me up the hill and through the busy parking lot of the hotel. We entered through the revolving doors and he followed me through the maze of escalators and elevators. When we finally got to my room, I stopped at the door.

"This is me," I said nervously.

I shouldn't have let him come with me this far. I should have stopped him at the first escalator.

"Thanks for walking with me."

He looked at me and smiled. "Are you going to ask me in?"

I looked at him and seriously thought about it, but something was holding me back from opening the door to him. I knew what, or who, it was, but he didn't. Or maybe he did and didn't care.

"I would like to, Taylor but, I'm kind of involved with someone."

"And I'll bet he's a detective."

"Kind of," I said, looking up into his eyes.

"Figures."

I nodded. "Thank you for dinner though, and everything else."

He held out his hand to me and I took it. He gently pulled me forward so I was against his chest.

"Anytime," he said quietly. "Give me a little kiss right there."

He pointed to his cheek. I knew that old trick, but figured it was all innocent enough, and he deserved a small kiss for helping me. I went to kiss his cheek and he turned his head quickly so our lips met.

So much for innocence. Holy crap, his lips are soft.

I loitered against him for a while, enjoying the taste and excitement of someone new. He leaned me back against the door of my room and kissed me deeply. Maybe it was the wine, or the fact that he was so unbelievably sexy, but I didn't resist him. He stopped, looked into my eyes, and pulled away slowly.

"You sure?" he asked.

I sighed, thought about it again, really, really hard, and nodded. "Yeah. I'm sure."

He nodded and pursed his lips slightly. "He's a lucky guy."

"Yeah, well, he might disagree with that. I've caused a lot of trouble."

"I'll just bet you have," he touched my chin. "And I'll bet you've got trouble written all over you." He took an obvious look at my cleavage and smiled slyly, "naughty boy" written all over him. And I had to admit, I was damn curious.

What would Indiana Jones be like in the sack?

"Give me a call and let me know how things are going," he said, backing away down the hall. "And let me know how you are."

I nodded again and held up my hand in a reluctant wave. "I will."

He waved and I watched him walk away. It wasn't quite the same as watching Varner walk away, he was a little wider through the hips, but all in all, the butt was bitable. I opened the door with my card key and went inside.

"Sexy bastard," I said putting my head back against the door.

Oh well, food for thought.

****

CHAPTER TWENTY-THREE

I regained my composure and called mission control.

"Fisher," he answered.

"It's Vic."

"Thank God! Little girl, you're killing me here. Are you all right?"

"I'm fine. I have some interesting information for you."

"Oh, yeah? What's that?"

I explained to him how I got in to see Fletcher. After he snapped off on me and hollered that I was completely insane, I explained to him what Fletcher told me.

"Christ," he said. "You could get a priest to admit he's screwing a nun."

I laughed at the analogy. "I guess I just have a way with people."

"Criminals. You have a way with criminals."

I neglected to tell him about the dinner date with Taylor Lowe. I figured I should keep that one to myself, to think about while I was lonely which seemed to be most of the time lately.

"So what are you going to do now?" he asked.

"Well, honestly, I haven't the foggiest idea."

"Listen," he said, "come back here. You can stay at my cabin. We don't have to tell Varner anything, okay? This is for me. I just want to know that you're somewhere safe, and somewhere you can get help if you need it."

Everything in my brain told me that it was the right thing to do. I usually listened with my heart. I needed to learn to stop doing that. If I had used my brain I wouldn't be in this mess to begin with.

"We'll see," I said.

"You're killing me!" he said with exasperation.

I smiled to myself. Driving Fisher crazy was starting to amuse me.

"All right," I said. "I'll call you when I'm back in town and you can show me the way out to your cabin."

He sighed. "Are you sure I can't let Varner in on this? He's practically frantic looking for you."

"Good."

"Come on, Victoria. He's crazy about you."

I sighed. "You can tell him that you've heard from me and I'm all right. But I don't want him near me anymore. I'm too dangerous."

"He's a big boy, he can take care of himself."

"Yeah, well, so can I. Besides, he made his choices."

Fisher sighed again, clearly frustrated. "All right, I'll wait to hear from you."

I ended the call and flopped back on the bed. I started thinking about Taylor Lowe. His confidence intrigued me, as did his bulging pectorals.

I was so freaking tired. I rubbed my face and practically staggered to the shower.

****

"I'm not going to watch. Just do it."

"You want me to layer it around this patch back here. This patch that has grown back around your scar, right? Are you absolutely sure?"

"I'm absolutely sure it's necessary," I said, cringing and closing my eyes.

Lucy, the stylist with pink hair and a pierced nose, went in for the first cut and I nearly burst into tears as she handed me a thick lock of hair that was about two feet long.

"No turning back now," Lucy said.

I stared at it, the tears bubbling up in my eyes. I'd had my long hair for as long as I could remember. It was my favorite part of myself, but it needed to go. I didn't want to make the mistake of being recognized by something I could have changed. Carnie was gunning for me, and she knew I loved my hair.

"You want to keep that?" Lucy asked me.

I nodded and closed my eyes. She wrapped a rubber band around it, handed it to me, and continued clipping.

"And you're sure about the color?" she asked. "Cherries Jubilee is kind of drastic."

"Yes. Make me the reddest head possible. I am henceforth your creation."

"Why all this change?"

I smiled but didn't open my eyes. "It's a very long story."

"Well start talking, we're going to be here awhile. You have the thickest hair I've ever seen."

It felt good to spill my guts to a stranger, and after an agonizing hour and a half, forty five minutes of it under an excruciating hair dryer, I prepared for the big reveal.

Lucy spun the chair around and I opened my eyes.

"My God," I squeaked.

"Do you like it?" Lucy asked hopefully.

Oh! God! No!

My brain screamed in agony at the shaggy, bright-red hair only a couple inches from my scalp, but I managed a smile. "You did a beautiful job."

"I think you'll like it once you get used to it. All you have to do is shake it around with a little product and go. And the color really brings out the gray in your eyes."

I nodded and gulped air.

Oxygen! I needed Oxygen!

Lucy checked that the sides were even, messed it up for the wind-blown look, and I paid and left the salon quickly so as not to burst into tears in front of everyone. Luckily the spa was in the Hyatt, so I didn't have far to go before my breakdown.

I put the key card in my lock and opened the door, tossing my shopping bags into the closet, and continued into the room. I flipped on the light next to the mirror overlooking the room and checked again, running my fingers through the long lock of hair I was holding. I sighed, swallowed, and ran my hand over my head gently.

"What the hell did I do?" I wondered aloud.

Then I saw movement behind me and I spun around quickly.

"My God!" Varner said, standing up from his seat on the bed. "What the hell did you do?"

My heart leapt up into my ears, and I started breathing kind of funny. Then my whole body just kind of slumped back against the dresser.

"I, I just, I cut…I don't know! It's gone, it's all gone!" I stuttered frantically, while he looked on with surprised and tired eyes.

"I look, I look like," my breath came in quick bursts and the more I tried to slow it down, the worse it got, until finally I was able to wail, "I look like Woody Woodpeckerrrrrrr!"

That was it. It was over. The tear dam had broken and my face was flooding.

Huge, open-mouthed crying jag now landing at gate eighteen!

He rushed to me and wrapped his arms around me. "Aw, Darlin,' don't. I didn't say I didn't like it."

I wrapped myself around him and sobbed uncontrollably into his chest and he rubbed my back in big, comforting circles.

"Vic, Sweetheart, it's all right. It's just hair. You know I don't care about that. It just took me by surprise, that's all."

Sometimes men just don't get it.

But God, he felt so wonderful! How could I have left this feeling?

"What are you…how did you…?" My tears wouldn't let me finish a single thought.

"A lot of people think we can't trace prepaid cell phones," he said gently. "But I have few connections. Flash a badge and a lot of people start talking."

I looked up at him slowly, and he took the long lock of hair from me. He looked at it for a moment, sighed, and laid it on the dresser behind me.

"I missed you so much," I sobbed, pulling him tight against me again.

"I missed you too, Girl," he said, his cheek against the top of my head. "Everything went to hell when you left. I couldn't get a decent night's sleep to save my life."

He kissed my tears gently and wiped them away with his soft fingers.

"You're not mad at me are you?" I asked him pathetically.

"How could I be mad at you?" he asked softly, touching my chin. "I practically pushed you out the door."

"I know, but I shouldn't have taken off and made you worry like that."

He took both of my hands and led me to the bed, sitting down and cradling me in his long lap. "It doesn't matter now."

He cuddled me until I stopped sobbing, and we kissed each other over and over, sighing with complete relief that we were together. He kicked off his shoes and scooted back on the bed, pulling me along with him so we were spooned together.

"I'm so glad you're here," I whispered as he wrapped me in his arms and snuggled against my back.

"Hum too," he said against my hair, just before he started snoring.

****

I'm not sure how long we slept. It seemed like every few hours we would wake up, say a few things to each other, and then burrow back down for a few more hours. I think at some point he got up and got undressed, and somehow I ended up in my underwear, but I'm not sure how that happened either. I guess I didn't realize how tired I was until I felt completely secure in his arms.

In the morning, I think, I scooted out from under his arm and went to the bathroom. I flipped the light on and caught a look at myself in the mirror. The blinding, red hair screaming at me made me physically jump back.

Ugh! Reality! Leave me alone!

I glanced at the clock on my way back to bed and it was five in the morning. By my calculations, I had slept twelve hours and he had slept even longer. I laid back down, preparing for another twelve, when I felt soft fingers running down my back.

"What time is checkout?" he asked.

"Noon," I said, rolling over to look at him. "Tomorrow."

He grinned. "We have another day?"

"Yep."

"To lay here, naked and pleasuring each other?"

"Mm hm," I said, kissing his chest.

"I must have died and gone to heaven."

I sighed with absolute bliss. "I hope heaven isn't anything like Chicago. I'm hoping to have a Ferrari when I get there and I'll need more room."

He chuckled and ran his fingers up my back gently. "How's the shower?"

"Very nice."

"Let's try it out."

What was I gonna say? No? I'm not that crazy!

****

We sat smiling ridiculously at each other over our room service breakfast after a long, hot shower and some long, hot sex. He was wearing the hotel robe that was way too short for him, but it just added to the charm of him, and his wet bed- head and sleepy eyes.

"I don't think I've ever slept that long in my life," he said, chewing his bacon.

"You must have needed it."

He nodded. "I can't seem to sleep without you anymore. Hell, I don't think I ever could."

"Nice to know," I said.

"I'm just glad you're okay," he said looking at me. "God, I can't get used to the hair though."

"I know, I'm sorry," I moaned, running my hand over my head. "I'll color it when this is all over and it's already growing."

"Don't apologize, Darlin'. I know why you did it. Beats wearing a mask."

I nodded and cut into my Belgian waffle.

"Can I ask you something?" he said.

"Anything you want."

"What are you doing?"

I looked at him for a few seconds. "Um, well, cutting my waffle and now I'm probably going to eat some…"

He exhaled and smiled. "You know what I mean."

"Sorry," I said. "I'm not sure I get it."

"Fisher told me you've been doing some research."

I licked my lips and scanned his face. "He's told you more than that, hasn't he?"

He nodded and pursed his lips. "How did you get in to see Fletcher?"

I chewed my waffle and debated with myself about what exactly I should tell him.

"Well, I talked to the Warden and he let me in."

"I talked to the Warden too," he said after sipping his coffee.

"And what did he say?"

"He said the same thing."

I wiped my mouth on my napkin. "And you don't believe either one of us?"

"Seems a little too easy to me."

"Easy?" I asked. "And what do you mean by that?"

He shrugged again and took a bite of his bacon.

I put my fork down. "All right, ask me. I know you're dying to."

"Okay," he said, looking me dead in the eye. "Did you sleep with him?"

"No!"

He pursed his lips again, nodded, and went back to his bacon.

"Oral sex works just as well," I said.

The bacon dropped from his mouth and his eyes rose to mine.

I laughed. "Kidding! I'm totally kidding. Lighten up."

He exhaled a laugh and rolled his eyes. "Well, I never quite know what to expect out of you."

I took his hand in both of mine and kissed his fingers. "You don't have to worry about that with me, okay? I'm crazy in love with you. There is no way in hell I'm going to screw that up."

He continued smiling. "You're in love with me?"

"I have been since I first laid eyes on you."

"Hm," was all he said. Then his eyes dropped to his plate and he continued eating.

I blinked once. Twice.

Oh, God! No! He didn't say it back.

Maybe he didn't feel that way anymore. Maybe he didn't even like me.

"Took me a couple minutes," he said.

I blinked again and shook my head. "Sorry?"

"I said it took me a couple minutes," he said, slowly grinning at me, "to fall in love with you."

I smiled and sighed with relief. "Just a couple minutes, huh?"

"Well, you were kind of bloody and delirious when I first saw you, you know."

"Yeah, and I still think you're an angel."

He grinned and his ears turned red. "I'm sorry I didn't trust you with the Warden. I just don't understand how you got in when Fisher called the guy a couple weeks ago and he wouldn't let us see Fletcher."

"Fisher?" I laughed. "Fisher is tactless. He probably tried to bully his way in. I told Warden Lowe what I wanted and why, and he let me in. End of story."

One of his eyes narrowed. "You charmed him."

"I suppose so, yes."

"You're very good at that."

"I guess, but it got me what I wanted."

"Listen," he said. "I appreciate what you're doing and why you're doing it, but you're treading on thin ice here. I really worry about you getting into situations like you did with Fletcher. You could have gotten into big trouble."

I nodded. "I know, and I appreciate your worrying about me. But I have to tell you, I'm having one hell of a time."

He chuckled. "Just be careful, you little hellcat."

"As a wise man I know once said, I'm always careful."

****

CHAPTER TWENTY-FOUR

"It's not much," Fisher said putting the key in the lock. "But you should be safe here for a while. I'm not sure I could even find it without a map."

We stepped into the cabin and were greeted by the smell of mold and fish. He flipped on the light to reveal a pleasantly furnished living area.

"It's really great," Varner said. "Thanks for letting us use it, Tom."

"No problem. The couch folds out if you, well, you probably won't need that, but…" He rolled his eyes. "This is so strange. I never would have thought that you, Jason Varner, of all people would be shtupping a witness."

"I'm not shtupping…I'm…she's not just a…ugh," Varner dropped his head and blushed.

"He loves me," I said with a grin.

Fisher grinned back. "No argument here."

I put my duffle on the couch and looked around. It had a small kitchenette with an ancient refrigerator, a microwave, a few cabinets and a sink. He led us up a staircase leading to a rather large bedroom that overlooked the living area. The bedroom had a queen sized bed, a dresser and a sink. Off of the bedroom there was a tiny bathroom that had no door with a tiny shower and a toilet. I had to chuckle at the thought of six-five Jason Varner folding himself into the pint-sized shower that was barely big enough for me. He was going to have to squat and wash in sections.

"Guess I'll be showering at the station," Varner said behind me.

I laughed. "I may join you."

"Use the place as long as you need to," Fisher said, handing the keys to Varner. "There's a Ford truck parked around the back. The keys are hanging on a hook in the kitchen. It's there if you need it."

"Is this okay with you?" Varner asked me.

I nodded, sat down on the bed and tried the mattress.

Lumpy. Perfect. I should have stayed in Chicago.

"Well, I better get home," Fisher said. "Give me a call if you need anything."

Varner shook his hand. "Thanks again, Tom."

"You bet."

He waved, grumbled a good bye, and left.

"I'm going to move my car around and bring in the groceries," Varner said. "I'll be back in a minute."

I flipped on the TV in the living area and again regretted leaving the comfort of the Hyatt.

Three channels. Terrific!

I had just settled on Jerry Springer when Varner slid the door open with his foot.

"Help me out here, will ya?" he said, holding up a bag of groceries.

I grabbed the bags from him and carried them to the table in the kitchenette as he went out the porch and grabbed a couple more. I opened the refrigerator to put the eggs in and almost dropped them.

A decayed fish on a blue plate was staring at me.

"Jesus."

I grabbed the garbage bags out of the groceries, picked up the dead fish by the tail and threw it in. Then I tossed in the plate. Then I wished I could toss in the whole refrigerator.

"Ugh," Varner said, coming up behind me. "Nice."

"Can we go home now?" I whined.

"Now come on, you said you'd make the best of it."

I poked through the kitchen for some sort of household cleaner, but all I could find was a prehistoric looking bottle of Windex. I opened it, poured the contents into the refrigerator, and started scrubbing with a paper towel. At least it was something with ammonia. After about ten minutes of scrubbing, it was much cleaner and smelled a little better.

"That smell will never be completely gone," I said. "I don't even want to look in the freezer."

"Fisher said his ex-wife didn't even fight him for this place in the divorce," Varner called from the living room. "None of them did actually."

"I can see why," I muttered. "Wait a minute, how many wives has he had?"

Varner smirked. "Four, I think. There might have been a fifth one, but no wait, I'm wrong. He married one of them twice."

I rolled my eyes, put the eggs in the fridge and finished putting the groceries away. Against my better judgment, I opened the freezer door. Thankfully, I found nothing but a tray of ice stuck amongst a mountain of frost and was very relieved. I stuck a few beer bottles in there figuring I was going to need them.

I finished up and sat down next to Varner on the couch. Something poked me in the back and I reached behind me and pulled a fossilized corn chip out of the back cushion. Varner chuckled. I rolled my eyes to the ceiling, flicked the chip across the room, and looked out the window.

"Sorry," he said.

"It's okay," I said, laying my head on his shoulder. "Thanks for coming with me."

He kissed my forehead. "I couldn't leave you alone out here. It would make me nuts. If I had realized that sooner maybe you wouldn't have felt the need to take off."

"At least we have a nice view of the lake."

"You want to go for a walk and look around?" he asked.

"Sure."

We walked around the lake shore and he found a flat rock and skipped it across the smooth surface of the water. The breeze was perfect and the chirping of the birds lifted my mood considerably.

"It is nice here," I said quietly.

We walked out on the boat dock and looked out at the lake. It was smooth and blue, and every once in a while a fish jumped excitedly. Varner took a long breath and stretched.

"I could get used to it out here."

I poked him in the ribs. "Don't you dare."

****

We sat at the table in the kitchenette going over our respective notes for the case. I flipped back a couple pages and chewed my thumb nail.

"What's K?" I asked him.

"Hm?" he said, obviously not paying attention to me.

"K," I said a little louder. "Fletcher said Carnie bought some K from him once."

He lowered the piece of paper he was reading and looked at me. "K is Ketamine. It's usually used in veterinary hospitals, but it's also a pretty popular date rape drug."

"I've heard about it recently," I said. "Somewhere. I can't place…"

"It's what Deborah used to kill herself," he said, reaching for my notes quickly. "Jesus!"

I stared at him. "You think Carnie might have whacked her?"

He spit out a laugh. "Whacked her? Who are you now, Tony Soprano?"

"You know what I mean."

"I don't know if Deborah was 'whacked'," he said, doing the little, rabbit gesture for the quotation marks. "Forensics wasn't called into her apartment because the Coroner ruled it a suicide at the scene. And I'm sure the landlord has the place cleaned out by now."

"But isn't the fact that she bought some Ketamine from Fletcher enough for a warrant to search Carnie's place?"

"I won't get a warrant based on any investigating you did," he said, tossing my notebook back.

"Why not?"

"It wasn't exactly obtained using legal means."

"Evidence is evidence, why does it matter where it came from?"

"It does," he said. "Let's just leave it at that."

I sighed. "Well, what did Deborah's suicide note say?"

He rubbed his face. "She apologized for running out on me. She said she was confused. She didn't like the way her life turned out, so she decided to end it."

I bit my lip. "Carnie would have been more dramatic than that."

"The handwriting matched Deborah's anyway," he said. "We can't finger Carnie for this. Deborah could have gotten Ketamine anywhere. And if we don't have the bottle it came from, there's no way to trace it."

I flipped through my notes again. "They found evidence of a meth lab at Fletcher's place right?"

He nodded. "He was cooking something. According to the reports from the scene, there was residue all over the house."

"But they didn't find any manufactured meth or the chemicals for it?"

"Nope, and they only found a couple ounces on him," he said. "Not enough for possession with intent."

"I'll bet he stashed it all at Carnie's house."

He scratched his head and rubbed the back of his neck. "It's possible, but it's the same argument all over again. No judge is going to give me a warrant based on a hunch of yours."

I smiled at him. "I wouldn't need a warrant."

"No!" he said, dropping his hands on the table. "Absolutely not."

"I could be in and out of there in five minutes. Then I could call in and place an anonymous tip."

"No!" he said, pounding his fist on the table. "You're not doing it! If she's got a meth lab set up at her house, just walking in there could be toxic!"

I felt my left eyebrow rising at him.

"We're questioning her tomorrow. If we determine there is probable cause, we'll get a warrant," he said, calming down slightly. "That's it. End of discussion."

"Fine," I said, slapping my notebook closed. "I'm going to bed."

"Now don't sulk."

"I'm not sulking, I'm tired."

I got up and walked past him, but he grabbed my hand and pulled me down on his lap.

"It's called breaking and entering, Darlin'," he said, kissing my cheek. "Laws are there for a reason. If we break laws, it doesn't matter what we find, we're screwed before we even have a case."

He cuddled me close. "You've got to trust me on this. I've been doing it for a long time."

I nodded and attempted a smile. "I said it's fine. I'm done."

He squinted at me. "Why am I having a hard time believing you?"

I kissed his lips gently. "I don't know. I'm a good girl."

He broke into a grin. "Excuse me?"

"Well, mostly."

****

CHAPTER TWENTY-FIVE

"Vic?"

I felt a warm hand on my face and soft lips on my forehead. I opened my eyes and gazed up at Varner. He was up and dressed in jeans and a blue button-up shirt. How could I have forgotten how incredible he looked in a pair of jeans?

"Darlin', I've got to go in to the office."

"Okay, is everything all right?"

"Well, not really."

I sat up quickly. "What? What's wrong?"

"Fisher went to pick up Carnie this morning and she was gone."

"Gone? Just gone?"

"Yeah, no sign of her at the office or her house."

I rubbed my face sleepily while my brain absorbed the news.

"Can you think of anywhere else she might be?" he asked.

I thought for a minute. "Well, you'll want to check the paper for any scheduled craft shows and garage sales. And antique shops. Oh, and her doctor's office."

"There were no papers or mail piled up at her house, but they're not being held. She must be around or in contact with someone. Then again, she may have just skipped last night or this morning."

"She's pretty close with an old couple that lives next door to her. You might check with them," I suggested.

"Okay, I'll do that."

"I'm coming with you," I announced, pulling the covers off my legs.

"No, you're not," he said, flipping the covers back over me. "You're staying right here."

"Jason, I'm coming."

Flip, covers off.

"You're not coming."

He threw the covers over my head and got up from the bed.

"You need someone watching your back," I told him, struggling out of the bed. "She's crazy!"

"I've got an entire police force at my back."

I stifled a snort. Fat lot of good they would do, especially if he didn't use them.

He held my shoulders and looked at me, his eyes serious and almost severe. "You're not to leave this cabin. You understand me?"

No, I didn't understand him, but I also knew there was no sense arguing with him.

"All right, you big mule," I said reluctantly, giving him a light punch in the shoulder.

"I mean it, Vic."

"I know you mean it," I said, meeting his eyes again and trying to look as serious as he did. His gaze softened and he smiled gently.

"I'll be back as soon as I can."

He leaned forward and kissed me softly. Then he turned and left the room with me close at his heels.

"You keep my forty-five with you, and your phone close," he said when we got downstairs. He holstered another pistol and clicked his cell phone on to his belt. "I'll call you with any updates."

"Jason," I started to say something, but thought better of it.

"What?"

"Just, be vigilant."

He smiled and walked over to me. He held my face in his hands and gave me one of his long, lingering kisses that I absolutely loved. I wanted to grab him and hold him. I wanted to wrap myself around him and not let him leave.

"I'm always vigilant," he said. "Don't worry."

I grabbed the front of his shirt and held it in my fist. "I'm always worried."

He kissed me again and tried to back away, but I held his shirt. He looked down at my fist.

"It's going to be okay, Vic."

I loosened my grip and he walked toward the door. He stopped with his hand on the knob and turned to me.

"I love you," he said.

"I love you, too," I squeaked, another stupid lump forming in my throat.

He grinned, grabbed his brown, leather jacket and locked the door behind him.

"And I'll be damned if I'm hanging around here," I said to the door.

I climbed the stairs and jumped into the tiny shower.

****

I jogged around the cabin, hopped in, and started up Fisher's old truck. It growled and snarled and stalled. It was like trying to get a bear out of hibernation before it was ready. I stomped my foot on the gas and tried it again. It growled and idled, and stayed running after a few loud coughs. I backed out of the driveway and started down the winding, dusty road that led to the highway. I noticed that the truck was nearly out of gas, so I pulled in to the closest gas station and filled up. I went in to the station, grabbed a pair of sunglasses and a ball cap, and paid at the counter. Not a very good disguise, but it might distort my features enough when looking through the dirty glass of the truck. I tucked my new red mop of hair up under the hat and put the sunglasses on. I checked myself in the rear view mirror.

Not perfect, but adequate.

Once I got into town, I drove past the police station to see what was shaking. I saw Varner's Tahoe and Fisher's Corolla, but there was no sign of either of them. They were inside, probably discussing what to do with me next. Bomb shelter? Basement? The highest tower in a castle with a moat and dragon?

Then I smiled thinking about Varner clanking around in a suit of armor, coming to rescue me. How was he going to get up to the tower? I cut my hair so he couldn't climb it. He'd have to use the stairs, which meant he'd have to slay the dragon. Or if Carnie found me she may have given me a poison apple and I would be asleep in the tower and he'd have to kiss me to wake me up. And we'd ride off on his…Tahoe.

Okay, daydreaming was once again getting me nowhere. And the last thing I needed was Varner to catch me sitting in Fisher's old truck in a daze and grinning like a fool.

Perhaps it would behoove me to drive past Carnie's house while Varner was still at the station. I figured there would be black and whites lining the street looking for her, but there was nothing. I drove around the block three or four more times just to be sure no one was coming. I parked a block away and jogged up the street to Carnie's house. It was a powder-blue, bi-level with three bedrooms, a detached garage and it was in bad need of a paint job. I stalked around the house and then back around the garage. She was manic about her garden and it looked like it hadn't been weeded or watered in a couple days. I went up to her back door, opened the screen and peeked through the window. There was a jar of pickles on the counter and a half-made sandwich next to it. Looked like tuna.

She obviously left in a hurry.

"Excuse me?" I heard from behind and to the right of me. I spun around and saw the old lady next door waving at me over her fence.

Shit!

"Hi," I waved back. "I was, uh, supposed to meet Carnie here. Have you seen her?"

"No, honey, she left yesterday afternoon."

I negotiated the rickety stairs headed down to the back yard and walked over to the fence.

"Did she tell you where she was going?" I asked politely.

"Sanibel, Florida. She was going down there to go shelling," the old lady smiled.

Shelling, of course, but she forgot her sandwich.

"We're watching her cat for her and picking up her mail," she said. "I'm sorry, my name is Ida Petty."

"Oh, I see," I said, looking around. "I must have gotten the date wrong."

"Well, she did seem to be in a big hurry when she left," Miss Petty said. "She was in quite a state."

When wasn't she?

"Have you noticed any changes in the way she has been behaving lately?" I asked.

"Well, now that you mention it, yes I have. I'm sorry dear, what did you say your name was?"

"I didn't," I said smiling. "I'm, uh…"

Shit! Shitty, shit, shit, shit!

I faked a sneeze and then broke into a coughing spell while I tried to think up a good name.

"I'm sorry," I croaked through the coughs. "I have bad allergies this time of year."

"Oh, I know what you mean, honey, my eyes are watering from sun up to sun down."

"So, what kind of changes have you noticed in Carnie?" I choked out, hoping she would forget her question.

"Well, she has lost a lot of weight, hasn't she? And then about a week ago she was working in her garden and she was really agitated and talking a mile a minute to herself. I mean, she's always been a talker, but she was almost out of control."

Meth! There has to be meth in that house!

"Yes, I've noticed she has been a little out of control as well," I said. "Well, thank you for your time ma'am. I'll be going now."

"I'll tell her you asked after her Miss…"

"Um, King," I said the first name that popped into my mind.

"King? My goodness. That's my maiden name. I wonder if we're related at all," she said.

Out of every name in the blasted universe!

"Oh, I doubt that, most of my relatives are in Tennessee," I said as I backed away.

She nodded. "Oh, well, have a nice day."

"You too."

I jogged down the driveway and back to the truck just in time to see Varner's Tahoe pull up in front of Carnie's house. I dove quickly into the truck, started it, and floored it heading up the street. I took a peek at the rearview mirror and he was headed up the front walk to her house.

Whew!

"I'm not cut out for this shit," I said to my reflection.

****

CHAPTER TWENTY-SIX

One close call a day was all I could handle, so I drove back to the cabin and pretended to be the good little prisoner who hadn't left the house all day. After several hours of cleaning the cabin, that included scrubbing the bathroom from top to bottom, dusting the antlers hanging above the fire place and scrubbing out the cabinets in the kitchen, I dozed on the couch and waited for Varner to arrive. I awoke to a screaming match on the TV. Apparently someone had just found out who the baby-daddy was on Maury Povich. I picked up the cell phone next to me and looked at the time. It read six-thirty.

He was late.

Oh God, Varner, don't be late. Please, please don't be late!

The phone rang and I answered it quickly.

"Vicki, it's Fisher."

"Hey, what's happening?"

"Have you heard from Varner?" he asked, with a touch of concern in his voice.

"No, come to think of it, I haven't heard from him all day."

Silence.

Oh God, Fisher, don't be silent. Please, please don't be silent!

"Do you think something's wrong?" I asked, trying to contain myself.

"Well, he went out to O'Leary's place to look around and no one has heard from him since."

I gasped and my heart rate shot up.

"You tried his cell right?" I asked, unable to disguise the panic. "He always has his cell on him. You tried it right?"

"Don't panic, Vicki, I'll check it out and get back to you, okay? Maybe he was staking her out and fell asleep. He said he didn't have a very good night last night."

The phone beeped in my ear. "I've got another call. I'll call you back, okay?"

"Yep."

I hit the talk button for the other line. "Hello?"

"Vic?" Varner said frantically. "Vic? Is that you?"

"Thank God, are you all right?" I asked him.

"No," he said, sounding more desperate. "Please, don't do anything she tells you. Call Fisher! Don't do anything…." his words trailed off.

"What!" I screamed, popping off the couch. "Jason! Where are you?"

No answer.

"Jason!" I yelled.

"Don't listen to him, Vicki. You always do what I tell you," the woman's voice said.

The icy gust of recognition blew up my spine and I shivered.

"Carnie?" I asked, trying to keep my voice from shaking. "Where is he? What did you do to him?"

"Nothing, yet," she said slyly.

I took a deep breath and composed myself. She obviously wanted to cause hysteria and I wasn't going to give her the satisfaction. No, I was calm, cool, collected…

And if she hurts one hair on his head I will hunt her down and blow her brains out of her head with the biggest damn gun I can find!

Okay, some hysteria certainly couldn't be avoided at this point.

"What do you want, Carnie?" I said calmly.

"I just want to talk. I miss you," she said.

"Okay, let him go and we'll talk."

"Him?" she said. I heard a slapping sound. "He's fine. He's just a little puppy. Yes you are, aren't you? He looks awfully sleepy though."

She was high as hell.

"Don't!" I started to yell, but thought better of it. "Don't do anything silly now. You don't want to hurt him do you?"

"He took you from me!" she wailed.

I heard another slapping sound and I heard him grunt.

Biggest damn gun I can find! Maybe even a freaking cannon!

"Where are you?" I asked her, trying not to sound panic-stricken. "I want to talk. Tell me where you are."

"Oh, I'm home, Vicki, you remember where that is?" she laughed.

"You're at your house?"

"Noooooo," her voice trailed off to a high-pitched squeal. "Not that home. And not the one that burned up. I'm at the home of the home away from home."

She giggled some more, and I realized she probably didn't even know where she was.

"Listen, Carnie, can you look out the window and tell me what you see?" I asked, hoping to get an idea of her location.

"It's dark," she whispered.

Dark? It wasn't dark outside.

"It's dark where you are?" I asked.

"It's dark out the window at the home," she laughed hysterically again and I heard another slap.

I tried to think of a place with dark windows. Maybe an old building that was boarded up?

No, she said home.

"What else do you see, Carnie?" I asked. "Tell me what's in the room."

"It's dusty," she said. "And it stinks."

"What does it smell like?"

She took a long sniff and giggled. "But he smells nice."

That's right bitch! And he better smell nice when I find him, or I will cut you into so many pieces they won't be able to find…

Focus, Vic!

"Carnie?" I squeaked. "Please, tell me more. Tell me where you are."

"There's a red window over there," she slurred. "Why? I don't know why."

Then I realized where she was. My Uncle Pete was a photographer and he sometimes used the basement for a dark room. The windows were blacked out.

Except for the one with red glass.

She was at my mom's house, which used to be my home.

Jesus.

"Listen, Carnie, I want to talk, okay?" I said as sweetly as I could. "I really, really want to talk."

"Shhhhh," she said. "He's sleeping."

Oh Jesus! Oh God! Did she knock him out? Did she give him something? Was he bleeding?

"Okay, we'll talk quietly," I said, wiping the tears away. "I'll be there in a little while okay?"

"When?" she moaned. "When will you be here?"

I looked at the fish clock on the wall. It was six-forty PM. I remembered a clock in the darkroom that glowed red in the dark so Uncle Pete could see what time it was while he was working.

All right, Carnie, you're acting like a child, I'll treat you like a child.

"Do you see the red clock on the wall?" I asked her.

"Ooh, yes, I noticed it earlier. It glows. I'll turn the light off so I can see it glow."

"I'll be there when the big hand is on the six okay? You watch that clock. When the big hand is on the six, you look for me, okay?"

"Okay."

"And, don't do anything until I get there. Just sit down where you are and watch the clock and wait for me, okay?"

"Will you bring ice cream?"

She disconnected.

I ran into the kitchen, grabbed the keys to the truck off the hook, holstered Varner's forty-five, grabbed an extra magazine for it, and clipped my cell phone to my waist band. I took Varner's denim jacket off the wall hook, figuring it would hide the gun better, and rolled up the sleeves. I jogged to the truck and started the motor. It growled loudly. As I backed it up, I called Fisher.

"Yeah," he answered.

"She's got him," I said. "They're at my mom's house. I think she's got him in the basement and she may have shot him up with something."

"Wait, hold on, what?"

I took a breath and continued driving down the dirt road past the cabin. "Just listen, okay? I got a call from

Varner's cell phone. At first it was him, but then Carnie got on the line, she was completely incoherent, but I got it out of her that she has him in the basement at my mother's house."

"Jesus, what a nut case," Fisher said. "What's the address?"

"Thirteen twenty-two west Sycamore," I said, turning left on the road that intersects with the highway. "I'm on my way."

"Let us handle it, Vicki," Fisher said.

"Yeah, you guys were handling it and look where it got us!" I yelled. "If you had let me help you to begin with I probably could have talked her into…"

Okay, Vic, now isn't a good time. You can tear him a new one later.

"She's crazy, she's on something, and she is begging to talk to me," I said as calmly as I could. "I'm on my way. Don't do anything until I get there. If she's got his gun…" The words caught in my throat. I couldn't think about that now. Jason needed me now.

"All right," he said. "I'll alert state police to let you go if they see you on the highway. Drive as fast as you can."

I disconnected, wiped the tears off my face, and floored it.

****

As I rounded the corner on my mom's block, I noticed several cars parked with several men sitting in each car. I also saw a large white panel van in front of the house. Then I saw Fisher's black Corolla. He opened the door, got out, flicked his cigarette, and leaned against the car. I parked about a half a block away and ran to him.

"What's happening?" I asked. "Has anyone gone in? Have you heard anything from inside?"

"No," he opened the back door of his car. "Get in and suit up. Put it on under your shirt."

I hopped in the car and found a Kevlar vest waiting for me. I slipped out of my t-shirt, velcro'ed the vest on as tight as I could, and threw my t-shirt back on. I honestly didn't care who saw me through the windows. I didn't have time for pride. But my boobs felt like they were going to explode out my armpits.

I opened the door and got out as I pulled the denim jacket over me. Fisher took me by the shoulders and looked me over.

"Looks good," he said. "Come with me."

We headed for the panel van where they wired me for sound.

"I wasn't expecting all this," I said.

"We want you to get a confession out of her," Fisher said.

"She is so high on something, I'm not sure that will be possible," I said as a guy I didn't know duct taped a wire to my hip and stuck a transmitter in my back pocket.

"Oh, I have a feeling she'll tell you anything," Fisher said.

I knew he was right. If she would tell me about pulling a bandage off her anal cyst when she was sober, she would probably tell me about a couple little murders when she was high.

The sound guy ran a wire up my shirt and clipped the microphone to the Kevlar vest.

"Say something," he said.

"Test, test," I said. "Four score and seven beers ago…"

"Sound is good."

"Okay," Fisher said, taking me by the shoulders again. "Don't be a hero. If it's too much for you to handle just say 'take down' and we'll come in and apprehend her. We've already got her on breaking and entering, and assault and kidnap of a police officer." He handed me a set of hand cuffs and the keys to them. "Good luck."

I put the cuffs and keys in my pocket, took a deep breath and walked up the steps to the side door of the house. I inserted my key and unlocked the door.

"Here goes nothing," I whispered. "Or everything."

****

CHAPTER TWENTY-SEVEN

"Carnie?" I called.

Silence. I hated silence. I could make up anything I wanted if it was silent, and I didn't want to make up what she might have done to him.

I tiptoed to the basement door, off the dining area, feeling behind my hip for the gun. I took it out of the holster, unlocked the safety, and held the gun in front of me as I descended the stairs.

"Carnie?" I called again.

Nothing.

Mom's house had one of those basements that went on forever in a dark, dusty maze like her own Underground Railroad. Carnie could be anywhere in the Underground Railroad. There was another entrance to the basement from the back of the house where Mom had her washer and dryer. I decided to check there first. I kept my back against the filthy brick walls and scuttled my way to the other entrance. I had a moment of "Victoria, you are completely insane," as I slid through the doorway of the laundry area.

I saw him there, upright but slumped against the washing machine and handcuffed to the water pipes. He had a cut above his left eye and his lip was swollen, but he was breathing. My angel was hurting and all I could think was, it should have been me. If he had let me do what I wanted in the first place, it probably would have been me. I holstered the gun, ran to him and fumbled with the hand cuff keys Fisher had given me.

"Ugh," he grunted. "No."

"Jason, it's me," I whispered. "I'm going to get you out of here."

I couldn't get the damn key to fit into the cuff lock. When I finally got it into the tiny hole, it wouldn't turn.

"It won't fit," he whispered in a moment of coherence. "Find mine."

"Where are they?"

He swallowed and his eyes rolled back in his head. "Jacket..."

I scanned what I could see in the dim light, but there was nothing that looked like a jacket.

Carnie was in the dark room when she talked to me. Through the door to the right.

God, please help me!

I scuttled over to the door and slammed my back against the wall as I grabbed the gun on my belt. Then I hurled myself around the corner with the gun in front of me. Nothing. I squeaked out a sob and opened the door to the dark room slowly.

"Please," I whispered. "Please, please, please."

Nothing. Only the red darkness greeted me. I flipped on the light switch next to the door and saw his leather jacket in a heap on the floor. I lunged for it and fumbled around for the keys, checking all the pockets.

No keys. No phone.

No gun!

Maybe he still had it on him.

No, she had it.

Oh Lord, help me, please!

I spun around quickly, looking for something, anything that would get him free. I saw a small hatchet in the corner and went for it. I'd cut through the pipe if it was the only way. Then my peripheral vision caught something. I turned my head slowly and saw it.

Carnie's navy blue jacket was hanging neatly on a hook by the door.

I ran to it, grabbed the keys and phone out of the left pocket and sprinted back to him.

I got one of the cuffs open and unhooked him from the pipes. He slid off the washing machine into my arms. He was so heavy, but somehow I was able to support him and I tried to get him to the floor gently. At that point I probably could have lifted a car off him.

"Jason?" I asked, squatting next to him. "Jason, can you hear me? Oh God, please, answer me."

I took his face in my hands and his eyes fluttered open.

"Vic?" he whispered.

"Thank God! Yes, baby, it's me," I said, quietly kissing his forehead. "Are you all right?"

He opened his eyes wide.

"Behind you," he whispered.

I stood up, spun around and came face to face with her. Her eyes were mascara-blackened and her face was gaunt and pale. She had on a black wig that was askew and looked like it was on backwards, and she was grinning like the devil she was.

"C….Carnie," I stammered.

"Hello," she said, lifting Varner's pistol to my face and pulling wig off. "Nice to see you, Vicki. And I just love your hair."

She reached to touch me but I stepped back quickly.

"What are you doing, Carnie?" I asked, thinking I could reason with her. "Stop this, please."

"But I need to talk to you," she said. "I need you to…I need you."

Varner tried to sit up but fell back stiffly.

"What did you give him?" I asked her gently.

"Just some Ketamine, he'll be fine," she said. "Unless, unless I kill him." She pointed the gun at him. "Should I kill him, Vicki?"

I slowly knelt down in front of him.

"You'll have to kill me too," I said. "I'll wrap myself around him and cover him from head to, uh, knee if I have to."

"Vic, no," Varner whispered. He scooted back against the washing machine and sat up breathing heavily.

I turned to look at him.

"Don't!" Carnie screamed. "Don't you look at him! You look at me, now! Me!"

"All right, all right," I said calmly. "Can we go upstairs maybe and talk about this? I'll make us some tea. I'm sure Mom has…"

"No!" she interrupted. "We're fine here!" She shook the gun at me. "Step away from him."

I stood up, taking care to stay in front of him, and took a step toward the gun. "No! I'm done with this stupid fucking game! You say what you have to say or you end this right now!"

She began crying. "Him! First he took her and then he took you away from me!"

"Took who?" I asked gently.

"Debbie," she sobbed. "He took my Debbie away. I loved her and he took her away."

I took another step toward her, the gun nearly against my chest. "Carnie, please put the gun down and let's talk about this."

She lowered the gun to the floor, but didn't drop it.

I looked down. The gun was black. Her shoes were black. Black patent leather shoes.

My mind flashed like a camera and I was there again…

I lay on the floor in the stairwell, on the landing. The back of my head is wet and I reach back to feel it. A sticky, thick substance covers my fingers, but it looks black to me…

It hurts…the light…

What the hell is that smell? I know it from working in surgery…it's coppery…

Animal blood?

No. Mine. My blood!

My head is bleeding!

Above me is a light, and then shadow.

Something against my cheek.

A black, patent-leather shoe.

She's nudging me to see if I'm alive.

Navy blue pants and jacket.

Carnie wearing a black wig.

Carnie wearing big sunglasses.

Carnie leaning over me.

"Why are you here? You shouldn't be here."

Carnie pointing the gun at my head, pulling the trigger.

"Click…Click…"

Carnie kneeling down and picking up my purse.

"You…you were going to kill me," I realized aloud. "Why?"

"You were going to tell that idiot Paul everything."

"Tell him what? I didn't see anything!" I said loudly. "I didn't even know you were there!"

"I'm sorry, please don't be mad at me," she wailed.

"You ruined my life, and you don't want me to be mad at you?" I yelled. "Are you out of your freaking mind?"

She wept uncontrollably into her hand.

"Who killed Judge Weinhardt?" I asked her, trying to calm myself.

"George," Carnie sobbed. She wiped tears from her face. "But I was there. And he wouldn't let him go. Stephen was my only friend left, but Weinhardt wouldn't listen to reason. I had to get rid of him so he couldn't hurt anymore people."

"Why did you put the gun in my purse?"

"I'm sorry," she wailed again. "I didn't know what else to do. You weren't supposed to be there. I had to do something with it. George was supposed to take it with him, but he dropped it. It wasn't supposed to happen this way."

My knees were weakening and I looked around for something to lean on. But she couldn't see me weak. I wouldn't allow it!

"Stephen Fletcher?" I asked her, regaining the gentle tone of her confidant, the tone I used with her accomplice. "Stephen was your friend."

"Yes," she said. "The judge said he deserved to be in prison. He ruined so many lives with his business. But his work helped people. He helped people see."

"His drugs, his meth," I said. "He took your pain away, didn't he?"

"Stephen helped me. He showed me with so many things, he showed me what it was like to feel free. The pain was gone, everything was gone." She sobbed on to the sleeve of her blouse.

"You've been using awhile haven't you?" I asked, trying to sound concerned.

"A month, a day, a year, it doesn't mean anything anymore. That's what he showed me."

"You killed Detective Raymer," I said. "You had to, didn't you?"

She nodded. "He ruined my life that night. He was going to tell everyone about me, about my life without pain."

"So you killed him," I said, knowing that she had to say it or the taped confession wouldn't mean anything. "You had to shoot him, didn't you?"

"Yes, I had to kill him," she sobbed. "I knew you would understand."

"And you've been housing Fletcher's drugs for him, haven't you?"

"In my basement," she said nodding.

"So all those letters you got from him…"

She nodded.

"What happened to Debbie?" I asked.

"I loved her so much. She was everything to me."

Sisterly love?

No, this was something else.

"Ev…everything?" I asked. "What do you mean everything?"

"My best friend. My life," she gasped. "My love."

I blinked and swallowed a gag.

Ugh!

"Debbie wasn't your sister was she?" I asked.

"No," she sobbed harder. "She was my life. I loved her so much."

"So, you and she were together. You were a…couple…for a long time?"

She nodded. "Yes, almost six years. Until he came and took her." She raised the gun again and wept. "She left me. She was all I had and she left me."

All right, I wasn't a homophobe in any sense. I had many gay friends, male and female, and I think I even had a cousin who was a lesbian. Fine! Beautiful! Whatever! And hell, we have all had our fantasies, right? I mean, I probably wouldn't turn down Beyonce, or maybe Jennifer Aniston. And whatever a person does in his or her bedroom with the partner of his or her choice is their own business.

But, the thought of Carnie O'Leary being intimate with anyone made me want to…

I heard retching behind me as Varner vomited on to the floor.

Hm! Apparently it's a universal reaction.

"Jason, baby, hold on," I said quietly, starting to turn again.

"Don't!" Carnie screamed at me again.

"Please let me help him!" I begged her. "He needs to get out of here. He needs a doctor."

"Step away from him, Vicki!" she yelled.

"Wait. Please just wait a minute."

She continued sobbing. "I'm tired of waiting. That's all I've been doing is waiting."

"If you loved Debbie so much, why did you kill her?"

"I didn't!" she screamed. "She killed herself. She killed herself because of him!"

Oops! Okay, so, a girl can't be right all the time.

"It wasn't his fault," I said calmly. "She wasn't well, Carnie. She needed help."

Varner coughed and gagged behind me. I started to turn toward him just as Carnie stumbled, but caught herself against the wall.

"You love him?" she asked me a little too coolly. "Don't you, Debbie?"

I took another step toward her. "Carnie, I'm Vicki, Vicki Childs."

Her eyes were swimming. Her touch with reality was completely gone.

"Debbie, my Debbie, why did you leave?"

"Carnie, please. Look at me."

"Say you love him!" she growled. "Say you love him and I'll set him free!"

"Yes," I said. "I love him very much. Please, Carnie, drop the gun."

She leaned and pointed the gun at him. And before I could think about it, I lunged.

"TAKE DOWN!" I yelled, grabbing the forty-five from my hip and firing, firing, firing.

A punch in the chest, and I fell back against the dryer.

A few more shots and then there was blackness.

****

CHAPTER TWENTY-EIGHT

"Vicki? Vic, wake up, Kid. Come on now."

I opened my eyes and looked around. I was still in that God-awful basement and Fisher was kneeling beside me.

"You okay?"

I sat up slowly. "Yeah, I think so."

He felt the back of my head and I flinched.

"Yeah, you've got a pretty good bump there. Looks like you hit your head on the dryer."

"I'm always hitting my head."

I looked down at the bullet hole in my t-shirt. Then I looked at Fisher as the reality of it all came crashing down on me.

Where is he? Oh, God!

"Jason?" I said, becoming hysterical. "Where is my Jason?"

"He's okay," he said quickly, holding my shoulders. "Paramedics have him in an ambulance upstairs. He took a bullet in the shoulder, but he was wearing a vest too. He's awake, sort of, and asking for you. Think you can get up?"

I leaned back against the dryer and he helped me to my feet. I was light-headed and clumsy, but I stayed vertical.

"Come on," he said gently. "Let's get you upstairs."

He put his arm around my waist and we carefully went up the stairs. I saw flashing lights throughout the house and heard voices coming from everywhere around me. Fisher walked me past the uniforms and down the front steps. He led me to the back of an ambulance and I saw a large pair of feet hanging off a gurney.

"How's he doing?" Fisher called to the paramedic sitting next to Varner.

"Oh, I think he'll make it. Ketamine is a bitch when you're coming off of it. You Vic?" he asked, nodding at me. "He's asking for you."

I climbed on wobbly legs up into the ambulance and the paramedic crawled forward into the cab. Varner lay there looking gray as a corpse. But he took a deep, raspy breath and I relaxed a little.

"Jason?" I asked, gently stroking his hair.

"Vic? Where's Vic?" he mumbled.

His blood was seeping through the gauze on his shoulder. I tended to do all right with blood, but for some reason the sight of his made me queasy.

Then again it could have been the fact that I got shot in the chest and knocked my head on a major appliance that was making me queasy. Who knows? I had a lot to be queasy about at that particular moment.

"Vic?"

"I'm right here, Jason," I took his hand carefully, avoiding the bandage around his IV.

A tear dripped down the side of his face and ran toward his ear.

"Is she okay?" he cried.

I leaned forward and kissed his forehead. "Baby, I'm fine, I'm right here with you."

He opened his eyes and looked at me. He looked disconnected and confused, but then he seemed to realize it was me relaxed somewhat.

"Is…Are you okay?" he asked.

"Just a little bump on the head," I said gently. "I'm fine."

"You go on with him, I'll follow you," Fisher called to me. He closed the doors to the ambulance and we started moving.

"Is she okay?" Varner whispered, closing his eyes.

I didn't answer him, it seemed pointless. I just held him and wept.

****

We got to the hospital quickly and they wheeled him in.

"Gunshot wound!" one of the paramedics called as they ran him down the hall.

"Miss, you need to stop and talk to admitting," another one told me.

I turned to the desk just as Fisher came in.

"Vic, I'll take care of this. I think you need to be seen too."

I shook my head. "I'm fine. I want to be with him."

He looked at me. "He will be fine. You took one in the chest and you could have cracked your skull on the dryer. You're going to be seen! Now go sit down!"

"But..."

"Park it, young lady!" he barked, pointing at the bench behind me.

I blinked.

It felt like my dad had just yelled at me.

I went meek, and parked it.

****

I was x-rayed, poked and prodded. They said I had some bruised ribs and a bump on the head. I thought, rather resentfully I might add, that I could have freaking told them that. But they gave me some Vicodin for the pain they said was coming soon.

Vicodin, sweet Vicodin, how I've missed the caress of your loving hand.

As I was sitting on the gurney in the ER waiting to sign release papers, Fisher came in.

"He's in surgery," he said. "They think he'll be fine." Then he cracked a smile. "I'm afraid the washing machine took one in the heart. It's a goner."

I took a deep breath and rubbed my sore chest.

"How ya doing?" he asked me.

"Oh, I hurt," I said, attempting to smile.

"You did a great job in there," he said. "Like a pro. We got everything we needed on audio."

"What happened to Carnie?"

He sighed. "Dead."

I looked at the ceiling and swallowed and prepared to be cuffed.

"Did…did I…" I looked at him. "Did I kill her?"

"Officially?" he said. "She was mine."

I stared at him and exhaled the breath I didn't know I was holding.

"How about unofficially?" I asked, even though I didn't want to know.

He rubbed his hands together. "No such thing, Kiddo."

He smiled at me and patted my arm. I held my hand out to him and he took it in both of his. He helped me up slowly and then seized me into a big hug.

"I'm so proud of you, Vic," he said quietly, kissing my cheek. "We couldn't have done this without you."

I choked out a sob and suddenly wondered if my dad was proud of me too. I wondered if he could see me, and he liked what I was or what I had become. Sometimes I missed him so much I couldn't breathe, but sometimes he felt close enough to take my hand or hug me.

Maybe Varner wasn't my guardian angel after all.

"Thank you," I whispered. "For everything."

He patted my cheek. "You take care now. I'll be up to see Varner in the morning."

****

I popped a Vicodin and was dozing in a chair in Varner's room when they wheeled him back from surgery. I moved out of the way so they could get him positioned comfortably.

"He's still pretty out of it," a pretty, Latin-looking nurse told me. "But he's been asking about you constantly. That is if you're Vic or Vicki?"

"Yeah, he didn't seem to understand in the ambulance that I was actually sitting there with him."

"They lose all touch with reality when they're dopey like that. He'll probably be fine in the morning."

"Can I sit with him awhile?"

She touched my shoulder. "You stay as long as you want."

I smiled at her. "Thank you."

"Vic?" Varner moaned quietly.

"I'm here, Jason," I choked out, tears rolling down my face. I went to his side and sat down. Then I took his hand and held it against my face.

"Vic?" he said again. "Is she okay?"

"It's me, Jason, I'm here."

He opened his eyes and looked at me. "It's you?"

I smiled. "It's me."

He touched my face and I put my lips against his palm.

"I thought you were an angel," he whispered with a soft, dopey smile.

I chuckled. "Not even close."

"I love you," he whispered.

"I love you too," I squeaked. "Rest now. Everything's all right."

And then he drifted off again.

I got up, took another Vicodin, and sat back down next to him. I leaned forward, held his hand against my face, lay my head on his thigh and watched him until I fell asleep.

****

The dreams came early and often. I was in a long dark corridor and I knew she was waiting for me. There she was, bloody, demonic, and almost dog-like. I shot and shot and shot and she kept coming at me, fangs bared, claws out.

"You left me!" she snarled. "You left me!"

"Leave me alone!" I screamed.

I felt a hand stroking my hair. "Vic? Honey, it's okay."

I gasped, jumped awake, and quickly sat up causing immediate pain in my back and neck.

"Ow!" I yelped. "Lord Jesus."

"Sorry, Darlin," Varner said with difficulty through his swollen lips. "You were yelling in your sleep."

I sat back and took a deep breath. Then I looked at him and the dream immediately disappeared.

"Hey, you're up."

"Sort of," he said weakly. He put his left hand on his bandaged right shoulder, grimaced, and tried to shrug. "Hurts. But I'm tired of being doped up on whatever it was they were giving me. Come here and kiss me."

I stood up and leaned over him. "It's going to hurt."

"I don't care," he said. "I need a kiss."

I kissed his puffy lips as gently as I could, but I lingered as long as he let me. I kissed back to his ear and held his face as we embraced in an awkward one-armed hug. I stayed against him until I couldn't take the pain in my back and chest anymore, and sat back down.

"So, what exactly happened?" he asked me, trying to adjust his bad shoulder again.

"What's the last thing you remember?" I asked, taking a deep breath and trying to will the pain away.

"Well, I was headed up the walk to Carnie O'Leary's house. The old lady was in her back yard messing with the garden. I talked to her for a few minutes. Then I think I got back in my car." He rubbed his neck. "Something jabbed me in the neck. I think I remember seeing you a couple times, but I don't remember what happened at all."

"Well…" started the outline of events as well as I could recall them. When I told him I went into the house alone first he began to look angry.

"Now don't you start," I said. "You were in trouble and there was no way she was going to talk to anyone else at that point."

"Fisher should never have put you up to that," he said furiously.

"He didn't. I didn't do anything I didn't want to do."

"Just because you wanted to do it doesn't make it right."

I took a deep breath, which hurt like hell. I got up and got a glass of water and swallowed another Vicodin. "Look, she wanted to talk to me. She would have killed you if anyone else had shown up. What would you have me do?"

"We have people for that kind of thing. Professionals."

I put my head back against the chair, took another deep breath, and willed the Vicodin to kick in. "Jason, there was no time for any of that. We're both alive, isn't that all that matters right now?"

"What matters is, you're not a police officer!" he yelled. "You don't have the appropriate training for the things you're doing and you need to stop pretending that you do!"

I stared at him lividly. "You don't need to yell, okay?"

"Well I'm fucking mad, why shouldn't I yell?"

"You're in a fucking hospital, that's why," I said with my teeth clenched.

He met my eyes and glared at me angrily. "You wouldn't happen to know a Miss King would you? Ida Petty says she looks just like you, right down to the obnoxious hair color."

"That's it," I said loudly, throwing my arms in the air in frustration. "I'm so sick of hearing about you and your 'appropriate training.' Where the hell did you and your training get you? Huh? Drugged up and hand cuffed to a water pipe, that's where! Poor, big, old Detective Varner didn't get to be the hero this time! He was outmatched by a woman! A tiny, little woman without any training and obnoxious hair!"

I walked closer to the door and turned around to face him again. "I did what I thought was necessary under the circumstances. I guess I should have just let her kill you. Yeah, that would have been a lot better."

I turned toward the door, and then back again.

"No matter how you look at it, I saved your ass pal! And I don't even get a fucking thank you!" I screamed.

I took two more steps toward the door and then spun around to make sure I hadn't forgotten anything. I knew I looked and sounded ridiculous, but I didn't care. For the first time in a long time, I was going to let myself be mad. In a different setting, I might have even thrown a couple things or at least kicked something.

"Vic," he said quietly.

"You're welcome!" I screamed. "You're welcome to kiss my stupid, untrained, little ass!"

"Hey!" a familiar voice called from the hall. My friendly nurse Mike opened the door and stepped in. "This is a hospital and you all need to calm down!"

Varner and I stared at each other. He was breathing heavily and his jaw was set. I looked away from him and swallowed several times, keeping the tears where they belonged, at least for the moment.

"Mike, will you escort Miss Childs out of here please?" Varner said.

I turned my glare back to him. "I don't need an escort."

"Sit your ass down," Mike said to me. "You all talk to each other civilly."

I shook my head. "No, I'm done."

I opened the door slowly and turned to Mike. "Tell Detective Varner to give me a call when he grows up."

I left the room and didn't look back.

****

CHAPTER TWENTY-NINE

"His pride is wounded," Fisher told me.

"Pride," I said, playing with my coffee cup. "I probably lost the best thing that ever happened to me because of my own damn pride."

A couple of weeks had gone by and I had been staying at my mom's. She returned the day after everything happened, to baby me. I had to admit, it was nice to have my mommy again. There wasn't much they could do about the livid bruise on my chest except wait and give me drugs. But I quit the Vicodin, it gave me nasty dreams of big, mean, blonde ladies with really sharp teeth and shiny shoes.

Fisher stopped by to see how I was doing, and I tried not to seem too curious, but I was dying to know how Varner was doing. I wanted to know if he missed me as much as I missed him. If his heart ached like mine did. If he could get through his days without crying. God knew that I couldn't.

"How is he other than his bruised ego?" I asked.

"Well, he's back at work. Actually, he's pretty much at work twenty-four/seven. His shoulder is still in a sling, but he seems to be getting around okay," Fisher sipped his coffee. "Aside from the broken heart."

"Right."

"Vic, if you looked up the word depressed in the dictionary there would be a nine by twelve picture of the man's face."

I put my forehead in my hand. "He made his choices."

Fisher nodded. "I know that. He's stubborn about the rules, and you broke a lot of them. I did too for that matter."

"Yeah and if we hadn't, he would be dead."

"He doesn't see it that way."

"Then he's an idiot."

Fisher chuckled. "Yeah, and I told him so."

"Yeah well, horse, water, you fill in the rest."

"Uh," he said, rubbing his mustache. "Hold its head under until it wises up?"

I chuckled and he gave my shoulder a playful little punch.

"Did you see the article in the paper?" he asked, "You're a freaking hero, little girl."

I shrugged. "I'll get fitted for my super bra and panties tomorrow."

"Now I don't want to know anything about that," he said, holding up his hands.

I laughed genuinely for the first time in a while. It felt good for a second, quickly followed by the awful feeling of not being able to share that laugh with someone.

He chuckled and finished his coffee. "Well, Kid, I better get going."

I nodded. "Thanks for stopping by."

I walked with him to the door and opened it. He put a hand on my cheek. "He'll come around."

I smiled. "We'll see."

He left with a wave. I closed the door behind him and a tear dripped down my face.

"Hon, why don't you call him?" my mom asked me from the doorway of the living room.

I shook my head. "You didn't hear the way he talked to me."

"You were both angry. I'm sure enough time has passed for those emotions to fade."

I shrugged and wiped the tear away.

The phone rang and mom went back into the living room to answer it.

"Hello?"

I walked in and sat down, slipping my shoes off.

"It's for you." She brought the phone to me.

"Hello?"

"Victoria Childs?"

"Yes."

"My name is Harold Van Patterson. I'm an attorney handling the estate of Carnie O'Leary. I'm obliged to inform you that she remembered you in her will."

"Excuse me?" I said, unable to believe what I heard. "Did you say I was mentioned in Carnie's will?"

My mom made a "wow" face and my eyebrows jumped up under my hairline.

"Yes," he said. "I need to you come down to my office and sign some papers before I can release your inheritance."

She probably left her cat to me. Wonderful.

"Can you tell me what she left me?"

"I'd rather discuss it with you in person," he said. "Are you free this afternoon?"

"Um, sure, I can be down there in about a half an hour."

"Good enough," he said. "I'll see you then."

I hung up the phone.

"Carnie left you something?" Mom asked.

I nodded. "Yeah, I wonder what it is. Probably her collection of ceramic Republican elephants."

Mom laughed. "Maybe we can sell them on Ebay."

I bent down and put my shoes back on. "Do I look okay to go to a lawyer's office?"

She nodded. "Jeans are fine. You might want to rethink the t-shirt though."

I looked down and the yellow kitties stared up at me.

Okay, so maybe an inherited kitty wouldn't be all that bad.

****

I drove my Honda to the attorney's office downtown, found a place to park about a block away and walked in the hot July sun. It actually felt wonderful to be out and about on my own again. I hadn't been able to do that since the beginning of April.

I opened the glass door to the office and looked around. A man in a suit came out of the office to my right holding a sub sandwich. He was pleasant looking enough, tall and slender with thinning hair standing up spiky on the top of his head.

"Can I help you?" he asked.

"I'm Victoria Childs."

"Oh, hi, Miss Childs, I'm Harold, come on in," he held out his sandwich toward the office.

I smiled at his informality and walked into his office. He closed the door behind us.

He put his sandwich down. "Sorry, you caught me eating. I'm due in court in an hour." He shuffled through papers on his desk. "Ah, yes, here we are, I need you to sign these."

He handed me three pages filled with legal mumbo-jumbo that outlined parties of the first part and second part and the deceased.

"I'm not buying a time share condo here am I?" I asked him.

He chuckled. "No, it's just saying that you have been informed of the passing of Miss O'Leary and that by law you are entitled to the amount designated in her estate. I will need to see your driver's license though so I can notarize your signature."

Amount? Nice!

I signed quickly and handed him my driver's license. He stamped all the pages, and flipped through the file.

"Okay. Everything seems to be in order," he handed me an envelope. "Thank you for coming down today. I'm sorry I have to rush you off like this, but I'm swamped."

"That's okay," I said, flipping open the unsealed envelope. I slid the contents out.

It was a check.

A check for five hundred thousand dollars!

I blinked and looked at the amount again.

Yes, there was a five and five zeros.

Five! Hundred! Thousand! Dollars!

"Seriously? This is mine?" I managed to get out.

"Yes, she left you the entire estate. We of course had to take some for her legal problems, but the rest is yours."

I was completely astounded, but I managed to thank him and get to my car without incident. I reached in my purse and pulled out the envelope again.

Where the hell did Carnie get a half a million dollars?

Do I really give a damn where she got it?

In a couple words: HELL NO!

I grabbed my cell phone.

"Toni, you are not going to believe this."

****

CHAPTER THIRTY

Construction started on V.C. Private Investigations and Process Service toward the end of August and was finished around the beginning of October. It was located on the south end of Brenton next to an enormous park owned by an insurance company and across the street from my old friend, Ronald McDonald. I had the property designed so my living quarters were above the office, and Toni had her own office as my assistant. We built another office as well, just in case we decided to take on another partner at some point if the business took off. I spoke with my new attorney, Harold, about it though and he said that since there weren't any other private investigation agencies in town, I stood to make a killing just on civil processes alone; serving people with divorce papers, foreclosure notices, small claims affidavits and the like. Especially since the police department tended to drag their feet about stuff like that. He said it, I didn't, and he was in a position to know.

Luckily Toni's husband had a lot of friends in construction, so my building was built for next to nothing. I invested a lot of the money with the help of my attorney, who also happened to be a financial wiz. Even if my business failed, I would still have money to live on. And hell, who knows, there was an election coming up and the town needed a new Clerk. I did, however, take some of the money and bought myself a Nissan 370Z Roadster in "Black Cherry." Reliable and chic as hell. I had always wanted a convertible. The thing cornered like it was on rails.

I studied hard and passed my online exams while they were building. I had no idea it would be so easy for me to get licensed, particularly since I already had a degree.

Studying also kept me from thinking about the incredible detective that I had lost, though I still missed him at night. I wondered if he missed me too.

We opened on October tenth which turned out to be cold and rainy, of course, so the opening day celebration had to be moved inside. It didn't really matter because the crowd consisted of me, Toni, Toni's husband, my mom, my lawyer Harold, and Detective Fisher who decided after a few beers that my mom was cute as hell. I nearly vomited when he planted a big wet one on her right in front of me.

Ugh!

About a week after opening, Toni and I were having a rubber band war in the office trying to kill time before I had to serve a Petition for Dissolution of Marriage on a guy who had an enormous chip on his shoulder. I had already served him with his Order of Protection, so I knew what he was like. I wasn't looking forward to meeting him again.

"You should just go and get back so we can take off early," she said shooting me in the ass with a gigantic rubber band she had taken off of an enormous pleading waiting to be served.

"Ow! Bitch!"

She laughed.

"You know you can leave anytime you want," I told her. "I can lock up when I go and I've got voicemail if anyone calls."

I wrapped a band around my hand like a gun and hit her in the forehead.

"All right! Someone's going to lose an eye!" she hollered, grabbing her coat. "Are you sure you don't mind?"

"Nah, go on. I'll get this jackass served and call it a day."

"Okay, I'll see you tomorrow."

She headed out the door. I shot her in the ass on the way out.

"You'll pay for that, Childs!" she said.

I laughed, grabbed my jacket, holstered my gun, stun gun, cell phone, and pepper spray and headed out the door. I hopped into my new baby and headed toward

Albert Palmer's house to let him know his marriage was about to be over. I pulled into his driveway and quickly noticed the place looked deserted. Then again, it always looked deserted. The house looked like it was constructed out of gray corkboard and the shingles were deteriorating rapidly. Palmer obviously took about as much care of his house as he did with his marriage, but I wasn't there to judge. I decided to put the stun gun in my jacket pocket for easier access. It was a "knuckle blaster" and I could easily grab it and turn my fist into a cattle prod. I armed the alarm on my car and started up the stairs to his door. The door burst open.

"What do you want?" the large man in the wife beater yelled at me.

"Albert Palmer?" I said without even flinching. I knew he'd take one look at me and know what was coming.

"You know who I am bitch, and I said, what the hell do you want?"

"I'm here to serve you with a civil process," I said calmly. I handed the papers to him and turned around to leave.

"I don't want this shit, you bitch!" he yelled, throwing the papers at my back.

"Sorry, sir," I continued walking. "You touched them, they're yours now. You've officially been served. Have a nice day."

A rock flew past me. Then another. Lucky for me he was a lousy shot. Then he began yelling something incomprehensible and I heard him coming down off the porch.

I hadn't really had this kind of trouble before. Last time he rattled off a few obscenities and slammed back into the house. I figured he was just blowing off steam, but I decided to turn to keep an eye on him. But before I could get around to face him, I was on the ground, with dirt in my mouth, and he was standing over me screaming, "You little bitch! I'll fuck you up and down!"

Alcohol dripped out of his pores as he stood over me and grinned.

"Aw, look, you got dirty."

"Back off, Palmer," I snarled. "You really don't want to do this."

"Oh, I do, I really, really do."

I rolled over on to my back and kicked him in the crotch, grabbing my stun gun in the process. Then I zapped him in the thigh. He let out a shriek and fell backwards.

"What the fuck are you doing?" he wailed.

Huh. It didn't knock him out. I always thought they were supposed to knock people out. Maybe I didn't hold it against him long enough. I looked at my stun gun and then at him again. I never had the opportunity to test the stun gun before. I enjoyed the effect immensely. Painful, but not lethal. At least, not yet.

I struggled to my feet and checked myself as I coughed and spit dirt. My jacket had a huge rip across the front pocket and it was covered with what I hoped was mud.

"Now you did it," I told him. "You ruined my favorite jacket you asshole."

I zapped him again, longer this time and right in the neck. He let out another cry, farted twice, and then he was still.

"Damn," I said, flipping the stunner off and looking at it with a new appreciation, nay, even a little awe, "I love technology."

I got my cell out and dialed nine, one, one.

****

"You bitch! You fucking bitch!" Albert Palmer yelled from the back of the squad car.

I smiled and waved at him as I outlined what happened to Officer Nathanial Starkey, who was the first on the scene. He was so adorable with his blond, spiky hair and clear, blue eyes that I almost found myself gushing and giggling a little bit. Fisher introduced me to him on a call once. It involved a burglary and I asked if I could tag along and watch the professionals work. I half thought that I'd like to go out with Starkey, but I knew my heart was still in pieces and starting a new romance would be counterproductive for my sanity at that point.

"He doesn't want a divorce, huh?" Starkey asked with a grin.

"Nope," I said, trying to brush more dirt off my jacket. "I can't imagine why she left him. He's such a catch and his vocabulary is outstanding. I've never been called a bitch so many times by someone I haven't dated."

I waved at Palmer again and he smacked his head into the window. Then he fell back, apparently out cold.

"Well, at least you're a cute bitch," Nate said.

I smiled my prettiest smile at him and batted my eyes. "Ain't I?"

"Damn straight," he said.

I giggled.

Shit!

"He's drunk as hell," I said, trying to hide the fact that I was about to turn the color of a strawberry. "He probably won't even remember me. At least I hope he doesn't."

"Probably not," Starkey said, closing his notebook. "Well, I think I've gotten all I need from you. You sure you don't want to press charges on him for shoving you?"

"Nah, I'm fine," I said. "He's in enough trouble with his wife, I hear."

"Yeah, he put her in the hospital last week. He'll be behind bars for a while."

I nodded.

"Catch you later, Vic," Starkey said, smiling. I watched him get in his car and kicked myself for openly flirting with a guy that must have been ten years my junior. He drove off with his precious cargo, and I was alone again, contemplating jumping in my car and going after him.

"You just can't stay out of trouble, can you?" I heard behind me.

I closed my eyes and swallowed. I knew the voice well.

Please God, if he's wearing the navy blue suit I'll just die!

I turned slowly and looked into his eyes. He smiled.

Navy blue. Of course.

I rolled my eyes to the heavens and I swear I saw a cloud in the shape of an extended middle finger, like a big old "F-you" from God.

"Hey," Varner said.

"Hi," I said quietly. "What are you doing here?"

"I heard the call and I was in the area. I stopped by to see if Starkey needed any help."

He kicked a rock into the street. Nervous. It wasn't like him to be nervous.

"Your hair has grown," he said.

I nodded. "Yeah, and I couldn't stand the color anymore."

"It looks nice. The brown is, uh, nice, I mean."

"Thanks. How's the shoulder?"

"Fine. Still twinges a bit, but I'm tough."

"I know you are."

Uncomfortable silence surrounded us again for a few moments.

"I heard about your new office," he said. "Congratulations."

"Oh yeah, thanks," I said.

I was suddenly aware that I was sweating and that I was covered with mud.

"Licensed private investigator, huh?" he said. "That's…that's really great."

I nodded and just stared at him. How could I have forgotten how beautiful he was?

"Oh I, um, I got you something," he said, his thumb pointing back to his car. "I've been carrying it around in my car for a while hoping to run into you."

"What is it?"

He grinned. "Now what kind of surprise would it be if I told you that?"

"You didn't have to get me anything," I said, following him.

He just smiled and opened the passenger side of his Tahoe and brought out a medium-sized box.

"Here you go," he said, handing it to me. "For your office."

I opened it, pulled the newspaper off the top and sucked in a breath.

"Oh, my God! Where did you find it?" I asked. "I've been looking everywhere for one."

"I told you, I've got connections," he said, grinning.

I pulled the Charlie Chaplin clock out of the box carefully and looked up at him. "Thank you."

"You're welcome."

I swallowed the latest lump in my throat and touched The Little Tramp's clock belly gently.

"Look, Vic, I…I never did thank you for what you did for me," he said as I put the clock back in the box carefully. "I mean for, you know, saving my life."

I smiled and gazed up at him. "No, you didn't."

"So, uh, thanks," he stuttered, kicking another rock.

"You're welcome," I said.

He smiled shyly and I was immediately in love all over again. Hell, let's face it, I never fell out.

"You want to go get some coffee or something?" he asked.

I looked down at my clothes. "Uh, well, I'm sort of a mess right now."

"Oh yeah? I hadn't noticed."

I snickered. "Oh come on, Varner, you notice everything."

He grinned. "I'm trying to quit."

We stood in awkward silence again and I was having great difficulty not picturing him naked in the shower.

"So, how about that coffee?" he asked.

I took a deep breath and considered my options.

"Um, not today."

Wait, what did I say?

"Oh," he said, nodding rather forlornly. "Okay, well…"

"But, I'm free for dinner on Friday," I smiled.

He grinned slowly. "Okay, I'll pick you up around six?"

I looked at him and licked my lips slowly. "How about I meet you at Betino's at six?"

"Hm," he said, narrowing his eyes and biting his lower lip. "You're not going to make this easy on me are you?"

"Nope," I said slyly. "I think I'll let you pursue me for a while. I think I deserve it."

He chuckled and took a step toward me.

"Pursue you," he said, taking the box from me and setting it on the hood of his car. "You know, I'm a cop. So your saying that, makes you even more...irresistible to me."

He grabbed the zipper of my jacket and pulled me forward against his chest. I looked up at him and smiled as he began leaning in for the kill.

"You'll get your suit dirty," I said.

"Don't care," he answered, kissing my upper lip.

"Jason," I said.

"Hm?"

"Angel."

"Pretty lady."

He stroked his lips lightly against mine.

"Suffer," I whispered. I grinned, backed away from him, grabbed my clock and hit the button disarming my car alarm. "See you Friday. I really like lavender roses."

He pursed his lips as he watched me walking away.

"Evil to the core," he said, smiling.

I smiled, flipped my hair, and hopped in my car.

THE BEGINNING

I hope you enjoyed reading my first novel as much as I enjoyed writing it.
Thank you so much for giving "Childs' Proof" a try.
Look for the next Victoria Childs novel, "Childs Abduction," available on November 23, 2012

I would love to hear from you

Please feel free to contact me at:

https://www.facebook.com/neeley.bratcher.5

neeleybratcher40@gmail.com

Twitter: @NeeleyBratcher

Read on for a sneak preview of
"Childs Abduction"
Victoria Childs Novel, #2

"I like the purple one you had on first," Toni said as I stood in front of her in a navy blue, sequined gown that hiked my boobs up to my neck.

My mom shook her head. "It was too short."

"She's got great legs though, really shapely and curvy. If she wears heels with the short skirt, it will have a lengthening effect."

Mom cocked her head and looked down at my legs. "I'm not sure heels would help."

Toni followed my mom's eye line. "Good point."

"I know, I have Munchkin legs, and it's definitely not this one," I said turning around in the mirror. "I look like Dolly Parton."

I shuffled back into the dressing room and tried on a green one that Mom picked out, and immediately took it off. The color was awful and it buttoned up to my neck. I hated shopping for dresses. Firstly, I never wore dresses or skirts because I hated them. Secondly, I could never find anything that would fit the top and the bottom concurrently. I needed large on top, short length, a small around my waist and butt and then a medium around my thighs. How one person could have so many sizes is beyond me. I always felt like Frankenstein's monster when shopping for dresses.

I turned sideways and groaned, "I'm just going to call him and tell him I'm not going."

"No you're not," Mom said. "We'll find you something. Here."

She poked her arm in and handed me a long, silver dress with a beaded jacket.

"Too matronly. I want to look like his date, not his mother."

I gave it back to her. Toni handed in another purple one.

"Too long. It will drag."

Mom handed in a baby-puke-green one with a giant silver belt.

"Mom? Seriously?"

"Well, I like it!"

We had been to five different stores and I had tried on a gazillion formals and we were getting on each other's nerves. It had been a very long day, and I was starting to panic because Varner and I were leaving in three days.

"I've got it!" I heard Toni yell from inside the store. "If you don't like this one you're crazy and I give up on you!"

She handed the dress to me. It was burgundy satin with a black lace over-lay. The neckline was low enough to be sexy, but high enough to be elegant and it hit me about mid-calf when I held it up. The straps were just wide enough for me to wear a regular bra with it, which was a major plus. I threw it over my head and Toni stepped in to zip it up. I stepped out of the dressing room.

"Oh," Mom said, putting her hand to her mouth. "Yes."

I looked at Toni.

"Yes," she smiled.

I stepped in front of the three-way mirror and spun around. It was absolutely perfect and I wanted to wear it home.

"Thank God," I said, turning around and checking the back. No bra straps. Beautiful!

"I don't think it even needs to be altered," Mom said, looking at the hem.

"No, I wouldn't change a thing," Toni said.

I tried to flip my almost-shoulder-length hair and smiled at myself. "Take that, Varner. He's never seen me dressed up before."

"He'll love it," Toni said quietly, looking me up and down. "But you should probably rethink the black socks."

"I'm more worried about the family," I muttered. "He'd love a burlap sack."

"It's very tasteful," Mom said. "A-line dresses are very flattering on you."

"It's not at all slutty?" I asked, waggling the boobs down a touch.

"No!" they both said together.

I sighed. "Okay. I need shoes."

"Thank God," Toni muttered.

****

I lugged my bags out of my car and struggled to get my keys out of my purse so I could open the front door to the office. I had my building designed so the bottom level contained three offices, a large bathroom, and a small kitchenette. The entire top floor was my apartment, and a sharp left at the top of the stairwell took visitors right to my front door. There was another entrance and another set of stairs at the back of the building to keep the building and zoning people happy, but it was a little inconvenient to use regularly as the parking lot was in front. If anything, it was sort of a fire escape with heat and air-conditioning.

As soon as I got the front door open, my Vic-senses told me something wasn't quite right.

It was the smell.

I recognized it.

Someone was baking vanilla cupcakes.

Or someone was burning the vanilla-cupcake candles I had just purchased from PartyLite.

"Jason?" I called as I dropped my purse and closed the door behind me.

I looked to my right. On the decorative end table by my office door was a votive burning in one of my PartyLite holders. I think it was one of the Quilted Crystal Pair, or something like that. Anyway, it was pretty, and I smiled as I hung my dress on the long coat rack on the wall.

"Jason? Are you here?" I called, a little louder.

I jumped when I heard the "thump" above my head. I did a quick mental calculation and decided that the room above me would be my bedroom.

"Well, someone is feeling excessively romantic," I said with a grin.

I grabbed my purse and my shoe bag and headed upstairs.

When I got to the top, I dropped my bags, and reached for my gun.

The doorframe was hacked all to hell. Someone had obviously taken a crowbar to it.

Or an ax!

Dear God!

I was frozen where I stood. I tried to get my feet to move, but they wouldn't do what I told them to do. I stood and stared at my front door, like an oblivious kid on his X-Box.

"Call Varner," I whispered.

Oh, right, I should call Varner.

Get a grip, dip shit!

I grabbed my cell off of my belt and punched a few buttons.

Voicemail.

"Damn it," I whispered as I disconnected.

I tried his home and got the machine.

I tried his office and got voicemail again.

"Where the hell is he?"

Footsteps! Heavy ones! Inside my apartment!

Shit!

I ducked down on the stairs, so if he opened the front door he wouldn't see me right away, and dialed 911. Before she even got her usual spiel out, I blurted out my address.

"Victoria Childs," I said quietly. "I need someone here now."

Most of the emergency operators knew me, or at least knew of me, and most of them knew I was dating Varner. And most of them were okay with that except...

"Well, Miss Childs," the lovely Alisha said in her oh-so-sexy phone voice. "And what kind of trouble have we gotten ourselves into this time?"

I had gone to high school with Alisha, and for a while we were good friends. But then, there was a big fight.

Yep. A guy. She liked him. He liked me. I wasn't sure about him, but we went out a couple times.

The sad thing is, neither one of us got him. He dropped out of school and worked as a farm-hand, and he apparently preferred the company of his cows. We later found out that he really preferred his cows, and his horses, and I guess there was a goat involved. It was all very sordid.

After that, Alisha decided that it was her mission in life to make sure I never had another boyfriend, or at least not a faithful one. It hadn't really been a problem until recently, because mostly, I dated losers until Varner. She really, really liked Varner. And she really, really wasn't shy about letting him know this, and making sure that I knew that she let him know this.

I sighed and pressed my fingers against my eyeballs. "Look, Alisha, there is someone in my apartment. From the sound of his footsteps, he's a big son of a bitch. Please hurry."

I could almost hear her smirk. "You can't handle it yourself? I thought you were supposed to be a big, old bad-ass now. That was the rumor. Or was it that you have a big, old, bad ass?"

"Hey! Leave my ass out of this," I snarled. "Just please, get someone here now."

"All right, all right, Starkey responded already," she said. "And I'll mention it to Varner, when I see him later tonight."

I growled and hung up on her.

Shit!

What if he is meeting up with her?

What if that's why I can't get a hold of him?!

What if he lied about not seeing anyone else?

No, he wouldn't lie to me.

But where the hell is he?

Do I really have a big ass?

Ooh, one of these days, I'm going to slap her stupid!

I heard a crash from the bedroom area, which sounded like a lamp, and I decided I had two options. One, run outside like a total girl and wait for the cavalry to arrive. Two, bust in on the bad guy and take him down myself. That's what Catwoman would do. Catwoman wouldn't let some big oaf break her lamps. And after she took care of the bad guys, she got to kiss Batman, also known as Bruce

Wayne, also known as Christian Bale. I'd walk over hot coals to kiss Christian Bale.

I took the last two steps silently, and skittered over to the door. After slamming my back against the wall, and letting out a very lady-like grunt, I nudged the door open with my gun, stepped inside and muttered, "This one's for you, Christian."

I ducked as low as I could, and sort of crab-walked to the living room. My bedroom was down the hall, off the living room, the second door on the left. But I didn't even make it all the way into the living room before he appeared.

He was dressed like Zorro, complete with mask, sans sword or hat, and he had a rather large bag slung over his shoulder.

"Stop right there!" I barked quickly, pointing my gun and standing up. "Don't you move or I'll..."

He moved. "You look good enough to eat."

"I'll shoot you! I swear to God!"

He chuckled. "Shoot me? A sweet, little princess like you?"

"I've done it before!"

"Oh yeah?"

He lunged.

I shot.

Glass popped behind him.

Suddenly, I was on my back and staring at the ceiling.

Then he was standing over me, straddling my hips with his feet and smiling down at me.

"The police are on their way," I squeaked, fumbling to point my gun at him again.

"Well," he replied, kicking my hand and sending my gun skittering away. "I'll see you in New Orleans then."

"What?"

He chuckled, stepped over me, and he was out the back door and down the stairs before I could get to my feet.

****

"You all right, Kid?" Detective Tom Fisher asked, sitting down next to me on the stairs.

Tom was Varner's partner and had become somewhat of a father figure for me. At least he wanted to protect me like a father. I think he kind of felt the same way about Varner. He had no kids of his own, and probably never would, so I think he felt the need to protect both of us. Plus he looked like a dad. He was somewhat squatty and bald with a lot of dark hair around the edges and a bushy mustache that he refused to shave off.

Varner and I likened him to the "time to make the donuts" guy, though we never told him that.

He put his arm around me and I shivered and hugged myself.

"I'm okay," I squeaked. "Where's Varner?"

"Hell if I know," Fisher said. "He said something about re-interviewing a witness. They were going to try to radio him at the station. It's not like him to be late for a party, especially if you're involved."

I shivered again and he gave me a squeeze. "Why don't we go on upstairs and take a look around."

We entered my apartment to find Nate Starkey checking out the bullet hole in the top glass of my living room window. Nate was a uniformed officer that I often called for back-up when I didn't want to get Varner involved. He was about ten years younger than me, and unbelievably cute with his spiky, blond hair and playful, blue eyes. We tended to do a little harmless flirting when we saw each other, and he turned when I entered and gave me a wink.

"Hey, Vic," he said, with his naughty, little grin. "I thought you were a better shot than this."

"I panicked."

A sort of ruckus erupted downstairs and we heard the clunk of a giant bounding up the stairs.

"Vic!" Varner boomed when he entered. When he saw me, he scooped me up in a huge hug and nearly squeezed me breathless. "Good Lord! Are you all right?"

"I'm...I just." He set me down and his large hands cradled my face as he searched my eyes.

His eyes always had a strange effect on me. They were like a truth serum, especially when I was trying to be calm and cool about something horrible.

"There was...there was a noise," I began coherently, but it was falling apart quickly as the heaving breaths began, "...through the ceiling, and so I called, but then she told me I have big ass, and, and, and she was meeting you, and, and, then he broke my lamp, and, and, and then I shot my window, and, and, and then...he kicked me...and my gun was gone...and then...then..."

Uncontainable sobs escaped me as he wrapped me in his arms, and I heard him murmur something about giving us a few minutes to Fisher and Starkey.

"Baby," he whispered. "Vic, it's okay now."

"Where were you," I cried against his chest. "Nobody could find you."

"Sh," he said, running his fingers through my hair. "My phone died while I was talking to one of the victims in this damn case. I'm so sorry, Darlin'. You know I would have been here quicker if I had known. Come on now, try and calm down."

He let me cry for a while, stroking away my panic with is warm hands on my back, and soon I was able to talk again.

"Let's sit down and you can tell me what happened," he said, taking my hand and leading me into the living room. We sat down on the couch just as Fisher entered.

“No sign of forced entry in the front,” Fisher said. “The glass in the back door has been broken out, so that's obviously how he got in. You need an alarm, little girl.

“You need a shave, big dude," I cracked, grabbing a tissue from the box on the coffee table.

He smiled and shook his head. “Smart ass.”

“Is anything missing?” Varner asked, rubbing my back.

“Not that I noticed, but I haven't had a chance to look around much." I shivered again and hugged myself. "He was carrying a bag when he left."

Varner took a seat on the coffee table across from me and took my hands. "Tell me again what happened."

I blew out a long sigh and stared at our hands as I hashed out the whole story. And it wasn't until I was finished that I looked at both of them. They looked at each other. Varner's jaw set and his lips pursed, as they always did when he was angry.

"What?" I squeaked.

"Did he say anything?" Varner asked.

I nodded. "He said..." I had to stop and swallow. "He said I looked good enough to eat."

"Jesus," Fisher muttered.

"Did you get a good look at him?" Varner asked, rather desperately. "Can you tell us anything about him?"

I rubbed my face. "He looked like Zorro."

"What do you mean he looked like Zorro?"

I shrugged. "He looked like Zorro."

"He had a mustache?" Fisher asked.

"No, he was clean-shaven."

"Zorro had a mustache."

"No, he didn't," I argued.

"Yes, he did. He had that pencil-thin moustache."

"Antonio Banderas didn't..."

"Oh, please," Fisher groaned. "He was not Zorro. Guy Williams was the only Zorro."

"Forget Zorro," Varner barked. "Did he say anything else?"

"Yeah," I said, "he said he would see me in New Orleans."

Varner's eyes narrowed and he exhaled angrily.

"Who knows you're going to New Orleans?" Fisher asked.

"I've only told Toni," I said, scratching my head. "She might have told her husband but...wait. He called me princess." I snapped my fingers as I remembered. "A couple weeks ago a guy called me that, but I didn't think anything of it until..."

Varner physically started, and Fisher inhaled deeply as their eyes shot to each other.

"What?" I said again. "Who died?"

"No one, yet," Fisher said.

I closed my eyes and took a deep breath through my nose and willed myself not to start screaming and clawing my face.

"Where were you when this guy called you 'princess'," Varner said. "When was this?"

"Well, a couple weeks ago Toni was worried about her husband cheating on her, so I went to the ice rink when he had practice and talked to him about it. This guy was there practicing. He asked me for my number and I told him I had a boyfriend."

Varner smiled and looked at Fisher. Fisher rolled his eyes.

"What else?" Fisher asked.

"He just told me to ask Jim for his number whenever I was free, or something to that effect."

"What does he look like?" Varner asked.

"The Christmas Story kid who couldn't put his arms down," I said. "How would I know what he looked like? He was suited up for hockey and he had a shield thingy over his eyes."

The men looked at each other again.

"What is going on?" I groaned. "Don't play this game with me right now, I'm not in the mood."

"We've had a series of reported sexual assaults in town recently," Fisher began. "We thought we found the guy, but it turned out to be a dead end."

"That's what these stakeouts have been about," Varner said. "Commissioner put us on this because there haven't been any homicides lately."

"All these cases have had the same M.O." Fisher said. "He stalks and calls them repeatedly after one or two meetings, leaves flowers…"

"And calls them all 'princess'," I finished.

They nodded simultaneously, like a couple law-enforcement bobbleheads.

"None of the victims seems to be able to identify him," Varner said. "He seems to be every man."

"One of those short, tall, thin, fat, blond guys with brown hair," Fisher said.

"And now we have Zorro and the Christmas Story kid to add to the mix," Varner said.

"Randy," I muttered.

"What?"

"The Christmas Story kid," I sighed. "His name was Randy."

"Honey," Varner said, reaching up to stroke my hair. "We need you in reality for a moment."

"A serial rapist," I said. "Terrific."

"You're definitely his type," Fisher sighed. "He likes small women with brown hair, usually parted on the left."

I swallowed, nauseous at the thought, and decided to buy platform shoes and make a hair appointment.

"He could have heard from Jim that you're going to New Orleans," Fisher said looking at his partner. "I'll bet he knows a lot more about her than we think he does."

Varner sighed. "There's one more thing we need to check."

"What?"

Fisher let out a grunt as he got to his feet. "Lead the way, Vic's boyfriend."

Varner led us into my bedroom and over to my dresser.

"I need you to open the top drawer," he said, putting a gentle hand on my back.

"Why?"

"I need to see what's inside."

"Is it going to be gross?"

He exhaled a laugh. "Probably not."

I took a deep breath. "Okay."

I slid the drawer open slowly and gasped.

Made in the USA
Charleston, SC
30 June 2016